PRAISE FOR THE AUTHOR . . .

"Forsaken is a striking end to P.J. O'Dwyer's Fallon Sisters Trilogy, a provocative, well-crafted romantic suspense series that's dark, dangerous, and addictive. In Forsaken, a sinister mystery shares the page with a problematic romance, complicated family dynamics, and a gripping woman-in-jeopardy plot as we follow O'Dwyer's feisty heroine from the dockyards of Dublin to the stable yards of Maryland, and finally to the racetracks of Saratoga."

With vibrant, confident narrative; irresistible characters; and a relentlessly edgy plot, the author immerses the reader in the world of horseracing, and it's a thrill ride."

—USA Today

"Money, privilege, horses, and the luck of the Irish are all bound up in a saga of high stakes in Forsaken. P. J. O'Dwyer's third and final book in the Fallon Sisters Trilogy promises to provide yet another perspective on the vision of love and freedom and completes a horse-and-romance-oriented journey begun in Relentless."

"The book [Forsaken] is a powerful analysis of what it takes to truly get a head—a lesson in life and love that we all need to not just survive, but thrive."

—Diane Donovan, Senior Reviewer, Midwest Book Reviews

"Highly entertaining . . . intriguing . . . This well-written novel [Forsaken] will keep you guessing until the end."

—Allbooks Review International

Novels Written by P. J. O'Dwyer

THE FALLON SISTERS TRILOGY

Relentless

Defiant

Forsaken

HUNTER'S MOON SERIES

Claimed

Black Siren Books

331 West 57th Street
Suite 510
New York, NY 10019
www.blacksirenbooks.com
inquiries@blacksirenbooks.com

This book contains an excerpt from the forthcoming book *Linger,* the first book in the Satin and Steel, Women of Law Enforcement Series by P. J. O'Dwyer. This excerpt has been set for this edition only and may not reflect the final content of the forthcoming edition.

Printed in the United States of America

LCCN 2014921795

ISBN 978-0-9848997-3-9 (trade cover)
ISBN 978-0-9848997-2-2 (e-book)

Cover design by Duncan Long, www.duncanlong.com
Interior layout and design by P. J. O'Dwyer

Visit the author's website: http://www.pjodwyer.com

FORSAKEN

P. J. O'DWYER

Black
Siren
Books

New York

To my sister Cathy Divver Walker, the bond we share is like no other. You're there when I need a laugh, a shoulder to cry on, or an accomplice to conspire with. I can't imagine life without you.

DEDICATION

Immigration is a controversial issue—one that is debated in our judicial system, by our politicians and our citizens of every ethnic background. There are no easy answers or magic legislation. Immigration is messy, heartbreaking, and fraught with strife.

It is easy to judge an individual based on the law. In truth, this is not a simple black or white topic. It is murky, clouded, and gray—like the futures of most illegal aliens.

In *Forsaken,* my Irish heroine Dani Flynn puts a face to the nameless people whose lives, struggles, and aspirations are hidden within a flashy headline or a one-sided sound bite from some world news organization. My character has hopes and dreams and real fears that make her human and worth saving.

And it is for those—the forsaken—who find themselves in the darkest place imaginable, standing on the threshold of freedom only to find they are the subject of ridicule and hate, that I dedicate my final installment of the Fallon Sisters Trilogy.

May God offer us acceptance and tolerance for the things we know nothing about.

ACKNOWLEDGMENTS

To my dear friend and editor Amy Harke-Moore. *You* are a blessing in my life that I count twice. Madeline Hopkins, your expert handling of the written word as a copy editor gives me the confidence that comes from knowing all my I's are dotted and T's are crossed.

My heartfelt gratitude also goes out to Irish writer and editor Laurence O'Bryan, author of *The Manhattan Puzzle,* for assisting me with creating an authentic Irish heroine in Dani Flynn. One of these days, I hope to find myself standing on Irish soil for a visit.

Thanks to my gifted illustrator, Duncan Long. You have given me three gorgeous heroines who, although different, could pass for real life sisters. You have been gracious and accommodating throughout, which makes working with you a joy.

A special thanks to attorney Cynthia C. Arn for her knowledge of immigration law; Steven Lewandowski for sharing his knowledge, expertise, and anecdotes of horse racing; Rita A. Noblett, field investigator; and Kelly King, of the Pennsylvania State Horse Racing Commission, who patiently explained the complexities of horse racing wagers; and, finally, to my dear friend retired Thoroughbred jockey Ricky Wilson, for imparting his life lessons from the track. As always, any and all mistakes are my own.

To the "Fabulous Four"—my father, Turk Divver; his wife, Pat Moran; my brother, Joe Divver; and my favorite cousin, Danny Divver. This would all be a pipe dream if it weren't for your steadfast support. I lift my glass to you—preferably good Irish whiskey. To our heritage. If you're lucky enough to be Irish, you're lucky enough! Love you with all my heart.

It's with great respect and admiration I want to thank my agent, Julie Gwinn. Thank you for your continued support and belief in me.

And to all my fans who have waited patiently for the third and final book of the Fallon Sisters Trilogy—it has arrived. I hope you enjoy meeting Irish heroine Dani Flynn and being reunited with a familiar cast of characters in *Forsaken*. Thank you for your unwavering support!

CHAPTER ONE

LAUGHTER FILTERED THROUGH DEVLIN'S ON THE OUTSKIRTS OF Rosslare. A local pub, it catered to the villagers living and working near Rosslare Harbour and the tourists who found their way to the seaside village Dani Flynn called home. On a cool Thursday night in June with a turf fire burning, Devlin's was brimming with business and many a tip to be had, except she wouldn't be afforded the extra quid to line her pockets.

There was more to be made along the docks.

Dani reached into the pocket of her apron and touched the crisp one-hundred-dollar bill a handsome Yank had shoved in it when she passed by his table. Even the unexpected tip would be no match for the income she would earn tonight.

She pulled her last pint of Guinness and leaned over the bar, the dark beer sloshing onto her fingers. She grimaced and wiped them on her apron. "That's the last you'll get from me, Rogan."

"And where might you be running off to?" Rogan Gillis's blue eyes twinkled.

He'd sized her up long ago—called her a fairy, no less, with hair the color of moon-kissed sable. He once wrapped his finger around it, tugging a long strand as she passed by him on her way to the bar. She'd eyed him, her blue eyes sharp and questioning. He only laughed, his hand falling away.

She'd known him most of her life. A few years her senior, Rogan Gillis was tall, dark, and would make for a prize of a husband, had she taken him up on his many proposals of matrimony. But at twenty-six,

Dani'd make no promise to a man unless her heart willed it, and, sadly, it didn't for Rogan.

He kept his eye on her still, smiling, and nodded toward Patrick Malone. Close to sixty, still holding on to his dark youthful locks with just a touch of gray at the temples, he was busy belting out a tune while his daughter, Darcy, a beautiful redhead, accompanied him on the fiddle.

"You'll not get me in trouble with the boss this day, Rogan." She slapped the top of his large hand and smiled. His fingertips, calloused from working his farm, reached out, curving around her hand. But she pulled it away just as quick. "I've already got approval from the barkeep himself." She gave a lift of her chin toward her employer. "I'll see you tomorrow, then, Pat," she called out.

Patrick Malone stretched the last line of "Danny Boy," his eyes black onyx, glimmering with purpose, fully aware of the emotion he drew from the soft, sad tenor of his voice.

Then his tall frame spun around. "Aye, tomorrow night it is, lass." He waved a hand. "And take your supper. Rachel gathered it up for you and something to drink, mind."

"I'll do that, and thank her for her kindness."

"I will indeed." His broad smile thinned. "And, Dani, I'll thank you to remind Kara she's walking a jagged cliff." Gone was the laughter in his voice, and with the added lift of his brow, he didn't need to say more.

"For sure, you've got my word." She nodded and headed toward the kitchen. Kara Gilroy was not a subject she wanted to belabor with Pat. He'd long gone round the bend with that girl for showing up late to work or not at all—tonight being one of those nights.

After clocking out, Dani took the brown sack with her name on it and a bottled water from the fridge. The Malones took care of her, and she loved them all for it. She unzipped her backpack, placing her supper inside, grabbed her sweatshirt as well, and slipped out the rear door.

She'd see Kara soon enough. It was Kara's message on her mobile earlier that had her begging an hour's leave at the end of her shift. She hadn't held out much hope since Kara's absence had put them one shy a server tonight. But Pat had granted it just the same. She'd thank her staunch work ethic for that. In the nine years since she'd worked as a part-time server and now barmaid, she'd not missed her scheduled shift or arrived late once.

She couldn't afford the luxury.

On her own since the loss of her dear ma at the age of eighteen, child protection services weren't responsible for her—which was just as well. Being a ward of County Wexford didn't appeal to Dani. As far as her da, she only knew of him, and it'd be a cold day in Hades before she'd reach out to him. Besides, she'd been earning a steady paycheck since finagling a job at Carrigan's Racehorse Stables where her ma had been employed 'til she'd . . .

A familiar pinch hit the back of her eyes, and she let the memory fade. She'd accepted her loss long ago—and the pity of Joseph Carrigan.

Grooming racehorses wasn't a chore. She had a knack for it, and taking care to bathe and care for them each day was more reward than hardship. She loved them. Her wage could afford her space in a boardinghouse in Rosslare Village and the bus fare from Rosslare to the O'Hanrahan Station, from there it was only a short walk to the stables each morning. And the pub, where she worked at night, gave her a bit of a cushion most months, barring any unforeseen expenses.

The night air blew cold across her bare arms. Dani shivered and pulled her dark blue sweatshirt over her head. She still had her misgivings about the extra euros from Celtic Trans-Atlantic Shipping but, like always, she put them out of her mind. Her pocket jingled, and she slung her backpack onto her shoulders and reached for her mobile, only to find she'd missed Kara's call. Squinting against the small screen, she frowned—10:43. She'd be lucky to make it to the docks—eight kilometers to the east—by eleven. There was no time to change or fancy her face with the makeup Tommy Duggan insisted she and Kara wear to meet his clients whenever their ship pulled into the harbor.

His clients...

She'd just as soon forget their faces and do what she was paid to do. It was just until she could catch up on her bills anyway. She only hoped Tommy made good on their arrangement. The five hundred euros would help ease the burden this month. She still owed the garage for the repair to her scooter. *It's historic,* she thought and smiled to herself. Or, as Pat would say, "Relic and undependable is more like it."

"Let him crack jokes," she muttered when she reached the bike rack and her 1980 yellow Honda scooter complete with rusty fenders. So it wasn't a shiny Fiat or some fancy Renault 5. It didn't matter—Dani didn't have a driver's license, it wasn't required for a scooter this size.

She wouldn't let her position in life or her lack of education dampen her spirits. She'd never had the privilege of finishing school, though sitting at a desk all day had never appealed to her anyway. She could read and write well enough, but she wasn't much for figures and memorizing.

Dani fumbled inside the small pocket of her backpack until she found her keys, then freed the scooter and tucked the stiff, coiling lock in with her clothes and a bag of peppermints she gave as a special treat to the horses. She next reached for her wallet. Her fingertips skimmed the soft leather grain and the teeth of a closed zipper holding her most important papers, and she relaxed.

The boardinghouse was affordable and clean enough. But many a thing went missing. Her valuables she always kept with her. Tucked inside her wallet was her ma's lucky twenty-pence coin, and an old photo of her taken at the racetrack in Saratoga Springs, New York. At eighteen it had been Dani's first and only trip abroad. She still had the passport with about two years remaining before it expired. It, too, sat in the wallet with a U.S. Social Security card that had been valid with her J1, a special work visa from when she worked that summer as a groom. Then there was that worn legal document her mother had given her, confirming whom Dani Flynn belonged to—even if *he* never wanted her.

Her fingers tightened on the strap of her backpack. He wasn't her business. It'd be best to remember that and put the ridiculous notion of finding him out of her head. With the weight of her belongings firmly against her shoulders, Dani hopped on her scooter and turned the key; the engine hesitated before it turned over. Tying her long hair up and trapping a dark, wayward wisp behind her ear, she grabbed her helmet and started out.

The stone pub with its thatched roof and chimney disappeared behind a hill, leaving only a curl of smoke from the turf fire to blow against a blackened sky. With no moon to brighten the gloom, she took the tarmac road running along the jagged coast and headed toward Rosslare Harbour. The air was damp and cool against her skin. Summers on Ireland's east coast could never be described as balmy—more windswept and temperamental, like an Irishwoman, giving way to bursts of sun and rain at a minute's notice.

Dani took the curve and followed the rise of the road. To her left the Irish Sea smacked the rugged cliffs, churning the water into an angry mix of dark waves and foam. On her right, the soft grass of the meadow swayed against a gentle sea wind.

It would be calming, if it weren't for the constant hum of her phone tucked away in the front of her sweatshirt. Dani had a fair idea it would be Kara's name backlit on her mobile but as she was already on her way, she wouldn't be fiddling with it—or she'd find herself in the hedges, to be sure.

A chain-link fence snaked along the harbor, guarding cold, industrial buildings. Large containers littered the shipyard, with the merest hint of a pilothouse behind the warehouse she would be entering. Turning left, her bike bobbled over train tracks. She pulled through where the gate had been left open and angled her bike next to Kara's battered coupe. With a quick turn of the key, the engine coughed and sputtered into silence. Lifting her helmet off, Dani hooked it over the handlebar and dismounted.

The docks at a quarter past eleven were dark, particularly so without the moon, and quiet. The eeriness shook her to her marrow, and she yanked her phone from her pocket and dialed Kara.

"You're a bold one, leaving me to the mercy of Patrick Malone to explain your absence. I still need to get dressed, and I don't suppose you have a mirror to—"

"Shh, Dani Flynn."

Dani frowned into her mobile. Still keeping it against her ear, she crossed the parking lot. She glanced back to account for the number of cars. "Where's Tommy, then? I don't see his—"

"He's not here."

"Why not?"

"There's no ship tonight. I've something to show you." Kara's usually calm voice shook.

A trickle of unease entered Dani's bloodstream, and she hesitated, just a fraction, before entering the warehouse and shutting the door. "Where are you, then?"

She squinted into the darkness and took a tentative step. Rows of towering shelves, filled to capacity with storage units, left her sandwiched between walls of metal. At five foot two, she couldn't begin to see above the first row.

"At the end, on the right."

She moved farther down. A hand shot out, pulling her around an enormous shelf, and she stumbled and fell.

Dani fought through the pitch black, clutching silky, long hair between her fingers; she knew the color to be blond. "Have you lost your feckin' head?" Her heart beat as though she'd climbed the highest hill in all of Ireland.

"Shut your gob, Dani," Kara hissed and slapped a hand hard across

Dani's mouth, her eyes wide and staring down at her friend. "We're in a load of shite, and I need you to keep your wits about you. Can you do that?"

Dani nodded, her own eyes growing rounder.

Kara removed her hand. "Did anyone follow you? You didn't see Tommy's black Spider?"

"No." Dani gave her a hard look and rubbed her lips.

"Shh."

"No," Dani whispered it this time. Straightening away from Kara, she sat up, the concrete cold against her bum. "What is it?"

Kara crawled over toward the edge of the shelf.

Dani pulled the straps of her backpack onto her shoulders and remained seated, blinking into the gray murk. They were in a corner of the warehouse closest to the pier, the thick metal walls making it difficult to hear anything but their heavy breathing.

Kara kept a steady watch toward the single door Dani had come through. "I went by Tommy's to get my cash. He carried on, complaining he didn't have it. He left me standing outside his apartment, the bollocks, too stupid to realize while he was laughing in my face and heading out with his mate O'Shea, he'd forgot to lock the door." She turned and reached into her jean pocket and handed Dani a wad of euros.

Dani hesitated. The last thing she needed was Tommy Duggan angry with her. She could have waited until he paid her. Kara was impatient and stupid. Tommy was a businessman, aware of how much cash he had down to the last shilling. He'd miss the money, and he would know who took it.

"I don't want it." Dani pushed the euros back and tried to stand.

Kara's mouth twisted. "Do you never take risks, Dani?" Kara yanked her down beside her. "Well I do. I wanted the money same as you, only I took the risk. He owed it to us. Calling us last minute to hand-hold his so-called clients—at midnight, no less. Did you never wonder who they are?" Their eyes met. Kara's usually light blue ones were dark and boring into hers.

Of all the things to say.

Heat pinched Dani's cheeks. She had, on more than one occasion, spoke aloud her misgivings. Only to be—

"So you're going to ignore me, then. Fine. But you're here with me now, so live with it."

The purr of an expensive motorcar brought their attention around.

"Did you hear that?" Dani whispered, a shiver shooting down her spine.

Kara's grip tightened. "It's Tommy." The words fell from her lips in hushed warning.

Dani's heart jumped. He knew they were in the warehouse. She could explain she had nothing to do with it—the money. He might believe her, but then he'd beat it out of Kara. She couldn't let him hurt her. Tall, blond, and at the moment incredibly without a brain wasn't reason enough to leave her to him and O'Shea.

"Let's go." She pulled Kara up with her. "We're only asking to get caught." Dani for one wasn't taking a fist to her face. "There's a back door. We double around while they're in the warehouse. If we're quick, we can escape and put the money back."

"It's not the money he's looking for."

Dani stopped, her fingers digging deep into Kara's sleeve.

"Ow. Let go of me arm."

Dani released her hold. "What did you do, Kara?"

"He lied to us. His clients are not what he'd have us believe."

"Who are they?"

The knob rattled and the door creaked open. Thick-soled shoes clicked on the concrete floor.

"We're lost if we don't move." Kara grabbed her hand. "Don't make a sound."

They ran along the back wall toward a single door that opened to the pier. Dani's trainers squeaked against the slick concrete floor, and she winced.

"Shite." Kara turned as they moved down the back row, her brows snapping together. "You're going to give us away."

"I'm—"

"Is that you, Kara?" Tommy's deep voice filled the warehouse. "Come out, luv, and we'll talk about a few euro and a certain thumb drive."

Dani swallowed and held tight to Kara's hand, still moving with her until they reached the door. Kara grabbed for the knob.

The male whispers behind them and the thump of heavy footsteps gave every indication O'Shea was with him. As much as Dani didn't like Duggan, O'Shea was worse. He was stocky and thick with muscle to the point he looked as if he'd burst. His blunt, wide features made him look angry, even the few times he smiled.

They needed to get out. The door? Would it be—

The knob turned in Kara's hand, thankfully, and they moved through the door without a sound, Dani shutting it behind them.

"Run," Kara whispered back, and then her grip on Dani's hand was gone. Kara headed left toward the shipping containers.

Dani caught up with her and silently cursed the pack on her back. They weaved between the painted containers, rusty and scarred, their height equal to that of most cottages in the area.

Dani stopped, grabbed Kara's arm, and held her in place. Both breathing heavy, Dani raised her chin, her eyes an accusing Celtic blue. "You don't own a bloody computer. Nor do I but I know what a thumb drive is. What the devil are you doing with one?"

Kara pulled out from her grasp and kept going. She shifted her head back, her blond hair whipping around her face. "I'll tell you." She gasped for air. "I promise. But move your arse before they catch us."

Dani's senses sharpened. The usual sounds along the dock became more disturbing. The wind had strengthened, whirling her hair about her eyes. The waves slapped the bulkhead with a ferocity only the Irish Sea could deliver. She clenched her hands, moist from a combination of the damp sea air and her own nervous sweat.

She followed Kara, legs pumping, looking for an escape. *To where?* Dani thought. They might outrun him tonight, but depending upon Kara's confession, she might never again rest her head in peace.

All her life she'd worked hard to survive on a pittance of income. She didn't require much, a dry roof and a warm bed. But she wanted more. Then Kara had talked her into taking Duggan's easy money. For what, mind you? So his clients could relax a bit after being locked up in tight quarters for a week or more at sea. And *her* looking ridiculous dressed in high heels, slim skirt, and blouse like a professional bitta fluff from Dublin.

How incredibly stupid, Dani.

Tonight she certainly wouldn't be afforded a moment's leisure under a blackened sky with the threat of rain.

Dani ran even with Kara. "They're going to catch us."

Kara slowed and eyed their surroundings. "To the left! We hop the fence and hide on the freighter."

The freighter loomed above several stories high, with containers stacked like children's building blocks. It was the one thing she could see. But unlike the blocks of a child, they offered no delight—only a desperate attempt to hide.

Kara darted around the last container in the row closest to the fence. Dani came behind her. They grabbed onto it and hoisted themselves up. The metal shook in Dani's hands and gave with her weight, making it bulge out and awkward to climb.

Cursing, she grabbed for the chain links above her and climbed higher, refusing to free herself of her belongings. No matter what it took, she'd scale the fence. Whatever Kara had taken, merely giving it back wouldn't suffice.

"He's going to kill us, you know. Whether you opened the files or not, he'll be a fool to assume you haven't." She kept climbing.

"Is that all you can do, complain and worry?" Kara breathed hard. "Next time I'll take me own money and forget about yours."

Dani gave Kara a sideways glance. "Like I asked you to put me in the middle and make me run for me life. I don't mind hard work, Kara. I've done it most all me life."

Angry, and with good reason, she'd been blathering on, climbing without a care for its difficulty and leaving Kara to struggle below. Above her remained only a few handfuls of chain before she reached the top.

Shite. Razor wire, gnarled and glistening sharp, ran the length of the fence. They'd both be bloodied and shredded once they made it over the top.

"Kara," Dani whispered down, her voice harsh with insistence. "Hurry—"

A door flew open and slammed, metal to metal.

"They're on the dock." Dani couldn't control the tremor in her voice.

Footsteps echoed in the distance. The height of the containers left Dani to wonder how close they were getting.

"The docks." Tommy's voice burst low with demand and impatience, and Dani froze, unable to move.

I'm going to die.

Kara's blond hair, a mass of tangles, spanned her shoulders and back. Her face tilted up, and she frowned. "I'm stuck! It's me jacket. It's feckin' hung up on the fence! Go on without me. I'll catch up." Kara gnashed her teeth and tore at the jacket like a snared rabbit ready to chew off its foot.

Leave her to Tommy and O'Shea? No. She couldn't do it.

Dani moved down. "Where are you stuck?" She angled her head to get a look.

"It's caught. The zipper." Kara tugged on the jacket, cursing.

"Leave it. I'll get it." Dani grabbed for the corner of the jacket and pulled, trying to free it. The full weight of her body and the backpack made it a burden to hold on to the thin metal of the fence. It dug into her palm and fingers. "It won't budge. You'll have to take it off."

Kara shimmied out of the left sleeve, and Dani helped with the right.

The footsteps came on—hollow, metallic, and much closer than before.

Dani glanced over her shoulder. Her body grew incredibly cold.

Chapter Two

"Is it a taste of death you're wanting? The Devil's henchman, lean and strong, sat perched atop a shipping container on his haunches in a black T-shirt and jeans. Duggan smirked as though he enjoyed the chase, a lock of raven hair sweeping his brow.

"Go feck yourself," Kara slung over her shoulder.

Dani's chest tightened. *He'll murder us for sure.*

She yanked down on Kara's jacket. "Don't. I'm not dying tonight."

Dani eyed Tommy. Unless he had wings, they had a bit of breathing space to free Kara and clear the fence.

But what of O'Shea?

"And here I thought gratitude would be in order." Tommy laughed then and nodded to his man O'Shea, coming from around the warehouse.

"Aye, it would," O'Shea shouted back, lumbering in their direction.

Dani closed her ears to their chatter and worked to free Kara of her jacket. Tommy only wanted to throw her off, keep her occupied until O'Shea could spring upon them.

Damn it. The jacket was caught between them, the remaining sleeve stuck on her wrist.

Dani bit down on her lip and gave one hard tug. The jacket came off in her fingers. She flew backward against the fence, clinging with one hand, her one leg dangling, her foot frantically searching until she found a foothold.

Her shoulders ached. Her mind screamed to lose the backpack. The clothes she despised, but the wallet she couldn't part with. It was her past and perhaps her future.

Kara slipped down the fence. "Don't lose the jacket." She peered up, her expression strained. "The thumb drive is in the pocket. I'm right behind you." Kara clung to the fence in a thin, white tank, shaking, chest heaving. "Go."

Dani shoved the jacket, best she could, inside the pocket of her sweatshirt. Ignoring the pinch and poke of the thin cold fence into her flesh, she climbed.

"Get the lying hoors." Hard-soled boots thundered toward them.

Dani peered down.

O'Shea charged the fence, shaking it like a mighty fist.

"Kara!" Dani held tight.

"Go! Don't be foolish, Dani." Kara's body visibly trembled, her hands slipping before she screamed and crumpled to the ground.

"Kara!"

O'Shea was on Kara, dragging her by her hair. Tommy grabbed the fence and began to scale it.

She had to move. It would be the death of her if she stayed. The bitter taste of cowardice filled Dani's mouth; but she clenched the fence tight and climbed. Her face crumpled in distress, hot tears rolling down her cheeks. The fence shook violently with Tommy's weight. His deep breaths grew closer.

She reached the top. The points glittered—she couldn't avoid them. With no mind to the pain, Dani heaved her leg over, the sharp tips digging into her hands and through her jeans. She grunted, ignored the blood, sticky and wet, from her palms.

She spotted a trash Dumpster. Thankfully, it was closed. She jumped. Her bum hit hard, pain radiating up her spine, her back falling against the fence as she landed on the other side. She struggled to get up. The neck of her sweatshirt tightened, and she angled her head back. Cold gray eyes met hers, and a sick dread held her bound, lost in Tommy Duggan's stare, his long fingers snaking through the chain links and digging deeper into the soft cotton of her sweatshirt.

"I'll slit your throat, feckin' bitch. Now give it to me."

His grizzly voice had her swallowing hard. He'd do it, even if she handed the jacket over. No, she'd fight him.

"Go to hell." She jammed her fingers hard through the fence. Tommy screamed, let go of her sweatshirt, and grabbed for his eyes while trying to hang on to the fence. "I'll murder you, hoor. Shoot you in the feckin' head and drop you in the sea."

Dani kept moving. She shimmied down the metal rungs of the Dumpster. He'd be on her soon enough. Duggan's moans and Kara's whimpers from somewhere to her right floated away. Only the roar of her heart crashed in her ears. She didn't ask for this. She should have worked her bloody shift and been paid right there from the till from Pat himself. What a fool she'd been. Her greed would surely get her killed tonight.

The ship with all its steely strength stretched the length of the pier. It was locked tight, the gangway sealed shut, her future just as gray as the paint on its wide hull.

What to do?

She slowed and peered over her shoulder. Tommy crested the fence, and everything around her swayed.

He's going to catch me for sure.

He was on the dock now, same as she, but toward the front of the ship. Still too close. Dani turned. She needed to get as far away from him as possible. She might not get on the ship, but she could hide.

Her legs twisted, and the notion fell away. Her chin hit first, the suddenness causing stars to swirl about her head. Had he caught her?

Flat on her stomach, she thrashed her head about. Tommy remained at a distance, unaware she was down. She touched her chin and winced. Scraped by concrete, oozing with blood, it burned without mercy.

Ignore it.

She pressed up onto her knees. The ship remained to the right of her. Thick braided ropes creaking above held the ship bound to the dock while the splash of the sea pounded the bulkhead. She had to find a way onto the ship. That, or the sea.

On her feet now, Dani sprinted toward the rear of the ship. A small platform jutted from its side. She ducked beneath it. Her heart fluttering in her chest, legs shaking, she pressed back into the darkness.

"Do you think you'll make it out alive, luv?"

Tommy's voice, smooth and taunting, made Dani stiffen. From where she stood in the shadows of the platform, she was sure she was well hidden. Black-soled shoes moved toward her on the dock. He was so close. Just one dip of his head, and he'd find her.

"I enjoy the chase, luv." He grunted with laughter. "I can hear your heart beating hard and fast in me own ears. I'll find you soon enough."

Trembling, Dani took shallow breaths and willed her heart to slow. She couldn't afford to do something stupid. Even her breathing could give her up. Dani grabbed the jacket from her sweatshirt pocket. The sweet scent of Kara filled her nose. Kara's whimpers from earlier had all but disappeared. Perhaps it was the distance. Dani dug inside one of the pockets. It was empty. Her heart sank. Had she lost it, then? Not that she cared a whit about his thumb drive. But as long as she had it, maybe she could bargain for her life. She tried the other. Her knuckles trapped a thin plastic case against the cloth. She wrapped her hand around it and drew it out.

So small . . .

What could it possibly hold that Tommy would kill for it?

Dani held it tight. Tommy continued to pace by the platform, never once bending his head to look under. Her bones shook so hard she thought for sure they were knocking against one another. He continued to pace.

Eventually, he'd think to duck his head. Then he would have her.

She prayed to God. *Protect me.*

Tommy walked away, heading in the opposite direction.

Dani tied Kara's jacket on a metal support pole beneath the platform, wrapping the extra material a few times to keep it from hanging. She had enough weighing her down. Shoving the thumb drive in her front jean pocket, she slipped out from beneath the platform toward the stairs. Her brain tried to make sense of the crisscross of metal.

No steps.

They had been folded up and chained in place, and that small chance she'd survive the night rushed past her like the last car of the midnight train.

There had to be another way. She could manage the height. The platform came to just below her chest. Dani slipped off her backpack, placed it on the edge of the platform. She shoved it under the bottom rail. Grabbing hold of the top rail with her bleeding hands, she hoisted herself up, her foot struggling to find a hold on the platform. When it did, the other foot followed, and she climbed over the top rail to the other side.

She snagged her backpack and swung it over her shoulder. It was all she had. If she escaped Duggan tonight, she couldn't go back to her apartment.

She started climbing the metal steps, leading onto the ship, her hand keeping a death grip on the support bar. The platform shook. She whipped her head around.

Two wide palms and long fingers, as bloody as her own, gripped the rail of the platform. Dani's hand tightened on the bar. Frozen, she remained staring into the eyes of death.

"You're a bold one, aren't you?" His lips thinned. "Pity I have to kill you." With that, he drew himself up and over the rail of the platform.

Dani flew up the steps, the metal rungs hollow beneath her feet. Once she cleared the steps, she found herself surrounded by walls of containers and no place to hide. She glanced back. Tommy's head crested the stairs of the ship, his body growing larger, taller, the more steps he took. He stood before her, perhaps twenty paces separating them. He sneered, his jaw clenching, the sharp angles of his face making him appear all the more dangerous.

"Tsk, tsk, Dani girl. You've got no place to hide, luv."

Dani searched the deck. To the left sat a metal barrel. She reached for it, and it tilted.

Tommy cleared the steps and came at her. She pushed the barrel to the deck and kicked it toward him with all her might. He jumped, his foot catching the corner of it, and cursed, stumbling onto his knees.

Dani ran toward the center of the ship. She'd seen the pilothouse—she only needed to reach it. She didn't dare look back. The metal two-story structure towered above her. She tried the door. It wouldn't budge. She searched for a window large enough to slip through, but the only window glinted high above.

Dearest Father in heaven.

She'd be dead before sunrise, make no mistake. And who would care? She was alone in this world. A poor misguided soul with no family to speak of. Something flapped in the wind, its white corner loose and waving to her right. A tarp, unsnapped from a lifeboat. She headed that way. Three feet below, the lifeboat hung down the side of the ship, the tarp open on one corner where it had come loose.

Dani climbed over the edge. Between the ship and the lifeboat, the Irish Sea, black and shimmery as the finest bolt of silk, roiled below. If she miscalculated the distance, it would be her death.

The clatter of heavy shoes came from behind the pilothouse. She jumped. Dani's body hit hard, her breath knocked from her chest when she landed. The weight of her backpack left her struggling for air.

Breathe.

She gulped in a mix of sea and briny salt air and sputtered.

Move.

She crawled on top of the tarp, heading toward the corner of the lifeboat where the flap lay open. Tugging until several snaps popped,

Dani then dropped down into it, pulling the tarp closed. If she held the flap down, he might not notice it had come loose. She sat hunched in the back corner of the lifeboat, her fingers straining to hold the tarp closed against the whipping winds. She only hoped O'Shea hadn't caught her abandoning the ship for the lifeboat from the dock. He'd surely call Tommy's attention to it.

Her chest hurt, her chin throbbed, and her fingers were becoming stiff. She refused to give in to the pain. Duggan paced the deck above, the sound growing louder until she was sure he stood right above her.

"You're some can of piss," Duggan called out. "I'll find you, you know? Make it easier on yourself and come out."

Dani shook her head, her body trembling.

Tommy's shoes, echoing against the metal deck, moved past the lifeboat—very close, too close. He stopped, and Dani held her breath and then released it when he moved on.

For almost an hour she waited, her hands frozen in place, refusing to let go. The metallic steps had long since subsided. Had he left the boat? She didn't know. But the sun would soon be up and the docks would awaken.

"Dani!"

Kara's voice tore through Dani, and she scrambled to the other side of the lifeboat. She couldn't see. On this side, the tarp was snapped down tight. She twisted her fingers beneath it, trying to quietly pop the snaps. She managed to pry open several, enough to peek under.

She could make out Kara's blond head below her on the dock. Duggan and O'Shea were dark shadows, forcing her to stand against the fence. The sky brightened; dawn was upon them. Just then light reflected off something.

Tommy's head rose, his attention drawn toward the ship.

Dani dropped down into the lifeboat, her heart hammering against her ribs. Had he seen her?

"Ireland's but a speck in the Atlantic, luv. I'll find you. Perhaps not tonight, but soon."

A scream, jagged and piercing, stabbed Dani sharp in her chest.

Kara . . .

It came only once before a single shot shattered the heavy air surrounding her, and Dani jerked as if the bullet had claimed her own life.

Dani awoke, her body gently rolling. Above her was a ceiling of white. Where was she? The lifeboat. Her nightmare came at her, and she scrambled to her knees. Dani's stomach heaved. Her hand flew to her mouth. What the devil? She poked her head out from the tarp closest to the ship, a cool wind caressing her cheek, the brightness making her squint. The sea roiled beneath her, whitecaps smacking the hull, the dock no longer in sight.

Shite! I'm at sea.

Dani fell back into the lifeboat. Tears leaked down her cheeks. She knew nothing of the world. Ireland was her home—and the one place she could not go. Shouts came from up above, and Dani stiffened. Would they find her? Her stomach gave witness and twisted; hanging her head down, she heaved. Nothing came out. And why would it? She hadn't eaten since . . .

Rachel's sack.

She couldn't even begin to think of eating. She'd only throw it up.

There was no telling how long until the ship docked or where it would land. Maybe it would only go as far as Dublin. Dani's spirits brightened. She would hold fast to that hope. She grabbed her backpack for a pillow, settled down into the corner of the lifeboat, and wiped her eyes. Yes, she would hold on to that hope.

She closed her eyes against the sway of the ship.

Kara's lovely face appeared, her words floating back to Dani, and starting her tears anew.

Do you never take risks, then, Dani?

Chapter Three

Sheriff Kevin Bendix headed west down Maryland's route 68. Part of Washington County—his county—he knew the road like the back of his hand but chose to turn on his spotlight anyway. Familiar or not, at close to two in the morning the county highway, with one lane in each direction and void of streetlights, could come up on him fast.

The spotlight caught the edge of the sign, growing larger with every mile his patrol car put behind him. He chuckled. He couldn't help it. *Grace Equine Sanctuary & Cattle Ranch*. He should have warned Texas cowboy Rafe Langston, who had lost his heart and proposed marriage to Kevin's childhood friend Bren Fallon. If she protected horses from the slaughterhouse, no way in hell would she allow him to harm a calf she helped raise.

It was one thing to buy a prepackaged steak at Ernst's Market, quite another to slaughter Julius, Buttercup, or Blackie. She'd named them. That should have been Rafe's first clue his Angus would never make it to market.

Kevin turned left down Grace's gravel drive. The farmhouse, lights ablaze, flashed between the wide trunks of the tall oaks lining the driveway. He parked in front and cut the lights, took a sip of hot coffee, and sat it down on the dash. He'd be taking it with him. He needed the pick-me-up. At thirty-nine and used to working the day shift, he could barely keep his eyes open past the ten o'clock news. But the third Saturday of every month was the only time he could meet with all of his men when the day shift overlapped with the night.

He'd been heading home when Bren called. With Rafe out of town and her pregnant with their first child, he'd oblige her by checking the grounds. Besides, with Bren, she'd do it herself if he didn't get there fast enough—probably, it had something to do with a certain teenager they both knew and loved sneaking in or out of his bedroom window. Whatever it turned out to be, he'd do his damnedest not to get sucked into the drama of one redheaded, emotional, pregnant woman.

That was one of the reasons he'd remained a bachelor. He had enough commotion in his life running the sheriff's department. He didn't need his love life spilling over into his perfect, orderly home. He discreetly kept his girlfriends a county's length away, far from the penetrating eyes of his neighbor, Mrs. Josephine Wiley.

Kevin reached around for his campaign hat hanging back on his headrest when his elbow clipped the coffee cup on the dash. His hand shot out, grabbing the Styrofoam cup. He jostled it, the top popped off, and hot coffee spilled onto his wrist, burning his skin.

"Shit." The cup tilted, spilling onto his lap. *"Son of a bitch."* Kevin pushed back into the seat, a river of hot coffee saturating his uniform pants, running under his legs, soaking his ass.

Pissed, he threw the empty cup over into the passenger footwell. He opened the door and jumped out, the cool, June mountain air smacking him square in the damp seat of his pants. A shiver shot through him.

Still holding on to his campaign hat, he placed it over his fresh military haircut, cursed some more, and grabbed his flashlight. He slammed the door and winced. If he kept up his tantrum, he'd wake her boys, Aiden and Finn—well . . . maybe not Aiden.

He had his suspicions on the boy's whereabouts.

Kevin hobbled across the gravel drive, pulling at his wet pants, and climbed the steps. He knocked and waited. The door flew open, along with the screen. He jumped back, the wooden frame missing his head by degrees.

"You pee your pants?" Bren, with her dark red hair spilling about her shoulders and wearing a pink fuzzy robe, her stomach out like a beach ball, said it with the utmost seriousness.

Which clued him in. Whatever happened tonight shook her up.

She lifted her head, which had been directed at his crotch. Her usual smiling brown eyes were flat, void of emotion.

Kevin shifted. His underwear stuck to him, and his legs had begun to itch. "I spilled coffee." He nodded to her. "You going to let me in?"

Bren backed away from the door. He stepped inside and smiled. Kate

Fallon, now Kate Parker, stood in the hallway leading into the kitchen.

"Hey, Kev, it's so good to see you." She moved toward him, dressed in a pair of boxers and a T-shirt. She gave him a hug, and he wrapped his arms around her.

She still looked the same, pretty brown eyes, long waves of mahogany hair. He'd had a thing for Kate when they were younger—much younger. Not that he ever got a chance to pursue those feelings. Bren would have beat the snot out of him if he had made a move on her little sister. Didn't matter. He'd gone off to the University of Maryland to get his bachelor's in criminal justice. When he returned, she had gone off to Georgetown and then on to law school.

"How's Colorado treating you?"

She gave him a tight squeeze and pulled away. "Good."

Funny thing was, in the end, she'd married a damn county sheriff. "How're Jess and the baby?"

"Jess's fine. Mineral County couldn't do without him for a few weeks. But Charlie's with me." She glanced upstairs.

He'd not met her daughter. But from what he'd learned from Bren, she was under a year. "You come to help Bren when the baby arrives?"

Bren came up behind him. "Let's take this reunion into the kitchen." She ushered them down the hall.

Kevin nodded toward the window over the sink. "Is this where you saw him?"

Bren leaned against the counter, her hand massaging the middle of her back. "I couldn't sleep. I made a cup of tea. When I went to grab the kettle, he was staring in the window."

Kevin pulled out a notebook and pen. "Can you describe him?"

She shrugged. "It happened too fast. He wore a dark sweatshirt, hood pulled over his head." She frowned. "He had the bluest eyes."

That let Aiden off the hook. "You could see that?"

Bren cocked her head, her brows furrowing. "When his face was pressed up to the glass, yeah."

He nodded. "How tall?"

"Not very," Kate piped in. "After Bren came up to get me, I went outside to check around. Beneath the window I found a potted plant dumped, the pot positioned under the window."

Kevin moved toward the back door and opened it. To the right on the back porch he found an overturned terra-cotta pot right where Kate had mentioned, the soft, pink petals of a petunia buried under a mound of dirt.

He glanced back from the doorway. "All the kids accounted for?"

Bren nodded.

"Which way did he head?"

Bren came toward him and motioned him out the back door. "He ran toward the barn. I thought about going after him. But—"

"I told her no," Kate said, stepping over the threshold onto the porch. "Whoever he is, it's not worth either one of us risking our lives."

He'd take a look around. At this point, the intruder was probably long gone. "Why don't you two go inside? I'll check the perimeter of the house and the barn."

"I'm staying," Bren said, slipping down into one of the porch rockers.

Kevin gave Kate a look.

Kate came up alongside him and whispered, "I had to fight with her to keep her from going in the barn. I don't want to argue over this." She moved past him, her voice rising to a normal tone. "We'll both sit and wait for you." She took the matching rocker next to Bren and sat down.

No way was he fighting the two of them. He'd lost as a kid against the Fallon sisters. He'd still lose.

"I'll be back." Kevin stepped off the porch and did a sweep around the house. Uncomfortable in soggy pants, he pulled at them, grimacing, and checked the windows on the main level. They were locked. Smart. Even though it was in the low seventies, he was glad Bren took the precaution. He came back around. The two remained—Bren rocking, her hands resting on her belly, and Kate making a move to stand.

He put up a hand. "I've got it, Kate. I'll check the barn."

He crossed the gravel drive and walked around the footprint of the barn, his shadow leading the way now that the moon had cleared a patch of clouds. Coming around to the front of the barn, he slid back the large door, interrupting the chorus of crickets as it screeched against a rusty track.

He stepped in and hit his flashlight. It was quiet, except for the movement of a few horses that were not well enough to be out in the pasture. Most were bedded down in their stalls. Only two remained standing foursquare, their large brown eyes twinkling when he caught them in the halo of his flashlight. Tack hung on the stall doors, bales of hay stacked in corners.

Kevin eyed the ladder to the loft and shook his head. He'd climb it. If he didn't—he rolled his eyes—someone else would. Scaling the ladder, he peered out over the hayloft with his flashlight. Nothing out of the ordinary—straw-covered floor, a few bales, and the pulley system. It was clear. Making his way down the ladder, he shoved the flashlight into the holder on his belt. He continued his descent until his uniform pants snagged something.

"What the hell?" he grumbled and bent his head.

A nail . . .

Movement from his right caught his attention. A figure darted from the shadows and out the door.

Kevin jerked. His pants tore, the sharp point of the nail scraping his thigh. "Shit." He jumped down the remaining rungs and cleared the barn.

In the distance, a dark figure ran across the gravel drive. Both Bren and Kate rose to their feet. Their cries of "get him" blended into one high-pitched squeal. He no longer needed caffeine. Every instinct that made him a cop jolted him awake. He dodged the tulip poplar and came from the left, cutting ahead of the intruder. Elbows and legs moved toward him and the cornfield behind him.

No way was the little shit getting past him. It'd be hell to chase him through the waist-high corn. No telling what he'd trip over. There was a good chance he'd fall on his ass and lose the perp.

Kevin waited until the figure passed by the wide trunk of the tree and swooped in. He knocked him facedown in the dirt, falling on top. A soft rush of air dwindled from the perp's chest. Gauging by the width of his shoulder blades poking into Kevin's chest, he was a gangly teen—a small, gangly teen.

But what he lacked in height, he made up for in determination. His legs flailed, feet kicking.

Kevin sat up, straddling the youth's waist. "Washington County Sheriff, you're under arrest." He grabbed for his cuffs with one hand, the other subduing the perp's left. He pulled it behind his back.

The moon glinted off the cuffs when he drew them around. A small hand, the perp's right hand, dug into the dirt. He twisted beneath Kevin. It happened in a split second. Granules of dirt flew into Kevin's face. He fell back and grabbed his eyes, dropping the cuffs, cursing.

It burned like a son of a bitch.

The perp, now on his back, squirmed away. Not going to happen. Kevin gritted his teeth, his hands landing on the perp's chest. He held him down. Only instead of a bony sternum and thin-ribbed youth, his hand curved around a nice set of soft . . . *shit . . . boobs!*

Kevin stiffened. He didn't move. Not his hands or his eyes.

He could make out the curve of her high cheekbones, a delicately shaped nose flaring with every breath. Eyes fringed with thick, dark lashes blinked at him.

Damn it. She was half his size, but a woman—not a child or a teen. *Shit.* He was still cupping her breasts. Kevin slid his hands onto her upper arms. "Relax." His breaths were coming in waves, too. She'd given him a workout. All . . . what? He glanced down the length of her. There was nothing to her waist. Her legs were firm and shapely against his thighs, but not long. She couldn't be much over five feet.

She said nothing.

The shadow of clouds floated by, and, for a moment, light landed square on her face. She pierced him with a pair of deep blue eyes—the same eyes Bren had seen in her window—but bright faded to dark, and he was left trying to memorize the depth of her face.

She took a deep breath.

He must be crushing her. At six two, muscular frame from working out—no way would he allow himself to be labeled out of shape by the young bucks he commanded—he moved back onto her thighs. Grabbing his flashlight, he clicked it on to get a better visual. "I'll let you up. But no funny stuff."

She nodded, biting down on a full bottom lip.

An odd thrill twisted his gut, and he ignored it, pulling her up to a sitting position by her elbow. The hood of her sweatshirt fell back. Shimmering dark waves caught the beam from his flashlight and cascaded down her shoulders, framing her face. The contrast against her smooth translucent skin was stunning, except for a rough scab running the width of her chin.

Kevin dipped his head. "You have a name?"

The heavy crown from the tulip poplar, high above them, rustled in the light breeze. She didn't answer.

Fine. He'd question hardened criminals before and gotten what he needed.

Kevin clicked off the flashlight, shoving it into the holder on his belt. He eased off and came to his feet, taking her to a standing position. "You hurt anywhere?" His hand ran along her arm, touching rough scabs along her palm and slender fingers. Her hand jerked, and she took a quick breath, exhaling it slowly.

He frowned. "Hurts, huh?"

Their eyes met. Hers were wary, darting from him to their surroundings. She couldn't escape. He'd be on her in seconds. Kevin kept his hand linked with hers. He leveled his gaze. "You want to tell me what happened to you?"

She stiffened, her eyes growing larger.

"I can help you. But you need to trust me."

A moan escaped her lips, and she doubled over.

Shit. Did she have internal injuries?

Pain shot through his wrist. "What the hell?" he grunted.

Like a rabid dog, she clenched onto him, sinking her teeth into the sensitive area near his pulse.

He let go. Couldn't help it—hurt like a bitch.

She took off, and the chase was on.

Kevin slammed into her back, taking her down to the gravel drive. She hit hard, a soft, feminine moan escaping her mouth, and he didn't give a shit. If she wanted to go the hard way—her choice.

He was more concerned whether she'd gotten her rabies shot.

He whipped her arm back and slammed the cuff around her wrist. She struggled beneath him. Kevin tightened his thighs. Her other hand dug into the gravel. Before she could arm herself, he grabbed her hand and shook it until she dropped every last stone then cuffed her.

Kevin placed his hand on her back and sat up.

"You ass. Get off her."

The voice, he recognized.

"She can't breathe, Kevin." Fingers dug into his shoulders. "Get up. You're hurting her."

Another familiar voice.

He glared up at Bren and Kate—both standing bare legged in slippers, their arms crossed over their chests, eyeing him with disdain. His youth flooded back to him.

He didn't have a chance.

Still breathing heavy, his words came in a rush. "Let me do my job." Kevin ran his hands up the back of her legs. They were stiff and glued together. "Spread them." Nudging her legs apart, he finished patting her down. He reached in the back pockets of her jeans, then the front. Nothing. He rolled her over and dug into the large sweatshirt pocket. Empty. "You have ID on you?"

She only lay there, her hair a tangle hiding her face. He pressed her hair back from her eyes, and he hesitated. Tear-filled orbs glistened in the moonlight. *Damn it.* She'd asked for this. He'd offered to help her. He wasn't the bad guy here.

Kevin pushed up and stood, taking his prize of a prisoner with him.

"Her chin." Kate's lips thinned, and she moved toward her.

Kevin moved to block Kate. "She bites."

"I'd bite you, too." Bren brushed by Kate and took a strategic position between Kevin and the woman. "I want you to un-cuff her."

"No way in hell, Bren." He pulled his prisoner toward his patrol car. His leg stung where the nail had gotten him, his pants were still wet along with his underwear, which, at the moment, rode up his ass compliments of Little Miss Innocent, and his wrist throbbed where she'd taken a chunk out of him. "She's spending the night in the county jail."

Bren and Kate blocked the passenger door of his patrol car.

Kevin shook his head. "You two called me, remember?" Keeping his hand around his prisoner's arm, he unlocked his door and motioned for the two of them to step aside.

"I'll drop the charges," Bren said.

Kevin laughed. "I don't need you to charge her. Trespassing is the least of her worries."

Kate grabbed his arm. "What do you have on her?"

He locked in on Kate. "I thought you gave up practicing law." He cocked his head. "In fact, as I remember, you were disbarred."

She nailed him with unsmiling eyes.

"Fine. Have an attitude. I'm charging her with assault on a police officer."

Bren's lips sputtered. "You're a big sissy." She grabbed his wrist, eyeballing it, and cast his arm away, giving him a less than sympathetic face. "She broke the skin. Big deal."

He had a head for people, especially these two. They weren't going to let it go. He also had a fair indication the mute leaning up against his patrol car would remain that way.

"I'll make you two a deal. You get her to talk. Tell me her name and where she came from, and she's all yours. But that means you have to take her in for the night."

He beaded in on his prisoner. Dirt smudged her cheeks. Grass and maybe a crunched up leaf stuck out of her hair. If she came to the height of his shoulders, he'd be surprised. But for such a delicate-sized woman, she could put up a fight.

He connected with her eyes. They flickered with something akin to curiosity. Curious as to whether he'd let her go.

He was a man of his word, except she didn't know that.

She wet her lips and glanced warily at Bren and Kate, then back to Kevin, and the eyes that drew him in with all their uncertainty hardened. "I'm Dani Flynn. I've come from Ireland to find me da."

Son of a bitch. He didn't doubt it—she had the accent, too.

"She's ours." Bren and Kate chimed in unison, throwing their hands up. A familiar smile tugged at Bren's mouth, one that effectively said, *You lose.* He clenched his teeth. When he had the chance, he should have kicked the small town dirt from his shoes and taken the FBI's offer of employment and moved his ass to L.A.

Bren held out her hand in a gimme kind of way. "The key."

He shook his head and moved toward Bren. Bending slightly, he whispered in her ear, "I guarantee you, she's illegal."

Kevin moved past and grabbed Dani Flynn's wrists. Her tiny hands curved inward. Didn't matter. He'd felt the wounds, had already deduced she had a story. He'd oblige the Fallon sisters tonight. But if Flynn remained in his county tomorrow—which was a big if—she'd be answering a few questions. He wouldn't be surprised if she robbed these two of everything valuable in the meantime.

He angled his head to get a better look at her and let her know in no uncertain terms who she was dealing with. "And it's Sheriff Kevin Bendix." He removed the cuffs and placed them inside the case on his hip. He held her hands behind her back, completely hidden in the width of his own. Small, vulnerable, and completely female, he ignored the dip in his gut. "I'll be by tomorrow to check on you, Miss Flynn."

CHAPTER FOUR

DANI STOOD ALONE IN THE YOUNG BOY'S BEDROOM. SCRUBBED CLEAN, her hair damp and hanging past her shoulders, she slipped the cotton shift over her head. Soft with a breezy spring scent, it fell to just above her knees. It was Kate who'd given it to her with a pair of silk panties and matching bra, which Dani had been grateful for. She'd been forced to wear the same clothes for over a week.

Getting to this farm over the past two days had taken every ounce of strength, the Yank's hundred dollar bill long since spent on transportation and a little food to get by on. She sat on the bed twisting the hem of her dress. She'd never planned to come here. But being afraid and flat broke had added a new perspective to that high-and-mighty attitude of hers. Kate and Bren had been kind to her last night, offering her food, a bed, and the use of the bathroom down the hall.

Would they continue their kindness if she told them the truth?

A car door slammed. Dani jumped to her feet, moving toward the window. She frowned at the brim of his hat, a hat like some American cops wore in movies, and the man beneath it, his long, determined strides, returning back to the house from his patrol car. He'd never left last night. She had heard his comment to Bren. Dani furrowed her brows at him and clenched her fists tight as he ducked under the porch roof, the screen door slamming.

I've never taken what was not mine.

Dani quietly stepped from the bedroom and made her way down the stairs in a pair of sandals from Bren. Voices mingling with laughter came from a doorway to the left. She swallowed hard and passed through it.

The voices slowed, stopped. Eyes from every direction landed on her. Her own darted from a young man with longish brown hair drinking from a container of milk by the fridge to Kate and Bren standing at the sink, their faces creased in question, to a young blond boy sitting at the table, his chin resting in one hand, the other stroking the head of a large brown dog with sad eyes. But it was the one in the sky-blue uniform shirt and dark blue pants with a gaping hole above his knee who had her taking a step backward.

Light brown brows, bunched over a pair of dark, brooding eyes, narrowed. "Sleep well, Miss Flynn?" He started toward her, and Dani turned the way she'd come, running into an elderly man holding a little girl in a pink outfit with small kitties on it.

"Well, you gave me a start." He kept the child in one arm, his free hand grasping tight to her elbow to steady them. "You must be the one from last night, then?"

Dani recognized the lilt in his voice. *Irish.* She took a closer look at the older gentleman and locked onto a pair of twinkling blue eyes similar to . . .

A hand hit the back of her waist. "Excuse us, Daniel. I need a word with Bren's houseguest."

The sheriff maneuvered her past Daniel Fallon before she could find her words. She stumbled down a hall, still caught in his strong grip, and into a living area with a large, flat television above a fireplace and plaid couches. Her eyes landed on the computer in the corner, her mind going back to the thumb drive and then to her immediate problem.

The sheriff's eyes bored into her. "They'll insist you eat breakfast."

Dani wrenched her arm from him, rubbing her muscle. "Aye, and I'd appreciate a bit of food." She kept her chin up. "You're rude."

"Honey, they don't pay me to be polite."

To be sure. Broad and looming above her, he made Dani tingle with uncertainty and a little irritation. "It would be up to Bren to tell me to go, I would think."

"Ms. Flynn, you're going to eat, gather your belongings, and move on—preferably out of my county."

"But I don't—"

"I'll escort you myself."

His lips thinned, and his firm, once clean-shaven chin now rough with morning whiskers nodded toward the kitchen. "Let's go."

He followed behind her, the shiny tips of his black shoes inches from her bare heels. They cleared the doorway. Everyone had taken a seat at a rugged, wooden, rectangular-shaped table and matching chairs. Three empty seats remained, two at the end and one by the child in the pink romper, her brown curls catching the morning sun from the kitchen window.

Dani headed toward the child.

"Ms. Flynn," the sheriff said with a stiff voice.

She stopped and peered over her shoulder.

Sporting a serviceman's haircut, his brass glistening his authority, he pulled out the chair next to the boy with the glasses, and nodded to it. "You'll sit next to me."

Bren laughed. "You plan on handcuffing her to you, too?"

Finn giggled. "Do you have real bullets in that gun?" He pointed across the table.

The sheriff eyed his holster and then Dani. "Twenty-one."

"Really?" Bren placed her hands on her hips. "Stop trying to intimidate her."

"I'm not." He cleared his throat. "And do I tell you how to run your rescue?"

"Dani, is it?" The soft blue eyes of Daniel Fallon held hers, his skin crinkled and tanned by the sun. "How do you like your eggs, dear?" He nodded to a bowl of fluffy, yellow eggs. "If you'd rather—"

"I like scrambled." She gave him a brief smile and sat down, pulling herself to the table. A rasher of crisp bacon sat to her left, and her mouth watered.

The boy next to her handed her the bowl of eggs. "Kev really handcuff you?"

"Finn," Bren admonished.

He pushed his glasses up. "Sorry, I'm Finn."

"I think she gets that." The young man across the table rolled his eyes.

"I'm Dani," she said and shook the boy's soft hand, then scooped a spoonful of eggs and passed it to the sheriff.

He said nothing, only took the bowl from her and nodded toward Bren. "You planning on heading out to one o'clock Mass after breakfast?"

"If we can get our act together." Bren connected with Dani across the table. "Are you Catholic, Dani?"

"Aye."

Bren arched a russet brow in the sheriff's direction. "Since when do you work on Sunday?"

He gave a sideways glance toward Dani and sent Bren an irritated gaze. "You rescue horses, remember?"

Bren's head tilted slightly, her expression hardening. "Couch put you in a cranky mood?"

"I slept fine," he slung back.

"I think you take your position a bit too seriously." She glanced over at Dani. "She hasn't slit our throats yet. Or stolen the family jewels." She laughed. "Dad, do we have any family jewels?"

Dani bit down on a chuckle. She liked Bren.

"Not that I'm aware." He laughed, too.

"Kevin," Kate said, "I don't see why Dani couldn't stay here at the farm until she can satisfy you with proof she's legally in the U.S." Kate winked at Dani across the table, and Dani's heart warmed. Maybe she wasn't so alone after all.

He stopped chewing, as if considering, and swallowed. "That's not how it works, Kate." His fingers tightened on the fork. "And you of all people know that."

Dani lost her appetite. He'd get his way soon enough. Finn had already walked away from the table. He said he had to brush his teeth for church. They'd be tidying up, and he would be escorting her with him. Dani grew cold.

"At least allow her to go to Mass," Daniel said.

"If you're so worried"—Bren eyed Kevin and pulled away from the table with her dishes in hand—"you could join us. Father Dooley would be glad to see you."

His lips compressed, and he stood. "Maybe some other time." He glanced down at Dani. "I don't recall you having much with you last night."

"Her clothes are in the dryer." Kate got to her feet. "I'll go get them." She frowned at Dani and moved away from the table when Bren caught her arm, the two exchanging a glance, and Kate remained.

Dani's heart beat, wild and desperate. She'd made it to the farm. It had been the devil to get here. She wouldn't be going with him. He'd send her back to Ireland, and Tommy would surely be waiting.

His hand encircled her bare arm—his tanned and rough against her dove-white skin—and he brought her to her feet, her chair skidding against the wood floor.

I can't go back. Dani wrenched her arm away, her other hand coming up to that very spot where he'd held her. She gripped her arm, the heat of his fingers still present along her skin. "I belong in America. I have a right to stay."

"Then prove to me you do."

Dani swallowed. She'd gladly do so. Only she'd hidden her backpack with her wallet in the barn last night. If she told him of its existence—the wallet—he'd surely march her to the barn and take it straightaway along with the thumb drive she'd tucked inside for safekeeping. She'd not be telling him just yet.

"Ms. Flynn," he said, his voice growing impatient.

Dani jerked. She didn't particularly like his tone. Her fingers tightened, and she made direct eye contact, refusing to shy away from those skeptical eyes of his. "You asked me last night, and I told you. I'm here to find me da."

"Are you saying he's an American?" He gave her a doubtful look.

Dani nodded. "Me mother was a celebrated jockey in Ireland." She gave Daniel Fallon a penetrating stare. "Her name was Rory Flynn."

Daniel Fallon sputtered his orange juice, his eyes widening. Both Kate's and Bren's heads swung toward him.

"You okay, Dad?" Bren came around to his chair and slapped him on his back.

He raised his hand and coughed. "Aye."

"Do you recognize the name?" Dani gave Daniel Fallon a questioning look. "She named me Dani for a reason."

Dani waited with the sheriff to her left. Across the table, Bren's and Kate's expressions slowly changed from confusion to understanding, and yet *he*—the one in the middle, her own flesh and blood—did and said nothing.

She clenched her hands and took a step away from Kevin Bendix.

"Man." The older boy's eyes grew larger, his mouth opening a bit before he laughed. "Granddad did someone other than Grandma?"

"Aiden!" Bren moved with purpose, her hand landing on his shoulder hard. "That's enough." She ushered him toward the door, scooped up the baby—Kate's baby—and handed her off to him. "Wash Charlie's face and hands, and check on your brother."

Aiden jostled the baby, a smirk on his lips. "I'm going, *jeez.*" His head swung back, the smirk more congenial. "Sorry, Granddad."

"Go, Aiden." Bren pointed to the stairs beyond the doorway.

Dani kept a guarded watch on her father, begging with everything in her for him to admit it.

Daniel Fallon sat his fork down and blinked. "There is no truth in what she says." His eyes darted from Bren to Kate to the sheriff, landing on Dani. "Is it money you be wanting, Miss Flynn?"

"*Christ,*" Kevin Bendix hissed under his breath and took an angry step in her direction.

"No," Dani snapped. "I want your honesty. I'm your daughter. That I've told you."

Both Bren and Kate gasped, their eyes focusing in on her.

Bendix came at her, his eyes edged with mistrust. "Ms. Flynn." He reached for her.

Dani swatted his hand away. "I'll not have you manhandle me like I've committed a crime." She stood firm, though every fiber within her trembled. "I have not," her voice broke.

His eyes turned to flint, his arm extending behind him, the glint of something catching the kitchen light from above. Strong fingers latched onto her wrist, pulling her arm behind her back. Cold metal touched her wrist bone, encircling it, the teeth of his cuffs ratcheting tighter.

"Kevin." Kate made a move in their direction. "Is that really—"

"Damn it, Kate, back off." He snagged Dani's free arm and faced her away from him. "She brought this on herself."

Dani tried to pull away, her heart knocking into her rib cage. He pulled her back snug against his chest, bent his head to adjust for her size, his lips grazing her ear. "Relax your arm, Ms. Flynn."

Tears hit the back of Dani's eyes, and she crumpled forward. "Please," she said on a whisper.

He brought her other arm behind her back and snapped the remaining cuff in place. He then yanked her up straight with her arms secure behind her back. Dani searched the blue eyes of Daniel Fallon, so like her own. He had to know she was his. She recognized it. The women, Bren and Kate—her sisters—remained quiet now. She'd shocked them. They'd not come to her rescue a second time.

The tears welled up. "I've come so very far," her voice cracked.

"That's enough, Ms. Flynn." Bendix's hand came down on her neck, and he steered her toward the doorway of the kitchen.

Dani blinked, and the tears ran down her cheeks, her head twisting back. "I'm not wanting to cause trouble. I'm telling you the tru—"

The angry arm of the sheriff caught her waist, the material of her thin summer shift rumpling inside the crook of his arm while he dragged her through the front door.

CHAPTER FIVE

DAMN IT! KEVIN LET THE SCREEN DOOR SLAM BEHIND HIM. HIS hand now against Dani Flynn's shapely neck, he gripped her tiny wrist with the other as he moved her along. He hated being a dick. She'd forced him to arrest her. All she had to do was eat her breakfast, gather her shit, and let him drive her anywhere, a bus station, train station—long as it was out of his county. He'd have even paid for the damn ticket.

What the hell had she tried to pull in there? He'd known the Fallons since . . . forever. Daniel Fallon had loved his wife, Deirdre. No way in hell had he . . .

"Step," he ordered and angled her down the steps to the gravel drive, ignoring the tremble of her body. She'd been crying since he marched her down the hall. He hated tears, especially a woman's. He'd seen his share of crocodile ones. He knew the difference.

He scowled. Hers were real.

Kevin moved her toward his patrol car, his grip now on her upper arm for added security. She'd bolt given the chance. Kevin unlocked the car and opened the door, guiding her down. "Watch your head." He tucked her inside and hesitated before gazing into those eyes of hers. They were wet and frightened—and a very familiar blue, now that he thought about it. Kevin's gut clenched. *Shit.* Was she telling the truth?

He kept himself bent, his face level with hers. "Ms. Flynn, I'm going to read you your rights. Do you understand?"

She snuffled and raised her chin, the tears streaming down her face.

He cursed under his breath and grabbed some napkins from the glove compartment. He gently wiped her face and placed the napkins to her nose. "Blow, Ms. Flynn."

She did, and then he crumpled the napkin in his hand, shoving it in his pocket. He stood, Mirandized her, and shut the door. Keeping an eye on her and the passenger door, he came around and got in. Dani Flynn's soft, feminine sobs filled his patrol car. She didn't resemble the young teen she portrayed last night in jeans and a sweatshirt. Womanly in the pretty spring dress he guessed she'd borrowed from Kate or Bren, it exposed her delicate shoulders, back, and the slight swell of her breasts, all of which trembled slightly.

Kevin gritted his teeth. She'd made him feel like a bully. He reached over and brought her seat belt around her waist, his arm brushing Flynn's tight thighs where her dress had ridden up. He clipped the belt in place, his eyes lingering on her slender legs, which he'd already checked out when he escorted her from the Langstons' family room to their kitchen. He grimaced. He was a cop, not a saint.

He sat back, took a long breath through his nose, and scrubbed his face hard. "Look. I'm not the enemy here, Ms. Flynn."

She turned slightly in her seat, her face puffy from crying. She stared at him for a brief moment before raising a sable brow over a less than friendly blue eye. "Isn't it only your enemies you handcuff?"

She had a point.

"You forced my hand in there."

She gave him her back. "I only spoke the truth."

"And I asked you for proof. The Fallons and Langstons are good people. Hardworking people. What is it you want from them?"

She turned back, fresh tears escaping down her face. She raised her shoulder and tried to wipe them away.

Kevin leaned in. "Hey, stop crying." He wiped her cheek with his hand. "Let me help you, Ms. Flynn."

"I don't like it when you call me Ms. Flynn."

He couldn't help but smile. "What would you like me to call you?"

"Dani would be fine."

"Okay, Dani." He started the car. He wouldn't put it past Bren to scout them out through one of the windows.

He couldn't say for sure if there was any truth to Dani Flynn's claim. But the similarity of their eyes—not just the color, but more the expression surrounding Daniel Fallon's and Dani Flynn's eyes—was uncanny. Maybe it was pure coincidence. Or, perhaps, now that she'd said it, his brain couldn't help but see it.

He pulled out down the winding driveway of the farm and turned left onto 68, heading toward 70 and the town of Hagerstown and the detention center. He glanced over at her. "I'd like to help you, Dani. But I need your cooperation. If you can't prove your identity—a passport, green card, birth certificate—I'll have to detain you."

"I told you. Me name is Dani Flynn. I'm from Ireland."

"I'd like to take your word for it. But I need documentation."

She sniffed. "I don't have it."

"Are your fingerprints on record?"

She swung around. "You don't believe me, then?"

"It's not that I don't believe you. In order for you to remain in the U.S., I need to be able to prove what you're telling me. It starts with documentation. If you don't have it, I'll have to fingerprint you and send it off to the feds for verification." That meant a couple of nights in jail. His hands tightened on the steering wheel. "Again, are your fingerprints on file?"

She moved away, angling her body in the corner of the seat and the door like the distance from him would protect her from the inevitable.

It wouldn't.

If he couldn't prove her identity one way or the other, and that she was in this country legally, by midweek he would be calling Immigration and Customs Enforcement—ICE.

He slowed and took the exit for 40. A lock popped, and the passenger door flew open. Kevin's head spun around.

What the . . .

He grabbed for her, but she rolled herself out, his gut tumbling right along with her. Kevin cursed, jerked his vehicle over to the shoulder, slammed it in park, and hopped out. He came around the car and caught sight of the floral print of her dress disappearing into the tree line.

The morning sun glinted off something in the tall grass beyond the shoulder. "Son of a bitch," he hissed and picked up the handcuffs she'd slid off her tiny wrists. Kevin kept moving while he attached them to his belt. The woods were dense with summer growth, making it difficult to see more than several yards in front of him. Since his world had collided with Dani Flynn, his life had gone to shit. He was still licking his wounds from last night, literally. He could deal with physical pain. Not sure how he would fare with the embarrassment of losing a prisoner, especially a wisp of a woman like Dani.

"Dani," he yelled. "You're going to get hurt."

Kevin slid down the incline, grabbing at tree limbs to steady himself. More like he was going to fall on his ass. "Backup's on its way," he yelled. Of course that was a lie. He had no intention of calling this out over the radio. He'd find her. She was wearing freaking sandals. She wouldn't get far.

He pushed through the thick, leafy bushes and pickers, his foot sinking into a pile . . . of . . . He angled his head. Dog shit. *Mother . . .* Kevin shook his foot, wiped it in the leaves, and continued the chase, wondering if it would be smarter to head back to the car. This section of woods would eventually dump her out behind a shopping center. Thinking better of it, he turned back, his mind battling whether he should call for backup. At this point, only he knew of the complete mockery the woman was making of him. As far as anyone knew, the sheriff of Washington County didn't work weekends unless it was a special event or some serious shit had gone down. Other than his shoe, this didn't count.

Dani slowed the moment she hit the narrow road and the rear of buildings just beyond, her heartbeat frantic, her breathing heavy. The woods had made a stinging, bloody mess of her feet, and her shoulder ached from where she'd hit the road. She ignored the pain and debated her next move. She'd been eighteen when she'd come to America. If they fingerprinted her for the social security card back then, she couldn't remember.

God.

All she had to do was hand him her passport. It was still valid, maybe not the visa. But how up was he on international documentation? The only two visa stamps were from her entry and exit from the U.S. all of those years ago. Surely he'd notice a thing like that. If only that damned thumb drive wasn't in her backpack, she'd gladly have given him the passport. Either way, she wasn't going to let him send her back.

It wasn't only Tommy she feared. She'd left a crime—one she'd witnessed. Not to mention stowed away. That had been an accident, of course. But would the Irish authorities believe her story? Duggan's threat grabbed hold of her.

Shoot you in the feckin' head and drop you in the sea.

They would never find Kara's body. Without it, they'd laugh in her face if she tried to explain she had no true intention of leaving Ireland.

Dani crossed the road, glancing back several times. She skirted the buildings until she came to a sidewalk and the front of a large beige building with a yellow flower and the word Walmart strung above its doors. Finally, something familiar from home, although Walmart was called Asda in Ireland. Bendix wouldn't think to look for her in there. She cleared the automatic door and nodded a hello to the older gentleman manning the entrance then went right for the bathroom. Grabbing a few paper towels, she quickly wet them under the sink. Dani dabbed the blood off her feet, wincing the moment it made contact. She'd surely cause unwanted attention if she left a trail. She glanced down at Kate's dress, now filthy with dirt after she'd fallen in the woods. Lifting her head, she caught her reflection in the mirror. *Oh, Lord.* She plucked a small twig from her hair. She was in a state, and not a good one.

Dani patted her hair down and dropped the towel in the trash. She had more important concerns. Slipping out of the bathroom, she grabbed a cart, her fingers trembling along the plastic bar of the handle. She had nothing. No cash to buy food, much less a few toiletries and clean underwear. Dani gnashed her teeth against those self-righteous thoughts from earlier on stealing. The store might be a way to hide. But it also had a few things she needed to survive. Not that she'd take much—only the essentials.

Dani pushed the cart through the teens' section, grabbed a set of bikini briefs. She'd be fine with Kate's bra. She swung through to the summer wear and snapped a small pair of khaki shorts off the hanger and did the same with a pair of jeans. She wheeled into the boys' section and took a package of medium, short-sleeve white T-shirts.

She cleared the aisle and headed toward the toiletry section, taking a toothbrush, paste, deodorant, soap, shampoo, and conditioner. Then she added a comb and hair ties. She eyed the hair dye and decided against it. She'd be back in that barn after midnight tonight. By tomorrow morning Bendix would have his proof. She wasn't going anywhere just yet, and Daniel Fallon would not dismiss her a second time. So what if he was embarrassed. She guessed fathering an illegitimate child could be awkward if your legitimate ones had no inkling.

Like that's my problem.

It wasn't. But a plan, and time, was. Dani pushed the cart down another aisle. She ducked into the handbag section and snagged a canvas tote from the hook, ripped off the price tag, and quickly emptied her cart into the bag. Slinging it over her shoulder, she glanced up, and jumped at the camera pointed in her direction.

Shite!

Keeping her hand on the bag, she cleared the small aisle, her sandals flapping on the shiny floor. Her shoulders slumped. The sandals, although pretty, wouldn't do. Dani backtracked to the shoe section, grabbed a pair of size five white Keds, dumped them in, and moved toward the front of the store.

"Miss," a sour voice came from behind her.

Dani angled her head back. A slightly overweight man with dark, curly hair moved busily down the aisle toward her, his hand waving. "Just a minute."

Dani kept going, her heart pounding, the doors her destination.

"Joel," he yelled. "Grab her."

Dani's head snapped up. A young man lumbered toward her, blocking the exit. She swung past his arm only to have another man, looming just as large, grab hold of her. She struggled. "Let me go."

"Grab the bag." The dark, curly-haired man came from behind, his fat fingers lacing the handles of the tote, yanking it from her. He dumped it on a nearby counter, and Dani's stomach churned.

"We've got a shoplifter." He shook his head and began punching numbers into a mobile he pulled off his hip. "This is Todd Beale, the manager at the Hagerstown Walmart. Can you send someone over for—" He picked through her things. "Maybe fifty dollars' worth." He clicked off and nodded to the one still holding her. "Take her in the back."

Dani yanked her arm, trying to get away. His grip only tightened, and he jerked her through a crowd of incoming shoppers and into a small room. The manager with the curly hair closed the door. The other one let her go and stood back. Over six feet tall, his arms crossed over a bodybuilder's chest, he said, "I'm Ken Dodd with Walmart security."

"I had every intention of paying." Dani looked toward the manager, her stomach in her throat. "You frightened me is all." It was a bald-faced lie, and she hated herself for it.

The manager opened his mouth. "We'll let the police decide, miss."

The door swung open. Two uniformed men with tan Stetsons stood in the doorway, and Dani pressed back against the wall. She just assumed it would be Bendix. They stepped in, the room growing more crowded with their bulk. Unlike Bendix, they had the air of conceit about them, and Dani grew increasingly afraid.

Both Beale and Dodd shook their hands, with Dodd excusing himself. The manager held out the bag he had refilled. "It's all inside."

The one took it while the other placed his hands on his gun. Both dressed in tan shirts and olive pants, their badges gold—not silver like Bendix's—with the words Maryland State Trooper embossed on them. Trooper? Before Dani could decide if that was a bad thing, one of the troopers—she believed his last name to be Archer based on his gold name plate—took a look inside the bag. His head shot up. "Go ahead and cuff her."

Dani couldn't breathe. She didn't like it when Bendix had done that to her. He, at least, didn't seem to enjoy restraining her. But this one smiled—viciously—when he rolled her around, pressing her face to the cold cinder-block wall.

"Please." The words ripped from her throat. She had to think of something, anything . . .

CHAPTER SIX

KEVIN SLAMMED THE STEERING WHEEL WITH HIS FIST. HE'D SEARCHED the side streets, hoping to catch the familiar, slender shoulders and that dusky, spiraling hair that reached down Dani Flynn's back. He eyed the radio. The woman was resourceful. He had no idea how long she'd been in the States or what city she arrived in. Hell. He didn't have a clue as to whether she'd flown or come by ship.

Ship? He didn't want to go there. Airports had security, immigration—no way had she come in by plane. He'd bet the farm . . . He chuckled. He didn't have one. But the Fallons did, and Dani Flynn's arrival and her claim meant she wouldn't go far. She'd be back. Maybe not today.

"Sheriff Bendix?" Marylou McHardy's voice, missing the usual serious tone he'd come to know from the dispatcher for the Washington County Communications Center, came across the radio edged with laughter.

He hit the mic switch. "Go ahead."

"Trooper Archer from the Hagerstown Barrack radioed in."

Great. They'd found her. It wasn't like Chad Archer, the asshole he'd known since they were kids, would cut him some slack. Dani Flynn might not say a whole hell of a lot. But to Kevin, when she did, she seemed irritatingly honest—especially about this thing with Daniel Fallon. As amazing as it was, he believed her story. It had been the eyes for him.

He sighed heavily. She'd more than likely fill Archer in on Kevin's ineptness when it came to securing her. That was what confounded him. She didn't fit the criminal profile. Her innocence and lack of street sense were genuine. Lost in thought, his brows rose. Funny. Marylou hadn't continued her radio transmission.

He keyed the mic. "Marylou?"

"Oh." Her voice came out sharp, and then she laughed. "I'm sorry, sir. Archer said to tell you he has a Ms. Dani Flynn in the security office at the Hagerstown Walmart."

Kevin's head dropped.

Marylou came on again. She cleared her throat. "She claims she's your girlfriend." Her laughter seemed to fill the interior of his car even though she'd ended transmission, and the heat of aggravation, and maybe embarrassment, crept into his face.

"Son of a bitch," he hissed and made a U-turn on 40, traveling around a mile until he made a left into the Walmart parking lot. Slamming the patrol car door, he strode into the Walmart and made a quick right into the security office to find Chad Archer *and* Stew Mitchell both smirking under those damned Stetsons that gave them the distinction of being one of Maryland's Finest. Which was bullshit. Any one of his men were just as capable of exercising their police duties as any Maryland state trooper. He blanched, of course. Today he couldn't be counted as one of them, thanks to the raven-haired beauty who, for the third time since last night, found her arms handcuffed behind her back.

His hands clenched at his sides. Now that he was on the outside looking in, it bothered him. "Un-cuff her."

"So it's true?" Chad pushed back his Stetson, his eyes agleam.

Did he even want to go there? "What she take?"

Mitchell handed him a canvas bag, and Kevin opened it—toothbrush, underwear, a pair of shorts. No electronics, no jewelry—only essentials. *Damn it.*

He gave it to Todd Beale, the manager. "How about you have one of the clerks ring it up." He'd also known Todd from high school, nerdy, but a good guy who'd stayed close to home after college. Kevin pulled out three twenties. "You think that's enough?"

Todd nodded. "No problem." He leaned in and whispered, "I noticed she has an accent. She not understand how things work?"

Kevin gave him a light rap on his shoulder. "Something like that."

"I'll be right back." Todd cleared the door.

Kevin shot a look at Archer. "So we good, Chad?" It pissed him off he had to even ask. Technically, Chad had the authority over him. If he wanted to be a dick, he could haul her off to the detention center. Kevin waited, his stance relaxing when Archer motioned to Mitchell. He complied and removed the cuffs, placing them back on his hip.

Archer nodded to Mitchell. "I think the sheriff has it under control."

They both moved out the door, their shoulders bobbing with silent laughter, leaving him alone with Dani. She refused to look up at him. He moved closer and put his finger under her chin and brought her face up. Ivory with a touch of crimson in her smooth cheeks—he assumed from shame—and blue eyes he'd known his whole life. Although prettier on Dani Flynn the way her thick lashes dusted her face when they fluttered, and they fluttered now, trying to keep from . . . *Damn* but the woman had a thing for tears.

"Hey, if you promise not to cry, I think you and I can work something out."

The words that left his mouth shocked her, as evidenced by the drop in the sweet curve of her bottom lip. *Shit.* He'd shocked himself. Even he didn't know what the hell he'd meant by that statement, except he'd made a promise, and now he was bound by his word.

"Here you go, Kev."

Kevin turned to find Todd in the doorway. "Thanks. I'm sorry for the trouble."

Todd grimaced and then nodded toward Dani. "No, I'm sorry. I didn't realize she was your . . . Plus she's got a sweet face—innocent."

Kevin would agree with Todd's description—maybe angelic was more like it. Only she wasn't innocent or an angel. She'd planned on stealing everything in that tote bag and *did* lie about being his girlfriend. He'd let her slide on this one. He understood the desperation behind both acts. That was probably why he'd paid for the items and went along with her guise.

Kevin shook Todd's hand. "Thanks for your understanding."

Todd handed him a plastic Walmart bag with his purchases. "Your change is in the bag."

"Thanks." Kevin latched onto Dani Flynn's small hand and tugged her forward. She grimaced, and Kevin loosened up on his grip, mindful of her wounds.

Todd took a step back, and Kevin nodded his thanks again and cleared the room with Dani beside him. She remained quiet, and, frankly, he was relieved she didn't strike up a conversation with him while they remained in the store. The automatic doors opened, and they stepped through, the summer sun warm against his face. Kevin checked his watch—close to two. This was not how he'd planned to spend his Sunday afternoon. He had yard work out the ass and a stupid vegetable garden he thought he'd have time to weed.

And then there was Dani Flynn—a petite little raven-haired beauty with just the right amount of curves to make her dangerous where he was concerned. Maybe he should have gone to church this morning. They continued toward his patrol car, and when they reached the passenger door, he jiggled her hand in his. She gave him a questioning look, her blue eyes wary.

"No cuffs, okay?"

She nodded. "Will you be taking me to jail now?" Her voice quavered.

No, not jail. He'd feel a lot better, though, if he could prove she belonged in the U.S. legally. "No."

Her sable-colored brows furrowed. "If not jail, then . . ."

Right. He hadn't thought that far ahead. There was only one place he could think of, and that was the peace and quiet of his home. His body sagged at the complications that presented. In fact, he'd be opening himself up big-time to a possible lawsuit. But he had a sense for people. Dani Flynn didn't seem the type, if left alone with him, to accuse Kevin of sexual assault. He'd go with his gut on this and hope it didn't come back to bite him in the ass.

"I know a place where we can sit down and figure things out. Are you agreeable to that?"

She nodded. "I appreciate your kindness, Sheriff. Bendix. Yes, I would be very much agreeable."

"Good." He opened the door, caught himself getting ready to cradle her head, and realized she didn't need his help this time. Once she was settled, he came around, got in, and shut the door, slinging her bag in the backseat.

Starting the engine, he pulled out, traveled the side streets to 40, heading toward the historic district of Hagerstown and the quick ten-minute drive to his house. He angled his head. Dani sat straight as a stick in the passenger seat.

"You can relax. I believe you."

She turned, her head tilting slightly. "Beg your pardon?"

"I said I believe you about your relationship to Daniel Fallon."

Her shoulders lowered, and Kevin's body sunk more comfortably into his seat. "I'll talk to Daniel."

Her eyes widened. "You're serious."

"As a heart attack. But don't make me regret my decision."

"You're a kind one, Sheriff Bendix."

Or a sucker. One that could easily fall for the lilt in her voice and the way his name fell from her lips. "I think we're past the formalities."

Her forehead furrowed in question. She remained quiet. He guessed she was figuring things out in that pretty head of hers. And then she laughed softly and smiled at him. Kevin couldn't say for sure, but it seemed they were making progress. For the first time since he'd met her, she seemed comfortable with him. "I can call you Kevin, then?"

"Do you think you can handle that, Irish?"

"Irish?" She did that thing with her face again. "Oh, you mean because I'm from . . ."

He nodded and turned left on Jonathan Street.

"You're very kind to talk to Daniel Fallon on me behalf."

"Don't get excited." He made the right on Charles Street and passed one of his yellow and black election signs.

Dani's head turned back when they passed it. "Sheriffs are elected?"

It was another reason he didn't need this thing with Dani Flynn blowing up in his face. "Primary was last week."

"Did you win?" She angled her head back, her eyebrows raised.

"Yes." He'd been the Washington County Sheriff for the last two terms, before that a deputy. If he lost it would be another four years before he could run again. Not to mention he'd need a job, unless his buddy at the Maryland gaming commission could get him one at the new casino in Cumberland as their director of security. "There's still the general election in November."

He took another right onto the tree-lined North Potomac Street where he lived and glanced over at Dani. "Getting back to you and Daniel. In order for me to talk to your father, you're going to have to tell me how you got in the States and all the proof you have on why you believe Daniel Fallon is your father. I can't go to the man and plead your case if I don't know what the hell I'm talking about." He knew Daniel Fallon—knew that if he explained all of Dani's reasoning, if it were true, he'd admit it.

Maybe not to his girls, not right away.

He narrowed in on her. "More importantly, it's the law you need to be concerned with, and it's my job to uphold it. If between the two of us we can't satisfy immigration in the next week, you'll be sent back to Ireland."

Kevin had always tried to be by the book with his law enforcement decisions. Only his objectivity where she was concerned was seriously on the line. But he'd promised to work with her. He'd worry about explaining his actions—or inaction—to immigration if it came to it.

"Agreed?" Kevin asked again.

"Y-yes, agreed." She gave him a quick smile and frowned before her head dropped, and she fidgeted with the hem of her dress.

Okay, so she didn't like it. Maybe she was reconsidering. He waited, but she remained quiet, leaving Kevin to wonder if he'd made a sorry-ass mistake trusting her.

He let it go for now. He was more curious how Daniel Fallon fathered a child and then kept it a secret for so long. Or—and this was a doozy—why, if it wasn't an act at breakfast, couldn't he place the exact encounter when he'd screwed this *celebrated jockey,* leaving Kevin to deal with his pain-in-the-ass mistake twenty-something years later?

That sealed it for him. She *was* Bren and Kate's sister. That trait—the pain-in-the-ass one—could only mean they were related. He gripped the steering wheel, glanced over. She was still quiet, only her focus had moved to the passenger window. Kevin had always been on the losing end with the Fallon Sisters Duo.

Shit. He wanted to slam his head against the steering wheel. Without a doubt, he could change that to a trifecta of trouble for him.

CHAPTER SEVEN

K EVIN BENDIX WOULD DEMAND THE TRUTH. DANI OWED HIM THAT
much for helping her. He could have easily left her in the company of
the troopers. She wasn't sure, but they—the troopers—seemed to rankle
him a bit. Although the embarrassment she'd caused him when she
feigned their relationship, which he said nothing about, would have
caused his discomfort.

Whatever she sensed, it wasn't her business. She'd best worry about
herself for now. Surely, when they were alone, he'd want those answers.

She wouldn't let it worry her just yet. After the trouble she'd caused
him, he had every right to arrest her and be done. But he didn't. Perhaps
it was his friendship with the Fallons that kept her in his company. If he
believed her—which, to her surprise, he'd claimed moments ago—he'd
want to protect them from her. Keeping her accounted for would do that
nicely. She cleared her mind of the wondering. Dani was more concerned
about what she could share—the truth, of course. But not all of it,
especially the thumb drive. Could she even begin to tell him about the
ship? Not likely. She'd stowed away—by accident, mind. Only, in order
to explain it proper, she'd have to tell him about Tommy and poor Kara.

She twisted the hem of Kate's dress. She'd created a fine mess with her
life—and been forced to live out of a grocery bag, no less. Of course not
literally, and the ridiculous image of Dani Flynn from Ireland wearing
nothing but a grocery bag from Walmart made her mouth quirk, and she
rolled her lips in to stop from smiling. Kevin could construe the gesture as
ungrateful. And she was not.

She had been worried when they first turned into this town. Old and run-down, it was nothing like the farm she'd been to. But the more turns he made, the more charming the streets became. The homes were close together, well-manicured lawns and tree-lined streets the deeper they went.

He slowed and then parked in front of a white Victorian—definitely historic—with black shutters, window boxes overflowing with colorful petunias, a lovely front porch that wrapped to one side, and a cute detached garage with the same matching black shutters. Actually, the entire street was lined with refurbished homes. Kevin got out, grabbing the bag from the back, and came around to open her door. He reached out, his fingers wrapping around her small hand. Her stomach tumbled at the strength of his touch when he brought her to her feet and shut the door.

They stood on a cobblestone sidewalk, the same cobblestone running straight to the steps of the front porch. Dani came just below his shoulders and strained her neck back. "Is it yours, then, the house?"

"You mean the money pit?" He was smiling down at her.

Perhaps it was, but it was the most beautiful money pit she'd ever seen. "It's lovely, Mr. Bend . . ." The heat rose in her cheeks.

"We're going to have to break you of that habit." He laughed just then. "Come on, Dani Flynn."

They took the walkway, and Kevin's hand tightened at the creak of a door. He cursed under his breath.

Dani hesitated. "Is there something wrong?"

"Nope," he whispered, his other hand coming up and waving to an older woman in a pink pants suit on the neighboring front porch. "How's it going, Mrs. Wiley?"

"Just fine, Kevin dear." She craned her neck. "Who's your . . ."

They took the steps, and Kevin fooled with the lock, cursing a bit more before calling back to his neighbor, "Have a good day, Mrs. Wiley."

He opened the door and gave her a light push inside, the door shutting behind them. Dani stood mesmerized by the dark wood of the staircase to her left and then frowned at him. "You were rude to her."

"Ya think?" He sat his keys down on a thin, ornate table in the hall along with her bag. "Trust me, before sunset she'll have created a hubbub about you and me, and you *will be* my girlfriend as far as the rest of the neighbors are concerned." He frowned. "Not to mention she's on the county council."

Dani grimaced. It was the same in Ireland with the elected officials.

She didn't want to hurt his chances for re-election. "I'm sorry for that. I'll not cause you any trouble with this Mrs. Wiley."

He nodded. "I'd appreciate it."

"But the . . . the troopers were very scary."

"And I'm not?" He took a step back.

Tall, blond, muscular, and very much alone with her—no, he no longer frightened Dani. She knew him to be a good man, especially after today. She shook her head. "At first, yes." She took his hand in hers and turned it over. She'd broken his skin last night. Her teeth marks, red and angry, remained an embarrassing reminder along his wrist. She touched him there, and their eyes connected and held. "I'm sorry for biting you. I know now you'd not have hurt me."

His eyes became distant, and he pulled his hand away. "How are you at making a sandwich?"

She folded her hands in front of her. "I do well at that. I worked as a barmaid at a pub."

His brows rose.

"And made sandwiches and served a fine glass of Harp as well."

He walked past her. "Come on."

Dani remained. "Can I wash me hands first?"

"Powder room to your right."

Dani flipped on the light. Rose-colored walls greeted her. Definitely not male.

"What is it?" He came up behind her.

"Ah . . . the walls."

"Preferred forest green myself." He shrugged. "Decided to plan ahead—not painting over it someday when my wife decides it's too masculine."

Wife . . . "You're married, then?"

"Not yet." He eyed her and then flicked off the light. "You can use the kitchen sink. I'll give you a quick tour and get you started before I go up and change."

She followed, her sandals slapping the beautiful dark hardwood. "Was I right, then?" Of course, she hadn't spoken it aloud. "Are the homes on the lane historic?"

He opened the fridge and pulled out meats, a tomato, lunch spreads. "Built in 1880."

"It's very old, then."

"It is and was a bitch to refurbish." He rubbed the back of his neck and turned, a smile tugging at his firm lips.

She couldn't help but smile herself. "You've done a fine job, Sheriff Bendix." Dani ran her hand against the smooth, dark wood of the entryway.

"I thought we had a deal?"

"Right." Her hand dropped to her side. She liked his name, all of it, actually. It was Irish, too. "How about you do whatever it is you were going to do, *Kevin*. And I'll make us something to eat."

"Sounds good." He moved toward the archway of the door. "Rolls on the counter. Mustard's in the fridge, on the door." He stopped, his expression thoughtful. "Knives in the wooden block for the tomato."

Had he actually questioned whether she'd use a knife . . . on him?

He walked away and called back, "Be down in a few minutes."

Dani let the thought go. She moved into the kitchen. The walls were papered in a classic print, keeping with a nineteenth-century home. He'd added modern conveniences such as a stainless steel dishwasher, fridge, and double wall oven. Dani had never been in such fine surroundings. She grabbed the bag of rolls and the knife he seemed a bit worried about and slit two rolls down the center. The inside was soft and smelled heavenly. She slathered mustard on both, sliced the tomato, and piled his sandwich with a generous portion of ham and turkey. For her own, she added only the turkey.

Cheese would be grand, and Dani opened the fridge and searched the meat and cheese bin, finding a package of Swiss and a head of lettuce. Once she topped the sandwiches with both, she cleaned up and went in search of two plates.

With the help of a chair, she opened up several cabinets and found two sturdy earthenware plates from a set of eight in a neat stack. After stepping down and fixing the plates with the sandwiches, she eyed the kitchen and the small kitchen table. She liked this kitchen very much. Dani carried the plates and caught sight of another doorway and couldn't help her inquisitiveness.

Her mouth fell open at the formal dining room. The walls had a dark blue floral print from the middle of the wall up to the ceiling, a chair rail and pale yellow walls below. She'd not have thought to mix the two. But as a whole, it was lovely. At the end of the room sat a brick fireplace, the mantel carved in ornate mahogany with a built-in beveled mirror above and a hearth made of the finest marble, inlaid inside the equally fine hardwood floor. On the long wall across from her, two sets of double-hung windows, trimmed in the purest white, looked out on the side lawn, a china cabinet evenly spaced between them.

Dani set the plates down on the dining room table. Her eyes transfixed on the china cabinet, she traveled the few steps in wonderment. Its glass was beveled, too. But it was the china behind the glass that fascinated her. Her heart sank a little. She'd lived in Ireland all of her life and never once had she been nose to nose with exquisite Belleek china. This particular pattern, with its basket weave and tiny green shamrocks, had her opening the intricately carved wooden door that encased the beveled glass. Her fingers trembled, and she touched the smooth edge of the fine bone china, lifting it from the wooden shelf.

"Ms. Flynn?" It was abrasive and full of . . . suspicion. Dani quickly placed the plate in the groove it had come from as though the cool surface had turned hot as a blazing ember, and spun around to find a pair of guarded brown eyes narrowing in.

"I'll not have a mind to stealing your precious china," she snapped. "I was curious is all." Her cheeks warmed to a nice guilty shade, and she got angry with herself and with him. She'd never stolen. Well . . .

She marched over to the table, grabbed the plates she'd planned to set up in the dining room because it was so feckin' pretty. Now he'd made her curse. In her head—but a curse nonetheless.

He grabbed her arm on the way out, holding her in place. "I'm sorry for assuming. But earlier—"

"If you had no way of support . . . No way to feed or clothe yourself and were dumped in a strange land—not by choice, mind—you might resort to stealing as a way to survive as well." She shook his hand off her and gave him a stern look. "I don't steal, Mr. Bendix, unless it's out of necessity. And I don't very much like doing it, even then."

A laugh rolled up his chest, and her cheeks deepened, she was sure, to a florid red.

"You're infuriating." She gave him her back and set the plates down on the small, round oak table in the kitchen. Sidestepping, she went to the fridge and pulled out two bottles of water she'd seen earlier and sat them down next to their plates. Handing him a napkin from the holder on the table, she took her seat.

He stared at her.

"You're not hungry, then?"

He sat down and opened her water and his. "I thought it was a myth," he said around a bite of his sandwich.

"A myth?"

"Irish women and their tempers." He wanted to smile; she could tell. But he remained the utmost of seriousness, sitting in a white T-shirt that hugged his muscular arms and a pair of faded jeans that hung low on his narrow hips. She couldn't see them—his hips—but she'd noticed them earlier in the doorway of the dining room. Only her concentration was diverted to his suspicious brown eyes tunneling into her equally angry ones.

"I'll not laugh at that." She took a bite of her sandwich. "It's funny. But I won't give you the satisfaction."

She continued to eat, and he continued to stare, his shameless interest in her unnerving. Not to mention the silly grin tugging at his well-shaped lips made her insides roll with a womanly sort of thing because he was a man—a man she found handsome and funny and bloody charming.

Chapter Eight

K EVIN COULDN'T TAKE HIS EYES OFF HER. DANI FLYNN—FROM THE Emerald Isle and with a temper that made him laugh out loud. Beautiful, petite with the face of an angel, and, the more he'd checked her out, the body of a sinner. He'd been a serious fool for bringing her to his home. Her world was foreign, her life messy. She was definitely in the U.S. illegally, and yet here she sat across from him in his kitchen, at his table, and, if he was correct, flirting with him—and he with her.

What the hell?

This was some major shit he'd gotten himself into. And thanks to his nosey neighbor, he'd be the talk of North Potomac Street. The sooner he could prove she had a right to stay—and it started with a birth certificate or some legal document that had Daniel Fallon listed as her biological birth father—he'd breathe easier.

"Have you always known Daniel Fallon was your father?"

She stopped chewing and swallowed. "Not always, no. Me mother told me on her deathbed."

"I'm sorry." Kevin fell back in his chair. His own mother had died from pneumonia when he was in college, which left him and his dad alone. At times, it felt as though he was the adult and his father the child. He knew now his mother truly possessed the patience of a saint because his father, Joseph Bendix, had required a watchful eye—from himself.

She waved a dismissive hand. " 'Twas long ago. I was eighteen. Rory Flynn, me mother . . ." Dani smiled and her eyes became moist.

Kevin immediately regretted her having to dredge up the past. But there was no way to avoid it if he wanted the truth.

She wiped her eyes and took a breath. "We lived at the racetrack, part of me ma's deal for being a jockey." She leaned in. "There was this race, an important one, mind. Had she won, we would have been living the life of kings and queens. But, as luck would have it, she lost—and I lost her."

"How'd it happen? The accident, I mean."

"The horse tripped, fell, and me mother tumbled from the saddle and was trampled." Dani fidgeted with her napkin, her head down. "She didn't die right away. She fought for three days—fought for me. But in the end her injuries were too great. She died holding me hand. I cried like a babe. They were selfish tears, I think. Loving me ma came easy. It was the letting go I found difficult."

Her head rose, those striking eyes filling with tears. "She told me that day while she lay dying about me da." Then her tear-filled eyes flashed with anger. "I couldn't believe it. I was so angry at Daniel Fallon for leaving me ma and me. She wanted me to go find him. Didn't want me to be alone, I guess." Dani shrugged. "He didn't want me. So I didn't see the point." She sighed, her expression distant like she was reliving it. "She died straightaway after that, her warm fingers losing their grip on me hand."

Kevin had seen enough sadness during his career in law enforcement. He'd never let it get to him. But the lump in his throat for Dani, he couldn't swallow. He'd treated her badly the first night. He was tired and wet, and he was an all-around irritated son of a bitch for not being able to go home to bed after he'd gotten Bren's call. Not that Dani had helped his disposition by throwing dirt in his face and taking a chunk out of his wrist, but he could understand her fear.

One thing bothered him, though.

"Why the change of heart about your father?"

She rolled her lips in, considering. "I had no choice."

"You saying you didn't come here intentionally?" He fell back in his chair, leery.

"As remarkable as it sounds . . . yes."

She continued to eat her sandwich. He guessed she believed his line of questioning was over. Maybe they were in a private setting, but he wasn't done with his interrogation—not after that bombshell.

"You care to explain how someone unintentionally arrives in a country not of their choosing?"

She set her sandwich down and took a sip of water. "I'll tell you, but I'm not prepared to fill in the details. Not just yet."

He'd accept it for now. He was an investigator, came with the job. If she gave him a lead, he could follow it. "Go on."

"By freighter."

His mouth dropped. When his mind had envisioned a ship, he thought more like the *QE2*. Maybe not that luxurious and not that he thought she'd gotten on it legally, either. But those tin cans were big, and she could easily hide. Plus, he didn't think the security at one of the Irish ports would be as stringent as it was here in the U.S. He shook his head at that. Obviously she'd slipped through.

Now he could envision her ordeal.

"I take it the crew didn't know."

She shook her head. "No, not likely. I remained in a life raft for the seven days before they landed in the States." She fooled with her dress, straightening it. "I never planned to stow away. I can't share the particulars. It was luck I landed a few hundred kilometers from me father's farm. I'd gladly go back to Ireland. But there are reasons it be best I don't, at least for a while."

Great, some type of international espionage. Kevin leaned into the table. "Have you done something that would warrant your arrest in Ireland?"

"Other than the freighter? And my lack of documentation?" She shook her head, averting her eyes. "No."

Uh huh. She was lying.

Kevin leaned in. "Who are you running from?"

Her dark brows rose. "It doesn't matter. He'd not follow me here."

So she thinks. He wouldn't say more. If she believed he was fine with the criminal activity she'd shared, or if she believed he believed it wasn't egregious enough for him to lock her up and contact Interpol, he could keep an eye on her. But she couldn't stay here. That was for damn sure.

Kevin stood up and stretched his back. "You think you can clean up? I have to mow the lawn. It'll take me an hour. I'll show you the bathroom if you need to get washed up." He had noticed her dress had gotten dirty— he guessed from her romp in the woods. "I put your bag in the spare bedroom upstairs—second door to your right as you come up. The bathroom's the first door."

She gave a quick smile and then frowned. "So will you be taking me to jail—now that we've talked?"

He should cuff her, Mirandize her for the second time, haul her off to the detention center, and forget Dani Flynn ever existed. But those eyes of hers, the way they looked at him like he could make every struggle she had endured and would continue to endure go away, made him inexplicably protective of her.

"Not unless you give me a reason to."

"Will I be staying here with you, then?"

Too tempting.

"We'll talk about it later." He started for the kitchen door and the garage where he kept his lawnmower and then turned toward her. "I didn't mean you had to stay in the house. But I'd appreciate it if you'd stay on the side with the porch, away from Mrs. Wiley's home. There's a swing toward the rear of the porch." He hooked his chin down toward the hall. "If you didn't catch the layout on the first floor, the living room's to the left, right if you're coming in the front door. I have some books and magazines." Hunting and fishing—probably not something she'd be interested in. "Maybe you should stick to the books."

She came around the table, her eyes moist.

"Flynn, I'm warning you. No tears." He sidestepped her, hit the laundry room, and grabbed his John Deere baseball cap off the rack above the washer and opened the door, hesitating. "Irish," he called to her. "What other work did you do, other than barmaid, in Ireland?"

"I was a groom at the racetrack," she called back as she cleared the table.

He nodded and shut the door, the oppressive late June heat smacking him in the face as he took the steps.

Horses. Why was he not surprised?

Kevin shook his head, and entered the side door of the garage. He wheeled the lawn mower out, checked the gas and oil, and pulled on the cord. It sputtered a few times before the loud, monotonous motor roared to life. He liked to mow. It gave him time to think. He started on the outside perimeter of the lawn and made nice, straight lines, the grass clippings disappearing, with the help of the mulch blade, into the soil.

He pondered Dani Flynn's skills, and he had an idea, one that would keep her out of trouble and give her a paycheck. He frowned. It would have to be cash. His grip tightened on the handle of the mower. Since he'd met her, he'd done a lot of things not in keeping with his by-the-book personality. Well, he wouldn't be the one paying her. Besides, to his ongoing dismay, the guy he had in mind paid some of his workers under the table. Another subject Kevin and he didn't agree on. He'd give Kevin holy hell for showing up when he needed a favor, especially since he'd been asking Kevin for weeks to meet with him about another issue.

Kevin moved closer to the house with every pass. Maybe two more passes and he'd be done. He'd glanced up a few times, but the porch swing remained empty. Maybe she didn't like the heat. It had to be close to ninety and humid. He'd already sweated through his T-shirt. Kevin angled the mower, made the turn to the back of the house, and almost ran the mower deck over the mulch bed of the dogwood tree. He cursed.

He'd been wrong about the heat. She'd changed into her khaki shorts, one of the T-shirts from the triple pack, and the white sneakers were discarded just outside the garden plot. Her long hair she tied up in a ponytail, exposing her slender neck. She remained on her knees on the perimeter of the vegetable garden from hell, a pile of weeds next to her.

The scene with her tending his garden and him mowing the lawn and the warm summer Sunday that spoke of barbeques, yard work, and family had him finishing up the last swath of uncut grass and heading straight for the garage. He'd remained a bachelor for thirty-nine years because he hadn't found the perfect mate. He had a list in his head. She would be tall, blond like him, a professional who, when the time came, would be willing to give up a career to raise their children. And this was important—and a point he hadn't thought about until now—she'd be a U.S. citizen same as him and above reproach.

Dani Flynn had ebony waves of silky hair—granted, sexy as hell, and he'd be lying if he said he hadn't fantasized about running his hands through it. But it wasn't blond. She was, at most, five two, and he had to bend down a good amount to be eye level with her. He swallowed a moan. He freakin' loved her eyes—curious, sometimes worrisome, and the color of exquisite blue sapphires. Nope. He wasn't going there. She had to go, and now. Dani Flynn wasn't the educated professional partner he'd envisioned. From what she'd said, she could man an Irish pub and muck out horse stalls. And the above reproach thing, well, he knew better. She'd hopped a damn freighter for crissake.

Enough said.

Kevin cut off the mower, stored it in the garage without first blowing off the grass. He didn't care. He had one purpose as he strode across the lawn to a vegetable garden perfectly suited for the gorgeous Irish lass presently standing barefoot, and teasing him with the hottest pair of legs he'd seen in a long time.

He reached her, his shadow looming above her. "Dani, let's go." His words were sharp.

She glanced skyward, placing her hand up to shield her eyes from the sun. "You're done, then. I hope you don't mind, but I've not a garden of me own. Yours was growing a bit wild, and I—"

"We're going in." He wrapped his hand around her arm and tugged her toward the back steps.

She pulled back. "K-Kevin, is there something wrong?"

There was that worried look. The one that had him circumventing the law and losing his good reasoning skills.

"You want a job?"

"Yes, of course." Her eyes grew wider, her mouth opening slightly. "I just didn't think it was possible, is all."

"It is." He motioned her up the steps, coming behind her. "If we hurry, we can catch him."

"Him?"

"You said you worked with horses, right?" He opened the back door and let her in first, then followed, shutting it.

She turned as they cleared the laundry room, a smudge of dirt on her cheek, her brows creased with concern. "Yes, of course. But I would think they need the documentation you spoke of."

Kevin wiped the dirt off her face with his thumb, the simple act more intimate than he'd planned, and his heartbeat raced. "He'll work with us, with you. Can you be ready in about twenty minutes?" he said, his voice agitated—agitated with himself, at her, and at the circumstance of having her so close, close enough to pull into his arms. But his damn, self-imposed, maybe a little snotty, agenda was getting in the way of the woman and the sweet, sensual curve of her mouth that he wanted to kiss.

He took a step back and checked his black sports watch. "Let's say about 4:35."

"Yes. What should I wear? I have Kate's dress."

"You're fine. You might want to wash your face. There's still a little dirt." He pointed to it, making sure he kept his hands to himself. "Right here."

Her hand came up warily and rubbed. "I've not interviewed for a job in a very long time. If you're sure I'm dressed appropriately, I'll wash myself, then." She turned away, heading down the hall and glanced back. "Aren't you going to as well?"

"In a minute. I have to lock up the garage. I'll meet you in the front hall."

She nodded, moving out of the kitchen.

"Oh, and Dani." He caught her in mid-step. "Bring all of your stuff with you."

She gave him a questioning look. "Will I not be coming back?"

He moved toward her. "I'm thinking it's not a good idea with my position."

"Oh." She frowned. "I understand it wouldn't be right. You've been more than kind." She waved a hand toward the steps. "I'll get me things. I won't be long." She disappeared down the hall.

Once she ascended the stairs, Kevin grabbed a white garbage bag and a napkin from the kitchen table and entered the dining room. His phone hummed on his belt, and he unhooked it. Bren. No way was he taking that call. He was surprised it had taken her this long.

He snapped it back on his hip and let it go to voicemail and opened the china cabinet. Kevin took his great-grandmother's china plate Dani had handled and picked it up with the napkin, carefully placing it in the garbage bag, and looked over his shoulder before he closed it, like he was committing a jewel heist. Why did he care if she caught him? Kevin clenched his jaw. He'd told Dani he planned to fingerprint her. He was saving her a trip, and if he were completely honest, keeping her under wraps . . . for now.

He needed those details—a confirmed identity for one Dani Flynn from Ireland, what she'd been involved in before she shanghaied it out of her homeland, and who she was running from.

What could a barmaid have gotten herself mixed up in? Whatever it was, he couldn't afford for it to blow up on him.

Kevin scratched his head. A woman like Dani Flynn didn't step off a freighter penniless on the shores of freedom and go in search of a father she despised unless she was running from some serious shit. Maybe this guy hadn't put it all together. But if he considered her a big enough threat, he'd still be looking for her, and when he found her, Kevin didn't think the Atlantic Ocean was a big enough deterrent.

He'd come for her.

CHAPTER NINE

KEVIN WAITED FOR HER AT THE BOTTOM OF THE STEPS, SHOWERED, HIS hair damp and nicely combed. He was dressed in a fresh pair of jeans and a yellow golf shirt with the shirttails pulled out. Dani's eyes landed on the bulge on his hip. She *hoped* he carried his gun everywhere.

She swallowed hard. *Not just with me.*

He ushered her from his house, into his patrol car, her sorrow palpable when he pulled away from a home she could only dream of having. He wound her through the neighborhood, more election signs dotted the lawns, and one in particular caught her attention: CHAD ARCHER FOR SHERIFF.

Dani's head swung around to Kevin. "Isn't he that trooper from Walmart?"

Kevin's jaw tightened. "Too good for us county cops until they're looking for another pension."

Ah. Now she understood his behavior from earlier. She wouldn't say any more. They turned off the main highway, traveling down a two-lane country road with horse paddocks on either side. The rolling green hills reminded her of Ireland.

Kevin remained quiet. Dani couldn't blame him for wanting to be rid of her. She'd caused him a great deal of trouble. And the longer he drove, the more her anxiety rose.

"You didn't say what type of job."

He glanced over. "Same one you did in Ireland."

"I'm not sure I know which one you mean."

He made a quick right down a gravel road, Dani barely having time to read the sign. "Whistledown Training Center?" She shot him a questioning brow.

"To be precise"—he smiled—"for Thoroughbreds."

"A groom, then?"

He parked in a gravel lot. "Come on. I'll introduce you to your new boss." They got out of his patrol car, and he motioned her toward a fence where a beautiful black horse grazed. "I'll be right back." He disappeared inside a large barn.

Dani placed her tote bag over her shoulder, filled with the items Kevin had bought her, and walked toward the fence and the black horse. She reached out an open palm. The horse eyed her and then came toward her, his nostrils moving feverishly, taking in her scent. "You're a pretty thing, aren't you?" she cooed. He moved closer. Dani smiled and rubbed his muzzle. "What's your name, then?"

"Hey, you!"

Dani pulled her hand in and jumped, swinging around. She recognized Kevin several yards away by the barn, standing next to a short older gentleman.

"You looking to lose a hand?" It came from the old man, the same irritable, craggy voice as before. The horse was . . . Dani tilted her head to check the horse from underneath. Definitely a male. Probably a stallion the way the old man had shot out the warning. Or was it a colt? It was hard to tell his age. Although, they could both be high-strung. In Ireland they'd castrate an unmanageable or vicious stallion, unless he was a stud with Arab or royal bloodlines. But Dani hadn't gotten the impression the horse was anything but friendly.

Kevin waved her over. She traveled the uneven ground, a mix of dirt and grass, and sidestepped a rooster that thought he had the right of way. She continued up the slight incline leading to the barn until she stood in its shadow.

"Dani, I'd like you to meet Turk Bendix."

Bendix? Dani reached out a hand of introduction.

The rough, calloused hands of Turk Bendix gave her a gruff shake. "Kevin said you've worked as a groom in Ireland."

"Yes. Going on ten years now."

"What track?"

"Tramore racecourse in Waterford." Technically she worked in her own county of Wexford, but they raced mainly in the county over. It would be best not to make that distinction to anyone. The less they knew of her origins, the better. Of course, she had no clue what gaps Daniel Fallon could fill in for Kevin if he asked. Although, at this point, his denial of knowing her or her mother played in her favor.

The old man pulled on his chin. "I know it." He glanced at Kevin and shook his head. "I'm doing this one a favor. Not in the market for another groom. Got too many as it is. The bunkhouse is full. But if you want to take the small room above the barn—it's not much more than a closet and stinks of hay and manure—I can accommodate you." He leaned back. "There's a john and a shower next to my office here in the barn you can use. The pay's twelve dollars an hour, twelve hours a day, six days a week, and includes evenings—room and no board." He checked his clipboard and gave a hard laugh. "Looks like you laid a golden egg, Flynn. You're off Sundays for rotation—but no holidays."

Turk Bendix folded his arms, tucking the clipboard under his armpit, and rocked on his heels. He seemed to enjoy making her uncomfortable. He was nothing like his son. Even their eye color was different. Where Turk's were an irritable blue, Kevin's were brown and held a softness she'd not seen before. But they changed to a stormy dark the moment he connected with Bendix's sour expression.

If he thought he scared her . . . He did. But not enough she'd refuse his offer. She'd dealt with ruddy complexion blowhards like Turk at the pub. Granted, they were patrons and not her future boss.

Perhaps the ragged look in Turk's face came from the hard life of a trainer. At least she assumed that was his position, standing as he was with his clipboard, dictating the offer of employment.

He'd purposely given her the downside to the job, no doubt hoping she'd squirm with disgust. After what she'd endured coming to America, he couldn't know how appealing an offer it was. In Ireland, on a good day at both jobs, she'd made half that. Maybe the room he spoke of was a shameful hole compared to Kevin's beautiful home, but she had no claim to such fine things and probably never would.

The upside would be the job itself. She had a knack for horses. She loved the beasts. Kevin and his father, although he hadn't admitted it as yet—the father thing—had done her a favor. "It's most generous, Sheriff Bendix. When do I start?"

His snow white brows knitted in aggravation, and he yelled above Dani's head, "Bonnie, got a new groom. I need you to grab a mattress from the bunkhouse." He smirked at Dani. "We're out of cots."

Those strong, controlled hands of Kevin's flexed at his side, and he cursed, leveling a scorching gaze toward his father. "Damn it." He grabbed Dani's arm. "Keep your—"

Dani pulled away. She wasn't Kevin Bendix's charity case. He'd been kind, but she was not his responsibility. "Your father's been more than fair, Kevin," she whispered. For reasons Dani couldn't explain, she rather enjoyed Kevin's intense expression of disapproval. She should appreciate all he had done for her, considering his position in the community. And she did. But his concern for her—if that was what she'd witnessed—made her feel significant where Kevin was concerned.

He steered her several paces away from his father and grimaced. "Guess you figured out we're related."

"The last name gave me a bit of a clue."

"Yeah, well, I'm nothing like him. He's an ass, and he's purposely screwing with you because he knows I . . ." His hand came down on her shoulder. "You don't have to take the job."

Standing in the strength of his shadow, she'd do almost anything to spend a few more hours with him. It was stupid, and just like her ridiculous notion that fairies truly existed under the green hills of Ireland—she knew nothing could ever become of her and the handsome Yank.

"You're not as tough as you would have me to believe, Kevin Bendix." She touched his cheek, still rough with whiskers. "I am perfectly fine with the job. It's not one I'm unfamiliar with." She glanced at Turk. "I can deal with the likes of your father. It's a matter of all bark and no bite, I think."

She took a step away from him, his hand falling from her shoulder, and caught Turk waving impatiently at her.

"You in or out, Flynn?" His rough voice lingered on the humid, late afternoon air. He stood with the clipboard in his hand, a pair of chunky reading glasses now sat oddly above the curve of his ear, pressed to the thick side of his balding, rose-colored head.

"I'm in," she called back. Dani had the overwhelming desire to hug Kevin goodbye. Instead, she stuck out her hand. "Thank you."

He shook it and then reached for his back pocket and pulled out his wallet and dug out a business card. "Use my cell if you need to contact me." He tipped his head down and frowned. "We still need to work out the legality of you remaining in the States. I'll be in touch."

She'd have looked forward to it. Except if he investigated her long enough—and she would be a fool to think he wouldn't—he'd find Dani Flynn, a usually law-abiding citizen of the Republic of Ireland, had gotten herself tangled in a web of murder and deceit, the extent of which she wouldn't know until she got a look at the thumb drive.

That would be her next dilemma, but first she needed to get back to the farm and retrieve her backpack with her wallet. Once Kevin had her birth certificate, Dani could prove her identity and her connection to Daniel Fallon, giving her the right to stay in the U.S. legally, and hopefully keep him satisfied enough he'd stop digging.

"Of course." Dani glanced back toward Turk and the woman still struggling with the mattress. "I should go." With her tote bag filled with all she owned, compliments of Kevin, Dani headed toward the barn.

"Let me help you." Dani took the other half of the mattress. "I'm Dani Flynn."

She nodded. "Bonnie Dunn."

Dani followed her through the barn, horse flesh and hay filling her nostrils, and she couldn't help but smile. They passed Turk's office, Dani's eyes lingering on his desk and the computer. Her mind went to the thumb drive. That would be a starting point once she went back for her belongings. But in the meantime, she could still search for news of Kara. Perhaps, she'd survived. Dani frowned. Not likely. Duggan wouldn't leave a loose end. It bothered her—the idea that Kara hadn't escaped him and Dani had.

Would he come for her?

Nonsense. She was letting her mind have its way. America was vast. He'd have no sense of where to look. She was sure of that. They came to another door—the bathroom. Dani peeked in. Small with little privacy, she'd be scheduling her showers at night.

"Are you a groom, then, Bonnie?"

Bonnie took a breath and angled the mattress up the narrow stairs located in the back of the barn to the right. "I am." Her blond head poked over the top of the mattress, and she smiled. "I like your accent."

"Irish."

"Yeah, that's what Turk said." She continued up the steps, bending the mattress around the corner. "The room's in front," she said on a heavy breath. Together they brought the mattress around and down the short hall through the narrow door, plopping it on the wooden floor, dirt puffing into the air when it landed with a thud. "Kind of dirty, huh?"

"It's more than adequate."

"I'll grab you a set of sheets and a blanket from the bunkhouse."

She liked Bonnie immediately—slender, close to her own age, a little taller than Dani with a bright smile.

Bonnie fell back a step, a sly grin forming around her mouth. "Gotta ask." She moved a pile of boxes, and peered through a small, dirty window and looked down to where Kevin stood with Turk. "How'd you meet the pissy, good-looking Sheriff Tightass?"

Dani laughed and moved to the window. "Through me da." Maybe it wasn't quite the truth. Kevin and his father's voices grew louder. "They don't seem to get along."

"That's how it's always been with those two."

"Why's that?"

"I think Kevin has always blamed his father for his mother's death."

"Surely he didn't cause it?"

"No. She died of pneumonia while Turk was up in New York at the Belmont. Guess Kevin felt if Turk had been home, she'd have gotten the medical attention she needed. I'm sure Lindy Bendix assumed she had what amounted to the flu." She turned to Dani. "Turk found her when he got home, still in her pajamas and tucked in her deathbed."

Dani shivered. "Oh, Bonnie, how awful."

"Yep, 'course that's been nearly two decades ago."

"They seem pretty animated." She shook her head at the pair, talking with their arms flying about.

"Turk's pissed."

"Why?"

She shrugged. "We're a fiercely competitive lot." She pointed out the window. Several stables lined both sides of the gravel road of the training center. "See the stable two down from ours?"

"Yes."

"It's owned by Blake Lansing. He's what you'd call old money and an elitist who thinks he's Rockefeller himself."

She'd heard the name, something or someone to do with American money. "What about the one next to us?"

Bonnie laughed. "That's Fritz Bailey's outfit—Cloverdale. I used to work for him until about six months ago." She became reflective. "It's a tough business, but it worked out for me. Fritz and Turk have been buddies for years. Turk agreed to hire me thanks to Fritz. You'll meet him."

"It's good that you were able to find employment so quickly." Dani cocked her head. "What does this have to do with Kevin and his father?"

She pointed her finger at Dani. "Fierce competition, remember?" She grabbed her hand. "Come on. Let's find a broom and a dustpan. If you help me, there's a small chest we can haul up here from Turk's office for your stuff, and we'll dump these boxes in the Dumpster behind the barn."

"Won't he be needing it?"

"Probably." A devilish smile tugged at her lips.

"Then we shouldn't take it."

Turk didn't much care for her already. She'd been foisted upon him by a son he didn't seem to be on good terms with. And taking his belongings wouldn't make him feel any more charitable toward her.

"He's more bark than—"

"Bite." Dani laughed when she said it.

Bonnie laughed with her. "He's harmless. I swear." Then her face turned serious.

"You all right?"

"It's that fierce competition I mentioned earlier."

Dani wondered when she'd get around to finishing her original thought. Bonnie seemed to be going in all directions.

"It can make people ruthless or paranoid. Turk is upset with Kevin, presently, because he's been blowing him off about the things that have been happening around here lately."

"What things?"

"Tack out of place. Horses off their feed."

"Isn't that commonplace? I mean the feed? And the tack—some aren't that organized."

"If you plan to stay here, you'll find this trainer doesn't tolerate sloppy grooms."

Not that she was, but she took note.

Bonnie shook her head. "Maybe it's nothing. Blake Lansing has the best Thoroughbreds his fortune can buy without sabotaging our stable. His aristocratic airs are what pisses Turk off the most."

Remaining in front of the window in her room, Dani's heart dipped at the brake lights of Kevin's patrol car as he pulled out and drove away. "Bonnie, do you have a car?"

She pointed to a yellow 1960s-something Volkswagen Beatle. "My pride and joy."

Parked down below in Starlite's lot, it sat with rusted fenders just like Dani's old scooter. "Would you be willing to take me somewhere?"

"Tonight?"

"No, not necessarily tonight, but soon."

"I can take you tomorrow after work."

"I'll pay you."

She snorted. "From the looks of what you brought and what Turk told me, you're broke."

The heat crept into Dani's cheeks. "When I get me paycheck, I meant."

Bonnie grabbed her hand. "Dani Flynn from Ireland, I'm happy to do it."

Dani's heart warmed. She'd hoped her own father and sisters would be as kind. And they had been until she'd told them the truth, a truth they were not ready to accept. By tomorrow night, with the help of Bonnie, she'd have her birth certificate, and they'd have no choice but to accept her for who she was—their own flesh and blood.

CHAPTER TEN

DANI WOKE AT HALF PAST FOUR IN THE MORNING ON MONDAY, HER first day as groom for Starlite Horseracing Stables and owner Jameson Porter. She'd learned of him from Bonnie while they tidied her room the night before. The eight by ten sized room remained cramped, but after they'd dumped the boxes, swept the floor, dusted out the cobwebs, and cleaned the small window to allow the light to come shining through, it wasn't bad at all. Even the mattress, which they'd raised with several plastic crates, allowed her a comfortable night's sleep with the fresh sheets and wool blanket they'd taken from the bunkhouse.

She went to the chest to pull out her clothes. She'd been a bit nervous when they'd carted Turk's chest up the narrow stairs last night, leaving what few papers there were inside it on his desk. Of course, they waited until he'd left to go home. She opened the first drawer of the three-drawer chest—one pair of khaki shorts and jeans, two T-shirts, two bikini briefs, Kate's bra and dress. She grabbed the khaki shorts, a T-shirt, briefs, and Kate's bra, then opened up the second drawer and grabbed her toiletries. Wearing only the shirt she went to bed in and her panties—it was early enough she'd have her privacy—she headed down the wooden steps in her sandals to the bathroom. Nickers and snorts filled the stable when she hit the ground level. They were hungry, too. Dani ignored her hollow stomach and entered the bathroom. She took a quick shower and dressed. Heading back to her room, she exchanged her sandals for the white tennis shoes, grimacing at the color. She'd be buying a pair of boots with her first pay. Dani checked the window. The bunkhouse remained quiet. While waiting, she repeated in her head the names of the horses

Turk had assigned to her. None of them were black like the horse she'd met at the fence yesterday, and Dani wondered who was assigned to him.

Dani moved away from the window when Bonnie and two Hispanic grooms came out of the bunkhouse, walking toward Starlite's barn. She wished she had her backpack now with her peppermints. They'd been like a talisman while she was at sea, a promise she'd again be with horses. Usually she fed the horses back home the special treat before bed, but having the peppermints this morning would have helped during their initial bonding. A bit disappointed, she took the steps down, meeting the grooms as they entered the stall area.

"Good morning."

"Hey, Dani." Bonnie smiled and turned. "This is Juan and that's Arturo."

She shook each of their hands and introduced herself. Bonnie waved them on, and they began feeding their horses.

Bonnie pulled her aside. "I'll show you where we keep the grain. Turk likes us to mix it with a little oil so it goes down smoother."

Dani nodded and followed her to the area where they kept the feed, still curious about one thing. "What about the black stallion I met yesterday?"

Bonnie's forehead crinkled, and she pursed her lips. "Oh, you mean, the colt Solitary Confinement."

Dani made a face. "It's a very dark name, don't you think? Did Turk pick it?"

"Yes and no." She laughed. "The name suits him, though. No one's been able to ride him since Turk bought him at auction. You'd think he'd show a little gratitude since he'd be dinner right about now in some fancy French restaurant overseas," Bonnie said and then entered the supply room.

Perplexed, Dani followed on her heels. The horse had been so friendly toward her, and she was a complete stranger. Perhaps he sensed she hadn't judged him yet. He obviously had a story and not an easy one it seemed.

"It's an awful thing, for sure. Even worse in Ireland . . . slaughter, I mean."

"Not a fan myself. Just glad Turk assigned him to Arturo and not me. I want to keep my fingers."

Dani swallowed hard. She'd all but offered her fingers as an appetizer yesterday. She'd do well to remember Bonnie's warning and let the silly notion go that they—the colt and her—had connected in some way during their brief introduction.

"Dani?" Bonnie gave her a curious look.

"Oh, I'm sorry." Bonnie had been giving her instructions, and Dani had not a clue what she'd said. "Me mind was on the horse. I'll heed your advice."

Bonnie nodded and gave her a few more minutes of the dos and don'ts according to Turk, and Dani locked Solitary Confinement in the back of her head for now.

Other than a few pet peeves of Turk's and his corkboard next to his office where he posted any changeups—feed, medication, farrier visits—it was a relief to find they ran their stables similarly to that of Mr. Carrigan. Bonnie gathered her a bucket and filled it with a rub rag, currycomb, soft and stiff brushes, large sponge, mane comb, hoof pick, and foot brush.

"Okay, that should do you." Bonnie handed her the bucket. "Last stop, the tack room."

A familiar mix of horse and leather greeted her, and she couldn't help but breathe deep. Exercise bridles hung neatly on hooks, and saddles sat one on top of another on a shelf with other accessories—saddlecloths, saddle and pommel pads, exercise girths and covers, and chamois cloths.

"Just remember, return it the way you found it." Bonnie leaned against the door frame. "We have a saying around here, 'Don't poke the bear.' " She grimaced. "Meaning Turk."

Dani only wished she'd known about it before they took his chest. "I'll treat the tack as if it were me own, for sure."

"Good." Bonnie motioned her out. "All right. It's breakfast time."

Dani fed her charges about four pounds of grain each, cleaned their water buckets with a stiff brush, and refilled them with fresh, cool water. After breakfast, out of the stalls they came. She cross-tied them in the middle of the aisle, brushed them, picked their feet, and saddled them for the next available exercise rider who would take them out on the track for their morning workout.

She'd lucked out for sure. Of the four horses she was assigned to, there was not a difficult one in the bunch. She had to chuckle at their names. If nothing else, Mr. Porter was inventive. George's Got the Gold, a handsome bay stallion, was a proud one the way he held his head. Down Under Joey, a chestnut gelding, had the saddest eyes and pulled at her heart. Nothing Like a Sister, a cute palomino filly who seemed to love attention, liked to nudge Dani with her nose, and Do It Again Harv

Man, another bay gelding, seemed to sense what Dani wanted him to do before she could instruct him. He truly was the smartest of the bunch.

Dani cleaned the horsehair from her currycomb, dropped it in her bucket, and hooked it on the wall next to the other grooms' buckets. Her own stomach growled just then. She had no money to buy even an apple or a candy bar. Turk had come in while she was finishing up her last horse. He'd be in his office, minus his chest of drawers. She was all too sure, even if he didn't use it, he'd give her royal hell for taking it. Of course, they'd swept up the cobwebs and the dirt left behind, but it remained a bare wall. Dani's stomach protested again, and she put her concerns aside and entered Turk's office.

"Good morning, Mr. Bendix."

Sitting in a high-backed swivel chair, he had his head buried in a racing book. He lifted his head, shut the book, and reached out to the general area where the chest had been and dropped the book. It landed with a slap.

Dani's stomach dropped. *Shite.* Their eyes connected. His were the same irritated blue she remembered from yesterday.

"Flynn," he said, his voice a rumble of discontent. "It's the damnedest thing. When I left last night, I could have sworn the old wooden chest was right where it's been for the past thirty-some years."

She had to tell him. Dani swallowed. "It's me own fault, Mr. Bendix. I should have asked. I had nowhere to store me things. Not that I have—"

"Save it, Flynn." He pulled on his chin. "Your strength surprises me."

Dani frowned. "Excuse me?"

He nailed her with his intense gaze. "Why are you here, Flynn? Don't like the accommodations?"

"N-no, you've been very generous."

He eyed the racing book on the ground and grumbled, "In more ways than one."

She ignored his comment. "I was wondering if you'd be agreeable to an advance until me first pay. I have clothes enough to get by. I'll need to wash them, of course. Bonnie showed me the laundry room in the bunkhouse. I would just need a little for detergent and"—her stomach gurgled loudly—"food." Dani's shoulders crept up.

Turk reached back into his pants pocket, pulled out his wallet, and thumbed through the bills. He pulled out five twenty-dollar bills. "Hundred see you through?"

"Mr. Bendix, that's more than enough."

He handed it to her. "Flynn," he said, sliding his glasses down his head and onto his nose. He glanced up through them. "You pull your load, continue to take responsibility—even though I know the chest had Dunn written all over it—and tell me the raw truth like today, we'll get along." He stood. "It's Turk, not Mr. Bendix."

Dani sputtered, trying to find her words. "T-Turk, it's very—" She cocked her head. "Is that a kitten?" In the corner of his office, curled in a box with the plushest black blanket she'd ever seen was a small kitten. With his eyes closed, it was hard to tell where the blanket ended and the inky puffball began.

"Horace A. 'Jimmy' Jones."

"Excuse me?"

"His name," he grumped.

Dani giggled. "It's a bit of a mouthful, don't you think?"

"Best damn trainer there ever was." He squinted over his glasses. "He answers to Jimmy."

Aw. Dani squeezed past and bent down. "He's adorable."

"Think so?"

"Oh, yes." She peered down. The kitty yawned and opened his eyes. "Green eyes like me ma's." She hooked her chin over her shoulder. "He's yours, then?"

"Not a charity, Flynn." He shook his head. "Feeding cats and penniless women," he muttered, pushed past her, and grabbed the box. "He's orphaned. From what that son of mine tells me, you know a thing or two about it." He shoved the box at her. "Don't have time to take care of a damned cat."

Dani blinked. "Are ya saying he's mine, then?"

He shrugged. "If you want him. Otherwise he's on his own."

She latched onto the box, her eyes locking onto Turk's. Surely he wouldn't stop feeding him. Granted, there were probably plenty of mice to keep him happy. But from the little she'd seen of Jimmy, he was coddled and spoiled, and she knew by whom.

"If you're sure."

"Hell yes, I'm sure." He let go of the box and waved her off. "There's food in the cantina in the bunkhouse. Get yourself something to eat." He walked past her, grabbed a small bag off the floor, handed it to her.

She juggled the box and took the food.

"He likes it with a little milk." He cleared the doorway to his office and then the open double doors of the barn and nimbly covered the distance to the track.

Dani's mouth fell open. She wanted the kitty, she did. Dani took the stairs, two at a time, to her room and sat Jimmy down next to her mattress. He mewed, stretched, and curled back up in a ball. She placed the food on her chest of drawers, her own stomach gurgling. *Grand.* Now she would have two mouths to feed once his food ran out. *Oh,* she'd need to buy milk, too. Another hunger pain ripped through her stomach. She gave the kitty a scratch behind his ear. He was a cutie, and she wouldn't mind at all spoiling him.

Dani smiled. "I'll see you later, then, little guy." She turned, sailing down the steps, and hotfooted it to the bunkhouse where she grabbed an apple, granola bar, and a bottle of water. She ate it quickly in the barn and then mucked the stalls, cleaned the grain buckets, refilled their water, and added a flake of hay to their stalls so it would be waiting upon their return.

Bonnie came up from behind her. "Come on. I'll show you where we bathe them." She headed out of the barn. "Grab your bucket," she called back.

Dani took it off the hook and caught up with Bonnie when she rounded the corner of the barn. "Wait. You move too fast."

"I'm sorry." She laughed and checked Dani's bucket. "Good, looks like you have everything." She motioned toward the side of the barn and a hose. "In nice weather we bathe them outside. They enjoy it, and it makes our job easier." She picked up the nozzle. "This hose is piped for warm water. Sweat scarpers are hanging on the wall." Her striking green eyes connected with Dani's blue ones. "You know the drill, right?"

"Yes, of course."

"Good." She turned toward the track behind them. "They should be bringing them in one by one, and we wash them and move on to the next, handing them off to Arturo."

"Bonnie Belle." The voice came from the track. It belonged to an older man, but not Turk.

Bonnie waved a hand and started that way. "Come on, Dani. I'll introduce you to Fritz Bailey."

Dani followed her. The closer they got to the rail, the more distinct the man became. He wore a tweed cap, dark trousers, white, short-sleeved dress shirt, and suspenders over a slight belly. She'd guess his age to be close to Turk's, although Fritz Bailey, from what she could see, had most of his gray hair.

"Hey, Fritz, how's it going?"

"Swell." He eyed Dani. "So who might this beauty be?"

Dani's cheeks warmed.

"Always a charmer." Bonnie smiled when she said it. "This is Dani Flynn from Ireland."

"I heard rumor." He stuck out his hand. "And it's a pleasure to meet you, Dani Flynn from Ireland."

Dani shook his hand. "Nice to make your acquaintance, Mr. Bailey."

He chuckled. "No need to be so formal. Call me Fritz. Starlite and Cloverdale are what you might call kissing cousins." He angled his head back toward the track. "We both have one thing in common . . ." His voice trailed off when a rider approached them.

There was something about the rider. Perhaps the way he sat in the saddle—aristocratic. He came very close to the rail, wearing black riding boots and britches, his short-sleeved white shirt damp from sweat and clinging to his muscular chest and shoulders. Horse and rider were a match of strength and beauty. Their muscles undulating, the man's in particular, with his forearm flexing as he held the reins in a skillful manner and moved closer.

"Good morning, Fritz." His voice was pleasant but controlled. He tipped his head toward Bonnie and then Dani. "Ladies." He smiled and winked, definitely at Dani, and she wanted to look away from his dark, curious eyes. He reined in his horse near the rail and stopped, his tanned skin glistening with perspiration under the early morning sun. "I don't think we've had the pleasure." He reached down his hand to shake. "Blake Lansing."

Her palms were moist, and she dried them on her shorts. "Dani Flynn." She shook his firm, dry hand.

"Charming voice."

"Irish, actually."

"I take it Fritz has snatched you up as his . . ."

"A groom, yes. But I'm employed by Turk Bendix."

His smile faded. "You find he's not treating you right, beautiful, come see me personally. I'm sure I can find something to keep you busy."

Dani's stomach dipped. He'd meant that in more than one way, she was sure. Although handsome with a sharply contoured face, arresting brown eyes, and short-cropped, jet black hair, she didn't know how to respond to his bold comment. She opened her mouth but shut it just as quickly.

He nodded toward Bonnie. "I see Chipper's on Midnight Edition."

"They seem well matched," Bonnie said, her voice missing its normal sweetness.

"We'll see," Blake said in a condescending tone. His horse seemed to echo the same sentiment when he stamped his foot and shook his head, snorting.

Bonnie fisted her hands to her sides but didn't engage him again.

Blake tipped his chin toward Fritz. "You've got some entries at Charles Town next week."

"Thought I'd give you some competition."

"Looking forward to it." Blake nodded to them, angled his horse toward the track, and took off at a gallop.

"I swear he likes to shove his fine breeding, and not just his flaming horses, in our faces."

Fritz shook his head at Bonnie. "I'd have thought with all the land he acquired since buying the Connelly place he'd have set up shop there."

Dani looked from Bonnie to Fritz. "Who are you speaking about?"

Fritz waved an impatient hand. "A big fat nobody that Rafe and Bren Langston are glad to be rid of."

"Are we close to them? I mean Grace, their farm?"

"Right up the road, hang a left, and you're there." Fritz gave her a look. "You know them, the Langstons and Fallons?"

Dani swallowed. "I met them once." Which was true, but the details of her relationship to them wasn't common knowledge. Turk might know, but Kevin would have asked him to keep it quiet. As it was, her family hadn't even accepted her.

"Good people. Daniel and I go back a long way." Fritz angled his head at Dani. "Getting back to horses. With your size . . ." He glanced at Bonnie. "She's built like a jockey."

"She is." Bonnie grinned at Dani. "Ever raced?"

Dani took a step back. "You're making a joke, then. I could only wish to have the ability like me ma. I could never—"

Fritz placed his hand, spotted with age, on her shoulder. "Don't sell yourself short." He gave a devilish smile. "Turk would skewer my ass for this, Dani, but you have the time, come see me. I'll let you take out one of my beasts, and you can have a go at it." He winked at Bonnie. "We work around Turk and his grumpy disposition all the time. Don't we, Bonnie Belle?"

She frowned. "What he means is Turk would be pissed if you took out one of Mr. Porter's Thoroughbreds to practice with." She shook her head at Fritz and gave him a disagreeable look.

"I'd like that, Fritz." Dani smiled. He was very kind.

"Well there you go." Fritz gave her a pat on the back. "Sounds to me like you were born with untapped natural ability."

She'd often wondered if she truly had it—the ability like her ma. But she'd never had someone willing to help her further her aspirations of becoming a jockey. "I'd be most grateful, Fritz, if you really have the time."

"Fritz!"

He lifted his chin, looking beyond Dani. "You leaving, Zelda?"

Dani turned.

An elderly woman shuffled toward a classic sedan complete with fins. "Water aerobics at eleven." She waved something at them. "Mailing out the bills."

He laughed. "If only she could remember to pay them on time." He shook his head. "Haven't the heart to let her go."

Dani pursed her lips. Aw. He really was sweet with a good heart.

Bonnie grabbed Dani's arm. "They're bringing them in. We need to get to work."

"Of course." She smiled at Fritz. "A pleasure meeting you."

"Same here, Dani."

Dani and Bonnie moved away from the rail.

"Dani," Fritz called.

Dani glanced over her shoulder.

"Not kidding about testing your skill."

"I'll let you know my schedule."

"Good girl." He tipped his hat and turned his attention back to the track.

"He's nothing at all like Turk," Dani commented.

"Fritz? He's laid-back. Takes his losses in stride and celebrates the wins when they come. Plus, he's the owner. He doesn't have a Jameson Porter breathing down his neck like Turk."

A horse's painful squeal stopped Dani mid-stride. "What the devil?" She glanced over her shoulder. On the track, several paces away, a black colt pulled viciously at the reins held firmly by, she guessed, one of Turk's exercise riders.

"Whoa, boy!"

The familiar colt jerked his head and snorted, and Dani turned. She shook her head. *Give him some slack.*

The horse reared up again, and the dark-haired guy yanked hard. Dani walked with purpose toward the rail. *You need to ease up.* He wasn't going to get anywhere with the colt by muscling him. The guy cursed and swatted him hard with the whip. The horse twisted his head, his eyes looking murderous with the whites showing.

Oh, Lord.

"Ease up!" Dani shouted and took off at a run.

The exercise rider swung his dark head around, the reins slipping through his hands, and the colt took off down the track.

"Shit!" He scowled at her. "You crazy . . ."

Dani slowed enough to shove her body through the railing then took off at a dead run, his words lost on her. The colt wasn't likely to run out of energy any time soon. He had his freedom . . . for now. Only if he couldn't hop the rail, he'd remain on the track and be a danger to those still on it. Dani relied on that connection from yesterday and whistled through her teeth. The colt slowed.

Come on, sweetheart. I'm not here to hurt you.

Dani jogged toward him, and he turned around. With his ears pinched back, he nervously pranced on his feet. Careful not to spook him into running, she slowed her step and held out her hand. Bloody fingers came to mind, but she ignored the overwhelming desire to pull them back. He wouldn't bite her, she was sure. Dani tuned everything out—the riders left on the track, the directions being yelled to her from the rail, and the reprimand she was likely to get.

"What do you say, boy? Make things a lot easier on both of us if you let me lead you back to the barn."

He snorted like he was thinking about her request, his ears now pricked up. And . . . could it be listening?

"Ah, see, you know a friend when you see one." Dani kept an even pace, hand out, refusing to believe when she got close enough the colt would take a bite. She was within a few steps of him when she stopped. If he trusted her, he'd find the courage to come to her. He only needed assurances. "I'll bathe you myself and plead your case to Turk if you come to me."

He nodded like he understood, a soft nicker escaping through his lips.

"Your choice, sweetheart."

He took a step and then continued toward her. Dani gently touched his nose, her other hand finding the reins. "I'll not pull on you like the eejit before," she whispered. "Let's walk together, your pace." Dani patted his side and waited. Solitary Confinement—she hated the name—took the first step. She only hoped it was toward the gate.

Dani held the reins, careful not to pull them tight. He wasn't a bad horse. He just wanted to be in control. She could understand. She'd lost control over her own life since hiding on the freighter. But she was finding direction and she could let the colt have some control and still give him the direction he needed.

Dani headed toward the outside rail, giving the rider and horse coming up on them a wide berth. She blinked as they passed by, trying to get a better view. A woman . . . and with fine form like a jockey. Whether she was or wasn't, she couldn't say, but Dani doubted she worked for Turk.

Dani and the colt came up on the gate, and she gulped. Turk held it open, his face taut and unsmiling.

CHAPTER ELEVEN

Dani grimaced when she passed through the gate. "I can expla—"

"Bathe him."

Dani clamped her mouth shut and walked to the barn with the colt content to be at her side, and Dani glad to be out of earshot of Turk. She removed the colt's tack and walked him around to cool him off.

"You really are a sweet one," she whispered to the horse and stroked his black face, no longer in fear she'd lose a digit. Of course she'd have to cross-tie him at the wash bay. They headed out of the barn. Expecting he'd fight her, she sidled up next to him once they made their way to the concrete wall with metal hooks cemented into it. "I'll only keep you tied up but a minute." She cross-tied him with little to no fuss, turning on the hose. The water shot out, and she gasped at its ferocity.

Laughter brought Dani around. Bonnie stood gauging the distance between her and Solitary Confinement. Dani frowned. She didn't like his name at all. There had to be something else, racehorses almost always had a nickname. Then it came to her. She'd call him . . . Solley. It was short and sweet and fitting. "He's quite friendly, I believe." Dani held out the hose as if it would bite. "It's got a kick, don't you think?"

"It's pressurized and won't bite like—"

"Do you think Turk would consider giving him to me to groom?"

Bonnie took the spray wand from her and turned it on. "Just let it glide over his coat." She handed it back to her. "*Oh, yeah.* He listens to you. Turk'd be a fool not to take you up on your offer."

The concern welling up in her chest subsided. Turk liked Bonnie. He seemed to respect her. Dani settled in with the sprayer, starting at Solley's shoulders on down. Now that he was nice and soaked, she wet the sponge and squeezed it. She started at his head, careful to avoid the colt's eyes and ears. She sponged around his mouth and cleaned away the sweat and saliva, taking care around his nostrils by squeezing the sponge of extra water and cleaning them thoroughly, reassuring Solley as she did.

She then grabbed one of the buckets and filled it with shampoo and water. Suds rose to the top, and she sponged down his neck, moving in circular motions down to his chest while Bonnie filled her bucket.

"You want to tell me what happened out there?" Turk's grumpy voice left nothing to her imagination.

Dani's hand stilled, and she kept her back to Turk. He made her nervous, especially his scowl. "He held him too tight."

"He's one of my best exercise riders. You telling me you're more seasoned?"

Dani winced. Although if he wanted her honest answer it would be a resounding yes. In Ireland she did it all—groom, hotwalker, exercise rider . . . She frowned. Except for jockeying. "No. Just that I understand him better."

"Flynn, turn around while I'm talking to you."

Grand. She dropped the sponge in the bucket and rotated slowly. "Yes, sir."

"His original owner told me he was no longer trainable. But I couldn't turn my back on him."

Something sorrowful and yet defiant flashed in those old blue eyes of his, and Dani wanted to hug him. "You did the right thing."

"You think you can handle him?" Turk placed his hands on his hips, narrowing in on her.

"Aye, and we'd both be better for it." Meaning she'd love nothing more than to care for Solley. She patted his rump. "He's an independent one. Not to say he doesn't need some reining in. But gently."

Turk nodded. "Then he's yours—if you think you can handle all five."

She could. It might take up more of her time teaching him ground manners, but the others were like cream-filled doughnuts compared to Solley. "Yes. You have my word."

"Then finish up. You've got four more to go."

"Yes, sir." Dani grabbed the sponge and scrubbed Solley down the rest of the way.

Turk headed back to the barn, Dani more than relieved to see him go.

"Don't let me regret my decision," he called back.

Dani smiled at that—Turk liked to have the last word.

Bonnie took George's Got the Gold and sprayed him down for her. "Let's be quick about it, Dani, and we'll be done in no time."

Dani didn't miss her attempt at an Irish brogue and chuckled. "You're a fine friend, Bonnie Dunn."

They laughed, and together they finished the two horses, taking care to dry them off just as Arturo showed up to take them back to their stalls. Solley and George followed Arturo into the barn. They passed the dark-haired exercise rider from earlier, coming out with two more horses to be bathed. He scowled at her. Dani swallowed hard, preparing for a confrontation. When he reached her, he shoved the lead to the chestnut nicknamed Joey at her. Without a word, he turned, handed Bonnie the lead to Dixie Bayou and whispered something into her ear.

Bonnie took one look at Dani and frowned. "Yeah. But I need to work something out first," she said to him.

He shot Dani an angry look and sauntered away, leaving her to wonder if their conversation had anything to do with her. Several exercise riders slowed their paces, nearing the gate. Bonnie had already moved onto scraping the excess water off Dixie, and Dani—still transfixed on the private conversation—fell behind with Joey.

Panic rose in Dani's chest. "They'll be coming in quick."

Bonnie caught her eye. "You're doing fine, Dani."

Dani gave a wan smile. It wasn't like she'd not done the job of groom before and well. She was just nervous. "You're very proficient, yourself."

"You will be, too, once you get your rhythm." She turned away when another rider came up. "Hey, girl, I think you have Lansing worried."

The female rider, the one from the track earlier, hopped down and took off her riding helmet. Her blond hair was short and choppy, yet stylish. She breathed hard. "I just ride." She patted her horse. "If he can keep us on this winning streak, Lansing may have a reason to worry."

"Great jockey, great bloodlines. I don't see a problem." Bonnie nodded to Dani. "Chipper, this is Dani Flynn. New groom working for Turk." She lifted her chin toward Dani. "Chipper Grant, Starlite's jockey extraordinaire."

"Stop it, Bonnie. I'm his only jockey." Chipper smiled at Dani. "She's a fan. Can you tell?"

"You handle the reins well." But more than that she *was* a jockey and, it would seem, Turk's only one. And no mention of an agent. Interesting, jockeys weren't usually tied to a single barn although of course they had their favorites.

"I try." Her eyes traveled over Dani. "You ride?"

"When time permits."

Chipper looked to Bonnie. "She's built like a—"

"Jockey," Bonnie ended Chipper's sentence, and the three laughed. "Fritz said the same thing," Bonnie added. She winked at Dani. "We're going to let her test her skills with one of Fritz's horses—of course, without Turk's knowledge."

Chipper wiped a smudge of dirt from her forehead. "Good idea. He'd think it was a conspiracy or something."

Just like Bonnie had mentioned with the tack and feed, Dani noted.

"So do you live in the bunkhouse, Chipper?" Dani asked.

"No. I live in an apartment in Hagerstown with my daughter."

"Hannah is three," Bonnie said, "and looks just like her mom."

"She must be very beautiful, then."

"Aw." Chipper pressed her lips out in a pout. "Thanks, you guys."

Bonnie stiffened, her eyes trained on something behind them. "Why would *he* be heading this way?"

Chipper turned, and Dani kept her eyes on Blake and his steed as they neared.

"Greetings, ladies." He hopped down with ease and motioned to Dani. "Do you have a minute?"

Dani's eyes widened. He didn't mean her, specifically, did he?

He reached out and took the sponge from her hand and gave it to Bonnie. "Appreciate it, Bonnie."

Bonnie took it, her own eyes growing larger. "Not a problem." She looked to Chipper who also had a look of surprise when Blake held out the reins to his horse.

"Chipper, could you hold Bart for a minute?"

"Sure." She gave him a quick smile and grabbed hold of them, her lips thinning.

Blake Lansing took Dani's hands, dripping with water, in his and directed her toward the rail. Her cheeks warmed, and Dani wished she hadn't allowed herself to be whisked away so easily.

"So how'd you do that back there?" He released her hands.

"Pardon?"

"The colt."

Dani shrugged. "It was nothing."

"You have striking eyes, Ms. Flynn."

His intense gaze had her lowering her lashes.

"You must be one of those Irish sirens. Full of black magic."

Dani's chin jutted a notch. "I'm not a witch, Mr. Lansing, of that I'm sure."

"Then tell me your secret." He chuckled, and the sense that he was accusing her of something sinister faded.

For the second time, Dani explained what she believed made for an irritable Thoroughbred. "But sincerity is key." Dani glanced back over her shoulder and chewed her bottom lip. "If we're done here, Mr. Lansing, I need to get back to me chores."

"Call me Blake, and I'll call you Dani?"

"Yes, it seems appropriate, I think, considering I'll see you around the—"

He laughed out loud. "You're a gem—an emerald, of that I'm sure, Dani Flynn."

"Are you making fun, then, of me—"

"Definitely not." Dark eyes flashed down at her, almost primal, but it was gone as quickly, and she questioned if she'd imagined it. Attentive brown eyes now held hers—unlike Kevin's that seemed more angry than not when he looked at her. "You have me intrigued and not just about horses."

Dani wet her lips. He was bold and making her nervous.

"I really need to—"

"Right. I know this is late. I had every intention of skipping the damn thing, but now I just might enjoy it."

"I'm not sure I understand."

"I'm not being clear." He took her hands in his, again. "Dani, would you be my date for the Horsemen's Ball?"

Her brain scrambled just then. *Ball?* She was sure Irish royalty—kings, perhaps—had them hundreds of years ago in their cold, dank castles. But these were not medieval times. Nor was she accomplished in any way, and the wealthy—from what Bonnie had said last night—gorgeous man standing so very near to her and holding her hands in his would know that. At least he should. Dani pulled her hands away, absently rubbing the scab on her chin. "Do you not know what you're asking, then?"

She glanced behind her. Both Bonnie and Chipper kept the unlikely pair in their lines of sight.

"Stop worrying about Bonnie and Chipper. Look at me."

She did, and she couldn't help but swallow. "I'm a groom, Blake. I couldn't possibly say yes. You're, you're . . ."

"A man who finds you incredibly attractive." His eyes connected with hers. "It's this Saturday at the Huntsmen's Club. I'll pick you up around seven. It's formal."

She wanted to laugh at the idiocy of it. Of course she couldn't go. She had a dress—a soiled dress that wasn't hers—and sandals battered from her flight through the woods. She doubted they'd let her in. An arm came around her shoulders, and Dani recognized the riding boots of Chipper and the horse that had been foisted upon her. "She'd love to, Blake," Chipper gritted through her teeth.

"But I don't have . . ."

Chipper's eyes tunneled into Blake like Dani was invisible. "You do. Remember, I saw it in your closet?"

Was she talking to her? Strange. Dani had only just met the woman. Chipper hadn't been to her room. If she had, she'd know there was no closet to speak of.

"You've kept her long enough." Chipper handed the reins back to him. "She'll be ready at seven, sharp."

She steered Dani around, and they walked back to the washing area, leaving Blake to stare at their backs.

"Have you gone completely mad?" Dani's brows knitted together in complete bewilderment. "How could you hear?"

"The wind. Depending on how it's blowing. You'd be surprised what you can pick up during a private conversation." She leaned in. "Although yours was quite salacious compared to others." She spoke with a laugh.

The heat crept into Dani's cheeks, and with Chipper's added humor, she let go of the idea there had been some type of friction between her and Blake.

They met up with Bonnie who gave the sponge back to her. "You're kidding me. You were actually going to turn him down?"

Dani's shoulders crept up. "I thought he was the competition."

"Who cares? When a guy like Blake Lansing asks you out, you go."

"But that's it exactly. I'm not like him . . . at all. He's rich. I-I have but a bag of me own possessions and a dress that isn't even me own. And even at that, it's not a dress that's sufficient to wear. I can't go." She eyed Chipper. "I don't know whether to thank you or curse you."

Chipper laughed. "My she has an Irish temper."

"Now you're taking the mickey out me."

"She's not." Bonnie handed Chipper her horse and motioned to Dani as another exercise rider brought her the palomino Nothing Like a Sister. "Chipper's your size."

"She's right. I've been to a few of these balls. They're a lot of fun, and why should you miss out on it?"

Because Blake Lansing frightened her, and she didn't know if that was a good or bad thing. Dani turned toward Bonnie. "Are you going?"

"Nope. Have to be asked by someone with an engraved invitation to such an exclusive shindig. Besides, got a date."

"With who?" Dani didn't remember her mentioning it.

"Jake. He's the one who brought you the chestnut a few minutes ago."

"Oh." The same one she'd surely pissed off earlier at the track when he had Solley. Dani rolled her lips in. "Well, if you're not going . . ." She twisted the sponge in her hands. "I can't go. I don't know him."

"You didn't know Kevin Bendix, either."

She didn't like being reminded of Kevin by Bonnie, even though it was true. But that was different. She hadn't had a choice.

"Will you two stop?" Chipper mounted her horse, glancing down. "I'll bring you what I have tomorrow, and you can decide which dress you like best. And relax, Dani. I'll be at the ball. I'll keep my eye on . . . *Blake.*" She laughed and trotted away, and Dani didn't feel at all good about the way she said his name.

"What did she mean?" Dani twirled her sponge up in the air. "The way she—"

"You worry too much." Bonnie pulled her hand down with the sponge. "It's exciting, be happy. But Turk won't appreciate our enthusiasm if we fall behind." She frowned at the exercise riders coming in. "We need to pick up the pace."

"Aye," Dani said, sudsing up Nothing Like a Sister, called Sister for short. Taking care to give her a good washing and rinse, she handed her off and then moved on to the next, feeling a tad embarrassed by how she'd treated this Jake—mostly because Bonnie seemed to like him. Only her mind couldn't help but go back to another dark-haired man.

Nice Bonnie found it exciting. If nothing else, it had given her an upset stomach. Did she even want to go out with this Blake Lansing? It had all happened so fast. Still, it was only a dance. She supposed she was a bit of a fool for her misgivings.

If it had been Kevin asking her, she'd need but a second to answer.

Chapter Twelve

D ANI JERKED BACK ON THE STICK SHIFT, THE GEARS GRINDING, AND quickly applied the brake of Bonnie's Volkswagen Beatle. She lurched toward the dash along with Bonnie who sat in the front passenger seat.

Jake Griffin, Bonnie's exercise rider, flew forward from the backseat. "What the fuck," he seethed in her ear, his head almost landing in the windshield.

Dani wouldn't have minded a bit if he'd suffered a concussion. He'd been rude to her since they'd been properly introduced earlier that night. She gathered—other than pissing him off at the track—she'd also put a chink in his plans for the evening.

"Shut up, Jake," Bonnie yelled back from the passenger seat. "She'll get the hang of it."

"I'm terribly sorry." Dani glanced over at Bonnie. "I'll wreck it for sure."

"You won't. Let off the brake, and let's try again."

Dani did and took the gravel road slow around the stable, turning left onto the main road of the training center. She passed the bunkhouse on the right, Fritz's place on the left. Picking up speed, she moved the stick into second gear.

"Good girl. See, you've got it." Bonnie patted her shoulder.

Dani relaxed and then caught Jake's scowl in the rearview mirror and tensed up again. His eyes were shifty, and his dark hair, long and hanging past one eye, reminded her of Tommy Duggan.

"Bonnie, I don't feel at all comfortable with taking your car." Her heart thundered in her chest. "I told you I've not been given a license."

"I'm fine with it."

"So take the damned car," Jake bellowed. "I want to catch the band before closing."

"You're impatient," Bonnie shot back. "We'll make it to the Purple Cow in plenty of time." She nodded to Dani. "Take her out, and make a right on 68. Go a few miles and turn around, and we'll see how you do before I cut you loose." She leaned back. "Not a word, Jake. I had promised to take her tonight."

"I didn't mean to cause a problem, Bonnie. I can wa—"

She waved her away. "We're good." She motioned to go, and Dani pressed on the gas and passed Blake's stable, looped around, and headed toward the entrance of the training center. She took a right and got up to speed, moving into third gear. It wasn't like riding her scooter with the open road and wind brushing her skin. But it gave her a certain exhilaration. Perhaps because she'd shifted gears and hadn't once grinded one. Jake silently pouted in the back, his arms crossed over his chest. Dani's foot hovered over the brake, debating, when the sign for Grace came up unexpectedly.

She took the left quickly into the gravel drive of her family's farm. Bonnie braced herself, and Jake slammed to the side in the back. "Son of a bitch, Dani." He straightened up, both his hands gripping the front seats, and pierced her in the rearview mirror with a pair of pissed off eyes. "You drive like shit."

She should have passed it and found a place to turn around, but the farm was like a magnet. Dani couldn't help but be drawn to it. At the very least she should have slowed down. But it had come up so quick and looked different driving by it than finding it on foot like she'd done the first time. From what she remembered, the house and barn were tucked back off the winding driveway. It wouldn't take her long to retrieve her belongings when she set out on her own later tonight.

If they'd traveled three miles, she'd be surprised. She could even walk it. She could do this.

Dani turned to back out and caught sight of Bonnie's ill-tempered boyfriend. She smiled sweetly. "Sorry, Jake. I didn't realize how touchy the brakes are." She bit down on her lip. If she laughed, he'd more than likely flip her off. Dani didn't want to ruin the night for Bonnie. Turning right onto 68, she traveled back then entered the training center and dropped them off at Jake's pickup.

Bonnie got out, and Jake crawled out behind her. She came around to the driver's side. "Registration is in the glove compartment, and everything is in working order. As long as you keep to the speed limit, no one will be the wiser."

"I'll have it back before midnight."

The headlights of Jake's pickup lit them up. Bonnie patted her hand, resting on the frame of the window. "Got to go." She sashayed toward Jake in a pair of wedge sandals, miniskirt, and tank top—very alluring. Dani never had the nerve to dress or walk that way. Even when she dressed up . . . like for Tommy. He'd demanded she and Kara look businesslike.

Dani waited until they made their turn. It should be late enough. The sky had taken on a thick layer of clouds. It would be a good night to retrieve her backpack and wallet. She'd be smarter this time. Like not peeking into windows. She grimaced. At close to eleven, her sisters would surely be getting ready for bed. Running a horse rescue had to be as grueling as running a stable. She yawned just then, her eyes widening, trying to shake off her exhaustion from the day.

She took a left and kept to the speed limit. The sign came up. *Grace Equine Sanctuary & Cattle Ranch*. This time, Dani passed it and looped around. She pulled off onto the shoulder and parked in the grass, turning off the car. Yellow. Of all the colors, it couldn't have been a dark one.

Dani got out, traveled several yards up, and slipped down the gravel driveway. She kept close to the trees and, when she came up to the opening, went directly to the barn. A few lights remained on in the house but only on the second floor. Her only worry would be the barn door. It screeched. That she knew from before.

She came up on the barn. To her relief the door had been left open slightly. Enough she could squeeze through. Sweet hay filled her nose, and horses peeked over their stalls. Dani ignored them and went straight back to the bales of hay stacked on the rear wall. She came around them, three rows deep, and reached back between the last stack and the wall, her fingers searching. Her chest tightened. It had to be here. She stretched the length of her arm, her fingers catching the familiar loop to her backpack. She gave a silent cheer and pulled it out. She opened the zipper, her fingers landing on the leather grain of her wallet. She flipped through the contents inside it and relaxed. Everything was there. Dani dug into the back pocket of her jeans and pulled out Kevin's business card she'd kept on her person since he'd given it to her yesterday. She placed it alongside her other papers and closed the wallet. Then thinking better of it, she checked the inside pocket of the backpack for the thumb drive.

Yes. All accounted for.

Dani zipped the pocket shut, then the backpack, and slung it over her shoulder. She cleared the middle aisle, wedging her body through the ajar barn door. She checked the house one last time—fewer lights—and ran down the gravel drive, keeping close to the trees. They opened up to 68, and Dani increased her pace and froze. Lights turned and headed toward her. *Shite.* She ducked into the tree line. Her foot caught a thick, dead tree limb, and she fell. Her ankle twisted as pain shot up her leg, and she swallowed a moan.

Of all the stupid things.

The old white truck drove by without slowing.

Her heartbeat regained its natural rhythm. They hadn't seen her. She was sure. Standing, Dani brushed off her jeans and put weight on her foot. Pain shot up her leg, and she gritted her teeth. "Work through it," she scolded under her breath. She leaned down and grabbed the damned limb that had caused her trouble to use for a cane. Hobbling, she continued down the driveway and to the car. She tossed the limb and climbed in, the engine sputtering to life when she turned the key. "Please, don't give out on me, you old bollocks."

Dani pulled out, using her left foot to accelerate. Three easy miles— she could do it. The road remained desolate at close to midnight until an orange furry flash skirted the road right in front of her. She slammed on the brake. Her injured foot smacked the floorboard hard, a jolt of pain shooting clear up her leg. Dani gripped the wheel, her head coming to rest against the soft lamb's wool steering wheel cover, and she waited until the pain subsided. Then she lifted her head and opened her eyes. Red and blue lights filled the car, and a cold dread filled her chest. She'd stopped—stopped in the middle of the highway. "Eejit," she growled under her breath.

"Move to the shoulder." The voice from a speaker, deep with authority, entered the small Beetle's interior, and Dani's stomach twisted.

She hit the gas, jerked the car, and grimaced. She resettled her left foot on the pedal and, this time, smoothly traveled the distance to the side of the road and parked. The lights from the patrol car followed behind her.

Dani prayed for only one thing.

CHAPTER THIRTEEN

K EVIN KEYED THE MIC, CALLED IN HIS STOP AND THE TAG NUMBER, AND sat back waiting. What idiot would park in the middle of 68? He'd seen the yellow bug recently but couldn't place where. He took the transmission from the dispatcher, the car coming back to a Bonnie Ann Dunn. If he recalled, she was a groom who worked for his father. He stepped from his patrol car, his dress shoes hitting the pavement, and grabbed his flashlight, cursing himself for being up on a work night after midnight.

He'd blame Dani Flynn. After dropping her off at the stable yesterday, he called up Kristin Jennings—single, attractive, blond, five seven, and the vice president of M & T Bank's lending department. He'd met her when he settled on his house, seen her occasionally since then, and got the impression—after she'd given him her business card with her personal cell phone written on the back—if he asked, she'd be open to a dinner date.

Eager, it turned out.

Dinner had been enjoyable—good food and great conversation—her condo even better. Only he couldn't get past some heavy petting before those bewitching sapphire eyes of Dani's fluttered in his mind, sweet and sensual. He had pushed away from Kristin. Both breathing hard, he made up some bullshit excuse as to why he had to leave, shoving his suit jacket on and walking away from a sure thing.

He neared the yellow bug, touched the rear with his fingers, using his fingerprints to link him to the traffic stop. Kevin flashed his light into the rear—nothing suspicious, one driver. Rapping on the window, he waited until the driver rolled it down. Slender fingers grabbed and held tight to the steering wheel. "Good evening, ma'am, could I see your driver's license and registration card?"

He kept a visual, giving her time to locate the items.

The usual scurry of opening up the glove compartment and digging into a wallet—nonexistent. Her hands retained their death grip on the steering wheel.

"Ma'am?" He bent down. "Is there a problem?" His first reaction confused him. His heartbeat increased, and the familiarity of her face had him trading the unexpected smile forming on his lips for his usual by-the-book frown. She'd only given him grief since they'd met. He wanted to be angry. He *was* angry.

She eased her fingers off the steering wheel and peered up, eyes unsure and searching his. The pouty curve of her bottom lip trembled. "It's me own fault—I shouldn't have stopped. Shouldn't be driving, for sure. I'm sorry, Kevin. All I seem to do is give you reason to—"

Another set of emergency lights lit them up, and Kevin turned. *"Shit,"* he hissed under his breath. He bent down, their faces inches apart. "Stay in the car." His words were abrupt, and she immediately rolled her lips in, brows furrowing, her body arching away from him, he'd guess because of the harsh tone he'd used with her. He would have thought she'd be used to it by now. She certainly should have expected it tonight. Kevin walked away, passed his patrol car, and caught Chad before he had a chance to exit his vehicle—a patrol car that always seemed to piss him off with its striping and Maryland State Police shield.

"Thanks for the backup."

"Whatcha got?"

"Disabled motorist. Called in for a tow."

"You want me to wait?"

That would be a resounding no. "Got it under control." He didn't need Chad recognizing the motorist. He'd never denied Dani's claim in Walmart. Kevin hadn't asked Dani, but he assumed since Chad and Stew didn't make an issue of her identity, they'd never actually ID'd her. Chad wouldn't know her immigration status. Or the fact she had no driver's license. Kevin intended to keep it that way.

Chad nodded, and Kevin gave him berth to pull out safely. Waiting until his vehicle lights disappeared around the curve of the highway, Kevin walked back toward the yellow bug. "You're two miles away from the training center. Can you drive the vehicle safely?"

"Yes."

"Let me get back to my car, and then you can pull out when it's safe to do so. I'll follow behind."

She didn't use the turn signal—probably didn't know where it was. But she eased out and picked up the necessary speed. Good girl. He followed behind, taking the left into Whistledown. She parked in the gravel lot, turned the ignition off, and got out while he parked next to her and did the same. He came around. "You're damn lucky it was me."

"I'd hoped."

He cocked his head, not sure how to take her words. "Dani, do you need me to go over what you can and can't do while you're here in the States?"

"No. I knew it to be wrong."

"But you did it anyway."

She wet her lips; they glistened under the security light of the barn. "I had asked Bonnie to take me. She had a date tonight and forgot her promise to me but offered the use of her car. I would have declined, but . . ."

"But?"

"Yes, your father had been kind enough to give me an advance on me pay. I only wanted to visit a market. I got a bit turned around, confused, actually, and couldn't find it—the market." She grimaced and redistributed her weight.

Kevin hadn't considered that. He wanted to kick himself for his own stupidity. Her Walmart bag filled with essentials missed one important element—food. He always took that for granted. He'd eaten a five-course meal tonight, topped off with a bottle of red wine. "What did you eat today?"

"Turk offered the snacks in the cantina."

"What specifically, Dani?"

"A granola bar, apple, and a bottled water."

"Christ, that's not enough to feed a bird."

"I don't require much." She twisted the handle of a backpack Kevin hadn't recalled seeing until tonight. "What are you going to do about the driving?"

"I should do what needed to be done when I met you."

Her eyes widened. She knew. "I won't do it again."

"I'm relieved. It's late. I'll watch you go in." He hooked his chin toward the barn.

"It's not necessary." She gave him a quick smile or another grimace. He couldn't tell. Her hand came down on the hood of the bug, and she shuffled her feet again.

"You're in pain." Kevin moved closer.

"It's nothing. I twisted me ankle is all."

"You ice it?"

She shook her head.

"When did you twist it?"

"Not long before you found me."

That opened a whole new set of questions. It wasn't pure coincidence he found her less than a mile from Grace. He let it go and concentrated on her. "Let me see you walk."

"It's not for you to worry about me, Kevin. I can make it to me room."

"Show me."

She squared her shoulders, took a deep breath, and put weight on her right ankle. Her leg crumpled under her, and Kevin scooped her up in his arms. She stiffened, not letting go of the backpack, and let out a soft moan before letting her body relax against his.

"You're going to fall on your ass, Flynn."

Her backpack sitting in her lap, her grip firm on the handle, she looked up at him with cautious eyes. "I interrupted your night." Her other hand came down to rest on his sports jacket, his biceps flexing beneath.

She'd interrupted it hours before. "Come to expect it with you."

She frowned.

He shook her playfully in his arms. "Come on. Let's see that fine room of yours and get some ice for your ankle."

She helped by sliding open the large barn door enough for them to fit through and shutting it once they entered. The emergency light remained on, giving the barn a bluish hue. Horses moved around in their stalls, a mix of straw, horseflesh, and that underlying manure his father had taunted Dani with when describing her living arrangements. He climbed the stairs. Dani's weight continued to be a non-issue when he hit the top landing, making him more aware of her slight body. She couldn't afford to miss another meal. He carried her down the narrow walkway, only a thin rail keeping them from falling to the barn floor below. He stepped into her room, his bulk filling the cramped dark space. "You got a light?"

"String right about where you're standing."

Right as she said it, his face connected with the metal piece at the end of the string, and he pulled the cord. A single bright bulb lit up the room and the age-old rotting plywood that made up the walls. The mattress sat to the right—raised off the floor by plastic crates. The room, a hodgepodge of mixed furnishings, was remarkably clean. He guessed that would be Dani's touch.

He placed her down carefully in the middle of the mattress, took the backpack from her and sat it down. Dani's eyes darted from the pack to Kevin and then back to the pack.

Oh, yeah. He'd get around to the backpack before he left. He grabbed the pillow from the head of the bed and positioned it against the wall for her. "Can you slide up, and I'll look at your ankle?"

"It's not necessary." She held herself up on her elbows, her hair cascading down her back in loose, dark waves.

He raised a brow. "Could have fooled me."

"Have a look." She peered over, her brows furrowing. "I think it's only sprained."

Kevin removed her tennis shoe. He'd guess he paid five bucks for them. They had no support and were no longer the crisp white they'd been, and she'd only worked one full day as a groom. He'd get her a pair of decent shoes and mucking boots—his charitable donation for the year.

Her ankle was swollen and slightly bruised, a sprain more than likely. "How'd you say you twisted it?" He connected with her eyes. He was good at spotting bullshit.

She pursed her lips. "I'll tell you the truth, but you're going to be angry."

Kevin sat back on his haunches. "Dani, if you're honest with me, I can work with anything you tell me."

"I went back to Grace."

Irritation niggled at him. "You went—"

"I didn't bother them if that's what you're thinking." She sat up straighter, lifting her chin. "I only went back to get me things. I'd hid me backpack in the barn. As I was leaving, I tripped when a truck, white I think, turned down the driveway."

"I thought you went grocery shopping."

"True, it would have been me next errand. But me driving had been compromised, and the fox ran in front of me. I slammed on the brake to avoid him and hit me sore ankle. I was working through the pain when you found me." She caught her breath. "It was stupid."

Kevin shook his head. "All right." He moved her ankle, and she gasped. "Hurts?"

She nodded. "I can't afford an injury. I'm hoping it won't interfere with me duties."

He rubbed his chin. "Okay. Sit back and relax. You need ice, and it needs to be wrapped." He stood and moved toward the door, then turned. "How do you change?"

"Pardon?"

"The door. You have no privacy."

She grinned. "Quickly."

"We'll fix that, too. I'll be back in a few minutes."

Kevin took the steps and slapped the corkboard sporting a hodgepodge of notes outside his father's office. The old man always had a thing for corkboards. He hit the light and ripped through his desk drawers until he came up with a box of thumbtacks. Shoving it in the pocket of his sports coat, he covered the distance from the barn to the bunkhouse. He entered, went for the small kitchen, found a gallon ziplock plastic bag, and filled it with ice. Then he hit the freezer, and dug into his father's stash of frozen food, grabbing a Salisbury steak dinner. Popping it out of the box, he tossed it in the microwave. Next he hit the supply cabinet and grabbed a wool blanket and an Ace bandage off the shelf. Good thing he knew his way around. He'd grown up in this stable. He swore then he'd never have anything to do with the business when he became a man.

Grabbing the hot meal and utensils, Kevin shoved it back in its box and humped back to the barn, entering Dani's room. She lay curled on her side. Both her hands tucked under her face, her eyes closed, pretty black lashes dusting her smooth skin, her backpack still on the floor next to her. He'd asked for her honesty. She'd given it to him regardless of the consequences. He wanted to get a look inside the backpack. She'd hid it for a reason—gone through a great deal of trouble to retrieve it. *Hell.* He picked up the backpack and sat it down on the chest behind him. He would trust that when he asked about it—and he would ask—she would continue to be truthful. Sitting down the ice and bandage on the floor, the dinner on the chest, he opened the blanket and spread it over her. She whimpered and snuggled inside it.

He got down on his haunches and pressed her hair back behind her ear. "Dani," he whispered. "I need to ice your ankle."

She took a deep breath through her nose, her eyes fluttering open. "You came back."

"I said I would." He studied her for a moment. She obviously lacked trust. No telling what type of life she'd had back in Ireland. If he had to guess, it was a difficult one. Kevin covered up a yawn and checked his watch—close to one.

He cocked his head. "What do you wear to bed?"

Those eyes of hers widened.

Kevin laughed out loud. "That came out wrong. I only meant you should get ready for bed before I ice your ankle."

She made a twirling motion with her finger, her other hand gripping the blanket. "Turn around."

He stood and gave her his back. Blankets crumpled behind him, a soft moan filling the cramped room while she shimmied out of her jeans. Kevin winced. The way she'd been hobbling—it must hurt.

"I'm done now."

He turned around. Their eyes collided. Hers were tired, ringed with dark circles. She'd been at sea for seven days, nearly two more working her way to Grace with what little money, if any, she had—meaning the U.S. port she'd arrive in couldn't be far—and another two in Clear Spring trying to escape him, and the last working her ass off in his father's racing stable.

He'd never met a woman with more courage and strength. Now that she was tucked under her sheet and blanket, he grabbed the extra one he planned to hang as a makeshift door and shoved it at the end of the bed. Kevin yanked at the blanket tucked under the mattress. "Mind if I take a look?"

She shook her head. "It's bruised."

Kevin lifted the sheet. Sure enough the thin-boned ankle he'd admired a few days ago had a purplish hue. He ran his fingers over the bruising. It appeared swollen—but not overly so. Without the other for comparison . . . "Let's see the other ankle." He didn't wait for approval, only pulled on the sheet to expose the lower half of her leg. He ran his hand over both ankles. Yep, it was swollen. He manipulated it slightly. Based on his training, he felt sure it wasn't broken. "Looks like a sprain." He gave one last approving glance at those shapely calves and pulled the sheet back down.

He placed the bag of ice on her ankle. "I'll keep the sheet as a buffer. If it gets too cold, let me know."

"You're not leaving, then?"

He noted the concern in her voice. She wanted him to leave. His eyes landed on that backpack. "Not yet," he said and took the meal out of its box, ripping off the plastic cover. "Sit up. You need to eat something warm." He helped her with the pillow, propping her up, and sat the dinner on the blanket. "It's still hot."

"I am a bit hungry."

He handed her the plastic knife and fork from his jacket pocket and cursed under his breath. "Forgot napkins."

"This is fine, really. You've troubled yourself enough."

"It's not a problem." Kevin took the extra blanket and grabbed the box of tacks and began tacking the blanket up over the door.

"Thank you for that," she said around a mouth of mashed potatoes.

He glanced over his shoulder. "If my father asks, tell him I owe him a box of thumbtacks."

She stiffened and got that worried look in her eyes.

"I'll call him myself." Kevin kept a visual on her and shoved the last thumbtack into the frame of the door.

Her shoulders visibly relaxed.

He nodded toward her ankle. "How's the ice?"

"Cold."

"Good." He took off his jacket and laid it on the chest and eyed the floor, debating if he wanted to sit down.

Dani moved her legs.

"Whoa, what are you doing?" Kevin caught the ice and redistributed it.

"Sit down."

He sat on the edge of her mattress, his elbows resting on his knees, his eyes on the backpack.

"You're wondering about the backpack, then."

He glanced over at her. "Pretty much."

"Will you give it to me?"

He reached over and took it from the chest and handed it to her, setting it on the space next to her on the mattress.

She unzipped it, dug around, and pulled out a large leather wallet. Opening it, she passed him an aged, and in some places, tattered, piece of paper. "Me birth certificate."

He sat up, his finger tightening on the document, and focused on the names. He recognized them: Dani Brianna Flynn, Rory Aileen Flynn, and Daniel Michael Fallon.

Son of a bitch. Just as she claimed.

"Why now?" He stood. "Why didn't you say something that night? At least the next morning." He ran his fingers through his hair roughly.

"It was silly, really, now that I think about it." She sat up and leaned back on the wall, her head falling slightly. "I had hoped he'd recognize me as his."

Quite possibly he had. "You ambushed him. Did your mother even tell him about you?"

"I always assumed. She never said otherwise."

More like, based on the story, she'd died before she could fill her daughter in. Knowing Daniel, Kevin would guess he knew nothing of his child.

Dani dug back in her wallet and handed him a worn business card. He recognized the logo as Grace's old one. Twenty-seven years ago, he would have been twelve and running the pastures with Bren, Kate, and Tom, passing through the big gate—not that it was there anymore—with the ornate letter G welded inside it. "Can I borrow these?"

She frowned and then nodded. "You'll be sure to take care they don't get lost?"

"Promise."

"I suppose it's fine." She fooled with her potatoes, refusing to make eye contact. "Will this buy me some time?" She raised her head, and that worried look was back. "You won't have to deport me?"

"I'll check with immigration. Got anything else in your bag of tricks?"

Something registered in those eyes of hers, and she flipped through the wallet, handing him a thin dark red book. "It's me passport." Her hand came to her lips, her eyes wide like she'd just remembered something important. "Oh." She dug some more and handed him a laminated card. "And a social security card from when I worked at Saratoga Springs."

Kevin did a double take. "You've been in the States before?"

She nodded and handed both to him. "When I was eighteen, before the fall of me mother's death. Me ma raced that summer in New York, she was really getting a reputation."

Passports were good for ten years. She really was a kid in comparison to him, and he'd better start making that distinction. He flipped the passport open to the front page, reading the expiration date.

"You still have two years."

He noted her birth date, then calculated the years in his head to be sure he had it right. Well, twenty-six, soon to be twenty-seven on December first. He glanced at the social security card. It looked like his, except for the words VALID FOR WORK ONLY WITH INS AUTHORIZATION and the social security number stamped across the top. It all seemed legit for an eighteen-year-old arriving legally into the States with her mother to work the summer—not the twenty-six-year-old who'd stowed away by ship almost ten years later. He handed it back to her along with the social security card, his lips thinning. "You know not to try and use this now."

She rolled her lips in, her eyes getting bigger.

Hell yes, she'd planned to use it. "Do I have to take it away from you?"

"No. Your father pays me cash. I'd have no need to use it."

Kevin scrubbed his face hard. He was in deep. He'd taken an oath to uphold the law—not look away. Ignoring his conscience he went back to examining the birth certificate and her father's old business card. "I might need these for a few days. I'd like to talk to Daniel. You okay with that?"

"I was hoping you would. I'd be uncomfortable approaching him again."

Kevin folded the birth certificate back into fourths and tucked the business card with it, placing both inside his billfold. He shoved it in his back dress pant pocket. "Let's check your ankle." He removed the ice and examined it. "Can't tell if the swelling's gone down, but I'm thinking it helped." He grabbed the bandage sitting next to him on the bed and wrapped her foot, careful to give her the support she needed without making it too tight. "How does it feel?"

"Much better." She smiled and tried to hide a yawn.

"What time do you get up in the morning?"

"Early, around half past four."

Kevin checked his watch. "It's almost one thirty."

"You have an early day I'm sure, too."

"Six."

She nodded. "I would think, once me father has proof, he'll be agreeable to helping me stay in America. It's me hope, anyway."

"If I know Daniel Fallon, he'll do the right thing." Something leaned against his leg. He glanced down and scooped up the black kitten. "He yours?"

"Your father's until a day ago."

Kevin laughed. "Old man's a magnet when it comes to cats." He sat the little guy down in his lap and continued to stroke him, his small body rumbling like a well-tuned car.

Dani's brows rose. "Looks to me you're a magnet yourself."

"Had about six at one time growing up, compliments of the man downstairs." He angled his head to get a better look at the kitten. "What's his name?"

"Jimmy."

Kevin lifted him up. "I wouldn't mind having one loyal, fastidious cat manning the place while I'm gone." He sat Jimmy down next to Dani.

Her small hand sank into the kitten's fur. He'd have to commend his father on a job well done. Dani seemed to need the little guy as much as he needed her.

"Getting back to Daniel."

"I trust your judgment. Leave him the papers. I'll make arrangements to collect them from him."

He gave her a hard look.

"Without being behind the wheel, of course." She picked up the dinner she finished, looking for a place to sit the empty tray, never letting go of the cat.

"I'll take care of it."

She gave it to him. "Thank you." She pursed her lips, her brows puckering.

"What?"

"I've been an unexpected burden in your life. I'm sorry for it. I'll do me best not to cross paths with you in the future."

She was giving him the royal boot. Three nights ago, he'd have given his left nut to be rid of her. Now he found it difficult to leave her behind in a room smaller than a walk-in closet, the walls rough with aging plywood and one single lightbulb positioned in the middle of a rafter.

Dani would be doing him a favor if she could hold true to her words. Not that it would be for lack of trying on her part. "We'll see if you can keep that promise."

"What do you mean by that?" Her cheeks flushed—he'd bet half from anger, the rest embarrassment.

"I don't know, Flynn. You can't seem to stay out of my path."

She opened her mouth and then snapped it shut.

Not that she'd planned running into him tonight. More to the contrary. But he called it, and she knew it.

CHAPTER FOURTEEN

$\mathcal{S}$ QUINTING AT THE MIDDAY SUN IN LATE JUNE, DANI REVELED IN ITS warmth. She sat low in the saddle, keeping her body one with the chestnut gelding with a white star on his forehead. His muscles rippled beneath her, his strides long and powerful. Wind tugged at her wisps of hair, sticking out from her helmet, and Dani let herself relax. Her wounds from that night on the dock had healed. She was alive and happy and starting a new life. God must be on her side. It had been pure divine intervention Kevin hadn't looked more closely at her passport after realizing her social security card was no longer valid. She herself hadn't realized, until his severe expression, the rules in which she'd received the card in the first place. She'd been a teen and had her mother to deal with such issues.

Her ma . . . Dani frowned. Sadly, she might never go back to Ireland.

Tommy Duggan's wicked smile flashed before her, and Dani's mood darkened.

Let him come in search of me.

He knew nothing of her real father. Even if he tracked the freighter to Philadelphia, she could be anywhere. She did need to know about him, though, and his movements. Not that it would be publicized—not directly. But indirectly she could track him. She'd had every intention of searching the Internet, particularly Rosslare Harbour, on Turk's computer—at night, of course. She just hadn't counted on her ankle or the exhaustion of putting in a full twelve-hour day's work.

There had to be news of Kara's disappearance. Pat Malone had a fair idea of who Dani was meeting that night. They—the Garda, the

Republic of Ireland's police—would question him about her and Kara's whereabouts. Dani swallowed hard. They'd never find Kara. Dani was sure of it—sure about a lot of things, actually. Like how stupid she had been to get involved with Duggan. Her only real concern now was Kevin finding out about her past. She couldn't risk being sent back to Ireland.

It could mean her life.

Dani frowned. It was more than that. She'd lied to him. Her dealings with Duggan were illegal. Not that she enjoyed her interactions with him or his clients. She'd only done it a few times and had planned to quit. But the bloody cash had been going toward her back rent and her scooter repair—living on the streets wasn't an option.

She took a deep breath. *Let it go for now.* She had bigger priorities than trying to minimize what she'd done. She needed Turk's computer. Not that she'd ever owned one, but she was capable of doing an Internet search. She'd done it a few times on Pat's at the pub—even went so far as to type Daniel Michael Fallon's name in the search bar. Nothing had come of it because she hadn't planned on coming to America. Dani shook her head.

Never say never.

"Come on, Dani girl. Put some muscle in it," Fritz called out from the rail.

Right. Her past wasn't going to interfere with her future. Dani patted the gelding named Delicate Maneuver. She saluted Fritz when she passed by him in his tweed cap and suspenders. Dani smiled so wide she thought her face would crack in two, and she had a lot to smile about.

She had been sitting at the picnic table, eating lunch, when Fritz showed up with a helmet and a beautiful chestnut Dani now knew to be Delicate Maneuver. She had a keen sense by the silly grin tugging at his mouth he would offer to let her ride him. A few days ago she'd have said no. Not because she didn't want to—she did to be sure. But her ankle wasn't in the best of shape. She'd managed to hobble around the past few days and done her chores—none of which would have been the least bit possible if it hadn't been for the support of her new work boots.

Today the ache was barely noticeable. She'd credit her quick recovery to one American sheriff named Kevin Bendix. It had been Wednesday around noon. She'd finished up bathing the last of her charges and had come in to change her wet shirt. The boots and a pair of black trainers—she'd seen him eyeing her dirty white ones the other night—were sitting inside her room. At first she wanted to give them back. She wasn't a charity case. Her mistake was trying on the boots. The relief that followed made it incredibly hard to return them.

He was peculiar, indeed. Her feelings for him ran hot and cold. As did his for her, she imagined. She'd caused him a lot of trouble in the last week—angered him. All the more reason not to be the least bit attracted to him—his temper. Dani frowned. But she was. She wouldn't let her mind run away with fanciful ideas of Kevin and her. He wanted more information about Duggan. She'd not given a name, of course.

Dani took a deep breath through her nose. She wouldn't let reality dampen her spirits today. She kicked the gelding in his sides, and he picked up speed. She came up on Fritz again.

He held up a timer. "Let it rip, girl."

She pumped the air with her fist and kicked the horse into gear.

Fritz jammed his thumb down on the timer.

The gelding flew, his hooves digging into the track, dirt flying. Laughter bubbled up inside Dani, and she giggled like a child. She'd missed it so. She came up on a rider, tall and lean, and passed him as though he stood still. Dani's eyes widened. She recognized him straightaway and grimaced.

Blake.

"Thirty-nine," Fritz shouted over the rail.

Dani gave a nod and clenched her teeth. She'd have done better around the half mile dirt track, if it weren't for the distraction. Patting Delicate Maneuver on his withers, she leaned into him. "You're a beauty and a fast one." She slowed their pace to cool him down before she took him back to be bathed. Keeping her eyes on the track, she scouted for Blake. She'd had every intention of speaking to him before today. She just hadn't gotten the courage to tell him.

"Dani!" Out of breath, she assumed from trying to catch up, he came up alongside them. "Damn good time, you're a natural."

She lifted her goggles. "You're too kind, Mr. Lansing."

His eyes landed on her, and he arched a brow. "It's Blake, not Mr. Lansing."

The heat crept into Dani's cheeks. "I'm sorry . . . *Blake,*" she said, making a point to use his first name. Although he was handsome, and it would seem, well-mannered, she didn't feel at all comfortable around him. She was a lowly groom. He owned a stable, and, from what she'd learned over the past week, did very well for himself.

They remained in the saddle and continued around the track in a slow walk to cool down their horses. Blake remained at her side, the silence between them awkward.

"You've been keeping a low profile."

Meaning she'd been avoiding him. "Turk runs a tight ship." Not to mention, after learning of Turk's paranoia where Blake was concerned, he wouldn't take kindly to her fraternizing with the enemy.

"I'm looking forward to tonight." He dipped his head, trying to gain her attention.

Dani swallowed. "About that." She rolled her lips in.

Tell him.

"I really don't think it's a good idea."

"You and me?"

She nodded. "I'm a groom, Blake. Surely, you have—"

"But I want to take you, *Dani.*"

Her stomach tumbled when he said her name. It was intimate, which made her all the more uneasy where Blake Lansing was concerned. Yet Bonnie and Chipper—well, definitely Bonnie would jump at the chance to go out with him. There was only one dilemma. With Chipper's schedule and her family, she must have forgotten her promise to play dress up with Dani. She literally had nothing suitable to wear. "I have no dress. Chipper and Bonnie spoke out of turn."

He slowed, which forced her to do the same, until they came to a complete stop in the middle of the track. His hand came down on her shoulder. "Sweet, Dani." His eyes took her in, and he smiled. "Size two petite."

Dani's bottom lip dropped in wonderment. Having the ability to size up a woman right down to her dress size couldn't possibly be a good thing.

"What?" He sat back in the saddle, his brown eyes twinkling with amusement. "I'll have it delivered in plenty of time."

Although tempting, Dani shook her head. "No. I cannot ask you to buy me dress. T'wouldn't be right."

"Dani!"

She jerked in the saddle, her nerves completely frayed as it was. Dani turned to find Turk walking swiftly toward the track with . . . Dani did a double take—her father.

Oh, Lord.

Kevin promised to have a talk with him. She swung back to Blake. "I have to go." She turned her mount and then, thinking better of it, glanced back to him. "It is a kind offer. The dress, I mean. But I can't, in all conscience, accept it."

A smile tugged at his well-formed lips. "I understand."

"Thank you." Dani galloped away, her stomach in knots, and it had nothing to do with Blake. She came up along the rail. Fritz swung the gate open, and she came through, hopping off Delicate Maneuver. "He's a beautiful horse. I loved riding him."

Fritz took the reins from her. "I'll see that he gets washed."

"B-but I promised I'd do it." It was the agreement she'd made with him before taking the gelding out.

He leaned in to her. "Talk to your father," he whispered and gave her a wink.

Interesting. She just assumed Daniel Fallon wouldn't be at all ready to admit their relationship, especially to others. If Fritz was aware, certainly Turk would be, too.

"Dani." Turk's eyes were not warm like Fritz's. She'd be a fool to think he'd treat her any kinder knowing she was Daniel Fallon's daughter. Although in all fairness to the man, he'd been more than equitable in his dealings with her. "Tighter on the reins next time and you'll shave a few tenths of a second off."

Her brows puckered. *Pointers from Turk Bendix?* Far better than the expected reprimand, she'd take it.

"You did fine, Dani. A real horsewoman like your mother." Her father stood there holding some sort of plastic bag and gave her a sheepish smile.

No doubt embarrassed for lying the other day. She wouldn't fault Daniel Fallon for that. She'd surprised him. It would be difficult to admit such a thing in front of his family when he himself was trying to make sense of it all.

"Don't suppose you'd let her ride Midnight Edition?" Fritz said.

"Too much money invested in both rider and horse," Turk grumbled.

He meant Chipper. It was nice of Fritz to put a good word in for Dani, but ever since her ma's death, she'd let go her dream of becoming a jockey. "Chipper's a fine horsewoman."

Turk checked his watch and gave Daniel a pat on his back. "Have your talk." He then made direct eye contact with Dani. "I can spare you ten minutes. But then I need you in the barn and, in particular, Nothing Like a Sister's stall."

He needn't explain. She knew and wanted to make it perfectly clear it hadn't been that way when she left Sister last night before bed. "Of course, thank you."

Light on his feet for his age, he headed toward the stable, and Fritz turned his gelding toward Cloverdale's barn. "Nice workout, Dani girl."

"Thanks for letting me take him out."

"You bet."

She smiled, and with that he had moved up the slight incline, leaving her in awkward silence with her da.

"I meant what I said, Dani. You've got it in you to be a world class jockey."

Dani turned toward him. "I gave up that dream long ago, I'm afraid."

Daniel Fallon let his head drop. "I'm sure it's been very difficult for you."

She wanted to blame him for all of it. "She never told you about me, then?"

He shook his head. "Not a word."

Dani nodded. "It must have been a shock."

"To be sure. My only regret was how I handled it."

"Do Bren and Kate know the truth?"

He motioned her toward the picnic table. "Do you have a mind to talk with your old man?"

Dani followed him over and sat down across from him. "I don't even know what to call you." She took off her helmet and sat it down next to her.

He grimaced. "It's an awkwardness we're both going to have to get over, I think."

"Would you prefer I call you Daniel, then?"

"I think it best under the circumstances. You'll know when it's right to call me da."

She hoped. But at this very minute Daniel seemed appropriate. "What do Bren and Kate call you?"

"Dad."

American, of course.

He reached over and patted her hand. "I'd hoped they'd call me da. But they never did."

"Do you miss it?" Dani cocked her head. "Ireland, I mean?"

"I went for a visit a few years ago. If I had known . . ."

"Aye. I take it Kevin talked to you."

"He did. But I knew it to be true the moment you spoke the words."

He picked at his nails. "I hadn't thought of Rory Flynn in . . ." He seemed to be counting the years in his head.

"Twenty-seven years."

He chuckled. "You're twenty-seven, then."

"Almost. My birthday is December first."

He nodded, a little forlorn. She guessed not knowing your own child's birthday could be construed as sad, although he shouldn't be. It wasn't his fault.

"Oh." He lifted the bag. "I almost forgot. Bren folded up your clothes." He handed her the bag. Inside were her jeans, white tee, and navy sweatshirt. "Kate said to tell you the tennis shoes fell apart in the dryer."

She wasn't surprised. "Tell them thank you."

"You could tell them yourself."

"I don't think that's wise under the circumstances." Dani shrugged. "I'm sure I'm the last person they'd want to see."

Daniel leaned in against the table. "That's nonsense." His cheeks flushed. "You're their sister. Not that it wasn't difficult explaining things. But they're adults, Dani. We've all done and said things we're not proud of. I should have never let it happen. I had just buried me own da. I was angry, grieving, and your ma was . . ."

"Available."

"It wasn't cheap." He smacked his fist into the table. "She was everything I was not that night."

Dani closed her eyes. Their union had created her. Not that she needed a detailing of their night together. She, too, was an adult. "You needn't explain yourself to me."

"No. But I do have some making up to do where you're concerned. You were right. You have every right to be here. Your sister Kate is"—he cleared his throat—"was an attorney. She can help you gain your citizenship."

At the moment, she really wanted an American driver's license. She'd been independent in Ireland. She could buy another scooter to get around on or a small car, possibly in a few months' time with her wage. "How would I go about this citizenship, then?"

"I gave Kate your birth certificate. You two talk about it next week. We're having our annual Fourth of July picnic on Monday, and we'd like you to come." He reached behind him and pulled out his wallet and handed her the worn business card. "You kept it all this time?"

"She did. I found it when I went through her things."

"How long ago, did she . . . ?"

"Eight years."

He frowned. "Why didn't you contact me then?"

"And say what?"

He remained quiet. She guessed he was thinking that through.

"You didn't say, and I'm curious. Where is Bren and Kate's ma?"

"She passed away several years back."

"I'm sorry."

He leaned in. "It would have been difficult, but Dee would have accepted you. She had a loving heart." He flipped through several bills in his wallet. "Do you need some money to get by on?"

Dani waved his wallet away. "Turk pays me a good wage."

He nodded. "I have room in the house. If you'd prefer to live . . ."

She could easily take him up on his offer. She'd seen both farmhouses on Grace—very quaint and she'd guess cleaner than her room in the barn. No, as tempting as it was, she was better off staying here. "It's very kind, Daniel, but Turk treats me fair. Me hours are early, and I haven't transportation to and from."

"I'd gladly take you."

She laughed. "That would be a bit embarrassing. I'm not a wee girl any longer."

"Aye. I guess it would be a bit awkward having your da driving you."

"You could pick me up for this Fourth of July party and bring me back, if you have a mind to."

"It'd be my pleasure." He reached over and squeezed her hand and then gave a nervous glance around. "We're past our ten minutes. I best let you get back to work. I don't want Turk fussing at you for being late."

"True." Dani stood and came around the picnic table.

Daniel got up and awkwardly climbed out from the bench. "Look at me. I'm getting feeble in my old age."

If Dani had to guess, he was in his mid to late seventies. She might not have many years with Daniel Fallon, and her sadness surprised her. He was a good man. She imagined. His daughters loved him very much. She hoped she could see her way to love him, too.

"Is that your truck?" Dani pointed to the white pickup she'd seen the other night at Grace.

"It's historic." He chuckled.

Dani laughed out loud. "To be sure."

Chapter Fifteen

Turk sat in his small unfinished office with stacks of *Daily Racing Forms* littering the floor when Dani stopped in front of his open doorway.

He sat staring through his reading spectacles into the computer screen with Jimmy perched atop his desk. It looked like they'd still be sharing the affection of one black cat that clearly enjoyed human companionship.

"You ready to go back to work, Flynn?"

Dani cringed at his sarcastic voice. "I—"

He spun around in his high-backed desk chair, missing her legs by degrees in the tiny office, his pupils but tiny pinpricks, narrowing through the thick lenses of his reading glasses. "That is, if you're done hobnobbing with Lansing, training Bailey's horses, and having a family visit."

Dani swallowed. She'd only trip over her tongue if she tried to explain. "Did you want to see the shoe I spoke of earlier?"

He pushed up from his chair, wearing a striped polo shirt, his belt conveniently securing his pants beneath his bulging belly. "I know I don't want to see you riding Delicate Maneuver or any other horse from Cloverdale."

Dani stiffened. She'd given him an honest day's work every day she'd been here. "It was on me own time. Is that a problem, then?"

He placed his hands on his hips. "When it's the competition."

Right. She'd forgotten to take into account Turk's paranoia for the opposing stables. She just hadn't thought Fritz—his good friend—would be counted as one of them. "It won't happen again."

"Glad to hear it." He motioned her down the aisle.

Dani followed with Jimmy on her heels, the bounce in her step from earlier nonexistent. She liked her job, appreciated Turk's generosity, and had learned to accept his disagreeable temperament. But after riding Delicate Maneuver, she'd realized how much she missed it—the speed.

"I'm assigning you exercise rider." He angled back, the tug on his lips more of a smirk than a smile. "You got a new job, Flynn."

Dani stopped in her tracks. "Pardon?"

"Like I said: tighten up on the turns."

Dani's forehead crinkled. "Not sure I'm following."

"Don't need a groom, Flynn. Not sure I need or want another exercise rider, either, but I saw something today I haven't seen in a long time." He stared at her.

Dani threw up her hands. "I haven't a clue what you're getting at."

He gave her his back and continued up the aisle, stopping in front of Sister's stall. Opening the door, he ushered her in by way of his hand. She followed.

"It's heart, Dani."

Standing inside the tight stall with him and the mare, she felt the first real connection to the man. "It's true what they say, then. About America, I mean."

"What's that?" He gave her a quizzical look.

"The land of opportunity."

He clucked his tongue. "If you have the desire." He touched the horse's rump to let her know he was back there then bent down toward the mare's hind legs. "You said it was the right?"

"Yes." Dani bent down with him, patting the mare's leg. She slid her hands down past the knee. "That a girl." She lifted the hoof. Dani could understand a missing nail from time to time, but more than that? *Very unusual.* "It's missing three." She pointed out the empty holes. It all seemed a bit strategic. If she connected the missing nails, it would form a complete triangle.

Turk peered through his spectacles. "You say she had them all yesterday?"

"I checked them meself before bed."

"You do that for all of them?"

Dani nodded. "I've seen many a shoe thrown. Not a huge problem—normally. But there have been others that have suffered lameness because of it."

He grumbled something under his breath and then straightened. "The farrier makes his rounds tomorrow. See he replaces them."

"Aye, I saw it on the corkboard. I'll be sure to take care of it."

He rubbed his chin. "Anyone else know about this?"

"Only the two of us." Dani rolled her lips in and considered what Bonnie had told her about the tack and the feed. At the time, Dani thought nothing of it, but in all of the years she'd tended horses, she'd never once seen a nail go missing between sundown and sunup. "Do *you* find it odd? The nails, I mean."

He blew out an agitated breath. "I can tell you it ain't normal."

"I agree."

"Well that's refreshing."

"Excuse me?" Dani's brows puckered in question.

"I want you to tell that son of mine exactly what you told me." He grabbed the mobile off his hip and punched in several numbers. A male voice came on the line, and Turk spoke into the mobile. "I need you to take another report."

Turk shook his head. "No, not me. From Flynn."

Kevin's voice rose.

Turk opened the stall door, motioning for Dani to follow. "Not Monday. Now." He shook his head. "Uh uh . . . Then bring her along."

Kevin spoke again, muffled but distinguishable, at least his disapproving tone. She guessed she wasn't the only one he used it with.

Turk ended the call amidst Kevin's objections. "He's not happy about it." Turk shrugged. "But he's on his way."

Oh, my.

She was filthy—smelled of horses. And her hair? Her hands came up automatically to the ponytail and stringy wisps that had escaped. Dani scooped up Jimmy twining between her legs. "I'd like to wash up, if you think—"

"Flynn." He laughed when he said it. "Relax. It's a simple police report."

He was right. She was behind in her duties and making a complete fool of herself. "I'll just finish up in here." She pointed back toward the stalls.

"You do that." He walked away, chuckling.

Grand. Kevin's father—her employer—sensed her jitteriness where his son was concerned. Not good at all. She only wanted to thank him for his kindness—the boots. Couldn't a girl say thank you without smelling like a stable? Dani kissed Jimmy on his soft black head. "Run along and stay out of his office," she whispered against his ear. Although from what she'd seen, Turk had been content to have him sit on his desk while he worked. She let the kitten go, and he sashayed down the aisle, slipping back inside Turk's office. Dani shook her head in defeat, and then headed back into Sister's stall. "Would you like some fresh water?"

Dani freshened up her water and that of the other four horses now under her care, including Solley. She attached the last water bucket to Joey's stall, gave him a peppermint out of her pocket, and caught those curious eyes of Solley's. "You know I wouldn't forget about you, boy." She kissed his head and slipped him a peppermint as Turk emerged from his office.

Dani straightened. She'd been giving them peppermints since she'd retrieved her backpack. They loved them, but Turk . . . maybe not so much, if he knew.

"Let's go." He waved her on and stepped out of the barn.

Dani let go of the breath she was holding and wiped her wet hands down the front of her jeans. Giving her ponytail a tight pull and pushing the loose wisps behind her ears, she headed out behind him. She'd make the best of it. It was silly to care. They were at best friends—at worst, he only pitied her. Or was it pitied himself after having met her?

Turk stood next to the sporty red coupe. Inside were two occupants. Dani narrowed in on the passenger. Blonde.

Bring her along. That was what Turk had said. Dani hadn't put it together until now, and she clenched her fingers. It was fine. She had no claim to him, and it was nonsense to think the man didn't date. It certainly was none of her business.

Wetting her lips, Dani continued toward the sports car. The door opened and Kevin got out. "I'm sorry, this won't take long," he called back to his passenger.

He walked toward Dani with his father next to him. He gave Dani a brief smile. "He's got you believing they are out to get him, too?"

Out to get him? No. She wasn't fearful in the least. But the nails were odd. "I'll leave the conspiracy theories for you."

"Good." He gave her a tight smile.

Strange. For a man who just spent a small fortune on footwear for her, he was being incredibly short with her. Or was it that Dani had just gotten a glimpse into his private life—one he'd rather not share with the likes of her? That would be a simple fix.

"Kevin, thank you for the boots and the black trainers." Dani turned to Turk. "Could you repay Kevin out of me pay this week?"

Turk's gray brows met over the middle of his pert nose, and he turned to Kevin. "You got the receipt?"

"At home." Kevin glanced at Dani. "I wasn't looking to be reimbursed."

"I can pay me way now." She eyed Turk. "Your father has given me a promotion to exercise rider."

Turk looked from Dani to his son, his blue eyes twinkling with what could only be amusement. Funny. It would seem she and Turk were both a burden and an annoyance to Kevin.

Turk nodded. "I forgot to tell you, Flynn. You got a raise. Two bucks on whatever it is I'm paying you." He folded his arms and rocked back on his heels.

Dani's eyes widened. "Oh, that's grand." She gave him a quick hug.

"Now, now, now." He pulled away, his face turning crimson while he checked his glasses she'd obviously smashed in his shirt pocket. He adjusted them. "Damn it, Flynn, you've squeezed me too tight."

"It was excitement. I'll not do it again." Dani stepped back, placing her hands behind her back.

Turk nodded and then craned his neck behind Kevin. "Who's the blonde?"

"Kristin Jennings. She helped me with my loan on the house."

"You dating her now?"

Kevin blanched. "She's interested in wine."

Turk rolled his lips in, trying not to laugh. "That's right. You're one of those wine connoisseurs."

"What is so pressing you had to interrupt—"

"Your date?" Turk snuffled.

Kevin put his right hand on his hip, unamused.

"It's in here." Turk led them into the barn. "Well, Flynn? Tell him."

"Can I show you instead?"

"By all means," Kevin huffed.

Dani brought Sister into the aisle and lifted the mare's back hoof. "There are three nails missing."

Kevin came around and took a look. "Is that so unusual? Horses throw shoes from time to time."

Dani shrugged. "Perhaps it's nothing. But it's odd—the pattern." Dani drew with her finger from one missing nail to another until she'd made a complete triangle. "You don't bed a horse down in the evening and expect to find three missing nails the next morning. It's highly unlikely they'd fall out in the stall."

"So put that in your report." Turk jammed a finger at Kevin.

Kevin took a deep breath. "Fine. I'll write it up."

"Kevin?" The soft feminine voice came from the front of the barn. The bank manager stood in the doorway, peering in. She was tall, dressed casually but chicly in a short skirt, breezy peach blouse, and sandals. "Everything okay?"

"Just wrapping up in here." He eyed his father. "Not a word. I'll write your report and file it with the rest." He shook his head. "Still think you're reaching, old man." He motioned to Dani. "I want to talk to you outside. Alone."

The authoritative tone he used with her prickled. She'd proven she had a right to be in America. Her own father had essentially opened his arms to her no more than an hour ago. She wouldn't forget it was Kevin's doing, but she was not the lawbreaker he'd met over a week ago. She had a job and thanks to Turk received a raise she hadn't even realized she was due. She could afford her own damned boots, and she'd be paying him back.

Dani grabbed the mare by her halter. "Let me see to the mare, and I'll be along."

He nodded and walked out.

"Take the night off, Dani." Turk's old hand came down on her shoulder. "And keep this between us."

Dani gave a half smile. Somewhere between resenting her a week ago and asking for her confidence today, they'd found common ground. "Not a word."

"Good. I'm knocking off myself. Just so happens I'm meeting your father for dinner and a drink." A smile tugged at his lips. "I'd say we both need one about now." He winked and trotted down the aisle, disappearing into the late afternoon sun.

Grand. She would no doubt be a topic of conversation.

Dani put the mare back in her stall. She cleared the barn, all the while debating how to handle Kevin. His date—she'd be a fool to think otherwise—was tucked back into his sleek red sports car. Interesting. When he drove her it was in his patrol car and not the shiny red apple he must keep hidden in his garage. Dani checked the parking lot for Kevin and caught the tail end of Turk's dark blue pickup turning right as another car turned into the training center.

"Dani!" Kevin called her over by the picnic table that sat between the barn and the track.

She marched over, her own irritation growing. "What is it, Kevin?"

"What is it, *Kevin?*" he mocked, his face twisting in anger. "Little snippy, aren't you?"

"If this is about the repayment of the—"

"Look, I didn't find you a job with my father so you could support this obsession he has."

The nerve.

Dani put her hands on her hips. "First of all, I'll not be beholden to you for finding me a job. I'll quit and find me own if you're going to throw it in me face."

He scrubbed his face hard. "This is not a conversation I want to have right now."

"Then go. I've got things I have to do meself."

The car that had pulled in parked. Chipper hopped out, and Dani's stomach lurched. *Shite.* She'd meant to get her number from Bonnie.

"Dani." She waved to her. Another woman got out. She was older and opened the rear passenger door. A little girl—Chipper's Hannah, she supposed—hopped out wearing shorts and a colorful tee.

Dani fidgeted. "I really have to go. I'll not add to your father's so-called obsession." She started to walk away.

"Wait." Kevin's fingers laced her upper arm.

Chipper slipped her sunglasses onto her head and came toward them at a clip. "Hey, Kev. How's it going?"

Dani jerked her arm free.

She glanced back at his car. "Nice car. Who's with you?"

"A friend." Now *he* squirmed. "Dropping her off before my shift."

"Didn't know the sheriff worked weekends."

"Working the Huntsmen's Ball."

"Then we'll see you there." She looped her arm through Dani's. "Come on. I've got two dresses I know will fit you perfectly."

"Dresses?" Kevin cocked his head.

"For the ball," Chipper said.

"Dani's not going." Kevin shot her a not-so-nice face.

"Sure she is." Chipper gave him an odd look of her own.

"With who?" Kevin said it with demand and a little disbelief.

Dani wanted to die.

"With me." A strong arm snaked its way around Dani's waist, pulling her against a lean sweaty body that was much taller than her own.

She recognized the voice straightaway and turned in complete distress.

Warm brown eyes connected with her panicked ones. "I'll pick you up at seven, beautiful." Blake Lansing leaned in and gave her a quick peck on her cheek, his eyes wandering toward little Hannah kicking gravel with her sandals by Chipper's car before he strode away in the direction of his stable.

Kevin's eyes blazed into Blake's back. "You gotta be kidding?" he huffed.

It appears not.

Dani swung on Kevin, spitting mad. Maybe she wasn't educated and didn't hold down a highfalutin' job at a banking establishment, but she wasn't without a brain. "I'll thank you to keep your nose out of me business." It was a bold statement, considering no more than twenty minutes ago she'd have welcomed his interference in her life and had, in fact, up until now.

Kevin's cheeks reddened. "Do what you want." He stormed away, got into his shiny sports car, and sped down the training center's drive.

Dani clenched her fists and stared after the angry dust cloud in his wake.

"Come on. Let's take a look at those dresses." Chipper put her arm around Dani, and they walked toward her car. "He's sweet on you, you know."

"Blake?"

Chipper stopped and angled her face toward Dani. "*No.* Kevin."

"*Bah.*" Dani laughed and waved the notion away with her hand. "He has a girlfriend. And even if he didn't, I'm not attracted to him in the least."

Chipper hugged Dani to her. "Then we have nothing to worry about." They continued toward Chipper's car and her family. "I've got the dresses and shoes, and Bonnie's bringing the makeup and bobby pins to put up your hair."

She truly had two wonderful new friends. She didn't need the likes of one Kevin Bendix. He was arrogant, opinionated, and rude. It was no wonder father and son had only a cross word between the two of them. If she were picking sides, she'd surely be on Turk's today.

Obsession was one thing. But nails didn't just fall out on their own overnight. Someone had removed them. *The burning question is why?*

CHAPTER SIXTEEN

S CRUBBED CLEAN AND DRESSED IN A PAIR OF FRESH SHORTS AND sleeveless, button-up top, Dani sat on a stool they'd taken from the bunkhouse while Bonnie blow-dried her hair. Suzanne and little Hannah Grant—Chipper's mom and daughter—sat on Dani's bed smiling at her with Jimmy in Hannah's lap.

Definitely not your normal barn cat. He loved people, slept with her most nights curled up by her head, and had become a squatter of sorts, taking up a strategic space on her bed during the day, sunning himself.

"I like cats." Hannah smiled at Dani.

"He's a sweetie like you." Dani patted her knee.

"She wants one desperately." Chipper winked at Hannah. "Maybe this fall."

Hannah nodded, her eyes agleam, and went back to petting Jimmy.

"You're a Fallon?" Chipper pulled two stunning sequined dresses out of their bags and hung them over the doorway against the makeshift privacy blanket.

Dani nodded. Chipper and Bonnie were the closest she had to family. She was bursting to tell them of her news. She hadn't been sworn to secrecy like with Turk and the missing nails. Besides, Daniel had told his friends. So it must not be something she'd have to hide.

"The Fallons are a wonderful family," Suzanne said while giving Dani's small room a sweep of her disapproving eyes. "I'm surprised they didn't offer to take you in."

"Oh, he did." Dani looked out from underneath her damp hair. "I chose to stay. Me hours are early, and I have no transportation. I couldn't expect me father to cart me to and from work."

"You need a set of wheels," Bonnie said.

"Driver's license first." Suzanne wagged a finger at both Dani and Bonnie.

Dani smiled up at Bonnie awkwardly from underneath the mass of hair. She'd told Bonnie of her stupidity that night with the Volkswagen and of Kevin. Dani reconnected with Chipper's ma. "Not to worry."

She liked Suzanne. She was very much a part of Chipper and Hannah's life. They shared a home together. From what Chipper had told Dani about Hannah's father, he didn't care to be a parent. And just like Dani at Hannah's age—which was three—she seemed to have little interest in knowing who her father was.

"Me sister Kate is going to help me get me papers in order."

Bonnie flipped Dani's hair away from her face with a round brush. Sectioning it off, she curled it with the brush and began drying it. "Let me know when you do. I'll take you to get your learner's permit."

"Learner's permit?" Dani arched a brow at Bonnie.

Chipper sat out two pairs of glittery shoes on the dresser. One was strappy, the other a closed toe heel. "It's what you get before they give you a permanent one."

"Mommy lets me drive her car." Hannah sat Jimmy to the side and hopped off the bed, her blond curls bouncing. She ran her small fingers along the straps. "Pretty shoes."

Chipper picked her up and kissed her head. "On my lap and only around the training center."

"Curling iron." Bonnie put her hand out to Chipper like a surgeon.

Chipper gave her a quizzical look. "Where'd you put it?"

"The bag." Bonnie pointed to the black bag on the corner of the dresser.

Chipper put Hannah down and dug through it then handed the curling iron to Bonnie, her elbow catching the corner of the bag. Chipper grabbed for it as a plump envelope beneath it fell to the floor.

"I got it." Hannah swooped down and picked it up, trying to decipher the writing. "I can't read yet." Hannah giggled and handed it to Dani.

"What's this?" Dani craned her neck at Bonnie and then Chipper.

"It's payday." Bonnie plugged in the curling iron. "I brought it up for you."

"Oh." How foolish! She'd never bothered to ask when Turk paid his employees.

"Bet you there's enough to start that car fund." Bonnie wrapped a section of Dani's hair around the iron.

Dani frowned. "Not anytime soon."

"Sure you can." Chipper came and sat on the bed, pulling Hannah onto her lap. "What does Turk pay for a groom?"

"Twelve bucks," Bonnie said.

"I make fourteen now. Turk gave me a job as an exercise rider today." The heat from the iron became much hotter. "Ow! Bonnie, the iron."

"Oh, sorry." She let the tendril of hair go, and it spiraled past Dani's shoulder. "So you're a rider now." She rocked back on her heels. "Huh."

Dani felt a flush of shame, she hadn't considered Bonnie's feelings on the subject. After all, Bonnie had been hired much before Dani. "Bonnie, I'll give the job back. I'm sure you'd make a better exercise rider than me."

"Dani, he gave the job to you. No hard feelings." She gathered up the ringlets of Dani's hair. "What do you think, girls? Up?"

"Definitely." Chipper sat Hannah down on the bed and got up. "Which dress?"

They were both very pretty.

"The one without sleeves," Suzanne said. "Dani, you have such beautiful, smooth skin."

"You're right, Mom." Chipper held out a sparkling sapphire dress.

"Mommy, it matches Dani's eyes."

It was indeed the most beautiful dress Dani had ever seen. "It's lovely."

"What do you think, ladies?" Bonnie stood back.

Dani'd been so consumed with offending Bonnie over the new position and the stunning dress she could only dream of wearing, she'd forgotten about her hair.

Bonnie stepped away and rummaged inside her bag. She came back with a large hand mirror. "Take a look."

Dani peeked at herself, her hand flying to her mouth. "I can't believe it." The tears pinched the back of her eyes.

Bonnie chuckled. "Good thing we saved the makeup for last."

"I'm sorry. I'll not cry. I promise. It's not the hair." Dani sniffed. "I've not had two closer friends."

Dani's eyes connected with her reflection again. Piled high atop her head, her sable hair shimmered with smoothness.

"Oh, hold on." Bonnie grabbed something sparkly from her bag. "Your tiara."

Dani's eyes widened. "I'm not sure . . ." It was beautiful but a little pretentious.

"I think we'll nix the crown thing," Chipper said.

Thank God. Dani didn't want to hurt Bonnie's feelings for the second time.

Bonnie dropped it back in the bag, and Dani grabbed her hand. "It is beautiful, though."

"Don't want you feeling uncomfortable wearing it."

If they only knew of her apprehension for tonight. She couldn't cancel. Not after Kevin and his comments. Of course, she couldn't really say if Blake had been serious about his offer in the first place. She'd find out soon enough, and who better to share in the rejection than her two closest friends.

Chipper checked her watch. "Blake still picking you up at seven?"

"As far as I know," Dani said.

"We've got about a half hour."

"But what of *your* date?" Dani directed her question to Chipper.

"We're going to be fashionably late." Chipper grabbed the makeup off the dresser. "What look we going for?"

"Smokey eyes," Bonnie said and took the makeup from Chipper.

Bonnie applied shadow to her lids, took a pencil, and drew around her eyes, tamed her ebony brows by way of a small brush, and applied mascara. "Last thing." She stroked Dani's cheeks with blusher and stood back smiling. "Beautiful."

Hannah came to Dani with the mirror. "You're pretty."

"Aw." Dani stroked her cheek and took the mirror. She gazed at herself, and her breath caught. She'd never seen herself this way. Her tear-filled eyes connected with Bonnie's. "Thank you."

Bonnie hugged her. "Don't you cry, Flynn."

Dani sniffed. *I'll not blubber.*

"Come on, you two." Chipper took the dress off the hanger. "Take off your clothes and your bra."

Dani grabbed her breasts. "But . . ."

"You don't need one." Chipper gave her a sympathetic smile and motioned Dani to her. "Everyone turn around."

Dani got up and handed Bonnie the envelope with her pay. "Would you put it in me top drawer?"

Bonnie took it from her and stuffed it in her dresser. "Under your T-shirts," she called back.

Dani slipped out of her clothes, careful to cover herself, and let

Chipper help her step inside the dress. She turned while Chipper zipped her up. The dress, although snug for obvious reasons, was a perfect fit, except she didn't feel at all comfortable with her cleavage.

"It's a bit revealing, don't you think?" Dani glanced down at the swell of her breasts.

"Stop being modest." That came from Suzanne, surprisingly.

"Yeah. You have a great body," Chipper said.

Dani gulped. That was debatable. Regardless, she'd never flaunted it.

"He's here!"

Dani jerked around to find Bonnie standing at the small window.

"Oh, Lord." Dani's heartbeat sped up. "I don't feel at all ready."

"We'll go down." Chipper motioned to her family, her eyes on Hannah. "Sweetheart, would you like to meet Mr. Lansing?"

"Yes." She smiled big for her mother.

Suzanne got up and gave Dani a quick hug. "You're stunning. If anyone should be nervous, it's your date." She fumbled with her purse. "Let me take a photo of you three girls." She motioned to Chipper and Bonnie.

They stood on either side of Dani and hugged her. They all smiled and then laughed after the flash went off.

"Mom, I want a copy." Chipper lifted the blanket from the doorway and waved them out.

"I'll text it to you." Suzanne took Hannah's hand. "Let's go meet Mr. Lansing." The three slipped under the makeshift door and disappeared.

Dani turned toward Bonnie in a panic. "Do I truly look all right, then?" She touched the sparkling stones of her dress, then her hair.

Bonnie laughed. "Relax. You look great."

Dani tried to control her breathing. "What am I missing?"

"Your jewels." A sly smile tugged at the corners of Bonnie's mouth. She reached inside the black bag and pulled out a silver box. Fingering a pair of glittery teardrop earrings, she held them up.

"Ooh." Dani brought both hands to her lips. "They're lovely."

Bonnie shrugged. "They're costume. But no one will know." She came to Dani's side and held them up. "I think just the earrings. Don't want to mess with your sexy neckline." With amused eyes, she handed them over and then held up the mirror for Dani. "Put them on."

Dani attached one to each ear. It was like the cherry on top of a decadent sundae. Not that she was decadent, mind, but the dress, her perfectly piled hair with spiraling tendrils, and makeup made her feel especially beautiful tonight. She wasn't sure how she would ever repay them for their kindness. "What do you think?"

"Perfect." Bonnie peeked out the window and then spun around, her eyes wide. "Your shoes!"

"Which ones?"

"Which do you like?"

She couldn't decide. They were equally flattering. "I'll more than likely fall on me bum." Dani grimaced.

"Open toes?"

Dani lifted up the dress and wiggled her unpolished toes in Kate's sandals. "They're not painted." She frowned up at Bonnie.

"Aw. You have cute toes."

Dani shook her head. "How about the pumps." They were shimmery with the same five-inch heel as the other.

"Done." Bonnie motioned her to the bed. "Sit down."

Dani complied, and Bonnie removed her sandals and slipped on the silver stilettos. Bonnie stepped back with a frown.

"Something wrong?"

"I know." She grabbed a tube. "Coral Lip Fusion."

Dani's brows knit together.

"Lip gloss." She applied it to Dani's lips and gave her a once-over. "Perfect." Taking her by the hand, she pulled her up, dropping the lip gloss inside a small clutch with a few of Dani's peppermints.

Dani's brows rose.

"What? You do plan on kissing him, don't you?"

Her cheeks warmed, and Dani didn't know how to respond.

Bonnie laughed, handed her the clutch, and grabbed her hand. "Come on, Prince Charming awaits."

Dani took her first step and wobbled. "I'm going to crack my head open, for sure."

"Baby steps, princess." Bonnie winked. "Now let's go."

They traveled down the wooden stairs with Dani gripping the rail. She took her first step onto the barn floor, her heels sinking into the dirt. She'd have to balance herself on the balls of her feet to keep the heels from getting dirty. Dani made her way to the doorway of the barn on tiptoe, Bonnie going ahead.

Dani's stomach plummeted. What a fine mess. She wouldn't have accepted Blake's final invitation had it not been for Kevin and his superior attitude. Dani took a deep breath and closed her eyes. She could do this. Her eyes fluttered open, and she walked from the barn with her shoulders pinned straight.

Her friends stood next to Blake's Mercedes convertible with the top up, which she was thankful for. He came around from the driver's side dressed in a white tux, looking quite dashing with his dark hair. He met her halfway. His eyes swept over her, and he gave her a most charming smile. "You're a knockout."

Dani's stomach fluttered, embarrassment stinging her cheeks.

"You're blushing."

Dani's hand flew to her warm face. "I am not."

"You're enchanting." He took her hand in his. It was firm and dry and covered hers possessively.

With Blake by her side, she picked her way gingerly to his car. He opened the door and Dani got in carefully so as not to rip the hem. He brought the seatbelt around her waist, his hand brushing her bare arm, and then he came around and got in.

Dani waved to her friends out the open window. "I'll take care to not ruin the dress—or the shoes."

"Just have fun." Chipper patted her hand on the car door, shooting a glance at Blake. "I'll see you soon."

"And I don't want to see you home until *after* midnight." Bonnie winked.

Indeed. Since coming to America, she had truly become a Cinderella.

CHAPTER SEVENTEEN

"**S**HERIFF, THE MANAGER SAID I'D FIND YOU OUT HERE." DALE Harmon one of Kevin's deputies, reached for the clipboard, his expression perplexed. "I got this, sir."

Kevin pulled it back. He guessed Gus Graham had sent Harmon over. The sheriff's department was responsible for keeping law and order—not directing drivers to their stadium-style parking spaces in the club's parking lot.

Usually with this gravy assignment, Kevin would be inside, sitting in the air-conditioned Clear Spring Huntsmen's Club office, thumbing the paper and drinking a cup of coffee. But not tonight.

"I'll see you inside," Kevin said. He motioned the next car he'd checked off the list to its rightful place.

"Yes, sir." Harmon shrugged and turned, heading through the parking lot and toward the club's front portico.

Kevin swung back to the next car in line, viewed their tickets, and quickly checked their names off the list. He frowned at the name above it—Lansing. Why did he care? She seemed to be figuring out things on her own. He should be relieved.

Yeah, right.

Lansing was a womanizing bastard. He should have told her no—*no, you're not going*—and come up with some bullshit excuse having to do with her citizenship. A lie. But one he was prepared to live with if it meant protecting her from Lansing. Instead, the sheriff of Washington County chose to stand outside, in the balmy night air, sweating his nuts off, doing the menial task meant for a teenage club employee.

His excuse? Glorified bodyguard for one Irish lass who had no clue how alluring she could be to the opposite sex.

"Lookie here, Daniel."

Kevin shut his eyes and shook his head. This night couldn't get any worse. Kevin turned and placed the clipboard under his arm. "Tickets."

In the same short-sleeved striped polo shirt Kevin had seen his father wearing earlier at the training center, Turk Bendix was far from fitting in at this swank, influential gathering of select, well-heeled horse enthusiasts.

Turk slung his arm out the window of his pickup. "You know I'm not here for this damned ball." His father's belligerent tone sliced the night air.

Daniel Fallon leaned over from the passenger seat. "How's it going, then, Kevin?"

Oh, it was going all right.

Kevin smiled at his old family friend. "Couldn't be better, Daniel."

"Good, good." Daniel rubbed his stomach that was almost the same proportion as his own father's. "Getting ourselves a nice carved turkey sandwich and a beer in the back."

It wasn't like these two old geezers would get remarried, but they enjoyed the company of one Elsie Morton and her famous twelve-inch subs. Kevin nodded and pointed them to a parking space. "Tell Elsie I said hello."

His father pulled away and then stopped. "Why you out here, anyway?"

A toot of a horn brought Kevin's head around. He caught the distinct grill of the Mercedes convertible. *Great.* Lansing.

"You're blocking traffic." With his hand, Kevin ordered his father to pull forward.

Toot.

"What in . . . the . . . hell?" His dad shoved his balding, speckled head out the window and sneered at the dark blue convertible with its top coming down. "Keep your pants on, Lansing," he called back. Then a wry smile lit his face, and Kevin got the sneaking suspicion his old man had put two and two together. "Daniel, your daughter's in the car behind us."

"Who, Kate?" he said with confusion as he swung his head back to peer out the sliding glass window.

"No. Dani."

"Dani?" he said, as though he had to be reminded he had a third child.

"She's with *Lansing.*" Turk said the last word in a hushed voice.

Totally done with his father's antics, Kevin motioned Lansing around and into the next parking space without even bothering to check his tickets.

"Wait. You didn't check his ticket." His father sat in his truck looking angelic—if that were possible—blinking up at him with his lips pursed.

"You're not funny," Kevin said through gritted teeth. "Now park the truck."

Turk waved him off and pulled forward into the spot next to Lansing's sports car.

With a line of cars piling up, Kevin covertly glanced in that direction. They remained in the car, Kevin only catching Dani's glossy sable hair, piled high on her head, and the shapely curve of her neck where she remained seated in the passenger seat of his Mercedes. He checked the next car's tickets and directed them to their spot as Lansing came around to the passenger door.

Kevin snorted. Dressed in a white tux—he had to stand out from the crowd—Lansing, looking like James Bond, graciously took Dani's hand and helped her up from her seat.

"Might want to put up the top," Kevin called over.

Lansing turned back. "How about I leave you my key, Sheriff?" He shot Kevin a sly look and dug into the pocket of his jacket.

What the . . .

Every muscle in Kevin's body tensed. Did the son of a bitch actually think he was his personal valet for the evening?

Kevin's chin shot up and he laughed out loud. "Good one, Lansing." Turning, he kept his back to them and feigned busyness. He was in no mood to start a volley with Lansing over, of all things, his damn ragtop.

Kevin checked several more tickets, moving the cars along before he caught a break. He then keyed his mic. "Harmon, send one of the club employees out here."

"Yes, sir."

Several minutes later, the parking attendant came out.

Kevin handed over his clipboard. "It's all yours." He gave him a friendly rap on the shoulder and strode across the parking lot, debating which door to enter. He didn't want to make it obvious he was scouting her out. Dani was like any other citizen of the community. He only wanted to be certain of her well-being. Although he knew *that* was total crap.

Choosing the side entrance leading to the kitchen, he grimaced. If his old man opened his mouth . . . Kevin took a cleansing breath through his nose and swung open the door. He stepped in, letting it automatically close behind him. The small bar with a couple of scuffed tables and chairs was set aside for the old cronies who had missed their chance at fame and fortune. Not that Daniel Fallon fit in to the same category as his father. He'd made a life for himself and his family at Grace. He had a world of respect for the man and valued the friendship he'd forged with him over the years.

"Go on." Daniel nudged Turk's shoulder in what looked to be disbelief. "A natural?"

Turk tipped back his beer and took a quick swig. "I seen it for myself."

"Seen what?" Kevin sat his campaign hat down on the bar.

"What can I get you, Kevin?" Elsie with her fifties do and cat's-eye glasses patted his hand.

"Water's fine."

"What? No cars for you to park?" his father said, smiling into his beer mug.

"Here you go, hon." Elsie sat a glass of ice water on the bar.

"Thanks." He took a sip and leveled his gaze on Daniel. "How'd your talk go with Dani?"

He swallowed a bite of his sub, setting it down on his plate. "She's a fine girl. We walked in with her and Lansing. But you were wanting to know about earlier now. Better than expected. Very forgiving, if you know what I mean."

"She's a good kid," Kevin agreed.

Turk sputtered in his beer. "She's twenty-six, built like a brick hou—" He blanched, realizing his error. "And . . . and . . ." He looked from Kevin to Daniel and back to Kevin. "*Old enough* to be my new jockey."

Kevin got the "old enough" and who it was directed to, and it was then that the tail end of his father's conversation registered.

"She said exercise rider earlier today."

"For now." His father laughed. It was genuine and full of awe, something Kevin hadn't witnessed in a long time. "You should have seen her."

"So you were saying, then." Daniel sat down his mug.

"She took off like a shot." Turk slapped his palms together and waved his fingers like a bird taking flight. "Took a furlong like it was nothin'."

Daniel slapped the bar. "Imagine that. She must have her mother's smarts for horses."

Turk shook his head. "You've still got some horse savvy in you."

"For rescuing—not racing."

"Like hell, old man." Turk took a swig of his beer. "Tell you what, come down tomorrow. It's Sunday. Fly—" He caught himself and then cleared his throat. "Dani's off. Let's put her on Midnight Edition. See how he takes to her."

Kevin tried to place the horse, and when he did and then calculated its height—almost seventeen hands—he clenched his jaw. "She's too small to ride that bruiser."

Turk's mouth fell open. "Did you hear yourself?"

Okay so she was the perfect size for a jockey. And his statement was, well, asinine. He didn't care. And he also didn't care to analyze why he had a problem with Dani riding the damned horse. "I'm warning you. Don't put her on that horse."

"And why the hell not?" His father arched an eyebrow his way.

"Because I'm asking you not to."

"You're a real piece of work." He slammed his fist on the bar. "You asked me to give her a job, pay her a decent wage, and put a roof over her head. Now you want to tell me how to run my stable?" Turk turned to his old friend. "Do you have a problem with it?"

"None that I can think of. I appreciate all you've done." Daniel shrugged. "Plus, I learned long ago not to hold on too tight."

Kevin shook his head. *Great.* Looked like he'd be driving out to the track on another Sunday when he should be working around his house.

"Then it's settled. How about ten sharp?"

"Looking forward to it," Daniel said and raised his mug.

"To Dani, then." Turk clinked his mug against Daniel's.

Kevin rolled his eyes and threw a dollar in Elsie's tip jar. "Okay I leave my hat on the bar, Elsie?"

She turned back from wiping down the bar. "You go ahead, hon. I'll watch it."

"See, ya." Kevin went to take a step toward the swinging doors that led to the banquet room when his father grabbed his arm.

"Don't forget to write that report."

Kevin nodded. "I'll do it Monday."

"Don't forget."

"I won't," Kevin grumped and walked away. *Damn* the old man needed to give it a break. That's all he needed with this election coming up, his father making a spectacle of himself in the horse community over something that was in his paranoid brain. Kevin shook it off and cleared the double swinging doors. He'd take a look around, spend five minutes tops in the ballroom before he made his way to the office on the other side of the dance floor. He could do that in the capacity of his job and not raise her suspicions.

"Sheriff." Bud Deetz, one of the county commissioners, sauntered toward him. "Like to talk to you for a minute about that speed camera on South Potomac Street and our budget."

Great. The speed camera located in Hagerstown City wasn't his deal. Now the budget . . . that he wanted to discuss.

CHAPTER EIGHTEEN

B LAKE BROUGHT DANI A FLUTED GLASS, FILLED TO THE BRIM. "IT'S
champagne." He handed it to her, his warm brown eyes holding hers.

"Thank you." Dani took a sip, the bubbles tickling her nose. She'd
tended bar and knew the difference—not that she'd admit as much. She'd
do well to forget her life in Ireland. But it was kind of him to make the
distinction.

Dani focused on Blake and tried to block out the last night she spent
on the docks in Rosslare Harbour. He seemed to take great care in her
having a good time with him. He'd tried to teach her the two-step and
suffered a heel to the foot because of it. The entire evening he'd opened
up a whole new world to her. Although she didn't much care for the
oysters. They were slimy and incredibly hard to swallow.

They stood with a group of his friends. Some were bankers like
Kevin's girlfriend. Others worked in the horse industry.

"So tell me, Dani, where is it you're from in Ireland?" Rick was his
name, she believed. He was tall and athletic and married to the redhead
Lisa.

She should be vague. "A small village on the east coast."

"I've always wanted to go to Ireland." Lisa had that faraway look.

"I hear the food's bland." That came from Tom. He was the bank
manager.

Dani smiled sweetly. "I wouldn't say that, not if you like potatoes."

Tom chuckled. "Where'd you get her, Blake?"

Blake placed the wide palm of his hand on her lower back, finding the
small cutout of her dress. Dani's stomach tumbled—in a good way. Still,

she hadn't been expecting it. Dani wet her lips. He still hadn't answered the question. The tingle of awareness for Blake, as a man, was quickly replaced with a pang of anxiety. He was embarrassed by her position.

"Do you know Storm Henderson?" Blake said.

Rick gave a nod. "Best damn female jockey on the West Coast."

"I want you to meet the best damn female jockey on the East Coast." His eyes held hers.

Dani was mesmerized. There was no doubt in her mind he'd sincerely meant it. But not only that. He had to have known about her fears—fears of being embarrassed in front of his well-to-do friends.

Before she could find her words, the small orchestra began to play. Blake took her champagne glass and set it down, catching Dani by surprise. "May I have this dance?"

"I'll only step on your feet." Dani grimaced.

"For you, m'lady, I'll risk it." He bowed like they did when kings and queens ruled empires, and Dani didn't have it in her to say no.

She took his outstretched hand and traveled with him onto the dance floor, careful not to twist an ankle. She'd give a day's pay to kick off her Cinderella shoes and dance barefoot. They hurt without end. Blake's arm went around her waist, his hand finding that familiar spot where he could touch her skin. She tingled, and for the second time she found herself trying to come to grips with her physical attraction to Blake.

Dani lifted her chin to him, which was not an easy task, considering he was a good foot taller than she. "That was very kind of you."

He gave her a questioning look.

"The jockey comment."

"No kindness at all, Miss Flynn. I seen it with me own—"

She pushed him playfully while he held her in his arms. "Now you're taking the mick."

His eyes that had been smiling down at her, changed. They were now thoughtful, if not sober. "You have good instincts. With the proper training, you could hone that natural ability and be a major contender."

"You're serious?"

"I make my living on the track—a good living. I know what I'm talking about."

"I'd be the competition."

"There's nothing wrong with competition, Dani." Those same serious eyes held hers. He wasn't joking. In an instant everything negative she'd been told about the man, prior to tonight, vanished.

Standing here in Blake's arms, with him gliding her over the dance floor, she could pretend to be that successful, accomplished woman she'd never be—like Kevin's bank manager. Yet Blake treated her as his equal. Welcomed the challenge of her someday—with training—giving him a run for those roses the Americans always talked about.

Bonnie had been wrong about Blake. Whatever was going on in the Starlite stable, if it was anything at all, couldn't possibly have anything to do with Blake Lansing.

Blake moaned, jarring Dani out of her meanderings. "Did I—"

He gritted his teeth and worked through the pain.

Oh, my.

"I'm so sorry. I should sit down. I have no bus—"

His arm tightened around her waist, and he lifted her feet from the floor.

Dani squealed and then laughed just as quick.

"That's better." Blake's eyes ran the length of her. "What do you weigh? All of about one hundred and two pounds?"

"One hundred and ten." She giggled. "You really must put me down, I think."

He sat her down gently and they continued to dance. They talked of many things—his life at the track, hers in Ireland, including the pub and the racing stable. She didn't give specifics. But not offering some details of her life in Ireland would be more suspicious. When the dance ended, he went back to get her another glass of champagne, and Dani went to freshen up.

Standing at the sink, she washed and dried her hands and checked her makeup. She slipped the small tube of gloss from her clutch and applied a fresh coat to her lips. Returning it, the light caught the cellophane wrappers of her mints, and her cheeks warmed, wondering what it would be like to kiss Blake. She got that warmth and tingle that only comes from pure utter attraction to the opposite sex. Dani closed her eyes. When it passed, she opened them and checked her hair. *God.* She was blushing, and the wisps framing her face only added to that soft feminine look a man might find alluring if he were thinking about kissing a woman. Dani shook her head. Was he even attracted to her in that way?

Dani opened one of the mints and popped it in her mouth. It was best to be prepared. Glancing up at the clock in the small sitting area of the ladies' room—11:59—she smiled. Cinderella would not be home before midnight, to be sure. She didn't want the night to end. Tomorrow she would go back to being Dani Flynn exercise rider. A step up from groom, but still a meager livelihood in comparison to others she'd met tonight.

Dani stepped from the bathroom and stopped short. Wobbling, she tried to stay upright.

Kevin grabbed her by her upper arms. "Not used to heels."

If it was a smirk she'd witnessed, it had disappeared from his face. But his inference still lingered like stale tobacco. Dani shook his hands off her. "It's no wonder. You walked straight into me." Dani glanced around. Most were on the dance floor or sitting at tables. And the entrance to the gentlemen's room was on the opposite side of the dance floor. "You were following me," she whispered with heat, trying her best to keep the dwindling mint between her cheek and gums.

"On the contrary, Miss Flynn, I was leaving." He pointed to the double swinging doors. "I'm headed out the kitchen way." His eyes lingered on her face and then took a southerly track before they reconnected where they should have been all along.

"What are you doing?" Dani checked herself to be sure she hadn't stained Chipper's dress, although she had a fair idea what his eyes were seeing.

"You clean up nice."

Clean up? Of all the . . . Dani clenched her fingers and twisted in his grasp.

He let her go. "Wait. That came out wrong."

"Do you have a point to all this? Because if not—"

"I ran into Daniel and my father earlier."

He wasn't telling her anything she didn't already know. "Yes, they were in front of Blake's car when we came in. We walked through the parking lot together." She gave him an odd look. "You were there."

A pained expression came over him. "Yeah, the parking lot."

Dani wanted to laugh at his discomfort. She didn't know much about American law enforcement, but it didn't seem at all normal that the sheriff would be parking cars.

"Kevin, is there a purpose here?"

"Ah, congratulations on your new job," he blurted out and then grimaced. "I should have told you earlier."

Only he'd been preoccupied with the bank manager. "Not to worry."

He nodded and attempted a smile. "I meant what I said earlier. You look very pretty."

She wanted to believe in his sincerity. Perhaps he did find her attractive. But there had to be more than a physical attraction, she was learning. She wanted Kevin's respect, and it wasn't a case of being a law-abiding citizen. He knew why she hadn't been, knew she was making strides to become one. It wasn't that. He was ashamed of her and her position in life.

Dani caught Blake standing with his group, holding up the promised glass of champagne. "I have to go."

Kevin followed her line of sight and scowled. "How's he treating you?"

"Like a gentleman. Why?"

"He's not."

"And I suppose *you* are the authority."

He looked down his nose at her, like she had to be out of her head to question his knowledge of Blake Lansing.

Dani only stared back.

"Look," he said, his expression softening. "I'm not here to slander the guy's reputation. Just be careful. That's all I'm saying."

Dani considered his words. She'd gotten to America, hadn't she? Had he not meddled in her life—had she not met him—she would have figured things out on her own. "I'll keep an eye out, then." Dani walked away, sure that Kevin was burning a hole in her back as she met Blake across the dance floor.

He handed her a glass of champagne. "You all right?"

She downed it, the slight burn of alcohol welcome as it slid down her throat. "I am now."

He took her glass. "Let's take a walk."

"That would be grand." Dani gave Blake her hand, and he led her out onto a back patio with fruit trees, fragrant flowers, and tiny Christmas lights strung all around. "It's lovely."

"No. You're lovely." He placed his hand on her lower back and drew her close.

Dani's hands automatically went to his chest and the expensive cut of his tux. "I've not had a more special night."

A faint smile touched his lips. "It doesn't have to end, Dani." His words were as smooth as spun glass.

Dani ignored her good senses and let her hands travel over his wide shoulders. Blake was accomplished, attractive, and, it would seem, attracted to her. "What did you have in mind?"

He cupped the nape of her neck and gently angled her face to his. His eyes were warm, attentive, and smoldering with desire. "I know a place."

He dipped his head and Dani closed her eyes.

The wail of a siren shattered the air around them, and Dani jumped, the top of her head knocking into Blake's chin. Her eyes sprung open, an odd purple glow pulsating around them outside in the garden. "Oh, my."

Blake cursed and grabbed his chin.

"I'm so sorry. Did I hurt you?" Dani's hands came up to examine his face.

"It's fine." He jerked away from her and scowled at the club's parking lot just beyond the fruit trees of the patio. "He for real?"

Directly behind them, through the tree limbs, Dani could just make out the white markings of Kevin's patrol car with its red and blue lights swirling. Dani clenched her hands at her side.

I'll murder him.

CHAPTER NINETEEN

KEVIN THREW THE CRUISER IN PARK AND JUMPED OUT RIGHT ABOUT the time Dani jerked the barn door shut. Okay, so she was upset with him. Maybe his job was not protecting a woman's virtue. Or maybe it was more he didn't want Lansing taking something he might eventually want for himself.

Stupid.

He shook his head and strode toward the barn. Grabbing the door, he jerked it hard, prepared to wrestle with the lock. It gave easily, and Kevin took the stairs two at a time, snagging the silver heel left on the step in Dani's wake.

He rounded the tight hallway, his destination the makeshift door on the left. He pushed the blanket aside.

"Arsehole."

Kevin ducked, a shoe hitting the wall. "You're mad."

"Mad?" Dani blew out an agitated breath. "You made me to look like a fool."

He'd waited until Lansing drove off from the club and followed him. It would have been uneventful if Lansing simply drove her back to the training center. "I wouldn't have had to use the lights and siren again, if he stuck to the road." He'd warned her about Lansing. Once he had her alone in his brick fortress, if she had a change of heart—more like she was clueless—she'd be at his mercy. She'd forced his hand, and he didn't regret it. "He offer you a nightcap, a little conversation before—"

Her eyes blazed back at him. "Get out of me room!" She dove for the small chest and a strappy stiletto.

Kevin dropped the shoe in his hand and was on her in one stride, his arm looping around her waist. He crushed her to him, his hand ripping the shoe from her grasp. He tossed it on the ground. Her eyes widened, and she swung at him. Grunting, Kevin grabbed her wrist and pulled her arm down. Now with her in a bear hug, he pushed her against the plywood wall. "Enough."

A whimper escaped her lips. "You're hurting me."

He pulled some of his weight off. "Stop fighting."

Her chin shot up, and a pair of ireful blue eyes locked onto his. "Stop following me, then. Stop buying me things. Stop feeling so bloody responsible for me. I can handle me own life."

"I'm not convinced." More like he was trying to convince himself. He could have simply turned his patrol car around once Lansing had finally dropped her off and Dani was safely in the barn. But he hadn't, thanks to the teardrop opening of her dress that exposed her shapely lower back. It had been the last he'd seen of her before she ducked inside the barn. "Lansing's not the man for you."

She stiffened in his arms, the slight flare of her nose giving every indication she wasn't thrilled with the conclusion he'd drawn.

"I'm not looking for a man, eejit." Dani squirmed against him, trying to get free. "I only wanted one night where I could be anyone but the shifty immigrant you seem to think I am." She stopped thrashing, gave one regretful breath before a frown tugged at those perfectly formed lips of hers.

"That's not how I feel about you." Kevin's eyes swept over her. She'd fooled with her hair. Piled high with soft wisps framing her face, it exposed the sensual curve of her neck. He followed her bare shoulders to the cut of her dress, his eyes lingering. His father had been right—full breasts pressed against the shimmering bodice. Trying to keep her contained, but giving him some needed space, Kevin readjusted his arm around her narrow waist. Bad move. His hand landed on the cutout of her dress and that tantalizingly smooth skin of her lower back. His body tightened, including his balls.

Shit.

Dani wet her lips. They glistened under the light, and his heart beat faster.

"Then how is it you feel about me?" She relaxed and concentrated on him with a serious pair of eyes, no doubt expecting the truth.

He only hoped his dick hadn't already clued her in.

He brought his chin down slightly, trying to find the words. Her eyes fluttered closed, dark lashes dusting her pretty face, giving him every indication she wanted to be kissed.

Ah, hell.

Kevin bent his head and kissed her. Dani parted her lips for him, and he slipped his tongue in. Hers was waiting, somewhat timid. He drew her closer, his hand cupping the back of her neck. Her lips were soft and moving against his, and Kevin ran his tongue across her teeth, and then deeper to explore the warm recesses of her mouth. She moaned against his kiss, her arms snaking around his neck. She was so warm and wet and tasted faintly of mint, and then he recalled the jerking motion of the Mercedes, his lights and siren behind it when Lansing turned it around, avoiding the right turn into his driveway.

She'd wanted to be kissed—but not by Kevin. He stopped the kiss and pulled away from her.

Dani's eyes opened, and she blushed. "Was I not doing it right?"

"No," he said, his throat rough. "I shouldn't have . . ."

"Kissed me." Her voice rose.

"It was wrong. You're . . ." *God.* She was perfect, and he was an idiot. So what if she'd had every intention of swapping spit with Lansing. She was here with him now.

"I see."

He didn't miss the edge to her voice, or the way her eyes darted toward the top of the chest and the lone strappy shoe with a five-inch spike that, if aimed right, could poke out his eye. She kept him accounted for and reached toward the dresser.

"Whoa." Kevin lunged and grabbed her arm. "You asked how I felt about you."

"And?" She wrenched her arm away.

"Protective." He shrugged. "It's my job."

"Which is a relief." Her brows knitted together as though she was thinking, and then she opened her mouth. "It was like kissing a brother. If I had one."

Ouch. Kevin tried not to laugh. He'd had his share of women. Knew when they were into a kiss. She was into his. "How about we both agree it was a mistake?"

"Fine. Now can I open me drawer? I haven't a weapon, if that's what you're afraid of."

He nodded and kept his eyes on her. She pulled out an envelope and thumbed through the cash. "How much do I owe you, then?"

"Excuse me?"

"The boots and black trainers."

"Dani." He grabbed for the envelope. "You don't—"

Dani jerked it away. "I'll not worry that I owe you any money." She stood as tall as she could in her bare feet. "I make a good wage, thanks to your father. Now, how much for the pair?"

He scrubbed his face hard. "Two fifty."

Dani's brows shot up. "Two fifty? What? Are they sewn with gold thread?"

He'd wanted her to have the best, and at the time he'd attributed it to her difficult start here in the States. But now if she asked him why, the truth would blow the protect-and-serve crap he'd offered up a few minutes ago. "The boots are made with Gore-Tex."

"I haven't a clue what that means."

"They're waterproof." He picked up one of the black tennis shoes beside the doorway. "And these have better arch support than your sneakers."

Dani frowned. "Well, you give up your hard-earned money too easily, then, to help a woman you barely know."

He opened his mouth to try and explain.

Dani waved a dismissive hand and counted out the two fifty and handed it to him. "We're even."

Kevin clenched his jaw and took the money from her, shoving it in his wallet. "I'm asking you not to see Lansing again."

She gave a hard laugh. "Aren't you a bold one?" She put the remaining cash back in her drawer and shut it. Turning, she lifted her chin to him. "I'll do as I please."

He took a step toward her. Her cheeks were flushed with anger, her mouth still slightly swollen from his kiss. After tonight, he should keep his distance. She was trouble with a capital T. It was high time he paid attention to that niggle in the back of his brain when it came to her past. He'd gone as far as looking into her ocean voyage and hadn't been very successful. He could chalk it up to lack of effort. Same for his grandmother's plate. It still remained in the grocery bag, shoved in the bottom of his desk drawer at the station. Fact was he feared the future. A future without one Dani Flynn. It was about time he started acting like a law enforcement officer. There was more to Dani, he suspected. And it started with her port of origin in Ireland. But first he wanted to clue her in on her little romance with Lansing. "I think he got the message, even if you haven't."

Her lips thinned, and she looked ready to deck him, but then a smile slowly formed on those pouty, kissable lips of hers, perhaps realizing the humor in it all. "After tonight . . ." She laughed, almost like she was reliving it. "He'll not ask me out again, I imagine."

Kevin chuckled. "Lansing?" He remained silent now, mulling over his handiwork. "Doubtful."

Dani nodded.

"That's not a bad thing." He took another step toward her, his fingers pressing a spiral of hair back behind her ear. "It wouldn't have ended with a kiss good night."

Her eyes widened, like he was talking out of both sides of his mouth.

He winced. "I should have shown the same restraint. I'm sorry, Dani."

She rolled her lips in. "It's good we know we're not attracted to each other."

"Makes it less complicated."

Dani searched his eyes with interest. "As for Blake . . . I'll take your word for it."

Only inches away from her in the cramped space, he fought the need to plant one right on those lips of hers. "I worry about you."

Jeez. He needed to be diplomatic here.

"I'd hate to see you or any young woman be taken advantage of." He dropped his hand to his side. Not touching her was going to be his biggest obstacle. Giving her every indication he shared her views, he laughed. "If I had a sister . . ."

Dani moved toward the door. "Aye. I've appreciated your kindness these past few days." She held open the blanket to her room and covered up a yawn. "You must be tired, too."

He guessed he'd overstayed his welcome. But he wasn't kidding about earlier. Maybe he was jealous, but he didn't trust Lansing. Kevin shoved his hands in his pockets and rocked on his heels. "I meant what I said earlier."

"I'll not search Blake out, if that's what you mean."

Yeah, like hell. She was Irish and every bit like her sisters. Meaning she *would* do what she pleased, and he'd be hard pressed to stop her. Kevin ducked under the doorway and turned back toward Dani. "Smart girl."

Her brows snapped together, and she pinned him with unsmiling eyes.

"Good night."

Kevin chuckled and headed for the steps. "It was meant as a compliment," he called back.

She had let the blanket fall into place. The I'm-done-with-you-tonight quite evident.

Ah, Dani, you're killing me.

Kevin groaned and took the steps. The woman was a knockout. Didn't matter if she was dressed to kill or dressed for yard work. But it was more than that. He enjoyed her laugh and her indignation when he razzed her. He shouldn't be attracted to her. But he was. Shutting the barn door, he strode over to his patrol car and then glanced up at the brightly lit window high in the peak of the barn.

Damn it. He was falling for her.

Chapter Twenty

Dani stood back from the window. Kevin Bendix could be the enemy she never saw coming. He *was* attracted to her. Well, her body and most notably—based on the way he was treating her—not her brain.

All these years she'd patiently waited for the man of her dreams only to have him look down his nose at her. She saw nothing wrong with her profession. If Kevin had given her a choice between the job she had now and one working in a bank like Kristin What's-her-name, she'd have chosen the stable. She connected with the horses. Loved them and, with Monday looming closer as Turk's new exercise rider—although exciting—she wondered if he'd still allow her to care for them as their groom.

Dani snagged her backpack off the ground and dug for the last of the peppermints. With all the to-do of getting dressed and going to the ball, she'd forgotten to give them their bedtime treat. Holding up the plastic bag, she counted eleven, and with the two remaining in her clutch, unlucky thirteen. Dani grimaced and popped one in, the zing of peppermint filling her mouth. There was nothing wrong with being superstitious.

Dani rummaged around for any loose mints at the bottom of her backpack. Her hand brushed the zipper of the small pocket inside, and her fingers stilled. The thumb drive. She'd had every intention before tonight of opening the files and doing an online search of the local paper from her village. At close to two, even if she tried to fall asleep she doubted she could. Dani touched her lips, her eyes closing. She'd never experienced a kiss like that. She hadn't wanted it to end.

But he'd pulled away.

God.

Why couldn't he accept the fission of heat building between them? It radiated along her skin like hot sparks. Did he believe her that inept at reading a man's body language? Dani ran her hand down the thin fabric of her dress. There hadn't been much separating her from him. He was pressed up long and hard against her stomach. His arousal was something she hadn't expected and he couldn't deny.

A sister, no less! She'd put the stupid idea in his head when she compared his kiss to that of a brother. They were truly a pair.

She shook her head and reached for the top drawer of her dresser and opened it. The plump envelope with her pay sat on top, and she grabbed it. She'd given Kevin two fifty. She had long since familiarized herself with American money. American tourists who hadn't taken the time to convert their U.S. currency often paid with it. Dani moved to her bed and sat down. Laying the peppermints aside, she opened the envelope and counted the bills. Six hundred and fourteen, plus the two fifty? She needed a pencil and paper to be exact, but it was close to one thousand dollars, for sure.

She couldn't possibly expect Kevin to treat her as his equal unless she worked hard to become one. First she needed a savings account. Dani's shoulders slumped. They'd probably ask for identification like they did in Ireland. Would it be smart to provide a bank with her passport and social security number to open up an account? Giving anyone information they could use to trace her back to Ireland could be risky.

Dani hoisted the backpack onto her bed. Unzipping the front pocket, she pulled out a pencil and small pad. She made a list. *Talk to Kate at Fourth of July picnic about citizenship, need help opening a bank account . . . possibly, learn to drive, buy a reliable used car.* Thinking if she'd missed anything, Dani doodled a woman's face, adding flowing long hair—Kevin's bank manager. Frowning, she tossed the notepad on the bed, got up, and carefully unzipped Chipper's dress and shimmied out of it. She hung it on the door frame, her hands running the width of its lovely beaded bodice. She'd likely not wear something as stunning again. Zipping the heavy-duty plastic bag shut, she turned her back on it and jotted down the words *pretty summer dress and heels,* and then added horns and a tail and the words *Kristin Jennings* to her doodle.

Jimmy hopped up on her bed and padded around. She gave him a teasing tug on his tail. If she wanted that storybook romance, she needed to compete with Kevin's bank manager. He'd more than likely be at the picnic *and* with her. Dani put the money back and grabbed a fresh pair of panties and her green polo shirt her father had returned to her earlier from Kate.

She ran her fingers along the stitching above the breast pocket—*Devlin's*. Thinking better of it, she dug the thumb drive out of the pocket of her backpack. Kevin was attracted to her, yes. Charmed or not, she'd be a fool to think he'd ignore her life in Ireland and what she had been involved in before she inadvertently stowed away.

Even *she* couldn't say what she'd gotten herself mixed up in—other than the obvious. Dani's head ached, and she pressed in on her temples. If anyone needed to make sense of her life back in Ireland—she did.

Dani rubbed her fist against the steam on the small mirror in the bathroom next to Turk's office, her stomach in knots.

If only I could take back every stupid thing I've done since meeting Duggan.

Kevin was a cop. He'd only want to be involved with a law-abiding woman. Even if she did everything right starting now, she couldn't erase the poor choices she'd made.

Dani brushed her hair hard, pulled it into a ponytail, and got dressed. She grabbed the breast pocket of her shirt and it crinkled. She relaxed. The thumb drive and peppermints were inside. Slipping on Kate's sandals, she clicked the wall switch off in the tiny bathroom and made her way to Turk's office in the dim murk of the barn's emergency light. If she wanted answers, it started with Turk's computer—in the middle of the night when no one was around.

Dani rounded the doorway and entered Turk's office, taking a seat in his chair. She touched the keyboard, and his home screen popped up, minus the need for a password. Dani sighed with relief. She just assumed with his distrustful nature he'd have one. Although, considering his age, he probably found technology a nuisance. Dani clicked into the Internet. She wasn't at all computer literate, herself. But she could do a search and typed in the URL for *Wexford People,* an Irish online newspaper which covered news from her village.

It had been over two weeks since that night on the docks. It wouldn't be at the top of the page. Dani grimaced at the first headline of a dog doused in petrol and set alight. Ireland wasn't all faeries and rolling green hillsides, to be sure. Swallowing her disgust, she clicked on Regional News. She scrolled down. It was all about borough councilors and local elections. One was about the new café. She didn't want to think of Pat's mood. He'd been vying for a place on the prestigious restaurant guide. Maggie's Café had taken it from him. She shook her head. He'd be murderous.

Thump.

Dani jolted upright in her chair, icy fingers running up her spine. She swiveled around so that she had a direct view of the aisle, which ran perpendicular in front of Turk's office. It was empty. The barn was old but still. She stood up, surrounded in the eerie glow of the computer screen, and took measured steps into the aisle. The barn door, which Kevin had shut on his way out, remained closed. She stood motionless. Only the gentle stirrings of the horses answered back. Now *she* was being paranoid.

Dani went back into the office and sat down. *Relax.* Like that was possible, sitting at her boss's computer without his knowledge, no less. Well, it wasn't like she was stealing it. She was only borrowing it. Dani scrolled down with an eye for anything that might . . .

Dani's breath caught. They had made mention of her—actually them—and her pulse quickened.

Two Local Rosslare Women Are Missing.

It had been easy to find, too. Dani read through the article, her heart beating in her ears. Kevin would surely find this. Even if she had a mind to lie about her origins, she'd bungled it the moment she declared Daniel Fallon her biological father. If Kevin needed a starting point, her father—who seemed to trust Kevin explicitly—could and would fill him in. Dani shut her eyes and shook her head.

I'm in a load of shite.

She was so focused on proving her identity she'd given him her birth certificate. Kate had it for now, but she'd be a fool to think Kevin hadn't made a copy. Maybe she had been born in Waterford County. But Wexford was only a county over. She fell back in her chair, rubbing her temples. It was only a matter of time. Her only saving grace, if she could count it as one, was that they hadn't found Kara's body.

Dani straightened and continued to read the entire article. After finishing the last line, her shoulders relaxed. There was no mention of Tommy Duggan—only a statement from Pat Malone confirming they were employees of his establishment and the women were friends. She hadn't mentioned Kara Gilroy to Kevin. He'd wonder why. She simply would hope he didn't ask.

Eejit.

He was going to ask, and she needed to be prepared. Dani dropped her head in her hands. Now she was digging a bigger hole of lies. How would she explain being connected to a corpse?

A cock crowed, and Dani jumped to her feet, her heart hammering in her chest. *Damn rooster.* Clutching the thumb drive in her hand, she checked the time on the computer—3:35. It would be sunup soon, and days started early in the stable. With the computer and its USB port only a fingertip away, she debated the risk.

Much too high.

She had too much going right to let Duggan, who was an ocean away, ruin it for her. Turk didn't lock his office. At least not that she was aware. She could come back same time tomorrow night.

Dani left everything as she found it and entered the aisle with the thumb drive clutched between her fingers. Catching her shoulder on the door frame, her pocket crinkled. Peppermints. Traveling down the aisle, Dani stopped at Solley's stall and clucked her tongue. His head swung back.

"Hey, handsome. I've got something sweet." Dani unwrapped one of the mints and held out her hand flat. His nostrils flared, and he came to the stall door and scarfed it up.

Dani giggled and roughed up his forelock. "You're a piggy."

Continuing down the aisle she doled out three more peppermints to Joey, George, and Hary Man, saving the last one for Sister. Not that she had a favorite, well, maybe Solley, but the mare had a sweet disposition.

Dani laughed when she neared her stall. She'd been tracking her in the barn, waiting, and, no doubt, wondering if there was a peppermint in Dani's pocket for her. She grabbed hold of her muzzle hanging over the stall and kissed her on the nose. "You know I'd never forget you."

She took out the last peppermint and was unwrapping it when the mare nudged her shoulder. "I'm hurrying." Dani shoved the plastic in her pocket and held out her hand with the mint. Sister's nostrils twitched before she sucked it up. Dani smiled. Kevin had done her a favor even if, at the time, she'd been panicked out of her wits. Dropping her off at the mercy of his bad-tempered father certainly hadn't—

Thump.

Dani's head shot up. Standing there in her panties and a shirt that barely covered her bum, she was ill-prepared to search the barn and find herself face-to-face with whatever it was that had actually gone thump in the night. Dani trembled at the possibility and tried to decide from which direction the noise had come.

Had to be the aisle on the other side of the barn. She was good at sounds and was sure it was the side door located directly below her room. It opened and thumped shut on a regular basis during the day, just like the thump she'd heard.

It was quiet now. Whoever it was, they were probably gone by now.

Shite. Maybe not.

Dani raced to the back door, her heart thumping in her chest. She pushed it open a crack. When she didn't see anyone, she opened it wider, the door creaking. Dani grimaced. A few paces away Jake had Bonnie pressed up against his pickup, his hand riding under her skirt, her soft moans drifting on the warm summer breeze.

Dani eased back on the door, but not before Jake whipped his head back and scowled at her under the parking light of the barn.

Dani blanched. "I'm sorry," she murmured and started to pull the door closed.

"Wait! Dani," Bonnie whispered harshly and pulled Jake's hand away, yanking down her tank top. Bonnie rushed over and grabbed for the door. "We were just saying good . . ." Bonnie's eyeballs seemed to roll, her lids heavy like she was fighting sleep. Then her eyes popped open and she continued in a bubbly voice. "We had an awesome time at the Purple Cow."

"Come on, Bonnie." Jake came up and took her arm, steering her toward the bunkhouse across the narrow gravel road of the training center.

"Wait. Is she okay?" Dani took a step toward them.

"Too much to drink," Jake said and placed Bonnie's arm around his neck.

"Oh . . . Did you see anyone when you pulled in?"

"No," he flung back, struggling with Bonnie who seemed to be having an animated conversation with herself.

Weird.

Dani let go of the door and rushed over. "Jake, can I help?"

"She's fine," he snapped, his eyes roaming her body before a salacious smile pulled at the corners of his mouth.

Dani gave him an odd look until she realized she'd run out of the barn wearing only her T-shirt and panties.

Heat crept into her cheeks. *Jerk.* She wanted to catch up to him as he crossed the gravel road and scream it at him.

She hadn't liked Jake from the start. She certainly thought less of him now, especially this thing with Bonnie. If he was such a great guy he wouldn't have allowed her to get pissy drunk. Thinking better of it, Dani shut the door, charged up the steps, and down the hall. Entering her room, she turned off the overhead. Surrounded in total darkness with only the filter of light coming from the thin window, she peered out.

Jake ducked inside the bunkhouse with Bonnie, and Dani relaxed until a small car looped around in the parking lot of Lansing Racing Stables.

Icy tingles shot across her skin.

The car passed by and headed down Whistledown's driveway, its brake lights popping on before making a left turn.

Blake.

Odd. He'd made no mention of swinging by his stable when he dropped her off. He hadn't. His car passed Kevin's coming in.

Dani shivered, and she wrapped her arms around her.

He'd come back.

Chapter Twenty-One

"**D**ANI!" TURK'S BOOMING VOICE ECHOED UP TO THE SECOND LEVEL of the barn.

It shook Dani's sleep-deprived brain. *Really?* He knew where she'd been late last night. Knew she had every right to sleep in on her day off. It was clearly Sunday. She opened one eye and was met with Jimmy's furry butt curled up against the crook of her neck. Pulling the blanket over both their heads, she moaned, recalling the last time she had seen Turk. *Ugh.* Lansing.

"Rise and shine, sunshine."

Dani whipped off the blanket, sending Jimmy flying, and creating a static mess of her hair. If he was going to give her hell for fraternizing with the enemy, she hadn't noted it in his voice. But still. She owed him an explanation. "I can ex—" Dani's brows furrowed.

Sunshine?

Turk poked his balding gray head through one side of the blanket, an uncharacteristic smile pulling at the corners of his mouth. "Here I thought you'd jump at the chance to ride Midnight Edition."

Dani blinked and shoved her hair back from her face. "You're serious?"

"Daniel and I were talk—"

"Me father?"

"In the barn as we speak." He shoved a helmet through the blanket and tossed it at her.

Dani shot up to a sitting position and caught it before it clunked her in the head. "What's this?"

"Flynn," he said with that I'm-going-to-enlighten-you voice. "I always thought you were smarter than that."

It was a silly question, but she hadn't been expecting his cheerful attitude or the chance to ride Midnight Edition.

"Don't analyze it. Get up," he grumped, more like the Turk Bendix she'd come to know, and ducked out of her room. Boots clunked down the hall and down the steps.

Dani jumped up in a flurry and threw on her jeans, her only bra, and a T-shirt. She'd promised herself, now that she'd gotten paid, to pick up some much needed clothes. She hoped to accomplish that today . . . sometime. Slipping on a pair of socks and her boots, she grabbed the helmet and stopped. This was her chance, and she needed a little piece of her ma with her. Dani ripped through her backpack until she found her wallet. She unzipped it and dug for the familiar round twenty-pence coin. Her mother had sworn by its luck. Dani grimaced. The woman had died young and tragically. But it was her ma's, so she tucked it into her front jean pocket and flew down the steps to the stalls.

Sister stood saddled in the aisle, and Dani stopped and looked around. "I thought . . ."

Her father slipped out from the mare's stall. "I didn't feel at all comfortable with you riding that colt."

She should be angry, but the thought behind the act melted the edges of her heart. "It's a fine choice for me, I think."

Dani continued down the aisle. "Did you saddle her, then?" She patted Sister's muzzle. She was a good horse with long legs meant for racing.

"While Turk took a phone call." He nodded behind her.

Turk came meandering out of his office holding some type of wire. He held out his hand. "Let's see the helmet."

Dani gave it to him, and he handed her a roll of black tape. He laid the wire inside her helmet. "Rip me off a piece."

"How long?"

"Four inches or so."

She tore the specified length off and handed it to him.

Turk pulled his glasses down onto his nose and taped the wire inside. "That should do it." He handed the helmet to Dani with a satisfied look.

Dani examined the wire. "What is it?"

"Earpiece." Daniel's hand came down on her shoulder. "From what Turk tells me—and the little I witnessed the other day—you have a knack for riding."

He'd offered her the job of exercise rider but she hadn't even started yet. This seemed a bit extreme. "I don't understand."

"Nothing to understand." Turk grabbed Sister's lead rope and started down the aisle. "Just ride."

Dani raised her brows to her father.

"Don't mind him, Dani." He reached out his hand to her. "I'll not be surprised to find you ride like your mother."

She took his hand. It was warm and solid and folded over hers with encouragement. She'd likely disappoint him. "I'm not me ma."

He shook her hand in his while they walked toward the open barn door. "No. You're not." He stopped in front of the door and turned. "You're me daughter and a Fallon."

They stood in the shadows, his expression difficult to read, but his voice resonated with sincerity, his brogue more pronounced than usual.

"Do you think it's possible, then?" She wrinkled her brows.

"As sure as the sun is shining, lass." He stepped out into the warm summer morning with her at his side. "If it's a jockey you want. Then it's a jockey you'll be."

"What's the holdup?" Turk called from the outside rail of the track.

Daniel waved to him. "Just a little fatherly talk is all." He leaned his head in conspiratorially. "Kick up some dust, me girl," he said and let her hand go.

It was what she needed and something quite unexpected. It warmed her heart. Dani slipped the helmet on her head and snapped it into place, the soft sponge of the earpiece against her ear. She strode with confidence toward Turk with one question on her mind. "How do I talk to you?"

He laughed. "Your job is to listen." He keyed the small radio in his hand.

Static filled her left ear, and she blushed at her arrogance. She should be grateful. The opportunity alone sent her pulse racing. Dani nodded and slipped between the rails.

Thick fingers laced her arm.

Dani angled her head back. Turk leveled a pair of serious blue eyes on her. "If my hunch is right, you prepared to go all the way?"

Racing for Starlite? That was what this was about. She just assumed her father had been talking about her distant future. She'd love nothing more than to follow in her ma's footsteps. But there were considerations to take into account. She wouldn't feel at all good about competing with Chipper.

"Flynn?"

Dani jerked at Turk's agitated voice. "Y-yes."

"Good." He let her go.

She grabbed for the reins, mounting Sister. It wasn't likely to happen, and if it did? She'd worry then. For now she'd concentrate on the track and the mare's capabilities. She pulled her reins to the left and positioned the mare onto the track. Leaning over, she patted her neck. "I'm depending on you to keep me from looking the fool."

Sister whinnied, shaking her head. "I know. You say that now."

"Flynn!"

Dani jerked in the saddle, Turk's raspy voice ripping through her eardrum. Perhaps this wasn't at all smart.

"Enough chitchat."

Laughter rolled up her chest just then, and she waved him on, giving the mare a quick kick in her sides. Did her ears deceive her? Or was that humor in his voice? The old bollocks did have a bit of fun in him after all. Kevin would do well to spend more time with his father.

"Warm her up." Turk's voice echoed in her helmet.

Dani gave Sister some rein and nudged her forward. She took to the dirt track well, kicking up that dust her father mentioned earlier. They passed a few riders and their mounts, and Dani got an awful thought. After last night, she'd be completely mortified running into Blake. Not that it had been her fault. But it had been awkward, to say the least, when he dropped her off. He'd made a joke, and gave her a peck on the cheek, and probably wished he'd never offered so gallantly to protect her pride where Kevin was concerned.

"Watch the turn."

Oops. Dani pulled the reins to the left. It was Turk's biggest gripe—tight on the turns. They hugged the rail, the mare taking it with ease.

"Nice."

Something close to pride filled her chest. Turk had trusted her—gambled with Mr. Porter's mare. She wondered if she'd ever actually meet him—Porter. He seemed more phantom than man.

"How's she looking?" Turk asked.

A bundle of nerves and pure exhilaration, she passed them and gave them a thumbs-up.

"Way to go, me girl." It was her father's voice, out of breath and laughing.

There was a tussle and a clunk. "Give me that!"

Dani rolled her lips in. *Someone's in trouble.*

Turk's voice was terse. "Take this lap and bring her in."

She took the last couple of furlongs at an even pace. Turk hadn't given instructions to speed up. She didn't want to incite him. Seemed her father had already done that. But then being a longtime friend he could more than likely get away with it. She reined the mare in alongside the rail and couldn't stop from smiling. "She's a fine horse." Dani grabbed the reins in her hand, preparing to dismount.

"Whoa, whoa. Where you going, Flynn?"

"But I thought—"

"Back up. We're just getting started."

"You looked great, Dani." That came from Fritz, who must have strolled over from his stable while she was taking the last eighth of a mile.

"You're too kind." She was breathing heavy and couldn't stop from smiling. *Did he say just getting started?*

"A real horsewoman, to be sure." Daniel winked at her, and it was as if he'd always been a part of her life.

"Thanks, Da." It was out before she knew what to do with it. The last thing she wanted to do was rush his affection—if he had any at all for her.

He beamed up at her, his blue eyes twinkling in the sun, and something told her that her worries were unfounded.

Turk handed Daniel a stopwatch. "You remember how one of these works?"

"Aye. It's been years but I can manage."

"Years?" Dani gave him a lift of her brow.

"Trainer in Ireland. 'Twas a lifetime ago I'm afraid."

He'd never said. But then she knew near to nothing about him. Plus, it was only yesterday he'd come, admitting the truth. Of course, she had a lifetime to get to . . .

Dani's stomach twisted. It wasn't like she was a child. The sad truth of it was, her da, the man she had wanted nothing to do with for the last eight years, had now become someone she wanted to get to know and to love. How much time did they realistically have together?

"Dani?" Daniel had moved close to the rail. "You ill, sweetheart?"

She shook her head, knowing she couldn't possibly share those thoughts with him. "Not at all." She smiled for his benefit. "Nervous mostly."

"You'll do fine." He reached through the rail and patted her leg.

"Turk, I think you might consider giving Daniel a try with the mic."

"Ya do, Bailey?" Turk placed his hand on his hip, the notion, based on his stance, an unpopular one.

"I'm perfectly fine at timing," her father said.

"No, no." Turk handed her da the radio. "Just push the top button."

Her father slid his glasses up on his nose. "This little thing here?"

The earpiece crackled in Dani's ear.

"That's the one, and don't yell into to it like she's deaf," Turk shot back.

"You might not be too far off, Turk," Fritz said, winking at Dani.

Daniel pulled his head back with mock disapproval. "Fritzy, you ganging up on me, too, then?"

"What are friends for?" Fritz rapped her da on his back.

"Enough yammering." Turk snatched the watch from Daniel's hand. "In case you two have forgotten, time is money."

Both Daniel and Fritz rolled their lips in, silently laughing with their eyes. Judging by the ripening shade in Turk's cheeks, he was more than done with *their* chitchat. And it seemed so was Sister, antsy and pulling on her reins.

Dani twitched in the saddle and patted the mare's neck. "She's more than ready, I think."

Turk leveled his gaze on Dani. "When I say go, give it all you got." He glanced at Daniel. "You got this?"

Daniel held up the radio, squinting, and smiled at Dani. "As long as I hit the right button."

Turk rolled his eyes, shaking his head.

Fritz went to the rail. "Show us what you got, lass," he said in an Irish brogue.

Dani laughed. She liked Fritz. She was sure it wasn't often the competition rallied behind its opponent. She certainly wouldn't see the likes of Blake Lansing supporting his foe, but then again he was all for stiff competition. Those Mercedes' taillights from last night forced their way into her head.

Could he have been in the barn last night? She was being ridiculous. It was only pure coincidence Blake had been at his stable around the same time she'd heard the thumps. Now she could believe that Bonnie's friend Jake would be up to no good. His eyes were shifty, unlike Blake's that were warm and—

"Fine day for a race." Horse and rider came up alongside Dani, leaving her in their shadow, and she cringed.

He's not serious. And where the devil did he come from? It was like thinking of him made him miraculously appear.

"How 'bout a small wager, then?"

"Da!" Dani swung on her father.

Daniel shoved the radio at Fritz and dug into his back pants pocket. "Twenty dollars says she'll be no more than three furlongs behind at the finish."

Dani's brows snapped together. Here she thought, as her father, he'd bet her to win.

"How far?" That was Turk and, interestingly enough, in support.

"What do you think? Eight furlongs." He connected with Dani. "That's a mile—twice around the track, sweetheart, in case you're wondering."

Dani knew good and well the distance, and she wasn't at all pleased about this race.

"Count me in." Fritz waved a twenty he'd pulled from his front pocket.

Her father gathered Fritz's and Turk's money with his own.

"No. Fritz. Me father spoke out of turn. I can't possibly compete against him." She locked her sights on Blake.

He sat atop his steed, the wind ruffling his dark hair, and flashed her a gorgeous smile as he, too, pulled out his wager—the scoundrel.

"It isn't a fair race," she whispered to Blake, hard under her breath.

"Watch and learn, beautiful," he whispered back and handed his twenty to her father.

Dani's mouth fell open in disbelief. He'd mentioned honing her skills last night, but she didn't need to learn from the likes of him. Oh, he was bloody handsome in his tight white shirt that left nothing to the imagination and his black riding breeches that clung to his muscular thighs. He'd only make a fool of her. Her first time racing on this track, where he rode every day. Even three furlongs behind weren't good odds against an accomplished horseman like Blake. This chance with Turk would be lost to her.

"Could I have a word with you?" She motioned to Blake.

"Absolutely." He reined his horse several feet in front of the three elderly men who had clearly lost their minds.

Dani brought her mount up next to his. "If this is about last night—"

"I don't scare that easily, Dani." His hand came up and caressed her lower back.

Dani's insides tumbled sweetly, and she blushed. She should swat his hand away, but judging by the angle and the deep conversation at the rail—or was it more argument—no one was the wiser. Dani lifted her chin to Blake. "Then is it only the women you're attracted to that you choose to embarrass?"

"Don't sell yourself short." His eyes connected with hers. They were warm and caring and not the least bit brash. "I meant what I said. Watch and learn. You're a solid rider. You just need to take risks."

She wanted to laugh out loud. Since leaving Ireland she'd risked it all. *Ask Kevin.* With that last thought in mind, she gathered her reins. "If it's a race you're wanting, Mr. Lansing, it's a race you'll get." She grinned at him and kicked the mare's sides, moving her to the middle of the track.

He shook his head and smiled. "That's my girl."

His girl? She was sure he'd meant it figuratively. But it didn't stop the frisson of awareness of him as a man from tinkering with her emotions. She *was* attracted to him, and the distraction was maddening. Surely having a fascination for two men counted as a risk.

"Time is money," Turk barked, taking all the cash from her da and handing it to an unsuspecting outsider—Kevin.

Dani's stomach churned. She was going to fail. They all knew this going in. The only question was by how much. Still, she'd been okay with that, until now.

"What's this?" He didn't take his gaze off her.

Oh, Lord.

Chapter Twenty-Two

S HE WAS UNDISCIPLINED, A RISK TAKER, AND THE WOMAN DISRUPTING his perfectly planned life. Kevin gripped the cash his father had thrown at him. He should be angry—angry that she was anywhere near Lansing—but as he had so earnestly pointed out to her last night, the kiss that had left him rock hard was a mistake. He had effectively placed her off-limits, his self-imposed policy leaving Dani free to do as she pleased—according to her.

"Look at her go, me boy!" Daniel smiled widely. Judging by the radio in his hand, Dani was aware of his excitement and, it would appear, pride each time he keyed the mic.

His own father was glued to the stopwatch and the track, his only thoughts—if Kevin was a betting man—the bottom line. He'd long said his piece in regard to his father's livelihood. It was a racket. One he'd never make a fortune in unless he was the man calling the shots. Even then it was a risky business, one fraught with expensive vet bills and overhead.

"That a girl, lass!" With an Irish lilt to his voice, Fritz raised his fist the moment she passed them after her first lap.

Kevin chuckled. Although not Irish, the man seemed enamored by Dani and her sweet brogue. Kevin couldn't help but smile. Fritz wasn't the only one.

Low in the saddle, her thighs pressed hard against the mare, she rode by on the half mile dirt track on the outside, close enough the ground pounded beneath his feet. Standing only steps away, it gave Kevin a whole new perspective on a sport he had grown to despise. Or was it the woman with her serious expression and dogged determination that had his pulse sprinting? He couldn't help but cheer her on.

"Move her to the inside," Kevin's father bellowed.

Daniel patted the air. "She knows, she knows. She's just waiting for a break is all."

And here he thought Lansing might cut her some slack. Kevin moved to the rail. Regardless, she was only four furlongs behind with another lap to go. Kevin leaned into his father. "What's her time?"

His father's eyes darted from the track to the stopwatch. "Sixty-nine," he said, the words rushing off his lips in a panic.

If Kevin didn't know any better, Dani had just become that lucky four leaf clover Turk Bendix had been searching for in the weeds all these years.

At least he had the good sense to listen for once. He recognized the mare, his shoulders leveling off—not too high. It was one of the reasons he'd put off the yard work until later this afternoon. He didn't want her riding that big-ass stallion. From what he could remember about Porter's horses, Nothing Like a Sister had a sweet disposition and, it would seem, tremendous heart. The mare hammered the track on the far side.

Damn. She had a chance of catching up.

"She's making her move." Daniel rapped Fritz on the back and keyed the radio. "Good girl, Dani."

She'd taken the inside rail. Kevin shoved the cash in the back pocket of his cargo shorts, his body wound tight like a coil. They remained neck and neck.

Daniel keyed the mic again. "You've got him now, sweetheart."

Dani and Lansing flew by, sending clods of dirt skyward as they approached the far turn. *Unbelievable.* Kevin gripped the top rail. She had a real shot at winning. Coming around the final turn, Lansing pulled ahead by a length.

"You're doing great, Dani. Hold 'em," Daniel said.

Lansing had her by three lengths when Dani took the corner tight on the homestretch. She was gaining, edging up.

"Holy shit!" Kevin grabbed hold of his father's shoulder. "She's going to—"

A projectile whizzed past Kevin's head, and he flinched. *What the . . . ?*

Dani's horse stumbled and fell, sending her airborne. Kevin's gut twisted—the sickening crack of her helmet deafening when she hit the ground.

Christ. Kevin hopped the rail. "Call an ambulance!" He hauled ass across the track, his whole existence riveted on the small broken form lying facedown and the riderless horse—skittish as hell—its legs erratic, hooves inching closer to Dani as it pranced around confused. "The horse!"

His father and Fritz charged past, trying to corral the mare as Kevin reached her.

"Dani." His voice shook, and he fell to his knees. He knew not to move her, tried telling his jackhammering heart to quiet. "Come on, Irish, open your eyes."

"*Jesus.* She okay?" Lansing tied off his horse and rushed over with his cell phone glued to his ear.

Footsteps came up behind him, a shadow cutting across Dani's slumberous dove-white face. "Dear God. She breathing, Kevin?" Daniel's voice quivered.

Kevin carefully opened the protective vest Turk insisted his riders wear and concentrated on her diaphragm. Her chest rose and fell in an easy rhythm. "She's breathing."

"Thank God," Daniel said on a heavy breath. "It's a relief."

Not to Kevin. He'd seen his share of motorcycle collisions. This was close enough. He wasn't so much worried about the scrapes on her elbows—they'd mend. It was the jagged crack running the length of her helmet front to back. He hoped the damn thing had protected her brain.

Lansing pocketed his phone, his usual arrogance tempered with concern. "Ambulance on its way." He came down on his haunches and brushed Dani's pale cheek with his fingertips. "Come on, beautiful. You're not off the hook."

Kevin gritted his teeth. If he knew this woman at all, he'd know she had a driving propensity to prove herself. *Damn it.* He guessed he could understand her need, especially with her father here.

But you don't give an addict a needle.

"It's me fault," Daniel moaned. "I bet money on me own daughter."

Kevin kept his gaze on Dani's dove-white complexion. Her dark lashes dusting her pretty face remained closed. With everything in him, he willed her to open her eyes.

CHAPTER TWENTY-THREE

GRANULES OF DIRT CRUNCHED BETWEEN DANI'S TEETH. HER HEAD thumped like when the band from Dublin came to play at Devlin's. Only she wasn't in Ireland, she didn't believe, except for the lilt in the man's sorrowful voice. What had he meant *bet money on . . . ?*

Then it all came flooding back . . . the race . . . the mare. She'd been winning, but against whom? Dani's eyes fluttered open. "It was a good . . ." Her head throbbed, and she grunted through the pain. "Wager . . . I think." She tried to push herself up to her knees to the protest of three men all hovering about her. She raised a tentative hand, slipping her fingers under the helmet to a pulsating knot on her head. She grimaced and tried to stand.

"Not so fast," Kevin said, his voice rough and, perhaps, a little angry. Practiced eyes and hands ran the length of her rib cage. "Any trouble breathing?"

Dani shook her head and was sorry for it when another stabbing pain sliced through her skull. She closed her eyes to the bright sun and waited for it to pass. "What of the mare?" She opened her eyes, searching.

"Turk and Fritz are tending to her, sweetheart," her father said.

"She hurt?" Dani couldn't live with herself if she'd harmed the sweet mare.

"We're more concerned about you." Her father's nervous blue eyes, cloudy with age, zeroed in on her face.

"You took a hard fall." The voice gave Dani a start. *Shite.* She'd been racing *Blake.*

Kevin's hand cradled her neck and the base of her head, tipping it back. "How's your vision?" He held up several fingers. "How many?"

"Three."

"Where is—" Her hair stood on end, and the last memory she had before going down was of the horseshoe. Dani's eyes clung to Kevin's. He was the only one she could tell. "I need—"

The wail of a siren, followed by the flashing lights of an ambulance, turned down the small paved road to the track.

"You think you can walk on your own?" Kevin unclipped her helmet, easing it off, and handed it to Blake.

"Yes. I can manage." She reached out to him for support. His arm went around her waist, lifting her to her feet. Something wet trickled down her cheek.

"Jeez, Dani." Blake took a handkerchief from his pocket and placed it against her temple and cheek. "You must think I'm a complete ass."

It was then she realized it was blood she'd felt on her face.

"That makes two of us," Kevin grunted under his breath.

Dani frowned at Kevin and then turned to Blake. "I was just as much to blame."

The four, including her da, made their way toward the waiting ambulance with Kevin's arm around her, Blake's hand pressing his handkerchief to her head, and her father leading in front.

Daniel glanced back. "How we doing, sweetheart?"

"Like I've been thrown from a horse," she said with complete seriousness.

Both Kevin and Blake chuckled, heading up the slight incline to the ambulance.

Her father beaded in on her, not the least bit amused with her humor. If she was looking for a scolding, it was coming. Kevin sat her down on a gurney, and the attendant took over for Blake, the two stepping aside and, as remarkable as it was, having a civil conversation.

"You're not the least bit funny, young lady. Here I've just been reunited with me youngest child. One I didn't even know existed until a week ago—and then thought I might lose—" He broke off, red faced and flustered.

"Da." She reached for his hand while the attendant examined her head. She'd thought the same of him—losing him, but because of his age. "I'm sorry. I only meant it as a joke."

He held her hand tight, his eyes moist with emotion. "No more jokes. Or races for that matter."

"How about I agree to no more jokes." She winced when the attendant dabbed her scraped elbow with a disinfectant pad. She couldn't give her word to not racing or even riding another horse. Until the thing with the horseshoe, she'd been living an incredible dream. Dani's shoulders slumped. Of course, Turk was probably none too pleased with the outcome of the race and what she'd done to his poor horse. "Da, would you do me a favor?"

The attendant flashed a penlight in her eyes. "Let's check your blood pressure." The heavyset medical worker wrapped a pressure cuff around her arm and pumped.

"Only if you agree to be more careful."

She nodded. "Will you check on the mare? Let me know how she's faring?"

"I did you one better. Your sister Bren's on her way. She's Dr. Winters's new, certified vet assistant."

Bren? Dani's brows furrowed with consternation. She was filthy dirty and not in the best shape to making her sister's acquaintance for the second time. Maybe her father had come to accept her—accept his own doing when it came to Dani's existence. But what of the two women who had believed they were the only ones?

An engine rumbled in the distance. Dani tried with her left hand to tuck her hair behind her ear.

"She's here, sweetheart." He kissed her forehead. "I'll bring her to you." He hurried off, leaving her alone until Kevin and Blake strode over, their expressions grim.

Grand. Either they were knocking heads, or they knew something about the mare she didn't.

"How's she doing?" Kevin asked the medical worker.

"Might be a concussion." The attendant removed the cuff. "Blood pressure's normal. I'd still suggest she get checked out by one of the ER docs."

Dani gripped the edge of the gurney. "I don't require a doctor." She'd need insurance for that. If emergency rooms in America were anything like Ireland's, the bill could be astronomical.

Kevin narrowed in on her. "You should get checked out."

She motioned for him to move closer. He took a step and leaned in.

"I haven't any insurance," she whispered.

"I'll pay for it," he whispered back.

Dani shook her head. "You've helped me enough," she said under her breath.

"Then you're taking the day off."

Considering that she was off, she could more than accommodate him. "After I check in on the mare." She gave him a sweet smile.

He shook his head like she'd become the biggest pain in his arse and then gave his attention to the attendant. "Have any discharge instructions for possible concussions?"

"Got it up front." He disappeared around the open door of the ambulance.

"Hey, beautiful, how's your head?" Blake bent down to her height while she sat on the gurney, waiting.

"It doesn't hurt as much."

He stroked the back of her head. "Let me make it up to you."

Dani's heart sped up. "You did nothing wrong. I should have paid more attention."

"How about dinner?"

"Not tonight." Kevin stood leaning against the frame of the ambulance with his arms crossed like a father refusing his daughter's suitor.

Dani's cheeks warmed. She had a brain. At the moment it was jumbled and painful but still capable of taking her health into consideration. "I think what Kevin meant was that I should rest today."

Blake looked from Kevin to Dani and then back to Kevin, perplexed. He pointed with his finger from Dani to Kevin. "You two . . . ?"

"No," Dani said forcefully, with Kevin not too far behind, echoing her same sentiment.

An awkward quiet fell on the trio until Blake's horse whinnied from the track, loud and sorrowful, and Dani was grateful to the stallion for breaking the awkwardness. He had to have been tied up on the rail for at least thirty minutes.

"I think Bart's expressing his displeasure." He dropped a kiss on top of Dani's head. "I'll check on you later tonight and discuss that dinner." He strode down the incline toward his stallion.

Bren rushed down in a pair of Bermuda shorts and a sleeveless pink maternity top with their father close behind.

"Bren, slow down. You're liable to fall and hurt yourself," Daniel admonished.

"You okay?" Holding a black medical bag, Bren pushed past Kevin to Dani's relief and, she hoped, interrupted his train of thought. He'd more than likely have something smart to say about Blake.

Bren's russet brows snapped together, her brown eyes taking in every inch of Dani's tousled hair, the bloody knot on her head, and scraped elbows.

"A bruised pride, perhaps." Dani smiled sheepishly.

"She's going straight to her room after you reassure her about the mare," Kevin said.

Bren laughed out loud. "You put her in timeout for wrecking a horse and getting dirty?"

Dani rolled her lips in, trying not to laugh. She'd missed a lot not growing up with these two.

"Always a smart ass." Kevin pushed off the ambulance door. "She might have a concussion and needs to rest."

"Here you go." The attendant held out a sheet of paper. "Ibuprofen, ice, and rest for twenty-four hours."

Kevin snagged it from Bren before she could grab it. "Rest. Just like I said."

"She will." Bren helped Dani down. "Show me your horse, sweetie, and we'll take a look." Bren's arm came around Dani's shoulders.

The more Dani thought about it, with Bren being almost nine months pregnant it didn't seem at all smart to have her working on a wounded thousand pound animal. Dani angled back. "But should you with the baby?"

"Officially I'm on light duty," she whispered "But for you and your horse I'm making an exception."

"But . . ."

She winked at Dani. "Don't worry I'll be careful."

All her misgivings, and Bren was nothing but kind, even loving. "Thank you. Turk took her back to her stall."

They went as a group with Bren holding Dani close at her side, her father shuffling next to them, and Kevin trudging behind like this had turned into a huge time suck on his Sunday. They entered the barn, the temperature dropping with the shade and the fans distributed throughout the stalls.

Turk and Fritz met them outside Sister's stall.

Turk shook his head. "She's limping pretty bad."

Dani started to move past Turk when Fritz caught her arm. "How's the head, lass?" A pair of worried eyes landed on the goose egg on her temple.

"A little banged up." She gave him a quick smile, gently pulling away from his grasp, and slipped inside the stall. "Hey, pretty girl."

Sister nickered softly.

"I know. It was my fault. I should have checked your shoes." She blamed it on the ball and her fanciful ideas. Dani ran her hand down Sister's right hind leg, lifting her foot. Just as she suspected, the shoe was missing. She also did a quick inventory of all her legs. She had some minor lacerations, and her coat was dusty from the fall. Dani stood. "I'll get you cleaned up," she said, lifting her hand to the mare's muzzle, hoping for that lick that meant she was forgiven. The mare's nostrils flared, sniffing for—

"Looking for those damn peppermints," Turk said with exasperation.

Dani swung around, her eyes wide with surprise.

With his arms folded over his protruding belly, Turk stared her down. "Flynn, there's not a lot that goes on around here that I don't know about."

Dani gulped. She wasn't likely to lose her job because of it. At least she didn't think. But if he was aware of the special treat she doled out to the horses, would he also know she'd been in his office using his computer?

"I didn't think you'd mind. They like them." She gave a half smile. "I won't do it again."

"I have a soft spot for sweets myself." He leaned over the stall conspiratorially. "I had Bonnie pick up a bag, seeing as you're out," he whispered.

Dani's bottom lip dropped in astonishment. He wasn't the grump she believed him to be, after all. If anything, he reminded her of a grandfatherly type with a penchant for doing little things that could put a smile on one's face. And amazing as it was, she couldn't wipe the silly grin from her lips.

Turk Bendix was a true contradiction.

Dani reached over the stall door and gave him a hug, her arm knocking his glasses. "I promise to see that their teeth are brushed every night before bed."

Rattled, he pushed her away. "What the hell, Flynn," he grumbled, straightening his glasses.

He wasn't the only one taken aback. Kevin appeared thoughtful. Perhaps remembering a man far different than the one he butted heads with as an adult. "Come on." Kevin waved her out. "You've seen the horse."

True. But she hadn't gotten to spend near enough time with her sister Bren. News of her unexpected visit had given way to a bad case of the nerves. Dani hadn't given either one of her sisters a reason to care about her. If anything, she'd turned their world on its side. She'd left them with more questions than answers. Still. Bren came and had immediately picked up where they'd left off—sticking up for her where Kevin was concerned.

Dani made her way out, feeling like the youngest child who had to go to bed before the older ones. "But I haven't had a chance to talk with Bren yet."

Bren patted her shoulder and winked. "I won't leave before coming . . ." She frowned and looked upward. "Dad says your room's upstairs?"

"Yes, and down the walkway."

"I'll come up and visit and give you a full report."

Dani nodded. "She tumbled hard. Lost her shoe."

"It missed Kevin's head by degrees." Her father shook his head.

"Which reminds me." Turk dug into his ample front trouser pocket and shoved a horseshoe at Kevin. "Imagine that. Found it near the picnic table." He didn't need to elaborate. His sarcastic tone put Kevin on notice. This wasn't by happenstance.

Kevin took it. "I guess you expect me to dust it for prints?"

"I don't care what the hell you do with it as long as you get me some answers."

Bren's brows snapped together. "What's going on?"

"Nothing you need to concern yourself with." Kevin opened the stall for her.

"Afraid I'll make it my business?" Bren winked at Dani and entered the stall with Turk slipping in behind her.

Dani eyed her father. Surely that comment had some underlying meaning.

"You'd think these two never grew up." Her father chuckled and put his arm around her. "How's that head of yours?"

If there was more to it than that, Dani couldn't say. She might never learn all there was about her newfound family. They had so much history together—history they didn't have with her. Dani cradled her head in her hand. "I'll take a pain reliever."

"I've got Advil in me truck," her father said. "How about I run get it?"

"Grand."

He shuffled down the aisle and cleared the door.

Dani pulled Kevin aside, still rubbing her head. "Can I speak with you in private?"

"You dizzy?" He grabbed her by her arms, concerned eyes tunneling into her.

"No. I'm fine. It's about what happened on the track."

His fingers tightened on her upper arms. "Lansing do something to cause this?"

"Of course not," she shot back. Dani lifted her chin to him. "That would make it easy on you, I imagine. Pinning it on Blake."

Something registered in those serious eyes of his. "How'd it all play out? The race?"

"What do you mean?"

"You initiate it?"

"N—"

Dani's brows knitted together. Blake had asked her.

"Something jog your memory?" Kevin peered down his nose at her.

She squared her shoulders. "He asked me." She wasn't going to dodge his questions or allow Kevin to poison her mind where Blake was concerned. She'd already done a lot of that since last night and with no good reason.

He chuckled. "An experienced horseman asking a groom to race?"

"So what are you trying to say? He purposely asked me to race, hoping the shoe would come off and I'd fall?"

He snorted. "I think there's way too much drama with you. If anything, judging by the way Lansing's sniffing around you, he—"

"You think he was going to let me win." Dani placed her hands on her hips. Of course Kevin would think that. He didn't believe she could swat at a gnat and kill it.

He shrugged.

Err. Dani clenched her fists. "Think what you want." Kevin hadn't been privy to her and Blake's conversations last night on the dance floor. It made perfect sense to her.

He grunted something under his breath, no doubt uncharitable where Blake was concerned. He didn't like him—didn't like that he showed an interest in her.

"You don't really believe a crime's been committed."

He took a deep breath through his nose. "I think there's a simple explanation for everything."

She hoped there really was a simple explanation. She rubbed her lower back that had begun to ache. People and horses were now getting hurt. "I thought so, too."

"But not anymore?" Kevin gave her a lift of his brow.

"Same horse, same shoe, twice in two days." Dani tilted her head. "You don't find that the least bit odd?"

He moved her down the aisle and into Turk's office. "Sit." He placed her down in the chair—the same chair she'd been in last night when she'd heard the thump—his eyes an exasperated shade of brown. "Look, Turk Junior. There's nothing going on here. If there was, I'd investigate it. It's just my old man doing what he does best—making something out of nothing."

"Yes, I know he has issues with"—Dani checked to make sure Bren and Turk remained in the stall—"paranoia." She pushed with her feet. The chair rolled back, and she stood. "Last night after you left, I came down to shower. When I was drying off . . ."

A smile tugged at the corners of his firm lips like his mind had wandered.

"Are you not listening to a word I'm saying?"

"Oh, I'm listening." His lips quirked again.

What the . . . ? Confused, Dani tried to recall where she'd left off. Shower. *Drying off.* Heat crept into her cheeks, and her mouth fell open. "You perv!"

"Shh." His shoulders rose like she was going to clobber him in the head. Dani spied the bag of peppermints sitting on Turk's desk and considered doing so. Although tempting, she'd probably knock him out cold.

"Do you think you could take what I'm saying seriously for a moment?" Dani placed her hands on her hips. "Shoes don't just fly off, nails don't simply fall out. Someone removed them, and a horse may be lame because of it. Not to mention, on a personal note, it hurt like bloody hell sailing through the air and landing like a sack of potatoes."

His lips thinned.

Ah, that got you. Now she'd drill it home.

"Someone came into the barn last night after you left."

His brows furrowed. "Is that odd?"

"Since I've been here I don't know of anyone being in the barn before five."

"I take it you didn't see whoever it was?"

Now that was a sticking point for sure. She shook her head.

"Dani, it's an old barn," he said, like *she* was paranoid.

Dani shrugged. "Don't believe me."

"Believe what?" Turk stood at the doorway to his office with his hands on his hips, eyeing them.

Kevin narrowed in on his father. "Now you've got her believing in your conspiracy theories." Kevin threw up his hands at Dani. "You may as well tell him."

"I . . ." Dani swallowed hard. Turk's incisive stare made it difficult to speak, much less know where to begin, and, as usual, she couldn't tell him exactly what she had been doing. "It was late, around half past three. I'd just taken me shower when I heard it."

"Heard what?" Turk said.

"A thump, like the way the back door of the barn shuts."

"Someone was in the barn?" Turk's voice rose.

"I didn't see anyone." Chills raced along her skin. Technically, she had not seen anyone in the barn. But she was leaving out an important detail. Knowing Turk, he'd jump on it. Still, she wasn't about to accuse a man without absolute proof. Blake had every right and reason to drive back to his stable whenever he liked.

Turk threw up his hands. "I guess this isn't enough for you to get off that duff of yours and launch a full-fledged investigation." Turk poked his finger in Kevin's face. "Before Bailey left, he told me they found compressed hay pellets mixed in with his chestnut's feed this morning. He's over there checking their horseshoes now."

Dani's head swung around. "Delicate Maneuver?"

"You got it," Turk said.

Dani trembled. Changing up a horse's feed could cause colic. "He okay?"

"A little gassy." He eyed Kevin. "It could have been worse."

Kevin raked his fingers through his hair. "All right. I'll check it out."

Bren came down the aisle rubbing her back and carrying her medical bag. Dani scooted out and met Bren, taking it from her. "Here, let me help you."

"Thanks." Bren gave her a tired smile and put her hand on Dani's shoulder. "She's sore. Must have twisted her leg when she went down. The horseshoe ripped off part of her hoof."

If only she'd taken the time before bed to check all of her horses' shoes.

Turk ambled out of his office, scowling. "Which means I'm down a horse, and a lame one at that."

Dani was beginning to think Turk never had a positive thought.

"In the meantime"—Bren opened up her bag, its handle still clutched between Dani's fingers, and handed her a tube—"give her this orally twice a day for the next three days. The bute will help with the pain."

Turk took the tube from Dani's hand. "Arturo's taking over for her."

Panic rose in Dani's chest. He really was going to let her go after what happened. "Mr. Bendix, I—"

"What are you rambling about, Flynn?" He gave her the oddest look. "Thought you'd be thrilled to train to be a jockey."

"Jockey?"

Turk scrubbed his face. "What did you think we were doing this morning?"

"I thought you said exercise rider."

"That was before you fell off the damned horse."

He made no sense, and she didn't think it was wise to argue the point, but she wanted to be sure she understood completely. "I just thought after what happened . . ."

Turk eyed his son. "Was going to happen to anyone who rode Sister this morning."

And there it was. The man was truly fair, and she gained a world of respect for Turk Bendix in that instant. But it was more than that. His words had also opened her eyes to the turmoil she had going on inside her. Blake seemed to genuinely like her. If he'd tampered with the horseshoe, then he knew once he saw her on Sister today, Dani would be in danger of getting hurt.

He wasn't behind it.

"If we're done here, I've got yard work." Kevin's abrupt voice brought Dani out of her meanderings.

"Don't forget that investigation." Turk wagged a finger at him.

"I'm on it." He turned to leave.

Bren put her arm around Turk's shoulders. "Kev, your dad's coming for Fourth of July. How about you?"

"What time?"

"Three to whenever."

"I'm working but I'll try and stop by."

"You coming?" Bren asked Dani.

"Da invited me, but I hadn't had time to ask . . ."

"She's going," Turk grumped and then raised his brows to Kevin.

"Bringing the bank manager?"

Shite. I wanted to go shopping.

Kevin gave his father a look that said *none of your business* and waved them off. "I'll see ya." He headed down the aisle and disappeared through the barn door.

Which meant he would be bringing her tomorrow, and all Dani had to choose from out of her vast wardrobe was her bitta fluff clothes from her backpack, Kate's soiled dress, or her barn clothes—none of which could compete with a woman like Kristin the bank manager.

Grand.

CHAPTER TWENTY-FOUR

"FLYNN!" TURK'S TERSE VOICE ROSE UP TO THE SECOND LEVEL OF THE barn. "You forgot these damn peppermints."

Dani stopped mid-step, her hand coming to her mouth. "Oops." She patted Bren's arm. "It's the first . . ." Dani blanched. She couldn't even say door. "Blanket on the left. I'll be right back." Dani hustled down the steps.

Turk came out of his office, holding a large bag of candy. "They are to be their bedtime snack. And . . . you just can't give them to a select few."

She grinned at that. "They'll all get a sweet bedtime snack. You've got me word."

He nodded and handed her the bag. "I'm giving you off for the picnic tomorrow afternoon. But I expect you out on the track at eight a.m. sharp."

"I thought I started at five."

"You're in training now, Flynn."

She should be grateful to sleep in a few extra hours. "Who will care for the horses?"

"I'll split them up between grooms."

"I don't mind the early hours. And I don't expect any extra pay. Would you mind too terribly if I remained their groom?"

Turk pulled on his chin, debating.

"At least allow me to feed them their breakfast."

"That's reasonable, I suppose."

"Thank you." Dani gave him a quick hug.

He didn't reciprocate it—the hug. But the slight smile tugging at his mouth when she pulled away told her, secretly, he was warming to the idea of receiving her affection. And as inconceivable as it seemed a week ago, she was becoming fond of the cantankerous trainer.

He waved her off, rotated his chair, and scooped up Jimmy, handing him over. "Go on. Your sister's waiting."

Dani juggled the cat and the peppermints. "If he's becoming a nuisance—"

"Nope. And it wouldn't do any good." His lips quirked. "Cats seem to seek me out." He turned and shut his door and locked it, pocketing the key. "I'll see ya."

Dani's stomach dropped like a piece of lead. Of all the times to start locking his door.

Damn horseshoe.

Perhaps her new life was falling into place. But her old one could be ripping at the seams, and she wouldn't even know it—unless she found out what was on the thumb drive.

"Ahh," Dani moaned and stomped her foot. She forgot to ask him about training with Solley. She didn't know who Turk had in mind for a horse. Chipper had Midnight Edition, and Sister was out. George and Joey were sound, but she'd connected with Solley. Even with his behavior problems, she felt sure they could work through them if only she could ride him.

Then Dani remembered Bren. "I'll be right up!" She sat Jimmy down, held tight to the peppermints, and flew up the steps in a nervous flurry. The blanket remained in place, and she moved it aside and stepped in.

Bren stood with her back to Dani, staring out the small window that came to just about her shoulders. "This isn't going to work." Her words were severe, her expression grim when she turned to face Dani.

A warm flash of panic rose in Dani's chest, and the pain of rejection pinched the backs of her eyes, hard. She willed her tears away and squared her shoulders. "I know it's a shock." She moved into the small room, her palms becoming damp with sweat. "I just thought—"

"There isn't even a door, much less a lock." Bren's lips thinned. "I heard the gist of what's going on. There's no way I'm allowing you to stay here." She sat down on the bed, testing the mattress out with her bum, and looked underneath. Her head popped up. "How do you sleep on this thing?"

Relief washed from Dani's shoulders, her bottom lip dropping in disbelief.

"What?" Bren gave her an odd look

"I thought . . . you seemed . . ."

"Oh, you mean . . ." Bren laughed, the sound light and cheerful. "Surprised definitely. But we, my sister and I, have a soft spot for wayward Irish-born sisters we didn't know we had until a week ago."

Dani appreciated Bren's humor on the issue of her legitimacy. It was an uncomfortable subject. One that could easily have been handled like the elephant in the room. "But a shock nonetheless, I imagine."

She chuckled. "Normally it's the child trying to explain to a parent an unplanned pregnancy." Her warm brown eyes held Dani's, and Bren reached over and took her hand. "Kate and I both connected with you before we knew the truth. Something to be said for that Irish intuition."

Dani squeezed Bren's hand. "I felt it, too." Of course, she should have done things right and knocked on the front door. "I'm sorry for frightening you in the window." Dani grimaced. "I'd have come out with it, ya know. The truth, I mean, about who I was."

Maybe not the whole story. Had Kevin even filled them in on me transatlantic voyage?

"But I was truly afraid once Kevin showed up."

Bren snorted. "We were, too, after he spent an unpleasant night on the couch."

They both laughed at that, and it was as if they'd been sisters forever.

Bren sobered and patted the mattress. "And speaking of an uncomfortable night's sleep."

"Ah, right, the mattress . . . It isn't at all bad."

"And it isn't at all good, either. How about I help you pack?" Bren made a move to get up. "You can stay with me. It's tight but never a dull moment. Or Dad's got—"

"Bren." Dani motioned for her to sit back down and make room. Dani sat down at the end of the bed. "I can't leave. I was thrown off a horse today."

Bren gave her a confused look. "All the more reason for you to sleep in a comfortable bed tonight."

Dani leaned forward, debating if she could confide in Bren. She ran a horse rescue and had to care deeply for them. "How long have you known Kevin?"

Bren opened her mouth and then shut it, her expression thoughtful. "Long enough to know he's struggling with whatever's going on around here."

"He's being difficult, I think."

Bren frowned. "No, it's not that. I'm guessing he is reminded of another place and time when his instincts were wrong." Bren cocked her head. "Missing nails and flying horseshoes, huh?"

"I know. It does sound commonplace for a racing stable." Dani smoothed the itchy wool blanket. She was more interested in knowing more about this previous incident. "This not following his instincts . . ." She didn't want to come off as prying, but she did want to know one thing. "What did you mean earlier when you said to Kevin, 'Afraid I'll make it my business?'"

Bren took a heavy breath. "Kevin is acting toward you the same way he acted toward me when my husband died."

Dani's mouth fell open. "But you're—"

"Rafe's my second husband. Tom—Tom Ryan, my first husband, Aiden and Finn's father—was murdered."

Dani's hand flew to her mouth, and she gasped. "Bren, how awful."

Bren shrugged. "It's been close to six years since it happened. My life is back on track." She smiled down at her belly. "I couldn't be happier. But back then, I was hell on wheels trying to catch his killer. Even accused poor Kevin of letting a murderer walk the streets of Clear Spring. Tom's death was officially ruled an accident."

Dani's forehead creased with concern. "Kevin ruled it an accident?"

"No. State police." She waved a dismissive hand. "It's a long story. One day I'll tell you all about it. But, interestingly enough, what I saw today between Kevin and you *and* Turk reminded me of my own fight."

She liked Bren, appreciated her confiding in her like she did. But more than that, Bren would understand. "Turk seems to think someone is sabotaging his stable. At first I thought he was paranoid, but now I'm not so sure. This is the second time in two days the mare has lost the nails to a shoe. Of course, today she actually threw one."

"You're worried about the horses."

Dani rubbed the cut on her elbow. "People, too, but mostly for the horses. I can't leave right now until I figure out what's going on."

Bren rolled her lips in, considering. "And I take it Kevin knows what you just told me. Only he doesn't believe there's more to it?"

Dani nodded. "He thinks there's a reasonable explanation."

Bren threw her head back and laughed. "That's Kevin for you." Her smiling eyes turned serious. "He really is good at what he does—the cop part. As for Tom's case, there was no evidence to support foul play. Only my gut feeling."

Dani frowned. "I'd think with this latest incident he'd take it more seriously."

"If it weren't for his old man leading the charge, maybe." Bren dug for something underneath her maternity top.

"I'd think after learning someone tampered with one of Fritz's horse's feed he'd think differently."

"Huh? That's odd." She leaned in. "And scary. Colic's always a concern, even without someone messing with the feed." Bren pulled a mobile off her hip. "I get why you feel you have to stay, but you need to have phone. I want to be able to get ahold of you. In fact"—she wagged a finger at her half-sister—"I expect you to check in with me every night before you go to bed."

It had been only Dani for so long. She forgot what it was like to have someone worry. "What will you use?"

"I have an extra one." Bren searched the top of Dani's chest of drawers with her eyes. "You have a piece of paper and a pencil to take down a few phone numbers?"

"In my backpack." Dani got up and slipped the pad and pencil out of the front pocket of her backpack and sat down. She opened it, took one look at her notes from last night when Bren leaned over. Dani quickly flipped the page.

"Can I see?"

Dani gave her a sideways glance. "It's just a list of things I need to do."

Bren held out her hand.

Dani took a heavy breath. "Fine." She handed her the pad.

Bren's eyes skimmed Dani's handwritten notes. "We can talk to Kate about your citizenship—no problem—but she and Charlie are leaving to go back to Colorado after the holiday with her husband, Jess."

"I don't remember meeting him."

"He's flying in late tonight for the Fourth. They fly out Wednesday to go home."

Now that she thought about it, she'd never met Bren's Rafe. "What about your husband?"

"He's in Texas. His family has a cattle ranch, and he helps manage it. He's flying in about the same time as Jess and bringing him home with him."

"What about the sign? I thought it said cattle ranch."

Bren made a face. "I thought I could handle raising beef cattle."

"Aww." Dani rubbed Bren's arm. "I know they're like pets. I couldn't cut them into steaks, either."

"So you like Kevin."

And there was *that* elephant in the room, thanks to the doodle with horns and the words *Kristin Jennings* scribbled underneath. The heat crept into her face. "I was mad when I drew that."

"The bank manager Turk mentioned?"

Dani picked at the wool blanket. "She's pretty, educated, probably very ni—"

"Say no more." Bren hit a number on her mobile and put it up to her ear. "Hey, no, she's fine. Couple of scrapes and a goose egg on her head." Bren smiled at Dani and then checked her watch. "It's close to two. Want to go shopping at the outlets in Hagerstown with Dani and me? She needs to pick up a few things." She covered up the phone. "You mind if she brings Charlie?"

Dani shook her head. She liked kids. From what she remembered of Charlie, she was a cutie.

"Meet us at Starlite, and we'll transfer the baby seat into my truck." Bren clicked off and connected with Dani. "Whatta ya say, sis? Wanna go shopping?"

"Oh, in the worst way." Dani hugged Bren tight. "Thank you," she whispered in her ear. She'd just assumed she'd be wearing her dirty khaki shorts tomorrow.

Bren hugged her back. "Of course, sweetie. What are sisters for?"

CHAPTER TWENTY-FIVE

"A LITTLE TO THE LEFT," KATE CALLED OUT FROM ON HER KNEES, trying to attach the hinges to Dani's new antique-white wardrobe. She moved the door a smidge. "Is that better?"

"Perfect." She tightened in the last of the screws, stood, and then tried the doors. "What do you think?"

"It's handsome, indeed." Dani frowned. "You two should have let me buy it, though."

"Nonsense. You work hard for your money," Bren said.

"And we wanted to." Kate took the hanger from Bren who slipped Dani's new navy blue wraparound dress onto it. It was casual, yet chic, and she loved it.

"What shoes are you going to wear tomorrow?" Bren handed each one of them a shoe box.

"What do you think?" Dani looked to Kate who had been her personal shopper while Bren pushed Charlie in her stroller.

"Depends what look you're going for."

"I like the flats," Bren said.

"They're nice, but if we're competing with this bank manager, I'd go with the wedges." Kate opened up the box in her hands and pulled out the strappy, brown leather wedge. "What do you think?"

Not too high and not too short, they were the most beautiful shoes Dani had ever owned. "I love them." She glanced from Kate to Bren. It would be very easy to love them, too. They didn't have to cart her around from shop to shop, showing a genuine interest in helping her pick out a nice outfit for the picnic tomorrow. "How can I ever thank you?" Dani's eyes filled with tears, and she blinked them away.

Bren picked up Charlie from the middle of the brand-new twin bed with built-in drawers and a headboard with shelves that matched the wardrobe. "You can hold Charlie." Bren grimaced. "I have to pee."

Dani took her niece, the idea of family—even down to the littlest one—hugged her heart. "Bathroom's down the steps next to Turk's office." With Charlie tucked in one arm, Dani helped Bren up. "Can you manage it?"

"I'm pregnant, not an invalid." She headed toward the door.

"Watch the paint!" Kate called out.

Bren slipped through, careful not to catch the doorjamb of the new door Kate had installed.

Dani sat down with Charlie, admiring her pretty brown curls. "She's beautiful, Kate." Dani slipped her finger through a ringlet of Charlie's hair as the child grabbed one of the floral peach throw pillows her sisters had bought to match the mocha-colored comforter. "Such lovely curls."

"She's my girl." Kate sat down next to them, putting the pillow back and handing Charlie her stuffed pink bunny she'd left on the cushy new area rug that fit perfectly inside her eight by ten space. "How do you like your room?"

"I love it. You and Bren really have a knack for decorating." The old plywood walls had been painted a pale daffodil yellow. It hadn't taken long, with Kate by her side, to paint the small walls with two rollers after they sent Bren and Charlie out for a stroll to avoid the fumes.

"I've always wanted to do a tropical room in our cabin in Creede, but it just didn't flow with the country theme."

"You like living out West?"

"Best move I ever made."

Dani was beginning to think hopping the freighter had been her best—although harrowing—move, too. She dug her bare toes into the brown frond area rug and smiled up at the twirling leaf-shaped blades of the fan and fancy light Kate had installed earlier and pointed upward. "You're very good . . ."

"At building."

Dani's face crinkled with confusion. "Da said you were a lawyer."

"A long time ago."

Dani remembered Kevin's snide comment that night when he'd first arrested her. She was sure disbarred meant the same as it did in Ireland. She wouldn't ask about that. "Do you think it's possible to get me U.S.

citizenship through Da?" Charlie reached out to Dani, and she scooped her up, placing her in her lap.

Kate patted Dani's hand. "We're going to try. I did criminal law, not immigration, but when I get back to the house, I'll search the Internet. I think we can use acquisition."

Acquisition. "What is that, exactly?"

"It's when a child is born outside the U.S. and out of wedlock to a U.S. citizen. I have to check the legalese. If we meet all the requirements, I think you automatically acquire citizenship."

"That would be grand." Dani hugged her sister, forgetting about Charlie who squealed between them.

Kate hugged her back and then took Charlie, kissing her on the cheek, and sat her down on the rug to play with her bunny. "It would definitely solve a lot of our problems." A frown creased her face. "But I don't want to get your hopes up until I check it out. I'll know more tomorrow when I see you at the picnic."

Voices rose from below, footsteps moving up the stairs.

"I don't even recognize it." Bonnie stood inside the door frame holding a glass jar like the ones Dani'd seen at The Chocolate Box, a candy shop in downtown Wexford. Not that she could afford to indulge in sweets, but once in a while she'd treat herself. It was their chocolate—well worth the tank of petrol for the forty-two kilometers it took to get from Rosslare to Wexford and back.

"Your head." Bonnie winced. "They told me about what happened. Are you okay?"

Dani touched her temple. She laughed. "I'd all but forgotten about it."

Bonnie nodded and took a tentative step. "Can I come in?"

Lost in memories of home, Dani jumped up, feeling like the worst friend ever, scooped up Charlie, who whined when her bunny fell to the floor, and handed her off to Kate. "Yes, of course. Bonnie, I want you to meet me sisters." She then grabbed the wayward bunny and gave it to Charlie before her round-eyed expression turned to tears. "This is me sister Kate and me niece, Charlie."

Both Kate and Bonnie shook hands as Bren slipped inside. The space, although beautiful, had become more cramped.

"And this is—"

"Yes, I know. Bren and I met downstairs." Bonnie couldn't stop smiling, her eyes taking in every nook and cranny of the refurbished space. "This is amazing. How long did it take you?"

"We started shopping around two. I'd only planned to buy something for the picnic . . ."

"Picnic?" Bonnie turned thoughtful.

"It's our annual Fourth of July picnic. You should come, Bonnie," Bren said.

"I'd love to, but I have to work until eight, and then Jake's taking me to fireworks."

"We're having fireworks, too. Come when you get off and bring him," Kate said and motioned to Bren, who stood massaging her back, to sit down.

"You're sure?" She handed Dani the jar and absently scratched up and down both of her arms. "It's for those peppermints of yours."

"Oh, it's perfect." Dani took it from her and sat it down on the chest of drawers. "Thank you." She fooled with the tie on the bag of peppermints, a little perturbed she'd have to be nice to Jake tomorrow. If it were up to her, she'd kick Jake's miserable arse to the road after allowing Bonnie to get plastered last night.

"Everything matches." Bonnie slowly twirled around the room. "A bed . . ." She pressed down on the plush mattress. "You're going to sleep like a babe."

"It's me hope, anyway." Dani carefully poured the wrapped peppermints inside the jar.

"What'd you do with the old mattress?" Bonnie asked.

"In the Dumpster out back," Bren said with a triumphant smile.

Dani couldn't stop the smile from forming on her lips. Bren had made it clear from the beginning it was either the mattress or Dani that would be leaving.

But her humor faded with one realization. "You think we should pull it out? After all, it is technically Turk's."

"Naw. It was disgusting. He'll never miss it," Bonnie said, scratching her arm again like she had a bad case of the hives.

"But I did put the crates back in the bunkhouse." Dani's brows furrowed. Had she had an allergic reaction to the alcohol?

"Good. He may miss those."

Kate checked her watch and then looked at Bren. "What do you say, Mama. You ready to go? It's close to nine."

Bren yawned and gazed out the small window. The sun had long since dipped below what Dani now knew to be Bear Pond Mountain. Her sisters had been with her most of the day, her injuries from earlier barely noticeable. Between shopping for clothes, some of which still remained in bags on the floor, and doing her best to pay for all of her purchases only to be told no in unison by her sisters, she simply hadn't had time to think about her head or Kevin's warning to rest.

Bren slowly got up.

Dani reached for her, pulling Bren the rest of the way. "Thank you so much." She hugged her tight.

"Aw, sweetie, I just want you to be comfortable," Bren said against her ear.

Dani let her go and turned toward Kate. "And you." She took Charlie from Kate's arms. "It wasn't until I picked you up, cutie, that I realized that I have a niece." She eyed Bren, too. "And nephews."

Kate hugged Dani, squeezing Charlie between them again. "Whatever you need, let us know." Charlie cried, and Kate pulled away and took Charlie from Dani. "Aw, don't cry, sweetheart." Kate kissed her forehead and smoothed her curls from her cherubic face. "She's just tired."

The two gathered the tools they brought, and Kate handed Dani two keys. "One's to your new door. Remember to lock it when you leave and at night. The other's for the lockbox I bolted inside your wardrobe."

Dani held them tight in her hand. "I will."

They took the steps. Dani stood by the railing as they descended, and the worst case of homesickness came over her. Only it wasn't for a place. She shook it off. She'd see them tomorrow. "Good night."

"Good night," they called back through Charlie's cries.

Dani turned and entered her room.

Bonnie remained on the bed. "They're great."

"They are, aren't they?" Dani shut the door. "Can you believe it? A door that shuts." She held up the key. "And locks."

"You must have been working nonstop."

"No. Not really. Kate's a builder. The door went up in minutes. The fan took longer, but she helped me paint." She sat down next to Bonnie. "They took me to dinner while it dried."

"I'm amazed for sure." She pouted. "Can I move in with you?"

"It would be tight . . . But sure."

Bonnie laughed. "I was kidding, but you're a true friend. If you had the room, I'd definitely take you up on it." She stood and took the two steps from the bed to her wardrobe, her hand resting on the brushed nickel handle. "Can I see what you bought?"

Dani jumped to her feet. "Oh there's more in the bag. And wait 'til you see the dress and shoes." She snagged the bag from the floor. "Can you hand me a hanger? They're inside."

Bonnie opened the wardrobe and gave her a hanger. Dani sat the bag down and pulled out the little black dress Kate had found on sale and held it up. "What do you think? Kate says every woman needs a little black dress."

"It's gorgeous." Bonnie fingered the nearly see-through shoulders and neckline of the dress. "Who's it for, Blake or Kevin?" she said with a sly grin.

She wanted to say Kevin. "Me."

"Good answer." Bonnie took it from her and hung it up. "What else do you have in the bag?"

"Oh, shoes to match, a pair of slacks, a breezy white top, and a sundress."

"Let's see."

Dani pulled everything out, and they both admired the black stilettos and new garments.

"What are you wearing tomorrow?"

"The navy wraparound dress." Dani pointed to the one hanging up.

Bonnie pulled it out. "That's nice. Very chic."

"That's what Bren said."

"Oh. I forgot." Bonnie opened the handbag on her shoulder and pulled out a booklet. "You want to learn how to drive, right?"

"In the worst way. But I'd need a car for that." Not to mention, she wasn't even sure with her status if she'd be able to obtain a driver's license. Although that would change soon, she hoped.

"I'll teach you with my car." She handed her the book. "It's the *Maryland's Driver's Manual.* It's got all the answers to the test."

Dani took it from her and frowned. "Isn't that cheating?"

Bonnie laughed. "No. They give these out for you to read and learn the laws of the road, silly."

"Oh." Dani flipped through the book, her heart near to bursting with emotion. Bonnie didn't have to be kind to her, especially with Dani's new position. It had to have stung a little to know Dani would be groomed by Turk as his new jockey. "I don't know what to say. You've been so wonderful to me from the beginning." Dani sat down on her bed. "I thought after the news of me new position you'd stop being me friend."

Bonnie took a step toward her. "Move over," she snapped.

Dani slid up toward the shelved headboard, perplexed by her sharp tone. Only it was her eyes that held her mesmerized. She didn't know pupils could look that small.

Sitting down, Bonnie grabbed one of the throw pillows. "You're an idiot."

Dani's chest constricted. "You have every right to be—"

"Offended, hurt, angry?" Bonnie raised a well-shaped brow and scrubbed her forearms hard with her nails.

"All of those." Curious and concerned, Dani touched the scratch marks inside her arm. "Are you bit?"

Bonnie gave her a confused look.

"You're scratching like a dog with fleas."

"Oh." Bonnie frowned. "It's the damn mosquitos. They're awful at night around here."

Dani relaxed. She could attest to that. She'd been bit a few times herself. "So you're not mad at me?"

"I was." Bonnie chuckled. "But not anymore. Truth is, even if Turk had offered me the job, I'd turn it down."

"But why?"

"I'm fine on the ground. Not so much in the saddle." She leaned in. "I'm not a jockey. Not even close. I can't do what you do. I saw you with Solitary Con—"

"Solley," Dani corrected.

"Right." Bonnie smiled at that. "The point is you connect with them on a much deeper level than I ever could."

Dani sighed. "I'm so relieved. I never would want to hurt you."

Bonnie waved a dismissive hand at her. "We're family, Dani. I'm happy for you. And whatever is good for the racing stable is good for all of us."

A knock came from outside the door, and they both jumped.

"Oh, my." Dani's eyes widened. "You think it's Turk?" Dani hadn't gotten his approval for the renovation job to his room. A reasonable man wouldn't have a problem with it, she didn't think. But Turk . . .

The knock came again.

"Answer it." Bonnie stood and pulled Dani up.

Dani swallowed, prepared to have her ears blown off, and opened the door.

Chapter Twenty-Six

THE RED ROSES STARTLED DANI—VERY PRETTY WITH BABY'S BREATH weaved throughout the soft red petals. But it was the man holding them in front of her smiling that had her hand tightening on the doorknob.

He nodded at the door. "Are you going to invite me in?"

Invite him in? To her room? No, she didn't think that was a good idea. "It's a bit cramped."

"I'm leaving." Bonnie winked at Dani. "So there's plenty of room, Blake."

Shite.

There really wasn't. Not for him. Not with those roses.

"Hey, Bonnie," Blake said as they passed one another in the doorway. "Where's the other musketeer?"

"Chipper?" Bonnie gave him an odd look. "She's home with Hannah," she said making her way toward the stairs.

Dani swallowed hard, her hands beginning to sweat on the doorknob when Bonnie took the stairs, her smiling face disappearing with each step she made down to the barn.

"Who's your decorator?"

Dani spun around. Blake had moved deeper into her room and sat the roses down on the chest of drawers next to the jar of peppermints. He opened the top and took one and began to unwrap it before he popped it into his mouth.

"Me sisters." It was out before she could take it back. She'd never told him about her circumstances—tried to avoid talking about it to anyone.

He stopped and turned around. "I didn't know you had sisters."

Dani let go of the doorknob and took a step in, which was all it took to put her within inches of the roses. "You shouldn't have spent the money, Blake."

Blake reached for her, pulling Dani toward him. "I wanted to." A pair of warm brown eyes searched her face. "How's the head?" He pressed a wayward strand from her ponytail behind her ear. "You had me worried."

Self-conscious, she touched the knot on her temple. "It's not very pretty, I'm afraid."

"Trust me. It doesn't detract. You're beautiful, Dani." His voice was low and seductive.

Dani wet her lips. He was close enough to kiss her if he wanted. That was the thing about Blake. She couldn't quite gage his intentions, and she couldn't stand the not knowing. "Are you thinking of kissing me?"

He chuckled. "It's on my mind, yes."

She withdrew from his embrace, needing the space to think. "We're not a match. You know that?"

"Opposites attract."

Not when it came to money. "I live in a closet." She held her hands out and laughed. "A nice one, thanks to me sisters, Bren and Kate."

He jerked his head back. "You're a Fallon?"

She nodded. What did she have to fear if Blake knew the truth? If he was thinking of a serious relationship with her—and, honestly, she wasn't sure how she truly felt about that—he needed to know some basic facts about her life. Besides, illegal or not, she wouldn't be for long once this acquisition thing went through. Kate made it sound as though it was immediate. "I'm their half-sister. Daniel Fallon's me da."

He sat down on her bed. "I had no idea."

Her gaze traveled his muscular tanned thighs and calves, beneath his plaid shorts, and landed on his russet-colored—she was sure, expensive—Dockside loafers.

"It still doesn't change who I am." Dani sat down next to him. "I'm not rich. I'm not educated. I'm not someone you should—"

Blake placed his finger against her lips and angled his body toward her. "Let me decide if you are someone I want to date." He frowned at her. "The word *should* doesn't even enter into the equation." He bent his head and kissed her. Pressing his hand into the curve of her lower back, he deepened the kiss.

She tingled, her lips moving against his until he pulled away, leaving her confused and trembling.

He laughed. "Don't ask me why, because, frankly, if you were any other woman, I'd have you undressed by now."

Dani's insides tumbled softly. She was attracted to him and a little nervous around him, too. A true dilemma, for sure. If it weren't for her obsession with Kevin—who made it quite clear she *was* truly beneath him—she'd be thrilled to have a man like Blake show an interest in her. Now she was just confused.

Blake pulled her up and caressed her cheek. "I get a sense it's not just my wealth."

And he was blunt and shameless about his money. But she appreciated his candor. Only she could never be candid about this thing she had for him and for Kevin. Frankly, it was embarrassing that she couldn't make a decision where they were concerned.

"You've been so kind and so attentive . . ."

"Then have dinner with me tomorrow night at Rocky Gap."

"I can't."

"There will be fireworks." He kissed her, and she moaned sweetly against his lips.

"I can't," she whispered against his mouth and then pulled away. "I promised me family I'd have dinner with them on the farm."

His dark eyes held hers. "I guess you can't be two places at once."

This time with her family was important to her. Blake was right. She couldn't be two places at once. Dani took his firm, wide hand in hers. "Come with me."

His brow shot up. "Are you asking me on a date, Miss Flynn?"

She couldn't believe it herself. Technically, he'd asked her. "I am, indeed, Mr. Lansing."

He laughed and pulled her toward him. "Then it's a date. What time should I pick you up?"

He had her there. She'd never really confirmed a time. Or if she had, she couldn't remember. But she had a phone, thanks to Bren. If she knew where she'd put it. She pulled away from his embrace. "I don't know, actually." She rummaged through the bags in the corner of the floor and smiled when her hand brushed the edge of the mobile. "But I have a phone now." She held it up for his benefit.

"Perfect." He took it from her. "I'll put my cell in your contacts."

He punched in several numbers and then smiled, handing it back to her. "It's under B for . . ." A salacious smile curved his lips. "You'll figure it out."

"I'll call you tomorrow with the time."

"Can't wait." He pressed his lips to hers in a quick kiss. "Now that you're a jockey in training—"

"How'd you know?" She cocked her head slightly.

"How hard did you hit that head of yours?"

Right. He'd been on the track today, raced her, and won. She smiled. He'd come close to losing if it weren't for the horseshoe.

"I guess after today you wouldn't still consider racing again?" Dani gave him a hopeful smile.

"Only if you promise to stay in the saddle." His words were low, controlled, and carried a hint of concern.

Dani trembled at the sincerity in his voice. "I promise."

He kissed her goodbye and opened the door. "Lock it."

"I will." Dani shut the door behind him and turned the little lock inside the knob until it clicked. She held up her phone and checked his number to be sure it was there. Oh it was, and she didn't know whether to laugh or cry at the entry: *Blake Lansing Boyfriend*—the last of it in capital letters. She didn't know whether to laugh or cry. He'd even put it under the Bs so she wouldn't forget it.

Dani threw herself on her bed. *I'm in a load of shite.*

CHAPTER TWENTY-SEVEN

WITH HER MA'S LUCKY COIN IN HER FRONT JEAN POCKET, DANI glanced skyward.

I'm livin' the dream, ma.

Dani smiled at that and put the exercise saddle square on Solley's back and brought him out of the barn. Turk hadn't said which horse she'd be training on. She wanted to ride this one. Solley more than proved to her, over the past week, he was ready to be ridden. If anything, she'd call him a gentle giant. Never once, since she'd met the colt, had he taken a nip or shown any aggression.

"Come on, handsome." She patted his withers. "We're more than likely going to have to fight Turk on this one."

He gave a quiet snort and followed next to her. The morning sun disappeared behind a dark cloud the moment they left the security of the barn. She wouldn't let that be an omen of what was to come. If Turk could see his way to give her a chance, she could get him to do the same for Solley. After all he'd saved him from slaughter. There had to be a reason.

Turk stood next to the track, clipboard under his arm, holding the helmet he'd rigged up from yesterday. He shook his head. "Why am I not surprised, Flynn?"

Dani trekked across uneven ground with Solley, never slowing until she stood a few paces from Turk. She looked him in the eyes. "Because you're a betting man. And you have a hunch he can go all the way." She couldn't stop from smiling. He'd used the same rhetoric on her yesterday. She knew in her heart it was the reason Turk had bought him. But not just for profit. Turk Bendix could try to hide behind that hardened disposition, but the softer side of the man kept poking out.

"Get on out there, then." He opened the gate and handed her the helmet, hesitating.

"What is it?"

"How's the head?"

They'd already gone at it early this morning about his concerns. "I'm perfectly fine. I'd tell you if I wasn't."

He gave her a doubtful look but handed her the helmet. "Chipper's waiting. Take a gallop around the track."

Dani juggled the helmet, managing, despite her unexpected surge of excitement, to finally get the damned thing on her head. "You won't be sorry," she said and mounted Solley, her bum plopping down into the saddle. "I can promise you that." She gave him a kick in the sides and took off down the track, smiling so wide she thought her face would split in two.

"Then breeze him," Turk called after her. "But let him run in your hands."

Dani gave him a wave. She understood. They needed to get Solley back to the races but easing him in was best.

Chipper slowed and waited for them to catch up. "Hey, you look like you've got your jockey on."

"It's me hope, anyway. He's letting me train with Solley." Dani rubbed the colt between his ears. "He's giving us both a chance."

"He's a good man."

Dani nodded. "I agree, and a fair one, too."

"What does he want you to do first?"

"Gallop and then breeze him. But not to push Solley out."

Chipper nodded. "Makes sense. It's been close to four months since he's been in training."

"Was he a fine horse, then? I mean, for racing?"

"From what I know he won several stakes."

"I'm not surprised." She patted him again. "Very regal, too." Dani only hoped given this chance, she'd find she'd inherited her mother's skill and could help Solley get to where he once was.

Chipper glanced over Dani's head and hooked her chin toward the track. "Better go."

Dani took a quick peek over her shoulder. Turk stood there with his arms raised.

"What are we waiting for?" he groused in her ear.

Dani grimaced. *Still a hothead.*

She pulled down her goggles and kicked Solley in his sides. He eased into a nice gallop, and Dani relaxed in the saddle. The sun came out as they neared the turn, warming her face. She couldn't be happier. Working for Turk had proven to be the best thing that could have happened to her, and she very much liked the way he ran the stable. The question was would Mr. Porter approve?

In most stables, jockeys rarely worked out a horse. But Turk's operation wasn't run like most stables. It was one of the reasons Dani was here breezing Solley with Midnight and Chipper now. Truth be told, Dani was nothing more than a glorified exercise rider until she could prove herself. That made her uneasy. If Porter ever did show up to check on his investment and review Turk's paperwork, or lack thereof, Dani was in a world of shite. She'd be sacked for sure. But more than that. She could find herself looking from the inside out of a jail cell.

Dani clenched her teeth when Jake galloped by on George's Got the Gold. She wouldn't concern herself with the likes of Jake. If anything, she was a step above him. She was now . . . Dani crinkled her brows. She guessed she *was* a cross between an exercise rider and an apprentice jockey.

"How's he feel?" Turk's gruff voice filled her ears, giving her a start.

She'd almost forgotten about the earpiece. She gave him a thumbs-up since she didn't have a mic to answer back.

"Get the timing in your head. Twenty seconds an eighth."

Dani came up on a pole and began counting. She passed the next one at twenty-two seconds. A little slow. But she wouldn't push Solley. She started over each time she passed the next pole. *Twenty-two . . . twenty-one . . . twenty-one . . . twenty-one.*

Turk waved to her when she rounded the last turn. "Come in."

Dani continued her counting and then reined him in, stopping in front of Turk, who stood on the other side of the rail.

"How'd you do?"

Dani lifted off her goggles, breathing heavier than when she started out. "Twenty-one."

"I can live with that." He checked his clipboard. "Do an open gallop. Try for fifteen seconds an eighth."

Dani nodded and put her goggles back on. Taking the next pole, she set the horse in motion and started counting again. *Eighteen . . .*

seventeen . . . seventeen . . . fifteen. Her heart sped up as Solley found another gear. *Fifteen . . . fourteen . . . twelve.*

"Whoa, Flynn, pull him back," Turk ordered on a laugh.

She did as he instructed, her hands slipping on the reins, and then clenched it tight. She'd fix that once—

Turk waved her in.

Dani stopped at the rail, prepared for a reprimand. "I didn't mean for him to go so fast," she said on a heavy breath of enthusiasm.

Turk smiled up at her. "I knew he had it in him."

Dani patted his neck. "He took the gallop easy."

"Breeze him in hand for this last lap. Let's see how he does." He held up his stopwatch. "On the count of three."

"Will do." Dani maneuvered Solley back out, knotted the reins to avoid what happened earlier when her hands had slipped, and waited for her cue.

"One, two, *three.*"

Dani gave Solley the go-ahead. Solley took off, and Dani clenched the reins. So much for allowing him that in-hand breeze. He took the first turn with ease, never slowing down the straight away. The second turn came up quick, and if he slowed Dani didn't feel it. The last few furlongs were a blur, and they passed by Turk within seconds.

"Holy hell," Turk yelled in her ear. "Thirty-nine. Thirty-freakin'-nine, Dani girl!"

Dani smiled and slowed to a trot to cool Solley down. She checked the track and looped around when it was clear, heading back toward Turk. Dani reined him in next to the rail. "He's very fast. Don't you think?"

"Hell yeah." He held up the watch. "He's still got it, no question that pace'd put him in the money in a stakes race."

Which made sense based on what Chipper said. "Should I cool him out?"

He nodded. "Catch up with Chipper."

Dani glanced out over the track. Her friend and mentor had already begun to cool out Midnight Edition. She peered over her shoulder toward Turk. "I don't mind at all bathing him, too."

Turk got a silly grin on his face. "See me in my office . . . After you bathe him."

"Thank you!" It came out louder than she expected, and she blushed, but she couldn't contain her excitement.

He waved her off and headed back up to the barn. Dani scratched

Solley between his ears. "We did good, boy." Well . . . Turk hadn't mentioned her specifically, but she hadn't fallen off like last time. If he made no mention of it, she'd assume her form was good, too. Dani kicked Solley in his sides and caught up with Chipper.

"Pretty impressive back there." Dirt smudged Chipper's face, making her teeth look whiter than usual.

Dani snickered and wiped at her own face, and then lifted her goggles up. "Thanks. It was mostly Solley."

"You handled yourself."

Dani couldn't stop from smiling. "I don't remember a better day."

"It's a great day." Chipper laughed. "I'm taking Hannah to the pool later. They're having games and relays for the kids for Fourth of July."

Dani had almost forgotten about the picnic—and *Blake*. "Aye." Dani rolled her lips in, debating whether to clue Chipper in on her date. "Blake's taking me to me da's."

"Oh." Chipper sobered.

"You think I shouldn't?"

"No." It came out a little shrill, and she shrugged. "I mean if you like him, why not."

Perhaps.

Dani kept even with Chipper, the clomp of horseshoes rhythmic and soothing as they made their way around the track. "You going to see fireworks tonight?"

"With Mom and extended family. Clear Spring has them at Plumb Grove Mansion."

Dani continued to cool out Solley with Chipper by her side on Midnight Edition, all the while her mind going back to her impending date with Blake.

"What about you? Blake taking you to the fireworks later?"

"Me family has them at the farm. You're welcome to come. Bonnie and Jake are coming."

Chipper frowned. "Jake, huh."

"You don't like him?" Dani's hands tightened on the knot in the reins.

Chipper shrugged. "He's a bad influence."

Dani agreed. "I worry about her."

"Something happen?" Chipper glanced over with a concerned look in her eyes.

Dani nodded and told her about that night outside the barn with Jake.

Chipper nodded. "They were drunk."

"They'd gone to a cow bar."

Chipper giggled. "You mean the Purple Cow."

"That's the one."

"It's actually a fun place."

"I was a barmaid in Ireland as well as a groom. A lot of fun to be had for the workers as well as the patrons." It wasn't so much the alcohol they'd consumed that night that bothered Dani. It was a combination of things. "Do you ever notice that Bonnie loses her train of thought?"

Chipper's head swung around, her brows snapping together. "How'd her eyes look?"

Dani jerked in the saddle, concern rising in her chest. "Constricted."

"Damn her and those pills," Chipper hissed.

Dani moved her mount closer to Chipper. "Pills?" she said, her voice edged with alarm.

Chipper grimaced. "Forget I said anything." She cantered away.

Dani kicked Solley in his sides. "Oh, no you don't. I want to know what you're talking about."

Chipper slowed her pace. "I'll tell you, but you have to promise to keep quiet."

"You've got me word."

"Did she tell you she worked for Fritz?"

"Yes, she said he helped her find the job with Turk when he let her go."

"A few months before that she got thrown from one of Fritz's horses. Messed up her back pretty bad. Gave her oxycodone for the pain."

"Who, Fritz?"

"No. The doctor."

"Still." Dani got a sick feeling at the bottom of her stomach. She'd heard stories like this before. "That's addicting."

"You got it." Chipper shook her head. "The doc cut her off. She told me she'd kicked it." Chipper connected with Dani, her eyes a sober green. "Question is who's supplying her now?"

"Jake?"

Chipper shrugged. "I don't know. Maybe."

Dani felt as though she'd been transported back to the docks with Kara and Tommy. Kara and Bonnie were alike in many ways. She didn't believe Kara had a drug problem though—more like impulsive and a little misguided. Not that Dani was one to talk, not with the mess she'd created of her own life. But if Kara hadn't taken the thumb drive, she'd be alive. Dani blinked back tears. She couldn't lose Bonnie, too. "Will you talk to her, then?"

"First thing when I see her tomorrow."

"Thank you." Dani reached out and squeezed Chipper's hand. "I feel better already." She tried to smile, but there was something else bothering her. "Why'd Fritz let her go?"

"From what I know of Fritz, he's in the game for the enjoyment. If it stops being fun or dents his nice retirement nest egg, he cuts costs." She became reflective. "Not that I'm looking to lose my job, but Turk could learn a thing or two from Fritz."

Dani understood. He'd taken on Bonnie, and then Dani after Kevin had pressured him. He'd said he wasn't looking for another groom. *Oh,* and the peppermints—he'd even supplied her with a new bag. Not that the sweet treat was a lot of money, but it was an extra he didn't need to buy. He'd done it for her. Horses could learn to live without the sweet, but Dani didn't think she could. It gave her untold enjoyment. He knew that—she was sure of it.

A smile tugged at her mouth. She'd make it up to Turk, and it'd start with winning a race.

Standing in the wash area, Dani dried Solley off and then handed his lead to Arturo. "Thanks. You may want to wrap his legs. He's had a hard workout."

"Sure thing, Dani. I check it out for you."

"That'd be great." Dani gave Solley one last pat and traveled up the uneven terrain of dirt and grass to the barn and ducked inside, entering Turk's office.

With his phone propped up against his ear, he motioned for her to sit down on a stool at the corner of his desk. "That's right—nominated. Who did I speak to?" He shook his head, looking rather exasperated. "I don't remember. Look it up." He plopped back in his chair, covered the mouthpiece, and spoke to Dani. "They always like to give you the runaround." Turk grabbed a piece of paper off his desk and handed it to her. "I need you to fill this out."

"Sure." Dani took a look at the form and gulped.

EMPLOYMENT ELIGIBILITY VERIFICATION issued by the DEPARTMENT OF HOMELAND SECURITY.

Shite.

Her head shot up. "What exactly did Kevin tell you about—"

Turk pulled his hand from the receiver and put it up to his mouth as he connected again with the person on the phone. "Did you say the Woodward?" His face twisted in question.

Dani's heartbeat sped up. Her ma had raced in it that summer up in New York. Could he be entering them in the race?

"No. *Travers,*" he snapped and pulled a sheet of paper closer. "Midnight Edition and Grant. Charlene Grant."

Dani's shoulders sagged. She felt like a balloon that all the air had been let out of—deflated. *Stupid.* Of course he'd be entering Chipper and Midnight Edition into the Travers Stakes. She and Solley hadn't proved anything to Turk except that she could manage to stay on and Solley could take direction. There was a lot more training to be done.

Turk shook his head a few more times. Motioning to Dani, he handed her a pen to work on the form, while he jotted down more notes from his phone call. Fine. She'd fill out the bloody form as best she could for now, but Turk needed to know about her status before this went any further.

She filled out her name, listed the training center for her present address, and skipped the social security card number because she couldn't remember it and had been told not to use it. Dani continued to scan downward and checked the box that made the most sense—an alien authorized to work. Only her authorization had expired almost eight years ago.

Turk hung up the phone, and Dani opened her mouth to explain her circumstances.

"Hot damn." Turk hit the desk with his palm, stood, and tried to kick up his heels like he was dancing a jig. Only he lost his balance and crashed to the floor.

Dani jumped up and grabbed for him. "Have you lost your head?"

He laughed out loud, his eyes agleam. "Hell no. I just might have myself two contenders." He pointed his finger at her. "We're going to New York, Flynn, and we're going to see how far we can go." He rose then again plopped down in his chair and opened his desk drawer. Taking out a peppermint—one from the bag he'd given her—he opened the wrapper and popped it in his mouth.

"What did you mean, 'two contenders'?"

"Ah, right. We've got a lot of work in front of us, but we're going to get you and that damned black colt ready for the Maryland Million Classic in October."

A stakes race. She should be elated, but the form she clenched in her hand had her dreading her next move. It was clear to her now that Kevin hadn't explained her situation. Knowing Daniel was her father, Turk wouldn't think to question her immigration status. Still she wouldn't let it worry her just yet. Soon she'd have her paperwork in order, and October was a long way off.

"Where exactly will you be sending this"—she glanced at the top right corner—"I-9?"

He waved her off. "In here where the rest of them sit." He opened his bottom desk drawer and pulled out a folder. "Damn bureaucrats and their paperwork. You don't think they want to store the mountains of paper they have us fill out."

Angst, so palpable, lifted from her chest. There was no harm in filling it out, then. "I need to get a few numbers from upstairs." She stood. "I'll finish it and bring it back to you."

He nodded. "Do it now. I want to lock up and get a shower before the Fallons' picnic."

"I'll be quick about it." Dani headed to the door and then turned back. "You're serious, then, about entering Solley and me in this Maryland Millions Classic?"

"I'm in the business to win. If what I saw today is any indication of the future, you and that horse can go all the way."

"You knew he could from day one."

"I knew the stories were true about him." He rapped his stomach. "Knew it in my gut."

Dani furrowed her brows. "What stories?"

"Solitary Confinement was a stakes horse." He cleared his throat. "Is a stakes horse. Last spring he won the Kentucky Juvenile Stakes at Churchill Downs."

"That's prestigious."

He nodded. "After that the Sandford Stakes in Saratoga, the Breeders' Cup Juvenile, and the Gulfstream Park Derby in January."

"And he won them?"

"You bet, and a few more after that at Aqueduct until I found him at auction in May."

"But why?"

His lips thinned. "Because the bastard who owned him used an electrocution device."

"He shocked him." Dani's throat went dry.

"I know this: if someone was shocking the hell out of me, I'd be mad as hell, too."

"They did this to him at the stable?"

"There and on the track, part of his training." Turk grabbed for the radio on his desk and opened up the back compartment, pulling out a 9 volt battery. "It's called a buzzer and it's the size and weight of this." He wrapped his hand around it. "Fits in your palm."

Where no one could see it. But someone must have for Turk to know. "How'd you find out?"

"Trust me. Word gets around the backside."

"Was the trainer punished?"

"It was never proven." He eyed the doorway and the horse Arturo walked around the shed row. "Didn't have to be . . . for me."

She understood. He knew horses—knew that Solley's behavior was through no fault of his own. Tears pinched the backs of Dani's eyes. "You're a kind man, Turk Bendix." She gave him a quick hug.

He did what he always did—complained—but he smiled when he did it.

"You won't be sorry you took a chance on us." She held up the form. "I'll be right back."

She cleared his office and headed for the steps, and then thinking better of it, turned around with one last question. "Who was the—"

Turk's phone rang, and he shut the door.

Oh, well. It was only curiosity on her part, and it didn't matter. She had what she wanted—Solley.

Chapter Twenty-Eight

"MOM, AUNT DANI HAS SOME MAN WITH HER!" FINN LEFT THE DOOR wide open and ran into the kitchen to the left.

Dani should have been happy he'd called her Aunt Dani. The last time she'd been with him she was the strange woman they'd taken in for the night.

"Finn!" Bren met him in the doorway, shaking her head. She then glanced up at Dani and Blake, and for a split second she seemed angry. Maybe at Finn. Or was it Dani?

She probably should have asked to bring Blake. But then Bren smiled, and Dani was left wondering if it had been her imagination.

"Come on in, you two." She handed Finn a thin, long fork. "Give this to your father, please."

He took it and galloped down the hall and toward the double glass doors.

"And no running, mister."

"I'm not," he slung over his shoulder, though he very much was.

"He's eleven and all boy," she said, smiling as she walked toward them. "I'm Bren Langston, Dani's sister."

"Blake Lansing." He handed her a bottle of wine he'd brought and shook her hand.

She eyed the bottle. "Wine. How nice," she said, her voice a bit short, and the feeling that Bren was not at all pleased returned.

"You don't like wine," Blake said, his comment only confirming Dani's own misgivings.

Bren laughed. "No, no, no. This is great. Come on in." She waved her hand, and Dani and Blake entered the foyer. "Everyone's in the back. Dani's met most of us."

Dressed in a red maternity top and white shorts, Bren motioned for them to follow her through the family room. Dani covertly did a sweep of the room until she found the computer. The thumb drive was tucked away in the small white handbag on her shoulder; she'd bought it yesterday with her sisters.

With a sunny day—and low humidity—everyone would hopefully remain outside for the duration of the party. It was Dani's hope, anyway. They stepped out of the sliding glass doors onto a gorgeous stone patio. Oblong tables were pushed together to form a large banquet table and she recognized Fritz in a group of men standing next to a built-in grill.

"How you doing, lass?" Fritz ambled over toward her with his trademark suspenders, holding a beer in his hand, and gave her a hug. "Good to see you, sweetheart. You had me worried." He angled his head, no doubt trying to get a look at her temple.

Dani moved her hair away for him. She'd worn it long and curled it with the curling iron she'd also bought yesterday, hoping to succeed at hiding the ugly purple bruise that had formed overnight.

He squinted. "No worse for wear, I suppose." Then he glanced up at the man standing next to her and laughed out loud. "You've always had an eye for beauty in horses *and* women." He winked at Dani.

"How you doing, old man." Blake shook Fritz's hand.

"Good. Better if I win at Delaware Park on Thursday."

"You must be Dani." Wearing a straw cowboy hat, faded jeans, and a T-shirt, the man came up behind Bren and put his arm around her waist, pulling her close.

Dani didn't miss his drawl or the way he cared for her sister. "You must be Bren's Rafe."

"The Stetson give it away?" asked a voice to Dani's left. An attractive man with sandy brown hair walked up carrying Charlie and gave her a hug. "I'm Jess. Kate's husband."

"Jess!" Kate came up on him from under the covered porch and swatted him. "Stop picking on Rafe."

"It's okay, Kate," Rafe said. "He's just mad because this *cowboy* beat his ass at croquet."

Everyone laughed. Both Bren's and Kate's husbands were ruggedly handsome and not the type to play a lawn game, but they'd no doubt made an exception for Finn, judging by the way he ran up on them with a mallet and ball, sporting a frown. Only it seemed Finn wasn't ready for the game to end.

"Dad, you going to play or not?"

Rafe roughed up his blond hair. "After dinner."

Bren angled back toward Rafe, her russet brows snapping together. "You're not letting my steaks burn, are you?"

"Relax, red." He playfully pulled her toward him and gave her a quick kiss. "I know how to grill up steaks." He winked at Dani. "I'm a Texan."

"Dani, is your friend Bonnie coming with her date?" Kate asked, holding a stack of thick plastic plates.

"She's coming around six," Turk said as he rounded the corner with her da and another man she didn't recognize. "I let her off early for the holiday." He smiled at Dani, his eyes landing on the man standing next to her.

If he was surprised, angry, or a mix of the two, she couldn't tell by his expression.

"Blake," he said in a pleasant voice—pleasant for Turk—and shook his hand.

Dani introduced Blake to Kate and her brothers-in-law. The older gentleman with a gray crew cut stepped away from her da and shook her hand. "I'm Paddy Ryan, Dani. Nice to finally meet you."

"He's also Aiden and Finn's grandfather and Rafe's dad," Bren added.

"Nice to meet you, Paddy." She cocked her head. "Are you Irish, then?"

"Irish descent." He chuckled. "But from very long ago."

Dani introduced him to Blake, all the while her mind trying to place the last name Ryan and why it wasn't the same as Rafe's.

Finn tugged on her hand. "I'll be right back." He took off down the stone patio, running in the direction of the croquet game, and it was then Dani realized her older nephew was missing.

"Where's Aiden?" Dani asked Bren.

Bren looked to Rafe.

"Out at the duck blind getting the bonfire ready for fireworks with a few of his buddies."

"What about Jenny?" Bren said.

"Her parents are dropping her off."

Dani gathered that was Aiden's girlfriend when Finn flew around the corner, juggling three mallets. "Aunt Dani, will you and your friend play with me?"

"Aw." Dani looked to Blake only to find him bending down to Finn's height.

"Call me Blake and absolutely." He patted his shoulder and took the two mallets, handing one to Dani. "I have to warn you. I play to win." He winked at Dani.

Her heart melted at the way he had treated Finn—but just a little. She knew he wasn't going to cut her or the boy any slack. Dani laughed to herself. She guessed he wasn't aware the game croquet originated in Ireland.

"I should have told you." Dani playfully nudged Blake's shoulder with hers, trying not to gloat. "But I didn't want to burst your bubble."

"You're a ringer." He chuckled and kissed her hand, which had remained in his since they walked away from the game.

"Will you teach me to play as good as you, Aunt Dani?" Finn followed close at her side as they walked to the patio.

She grabbed his hand, too, and squeezed. "Aw, of course, sweetie. I'd love to." She and Finn seemed to have a special bond since that first day at breakfast, and she exchanged that hand for a one-armed hug before they took the brick step.

"Plates are here and food's on the bar." Bren came out from behind it, her cheeks flushed.

Dani let go of Blake's hand and rushed over. "You should sit and rest. I'll make you a plate." Here she was playing croquet, enjoying her date, and her sister, who was going into her ninth month of pregnancy, looked ready to drop.

"I think I'll take you up on that." Bren made a move toward the long picnic table, covered in red and white checks, when Rafe came up behind her, holding a plate of food. "I got ya, darlin'." He took her down the one step of the patio and sat her down with her dinner.

Dani got her own plate and helped Finn as she rounded the bar—filling his plate with the food that was out of reach. There were a multitude of salads, perfectly seared strip steaks she could only dream of eating in Ireland, and the funniest orange-colored shellfish. "What is this?" Dani asked Finn.

"Crabs." He laughed. "They catch them in the Chesapeake Bay."

"Oh." They didn't look the least bit appetizing. Not that the Irish didn't eat crabs too, being surrounded by water. But it was only the wealthy and she believed they boiled theirs.

Aiden grabbed one by its claw and plopped it on her plate. "Try one, Aunt Dani."

"Oh, no. I couldn't begin to figure out how to open it, much less eat it."

"I'll help you," Blake said, his hand caressing her lower back.

Dani tingled with his touch, feeling all the more confused where Blake was concerned. If it weren't for this tug-o-war on her heart between Blake and Kevin, she'd be content. At least her confidence was at an all-time high, dressed in her trendy navy wraparound dress and wedges. If Kevin did show up with his bank manager, she could hold her head up.

Dani followed Blake and Finn to the table and sat down between them, her gaze shifting to the back patio door into the house. She'd do best to stop torturing herself where Kevin was concerned. If anything, she was making a fool of herself.

Dani willed her eyes down and frowned at the crustacean on her plate. She liked fish—sea bass mostly. She'd found it to be quite tasty the few times she'd eaten it. Dani took her plastic fork and tapped the hard shell of the crab. If there was any meat to it at all, she'd be surprised. But more disconcerting, she hadn't a clue how to get to it.

Finn nudged her side. "First, you rip off their legs." He held his up and proceeded to remove the two claws and the rest of the spindly legs beneath the shell.

Dani grabbed it off her plate and followed her nephew's instructions. "Like this, then?"

"Yep."

Rafe handed her a mallet and a stainless steel bread knife from the center of the table and grinned. "It took me a while to figure out the damn critters myself."

"Thank you." She liked Rafe. Out of all the people she'd met, only he seemed to understand her awkwardness around her new family. He was different than the rest of them, too. She supposed Texas was different.

Finn nudged her side. "Take the knife and stick it under this thing here." He showed her with his and lifted the shell off. Then he scraped out a green coiling goop.

Dani's stomach pitched, and she swallowed hard.

Finn continued his instruction. Breaking the shell in two, he dug his fingers inside and pulled out a clump of white meat which he held out to her. "Here. You try it."

"You're sure?" Dani raised an uncertain pair of brows at him.

He nodded his head. "Yeah. Try it."

She took it from him and gazed into those expectant blue eyes of his as she debated whether she really wanted to put it in her mouth. Then she ate it. The tender meat melted in her mouth, the spices different than anything she'd ever tasted.

"Well?" Finn said.

Even with the zing of spice, she found it delectable. "It's good."

"Now you try."

Dani took the knife and proceeded to dismantle her crab. Disjointed conversations took place up and down the table, but one caught her attention.

"Had to put him in a claiming race to raise more capital," Fritz said around a swig of his beer.

"Only thing worse is when they don't get claimed." Blake chuckled to the right of her, took a bite of his steak, and squeezed her thigh. "Then it's off to the butcher."

Dani swallowed the crab meat in her mouth. *Off to the butcher? What an uncaring thing to say.* She glanced at Turk. His lips thinned, and he jammed his plastic fork into his potato salad.

And the man who said it continued to eat his dinner and fondle her leg. *Err.* She wanted to say something—anything. She wasn't at all fine with his way of thinking.

"Hey, guys. Sorry we're late." Bonnie rounded the patio dressed in a short—although pretty—sundress with Jake. Dani pushed Blake's hand off and made a move to get up.

"I got it." Kate shut the slider on her way out after putting Charlie down for a nap and waved her down, meeting the late arrivals as they stepped up onto the patio. "We've plenty of food."

The three passed behind Dani on their way to the bar.

Dani put her hand out. "I'm so glad you came."

Bonnie squeezed it. "Me, too."

Dani went to stand, more than ready to move away from her date. "I'll help you—"

"Don't get up. Jake and I can figure things out."

The two followed Kate who got them started with a plate. Within minutes they had taken the empty seats across the table and a little to the right of Dani.

Bren brought them two beers from the cooler against the wall of the house. "You like Corona?"

"Sure." Bonnie took them from Bren, handing one to Jake. "Ooh." She cocked her head at Bren. "I love your necklace."

Bren grabbed the silver pendant between her fingers.

"She made it," Kate said, coming from the house, minus Charlie. "She's an artisan."

"No, I'm not. I only make jewelry when the mood strikes and if the piece has meaning."

"Spoken like a true artist." Rafe chuckled.

The same thought had run through Dani's head as well.

Jess came over from the bar and put his arm around Kate. "All I know is your design helped me find Kate in Creede."

Find Kate? Dani didn't even know her sister had gone missing.

She looked from Bren to Kate. Kate came over and bent down, dangling the pendant at the end of a silver chain between her fingers. "It's a butterfly." She held it out for Dani to see.

The delicate design fluttered on the silver chain. "It's lovely."

"What's the meaning behind the—"

"Bren, come show Dani yours." She smiled at Dani and the thought that Kate didn't want to elaborate vanished. "It's a horse."

Bren walked around, sidestepped Finn who jumped up, almost colliding with her. "Finn, watch where you're going."

"Sorry, Mom." He darted by her, heading toward the bar with an empty cup.

"I'm taking your seat," she called after him and sat down. "I made it from a quarter."

Dani gently took the piece of silver in her hand. In the face of the coin, Bren had cut out a beautiful horse's head. "You did it yourself?"

"With a special saw."

"It's so intricate." Dani marveled at the necklace and the matching bezel with the black leather cord. "Was this a horse of yours?"

Bren's brown eyes glistened. "His name was Smiley. He was an Appaloosa I had when I was about six."

"No tears, Red." Rafe handed her a napkin from across the table.

"I'm sorry." Dani rubbed Bren's thigh. "I didn't mean to bring up—"

"It's not your fault." She took the napkin from her husband. "Wait 'til you're pregnant. Everything makes you cry."

Dani hadn't thought that far ahead. She'd heard a woman's emotions were all over the place, but she didn't think Bren's sadness had to do with her pregnancy. She understood how a piece of metal could cause a person to cry. She'd done it many times with her ma's coin. Dani pulled on the leather tab of her purse, struggling with the zipper. When it finally opened enough, she reached in, trapping her ma's coin between her fingers and slowly pulling it out.

"This was me ma's."

Bren reached for it. "Can I see?"

Dani gave it to her. "She said it was her lucky coin." Dani pointed to the front. "The horse for her racing, and if you flip it over . . ."

Bren did as she asked.

"The year of me birth."

"It has a nice weight to it," Bren said, fingering the coin. "I could make you a necklace out of it, if you like."

"I'd love you to."

Bren laughed and handed it back to her. "Sure, but I'm thinking you want to wait until after the racing season."

"We need all the luck we can get." Turk winked at Dani.

Dani went to put it away when Blake put his arm around her. "Can I see?"

The truth was, no. After his earlier comment, she wasn't sure how she felt about him.

"Hey, you can smell the crabs from the front of the house." Kevin came around the corner in his uniform, bringing with him the swell of chatter burbling from the radio strapped across his chest. He reached up and hit a button to turn it down, his tired eyes landing on her and Blake.

Dani dropped her coin back in her purse and moved her chair away from Blake. He removed his arm from her shoulder and took a sip of his beer, and she wondered if he sensed a change in her behavior toward him.

Turk got up. "Take my seat. I'm done." He grabbed his plate and frowned at Kevin. "You look like hell."

Dani thought so, too. Lines bracketed his strong mouth, and his forehead glistened with sweat.

"Take off the vest," Turk said. "That's half your problem."

He shook his head. "If I expect the rank and file to wear it, I have to wear it."

Turk nodded. "I'll get you a beer."

"Water, Dad. I'm on duty."

"Right." He patted the air as if to say he knew that.

"What do you want to eat?" Kate asked.

"I can get it." He came around the table and walked with Kate to the bar area.

"Oh, Dani! I almost forgot."

Dani turned away from Kevin and focused her attention on Bonnie.

Her friend pulled out a folded piece of newspaper from her bag. "I found a car for you."

"A car? But I'd need a driver's license first."

Jake mumbled something under his breath, and Bonnie shot him a not so nice face before turning back to Dani. "Doesn't hurt to look."

"Can I see, Bonnie?" her father asked.

She handed him the newspaper, and he slid his glasses from the top of his head down onto the bridge of his nose. His brows crinkled. "A two thousand and one." He raised his head. "It's a bit old, I'm afraid."

"What's old?" Kevin returned and sat down next to Daniel with a plate of food.

Oh, Lord. That was all she needed. He'd have something negative to say. She was sure of it.

"A Ford Escort."

Kevin took a bite of his steak. "Aiden looking for a car?"

Her father shook his head. "No, Dani."

A pair of serious brown eyes narrowed in on her. "You need a driver's license for that."

Kate came over and stood behind Jess who sat across from Dani, still picking crabs. "No, she doesn't. She can buy a car and insure it as an excluded driver through Maryland Auto Insurance Fund until she gets her license."

"Maybe." Kevin took a sip of his water. "But she still needs an authorized driver to drive it off the lot."

Blake slammed his beer down, his eyes narrowing in on Kevin across the table. "What are you, man, her gatekeeper?"

Dani tensed.

Kevin's eyes blazed back, and then he sneered. "Why don't you—"

"I'll be that authorized driver until you get the license, lass," Fritz said from down the table.

Dani smiled at Fritz, grateful for the interruption and a little amused with the special named he liked to call her, knowing full-well his Irish roots were from long ago.

"Now if anyone's going to be an authorized driver, it would be her father." Daniel sent a look of rebuke down both sides of the table, his expression softening when it landed on Fritz. "It's a kind offer, Fritzy, but I'll take on the responsibility meself."

Fritz nodded, lifting his beer. "Then how about I help you pick it out at the dealership."

"It's a date." Her father lifted his beer as a toast.

Now they were moving faster than she could catch up. She didn't want to continue to depend on others for her bare necessities like transportation and food. But first she had to save the money. She'd even settle for a nice scooter like she had before. "How much is it, then?"

All eyes landed on her, including Blake's, and Dani's face warmed. "I need to know if I can afford it."

Her father glanced down at the paper. "Fifteen hundred."

It was more than she'd put by. "I think I'll wait until I have a little more put away."

Kevin winked at her from across the table. "Smart girl."

Dani's stomach tumbled softly at the rasp of his tired voice, and she lowered her eyes. She was still hopelessly attracted to him.

Her father patted the table with his hand. "I just might have that fifteen hundred you need, Dani."

Dani's eyes widened. "Da! I can't expect you to pay me way. I can manage the car in a few weeks' time. What's the hurry?"

More to the point, this was becoming a bit embarrassing with Blake sitting silently next to her, drinking his beer, and learning the details of her meager existence.

"Nonsense." Her da's cheeks turned rosy with frustration. "If I want to buy me daughter a car, there's nothing to be done about it." His sparkling blue eyes hardened with unwavering determination—the expression so unlike anything she'd witnessed before.

Aw. Dani pushed her lips out into a pout. He was her da. Maybe twenty-six years too late. It didn't matter. She loved him in spite of it. "I guess there's no harm in looking." She smiled across the table at him.

"We could go tomorrow. They're open until nine," Bonnie said.

Dani smiled at her friend. She seemed completely put together tonight—her thought process clear and uninterrupted. Dani couldn't help her growing enthusiasm. "How about after work, then?"

"Let's make it a foursome," Fritz added from down the table.

"Then it's settled. I'll pick you up around . . ." Daniel looked from Bonnie to Dani.

"What do you think, Bonnie? Half past four?" Dani said.

"It's settled." Her father smacked the table with both his hands. "I'll pick everyone up outside Starlite, then."

Kevin grunted when he stood and walked away from the conversation. So he didn't approve of the car. It wasn't his business to begin with. He'd do well to remember that.

Jess wiped his spicy hands on a paper towel. "So, Dani, Kate tells me you worked at a pub in Ireland."

"Aye. I miss it sometimes." The sound of Pat's voice, singing his favorite tune filled her head. "Mostly the music."

"Do you like the Irish band The Cranberries?" Bren asked, sitting next to her.

Dani looked to Bren with surprise. "They were me ma's favorite."

Kate sat down in Kevin's chair next to Jess and laughed. "I'll never forget that song"—she pointed at Bren—"you played over and over again your senior year."

" 'Linger,' " Bren shouted across the table. "I loved that song," she said in a melancholy way and then motioned to Dani's purse. "Did you bring the phone I gave you?"

"Yes. It's in me purse."

"Remind me to give you a pair of earbuds. The album is on my iTunes account. You can listen to it."

"Oh, that'd be grand. I haven't heard it in years." Dani blinked back tears. Some days were harder than others when it came to her ma.

Her father pushed up from the table. "I need to get the truck ready." He motioned to somewhere in the distance past the house. "The bonfire. You know . . . and the fireworks." He walked away, no doubt feeling awkward at the mention of Dani's ma.

"Come on. Let's help your grandfather." Rafe motioned to Aiden.

"I'll give you a hand." Blake stood and caressed the back of Dani's neck. "I'll see you in a few."

Dani nodded. "I'll be inside washing up." Her hands had grown stiff with crab spice. Plus, if she wanted to get a look at the thumb drive, now was her chance. She cleared the table and headed across the patio. Slipping inside, she wondered where Kevin had gone to. He'd made it clear he didn't approve of her having a car before she'd gotten a license. She imagined his superior attitude—about certain things—came from being a cop. She could see his logic about the car, but it didn't change the way she felt. She wanted it—childish . . . maybe.

Dani traveled down the hall to the bathroom when the door opened.

Turk walked out and grimaced. "Jeez, Flynn, almost clocked you upside the head."

"You weren't even close. I saw you out the corner of me eye."

"See ya outside." He continued down the hall.

"Ah . . . Turk?" She raised her stiff, crab covered finger toward him.

He stopped and turned, raising his brows. "What's up?"

"Blake was Solley's owner." She bit down on her lip. "He was the one who sent him to auction."

He shrugged. "I guess that pompous ass gave himself away at dinner."

"Why didn't you tell me?"

"Wasn't my place. Lansing saw how you connected with the colt that day on the track. He could have 'fessed up." Turk shook his head. "Of course he doesn't see anything wrong with his practices."

Meaning this wasn't the first time he'd shocked one of his horses.

The day on the track when Solley had gotten away from Jake came flooding back. What a fool she'd been. It wasn't mere curiosity on his part. He wanted to know her secret. There wasn't one, unless compassion counted.

"Hey, why the long face, kid?" He gave a hard laugh. "If there's any justice for what he did . . . we'll get it on the track."

Right. Solley was a Starlite horse now. And with any luck, she'd be the one taking him over that finish line and into the winner's circle. "I'll see you outside, then. You're staying for fireworks?"

"You bet, kid." He waved her off and then turned back. "How about taking the day off on Thursday? Come up with us to Penn National and watch Chipper race."

She'd love to. But getting on the backside, if it was anything like the tracks in Ireland, required an ID. She'd been warned not to use it. Dani frowned. "Did Kevin ever, huh, speak to me circumstances...in regard to me citizenship?"

Turk made a face like he was trying to recall and then beaded in on her. "Is there something you need to tell me, Flynn?"

"It's nothing to worry about. I'm not quite legal."

His face fell. "Nothing to worry about," he echoed with disbelief.

"But I will be as soon as Kate helps me fill out the necessary paperwork."

"But you have a social security number?" He looked skeptical.

She grimaced. "It's expired."

"Well, damn. Good thing that I-9 won't see the light of day." He winked at her. "If it was New York, we'd have a problem. But Pennsylvania . . . we got some leeway. I'll see what I can do and talk to you tomorrow. If nothing else you can sit in the grandstand." He turned and headed for the patio doors.

Dani entered the bathroom feeling somewhat relieved she'd come clean with Turk and rather foolish about her flirtation with Blake. To think he had her believing his nonsense about fair competition. He wouldn't know fair if it bit him in the arse. Dani washed and then dried her hands. She'd deal with him later. For now she needed to get into Bren's computer and access the information on the thumb drive.

Clearing the bathroom, she went back toward the patio doors and took a right into the family room. She remained completely still, listening. The house was quiet. She skirted the brown leather sofas positioned to form an L. Between them sat an oval table with a small mahogany table clock. She recognized it immediately. A Charles Craig of Dublin clock was very rare. She'd only seen one other in her life—in Mr. Carrigan's home, during his annual Christmas party for all the workers at his stable. Ignoring the urge to touch it, Dani took the seat in front of the computer and pulled on the tab of her purse. The confounded zipper moved a wee bit, and she cursed under her breath for ever having bought the damned thing. And to think she only needed it to open a fraction, and it couldn't even accommodate her on that.

Of all the stupid things.

Chapter Twenty-Nine

"Y OUR'E THE BIGGEST ASS." B REN BEADED IN ON K EVIN.
"I love you, too." Kevin dropped back down in his chair across from
her. At least she'd had enough tact to wait until no one was around to call
him names.

"That's the problem. I do love you."

It was mutual. He'd know this woman his whole life—mourned with
her when her husband Tom, also his best friend, died. Fought like hell
with her while she ran amuck, trying to prove his death wasn't an
accident. She'd been right, too . . . at least about Tom's death. "What's on
your mind, Bren?"

She leaned in. "You need to lay off Dani."

He threw up his hands in defense. "What'd I say that wasn't true?"

"Stop treating her like a child."

"In many ways she is."

Bren's brows snapped together. "That's the most ridiculous thing I've
ever heard."

"You don't know the half of what's she's done."

"What's that supposed to mean?"

"Has she confided in you or Kate about how she got into the States?"

Bren shook her head.

"Kate fill out that immigration paperwork yet?"

"Tonight." Bren glanced at her watch. "Although, judging by the time,
it's going to have to wait until tomorrow."

Kevin checked his own watch—8:15. He'd have to get a move on it if
he wanted to get back to the command post at the Hagerstown Speedway

before the fireworks. He leveled a serious gaze at Bren. "Look. Your sister's running from something. Definitely from Ireland. I can't help her or stop whoever or whatever it is if I don't know what I'm dealing with."

Bren's lips thinned. "You think this threat would come here?"

He shrugged. "Depends on how big a threat it is. I need to know where she originated in Ireland."

"Did you ask her?"

He snorted. "She said and I quote, 'I'm not prepared to fill in the details. Not just yet,' " he mimicked Dani and her sweet Irish brogue, trying not to crack a smile.

Bren laughed. "You're falling for her. And if you don't make your move"—she looked past him—"she'll be someone else's."

Kevin turned around. Lansing was helping Rafe, Jess, and Daniel load the pickups with coolers and chairs. The three were laughing at something Jess had said.

Bren leaned over the table conspiratorially. "You and I both know he's an asshole."

Unable to stomach Lansing's theatrics, he gave Bren his full attention. "Then tell her. She won't listen to me."

"I'll talk to her tonight." Bren patted his hand.

Kevin connected with those grim brown eyes of hers. "You going to give me the you-need-to-settle-down lecture?"

"No. But I hate seeing you so miserable."

He'd stay miserable until he figured out a few things about Dani. Bren wasn't telling him anything he didn't already know. He was attracted to Dani—in a major way. Was it something more than lusting after his best friend's sister? He blew out an agitated breath. Yeah. Oh, yeah, and it frightened the hell out of him.

"I gotta go." He stood up. "She tells you anything about her past, I need to know."

"Just remember what I said about Dani."

"I'll try to keep my opinions to myself." Kevin took the patio step down to the lawn. The sky had turned cobalt blue, making the stars more visible. Fireflies blinked in the distance, and for once he wished he could share the holiday with his family, close friends, and a bewitching Irish beauty. He shook it off and unbuttoned his front uniform pocket and pulled out a folded sheet of paper, heading in Daniel's direction.

"Kevin, you leaving us so soon?" Daniel called from the bed of the truck.

Kevin waved at him as he neared the truck. "You have a minute?"

"Sure, sure." He patted Jess's shoulder on the way down.

"Gotcha, Dad." Rafe helped him the rest of the way and then rapped Kevin on his shoulder. "When you got some time, let's go fishing."

Kevin smiled at that. "You bet." He shook Rafe's hand.

"Good to see you, man." Jess slapped him on his back.

"You, too. How long you here for?"

"Wednesday."

"Have a safe trip home." Kevin turned his back on the group—Lansing in particular—and motioned for Daniel to follow him.

"Is there something wrong?" Daniel fell in step with him, his worried eyes searching Kevin's face.

"Nothing we can't solve together."

"Then there is a problem."

"Let's take a walk."

Daniel pointed to the far side of the house by the barn. "We could sit on the side porch and talk there if you'd like."

It was as good a place as any. Kevin nodded, and they made their way around the house. They each took one of the country rocking chairs—the same pair Bren and Kate had sat in that night when his life had collided with Dani's, literally.

He handed Daniel the paper. "It's a copy of Dani's birth certificate."

He looked to Kevin, then the paper, and back to Kevin, his old eyes filled with concern. "Is there a problem with it, then?"

"It says she was born in Waterford. I looked it up. It's on the east coast."

"It's a fine area."

"I'm worried about your daughter, Daniel."

He nodded. "We're working to get her all legal."

Kevin chose his words carefully, knowing they were going to sting. "She didn't come to the States looking for her father."

His brows rose. "What do you mean? Of course she did."

Kevin scrubbed his face hard. "She hopped a freighter—illegally. It was by chance it docked in the U.S."

"A freighter? You mean she stowed away?"

Kevin nodded.

"She could have been killed! Why would she take that risk..." Daniel's voice rose and then fell as understanding dawned. "So you're saying she had no intentions of finding her family—her sisters?"

Kevin placed his elbows on his knees and leaned over. "I think it was a bonus she hadn't counted on."

He shook his head. "I don't understand."

"She's running from something or someone. If she's a big enough threat, they'll come looking for her."

"Surely they wouldn't cross the Atlantic."

"I'm not willing to take that chance. I need you to tell me everything you remember about Rory Flynn. Where she lived, worked, might have settled. I need to know what Dani was involved in. But first I need to trace her back to her origins."

"Why don't you ask her yourself?" He fell back in his chair, no doubt shocked and maybe perturbed with the messenger.

"I did. She's not talking."

"Make her," he shot back.

"That entails arresting her, notifying ICE."

"What the devil is this ICE?"

"Immigration and Customs Enforcement."

His eyes widened. "They'll send her back. Whatever is there waiting for her surely hasn't gone away."

"That's my thought."

Daniel slid his glasses down onto his nose. "Let me take a look at that again."

Kevin handed it to him.

Daniel read the blocks off from the birth certificate, his expression thoughtful. "I'd gone back to Dublin to bury me da. We'd had a falling out years ago, hadn't really spoken since. I was angry at him 'til the day he died." He gave a wistful laugh. "Then angry at meself mostly for being so stubborn. I was sitting at a bar after the wake, in me cups, drowning me sorrows when this group from the Leopardstown Racecourse came in. They were hootin' and hollerin' about something or another. That's when this female jockey sat down next to me. She was a longshot, see. Won the Irish Champion Stakes, breaking her horse's maiden to boot."

"What county is Dublin in?"

"Dublin, same as the city." He scratched his head. "If you're looking to pinpoint where Rory lived, I couldn't say. Me own father was a trainer, and not a kind one at that. It was one of the reasons I left Ireland and started the rescue. But I'm getting ahead of meself. They—the racing stables—travel around, Rory would've been all over. But the county where Dani was born would be a starting place. Waterford is south of Dublin.

I'd start there." He tapped his fingers to his lips. "There's a port. It's actually in County Cork, right over from Waterford. It's called Youghal. I haven't the faintest idea if it's remained a bustling manufacturing town, but freighters were known to dock there in me youth."

Kevin pulled out his notepad and jotted the town down. "Anything else?"

He pursed his lips. "There's the next county over—Wexford. As I recall there was a seaside village named Rosslare and a harbor."

Kevin made additional notes. "I'll check it out." He stretched his legs and stood.

Daniel came to his feet. "I'm worried, Kevin. With all you've told me, how do I keep me girl safe?"

He patted Daniel on the shoulder. "That's my job."

Daniel nodded. "What of Bren and Kate? Have you told them?"

He'd told Bren the bare minimum. It hadn't been that long ago the two Fallon girls trampled a few laws themselves. They'd do it again to help their sister. "I'm asking you not to share with them what I've told you." Kevin gave him a knowing look.

"Aye. Those girls think with their hearts and not their heads."

Kevin grunted. "That's a nice way of putting it."

"I'm their father. I tend to sugarcoat things a bit." He chuckled. "It's more of being betwixt and between, I think." Daniel took hold of the knob of the back door. "Need to visit the head. You leaving, then?"

"Got to get back into town." Kevin shoved his notepad in his back pants pocket.

"You'll let me know what you find out?"

"Yeah." Kevin pulled his iPhone off his hip. "Soon as I know something."

Daniel nodded and slipped inside the house, and Kevin pulled up the Internet on his phone, typing in "Waterford news." It'd been almost three weeks since Dani had left Ireland. He scrolled down the headlines until he came to the beginning of June. Nothing. Then he pulled out the notepad, checked the other county, and typed in "Wexford news." A rag called the *Independent* popped up, and he clicked in, hitting the next tab for *Ireland Regional News*, and finally *Wexford People*.

Scrolling in the dark, trying to avoid stepping in a hole, he rounded the side of the house and headed toward his cruiser when a headline caught his attention: TWO LOCAL WOMEN FROM ROSSLARE MISSING.

Kevin read the first paragraph and clenched his jaw. "Son of a *bitch*."

Pulling the thumb drive out of Bren's computer, Dani sat perplexed. She'd recognized hers and Kara's names right off. Tommy Duggan had them under payroll. There'd be no denying they worked for him if the Garda caught up with her. But now it was becoming increasingly confusing. What exactly *was* her business on the docks—barring the obvious?

She could contemplate the other names on the thumb drive later tonight when she got back to the training center. For now, she needed to get back outside. Dani stood, made sure she'd left the oak desk the way she'd found it, and was skirting the two couches when she spied the lovely mahogany clock on the oval table between the sofas again.

A wave of melancholy swept over her. She missed Ireland—missed the music, the people who were good to her, and the sound of an Irish clock's chime. Drawn to the timepiece, she squeezed between the sofas. Thinking better of it, she worked the infernal zipper, trying to put the thumb drive away for safekeeping. The zipper didn't budge. Dani gritted her teeth and gave up, her interest turning toward the clock. She bent over to examine it.

This was a rare one, indeed. It still had the key and tassel that opened the wooden-framed door to the face, allowing one to change the time. Dani turned the key and opened the door, she couldn't help but touch the fine gold and silver front. Embossed black Roman numerals spanned the hours of the day on the round face. Corresponding minutes, also embossed in black, sat above each hour in intervals of five. The intricate minute hand moved a fraction to 8:59 p.m. *Sixty seconds.* Dani moved her head side to side with the ticktock of the clock, waiting anxiously for the chime to sound.

Hard-soled shoes hit the foyer behind her, and Dani stilled. Fear held her in its vise, her chest constricting. She let go of the key and fumbled with her purse and thumb drive.

"You lied to me!"

Kevin's sharp words filled her ears. She blanched and tried like mad to open the damned purse. The click of his shoes stopped the minute he stepped onto the carpet. Dani eyed the clock. It would have to do. Holding her breath, she placed the slim black thumb drive along the inside wooden ledge of the clock and shut the door, letting out her breath when the key turned easily in her hand.

She spun around. "It's a lovely clock, don't you think?"

His eyes tunneled into her. "Stop with the bullshit."

Dani swallowed hard. "I don't know what you're referring to, Kev—"

"Dani?" Blake walked in, followed by Bren, but it was her sister's concerned expression that made her heart beat faster.

Dani sidestepped Kevin, knowing full well he was burning a hole in her back. He'd be smart not to engage her again with that attitude. Whatever he wanted—based on his tone—it wasn't something he'd be sharing with Blake in the room. "Are we ready, then?" She slipped her arm inside Blake's though it was the last thing she wanted to do.

Blake looked from Dani to Kevin and back to her with one curious eyebrow raised. How incredibly Neanderthal. He was jealous of Kevin. Dani led him out the sliding glass doors. He had more to worry about than Kevin. She shut the door behind them. If Kevin had the nerve to follow them, Bren would intervene. She was sure.

Dani removed her arm from Blake's and looked up at him. "There's a matter I need to discuss with you."

He looked back at the house. "What's going on with you and Bendix?"

Dani crossed her arms. "You'll not be staying for fireworks. I'll find me own way home."

His eyes blazed heat, dark brows meeting in the middle, above his aristocratic nose. "What the hell are you talking about?"

She didn't miss the edge in his voice.

"Solitary Confinement."

He laughed out loud. "This is about a damned horse."

Dani tapped her foot on the stone patio. "That's how you think of them, I imagine. A piece of property you can ship off to auction if they aren't winning." She shook her head with disgust. "Me mistake was believing you actually cared."

"Dani." He tried to caress her face.

She jerked away. "You had me believing your song and dance about honest competition. But you shocked your way to the winner's circle and the hell with the horse that got you there."

He fell back a step. "Who told you that?"

"Word gets around."

He mumbled something under his breath, his face stiffening. "You don't know what you're talking about."

Dani clenched her teeth. "I know what a buzzer is. I know what it does to a poor horse who's trying it's best to win a race."

"Kevin tell you this?"

"No, not Kevin. His father."

"Turk." He snorted. "That wash-up would do anything to cause me trouble."

"You better watch your tongue, Mr. Lansing. That so-called wash-up has more heart and integrity in his bloody pinky than you'll ever have."

"Dani?" Bren stepped out onto the patio. "Everything all right?"

Dani hooked her chin over her shoulder. Bren stood in the lee of her covered porch, her expression hidden in shadow. But Dani recognized the concern in her voice, and the immediate love she had for Bren and all she'd done for her warmed her straight down to her toes. "Blake won't be staying for fireworks."

"Dani," he whispered under his breath, "don't . . ."

Dani called over her shoulder. "I'll just walk him out and meet you at Da's truck."

"Okay. I'll meet you out front." Bren stepped inside, leaving the spotlight on.

Dani took the step down from the patio. "I'll walk you out."

"This is ridiculous," Blake huffed and fell in beside her. "You could have at least asked me if it was true before you judged me."

Dani stopped and nailed him with a pair of irritated blue eyes. "Is it true, then? Did you electrocute the colt?"

He only stared at her.

She threw up her hands. "You *are* guilty."

He said nothing more and continued to his car. Of course he wasn't going to come out and admit it. If he did, he ran the risk of her telling Turk who would then run to the racing commission. Only he *would* keep doing it if she didn't do something to prevent it. Dani stopped in front of his Mercedes with the top down. "You don't have to admit it—I know the truth. But I warn you. Shock another horse into despondency, and I'll make sure you're arrested and held accountable."

He opened the door and got in. "That coming from an illegal alien is . . . laughable and unwise."

Panic rose in Dani's chest. No one had mentioned her status at dinner. He had to be bluffing. "I don't take kindly to threats, Blake."

Shutting the door, he placed his tanned, sinewy arm on the frame of the door. "Seems we both have a lot to lose." He punched the gas and took off down the gravel drive.

Dani remained, the lights of his Mercedes growing smaller until the car disappeared around the bend of the driveway. She didn't like to be threatened, but if she made trouble for him, he'd make sure this ICE Kevin talked about knew where to find her.

Tommy Duggan's cruel face invaded her thoughts, and Dani shivered in the humid night air.

Chapter Thirty

"**G**ET IN," KEVIN ORDERED FROM THE SEAT OF HIS PATROL CAR. HE couldn't hear what had transpired between Dani and Lansing from his parking spot by the barn. But if peeling wheels were any indication, he'd hazard a guess they'd had their first fight.

"So you can gloat?" she slung back, then walked in front of his car, her slim body and sexy bare legs caught in the beam of his headlights.

Kevin pulled ahead, angling his patrol car in front of her, and jammed it in park. He got out. "You're going to gather your things, say good night to your family, and we're going to settle things between us once and for all."

She laughed at him, the sound harsh yet pained. "Are you going to dump me in the next county over, then? Like you warned the first day?" Dani marched toward him, wiping hard at her face. "I'll save you the trouble," she said, her voice hitched as she tried to hold back a waterfall of emotion. She passed him and continued down the gravel drive.

Shit.

He'd been the competent, unruffled sheriff of Washington County for two terms. There wasn't a council member he didn't get along with or a deputy under his command who questioned his authority. Yet this woman was making a complete mockery of him. Kevin's radio went off, and he keyed it at his shoulder. "Go ahead." He kept her in his sights.

"I have that update, sir."

He keyed the mic, again, losing Dani in the tree line. "Give me the rundown."

"Two disorderlies, one drug possession, nothing further."

Kevin checked his watch—9:10. Fireworks didn't start until 9:30. It would be quiet, he hoped, until a little after ten. "Reach me by radio if you need me." He clicked off, with Bren moving at a fast clip toward him. *Great.*

"Where's Dani?"

"Running away." He flung open the car and grabbed his flashlight, slamming the door shut.

"What?" She zeroed in on him. "This isn't a game. She's hurting."

"I'm supposed to feel sorry for her because she and Lansing had a fight?"

Bren pushed past him.

Kevin grabbed her arm, holding her in place. "You're in no condition to traipse through the woods. I'll go talk to her."

She spun around, yanking her arm from his grip. "The same way you did in the house?" She gave him a lift of her brow.

Kevin clenched his jaw. Since he'd met Dani, he'd been labeled the bad guy. "It was concern, Bren. Concern for her well-being." Which was true, except now that he was thinking it through, he'd have to admit the advent of Kara Gilroy, although new, didn't change what Dani had already told him. So there were two. He only cared about one, and she was here with him. Well, maybe not, if he didn't go after her. "Okay. I shouldn't have yelled." He grimaced. "I'll handle Dani. *You*"—he motioned with his flashlight—"go watch fireworks."

"But what about—" She pointed a slender finger at the woods.

"I'll find her and see that she gets home."

Bren's mouth twisted with indecision. "Fine." She headed toward the corner of the house and the backyard where the pickups were parked and waiting and then turned. "Call me later."

Kevin nodded. "When I get a chance."

He took off down the gravel drive and ducked inside the wood line. Surrounded in pitch black, vines twining about his ankle like tripwires, he flicked on the flashlight, cursing Dani and himself. He should have turned her in to immigration that first night. If he had, he wouldn't give a damn what happened to her now.

Kevin swatted at branches and moved deeper. That was the problem—had been since taking her to his home that first day. He could see a future with her, if it weren't for her past. Whatever it was, it had been keeping her from being honest with him. He'd accepted that, and it was only now, as he fended off sharp barbs in the dark, his bare arms rubbing against supple leaves that quite possibly could be poison ivy, that he understood why.

He wanted her regardless of what lurked below the surface.

Fanning the light in front of him and then below, he stepped over a log. He should yell her name. He was close, had to be. She couldn't get far in her heels. That bothered him, too. This was the second time she'd gotten all made up for Lansing. He'd been pissed off from the moment he turned the corner onto the patio and found lover boy's arm around her.

Okay. If he wanted that future, it started with a few truths of his own. He was jealous. This thing with the Gilroy woman had been more about Lansing. His anger and frustration had been climbing like mercury inside a thermometer since he arrived.

Tonight, when he found her, he was going to lay down some new ground rules. He couldn't force her to give details of her life in Ireland if she was afraid. It would be up to him to find those answers. But he did expect her complete cooperation when it came to following his directives. This stunt wasn't earning her any brownie points. If anything it was childish. Not to mention dangerous—she'd already twisted her ankle doing the same damn thing.

That was what he struggled with the most. Should he turn her in to protect her? He wasn't so concerned about deportation now that she could prove Daniel was her biological father. Not to say she wouldn't find herself—until the paperwork went through—in an immigration detention facility. But they had their own set of problems—in-custody deaths for one.

Would she be safer? That was debatable. Accounted for? Sure. No longer a moving target? That last thought had him picking up his pace, his heart jackhammering in his chest. If he lost her tonight and she slipped through to the next county, she'd be another lawman's responsibility if she got caught. Whoever was after her, he—they—would have a better shot at getting her if she were arrested and sent back to Ireland.

"Dani!"

His head was on a swivel, the beam of light erratic. He slowed and came to a complete stop, hoping for a sound—twigs breaking, anything. Nothing.

"Dani!"

Kevin cursed, debating which direction to head next when a woman's soft sobs came from the right. Kevin aimed the light in the general vicinity, his shoulders relaxing. Ahead of him, maybe forty feet, Dani stood immobile.

Dani couldn't stop crying. She'd made a complete mess of her life. Her new one couldn't seem to gain enough traction before the old one flattened her with its cold reality. Lost, frightened, and caught in a vicious sticker bush that had her pinned in all directions, its sharp gnarled points digging into the soft fabric of her new dress, she couldn't even escape Kevin and the distrust he had for her.

Kevin pushed through knee-high vegetation, his flashlight stark and bright, illuminating her. It was no wonder he couldn't see straight through to her lying soul. She squinted and put her hand up.

"Hold still." He came up to her and shoved back the stickers with the long metal club of his flashlight, the thorns ripping at her clothes. "You hurt?"

No, she didn't think so. She bent her head to see, sucking in air at the thorns pulling on the pretty blue fabric. "Me dress," she squealed.

"I'll buy you a new one you can flaunt for Lansing," he said through gritted teeth and continued to attack the vines with little to no regard for the dress he was ruining.

Dani cried harder, her body shaking. "I bought it for you."

His head shot up. "What the hell are you talking about?"

"Nothing." She wiped at her face. "It was stupid. You're not the least bit interested in me."

"Whoa. I never said that." He pulled her from the thicket and handed her the flashlight. "You're in charge of navigation."

She gave him a questioning look. "And what are you—" She shrieked when he lifted her into his arms.

"Protecting you." He angled his head down to get a better look at her, his serious face caught in the halo of light coming from the flashlight. "For me, huh?" he said, with a quirk of his mouth, somewhat amused. "You and I have a lot to talk about." He held her tight and trudged through the forest, woodland debris cracking beneath his weight. He bent to avoid a low lying branch and eyed her. "You need to start trusting me."

Dani wet her lips, her body trembling. "It's not that I don't."

"You cold?" he said with concern and dipped his chin so that they were close to eye level.

She shook her head. "Mostly . . . scared."

He stopped, and even though she couldn't see his face clearly, she knew he was giving her that stern look of his. "This is when you start trusting me."

She did—with her life. But how would he handle the truth? It was her biggest fear.

Best to remain quiet.

He must have gotten the message because he nodded to the flashlight that she had moved to her lap. "Shine it out in front."

She did, and he continued with his determined strides. She remained silent, wrestling with her demons, trying to find the words he wanted to hear. She couldn't. But there were other things she did want to tell him.

"I accused Blake of electrocuting his horses and warned him not to do it again."

He shook his head. "Let me guess. He threatened you with deportation."

"How'd you know?" Dani narrowed in on him.

"The longer you're here, the more people you meet, the more you're going to drop unintentional hints." He sighed. "Look. Not everyone is like Lansing in this town." He chuckled. "Or like me. Although you know why I want and need your honesty," he said pointedly.

Kevin wasn't telling her something she didn't already know and respect about him. It bothered her, too—the lies. But she'd weighed the consequences, especially after getting a look at the thumb drive. How could it be that Tommy Duggan knew John Derry, the Deputy Prime Minister of Ireland or Mick Ryan, another almost equally well-known Irish politician? The names themselves wouldn't have raised an eyebrow, but finding them together in a document from a thumb drive Tommy Duggan would kill to have back in his possession surely meant something.

But there was one other problem that could cause her trouble, and he had nothing to do with her past. "I'm a little worried about Jake Griffin."

Kevin stopped a few feet from the wood line. "One of Dad's exercise riders?"

She nodded. "He doesn't like me very much."

"You know why?"

"Me friend Bonnie is his girlfriend."

"Ah. The blonde who let you borrow her car." He remained quiet, perhaps thinking it all through. "Sounds to me like he's jealous of your friendship. I'll keep an eye out, but Lansing is the bigger threat."

Dani's forehead creased with worry. "You should have turned me in to immigration." She lowered her lashes. "I'm sorry."

He stepped from the dark canopy of trees onto the gravel drive, the full moon illuminating his determined brown eyes. "I'll worry about Lansing, but I'm asking you to stay clear of him. Animal control has already investigated those allegations of abuse. There wasn't enough evidence to charge him with a crime."

"That doesn't mean he's not guilty," she shot back.

"I agree. But I meant what I said. You are in no position to intervene. That's my job."

Dani understood. Her hands were bound until her citizenship went through, but she did want to know one thing. "Who alerted them?"

Kevin frowned. "Who do you think?"

Dani knew of only one person. "He's a good man . . . your father."

He shrugged. "We've had our differences. When I was young I resented his profession—horses don't take Sunday off and neither did Turk."

A lump formed in Dani's throat. "And now?"

"As an adult, as a law enforcement officer, I still disapprove of the things that go on behind the scenes."

"But your father is good to the horses."

"I know he is. But others are not so kind."

Horse racing had a darker side from the pageantry of well-dressed owners, flashy silks, and grandstands full of exuberant spectators. She only needed to look as far as the next stable over to be convinced of that. But that wasn't what had her stomach twisting into knots.

"What's wrong?" He sat her down on her feet and began checking her legs, she assumed for scratches from the nasty thorns. He wouldn't find any marks. The lacerations were on her heart. He took the flashlight from her and shined it on her legs. "You cut?"

"No," she said, her throat tightening. "Horse racing. It's one of the reasons you don't respect me."

"It's not you, Dani," he said, his voice rough. "Your dad was more of a father to me than my old man. I grew up on Grace. My father's livelihood made it hard for me to compete for his affection or time. I hated everything that had to do with horse racing."

The sadness of his voice was palpable. Dani caressed the rough angles of his cheek. "Your father loves you. If anything, I think he longs for *your* acceptance."

"Maybe." He placed his hand against hers, still resting on his whiskery face, and brought it down. He kissed her palm. "I had this plan. College. FBI." He had a faraway look. "That changed after my mother's death. Couldn't leave the old man to his own devices." His gaze held hers. "Eventually, I planned to settle down—find the perfect partner." He shook his head. "I had this checklist, see. Then you showed up, totally blowing my preconceived ideas on what I wanted in a woman, a wife, and the mother of my children. Hell, Dani, I don't know where this is going. Your life is messy and complicated and could cost me the election. But I don't care."

Dani's heart beat furiously in her chest. "What are you saying, then?"

He chuckled. "I know you're just a kid . . ."

She stiffened. "I'm twenty-six. Almost twenty-seven."

"December first. I know." He pressed back her hair. "I'm thirty-nine, Dani. Does our age difference bother you?"

Her forehead crinkled with consternation. "Why on earth does it matter?"

"Because you're screwing with my perfect, orderly life. That's why," he snapped.

"You don't have to get so angry. I told you I'd leave."

"That's the problem. I don't want you to." He gave her a stern look. "I'm going to kiss you."

Dani's eyes widened, and she snickered. "You Americans are a strange lot. In Ireland we don't warn of an impending kiss we just—"

Kevin gave a rough tug, pulling her against him. "Just work with me." He bent his head, his eyes heavy with wanting, and kissed her. It was slow and deliberate.

Dani closed her eyes and threaded her arms around his neck, splaying her fingers through his short-cropped hair. He cupped her bum, his hand a sizzling brand, and she moaned into his mouth.

A firework exploded high above in the treetops. Kevin broke the kiss, leaving her tingly and confused. Dani's eyes flickered open under a colorful burst of oranges and reds fanning the night sky. She then concentrated on Kevin. He was breathing heavy, his gaze intent on her face. It was then she realized what he was about.

"It's not the kiss of a brother." She blushed. "Or a sister for you, I imagine."

"Not even close." He stroked her hair. "You leaving isn't going to solve the problem."

He spoke to her like they had a future. Like he was committing himself to her for however long this thing between them would last.

What of her activity in Ireland—was he piecing it together?

She knew this was the moment to come clean. But to tell him she'd been involved with a hustling, murdering scum like Tommy seemed too big a risk. He couldn't have a clue where to look for her but if Dani admitted she'd taken his filthy money even when it felt wrong, she'd lose everything for someone and something that quite possibly could never pose a threat.

She trembled in Kevin's arms. It was a huge gamble. One she could lose . . . in more ways than one.

CHAPTER THIRTY-ONE

THE CAR HAD BEEN MADE FOR SWEET SUMMER LANE DRIVES. THE DEEP sapphire blue two-door, Dani thought, looked best with its matching convertible top down, twinkling under the last bit of the sun's rays as her da took the right into Whistledown.

He parked the car with its automatic transmission—a plus since she didn't know how to begin to drive a stick shift—in the lot in front of Starlite's barn, a satisfied smile tugging at his lips. "We got him down, Dani girl, didn't we?"

Her father, she learned, liked to dicker. The salesman didn't have a chance at his asking price of forty-three hundred. Dani narrowed in on him. "I meant it when I said I'll be paying you back the thirty-six hundred."

"I told you, sweetheart"—he tweaked her nose—"it's a gift. I've spent far greater amounts over the years on both your sisters." He wagged a finger at her. "Your job is to pass that test and get your license so you can drive it." He patted her knee and got out, favoring his back.

"Aye," Dani whispered, her voice edged with concern for him, his age, and what little time she might have left with him. But she eased these concerns from her mind when she ran her fingers along the sporty black and tan leather upholstery of her Volkswagen Cabrio. She loved the car—loved her da for helping her and putting it on his insurance until she could get her own.

Dani tinkered with the knobs on the pristine dashboard. It could pass for brand-new with a working radio, cup holders, and automatic door locks. Considering she wasn't even close to having a license, Kevin would more than likely complain about its existence and expense, not to mention the high miles, but she knew the quality of a German-engineered car. At one hundred and thirty-two thousand, it was just breaking in.

Fritz and Bonnie pulled in next to them in Daniel's white pickup. Bonnie jumped out, wide-eyed and smiling. "It's stunning," she said, laughing as she picked her way through the gravel parking lot in a pair of strappy sandals.

Dani got out of the passenger side, giggling. *Stunning* had been the preferred adjective used by the barrel-chested used car salesman who sold them the convertible. "I'm pinching meself. I can't believe it's really mine." Dani met Bonnie next to the car, wearing her new crocheted cream-colored sundress and leather wedges. They grabbed for each other's hands, squealing with delight.

Fritz ambled toward them and shook her da's hand. "You're an excellent negotiator, my friend."

Her da slapped Fritz on the shoulder. "It was good thinking on your part to check the ragtop."

"I just remember that Ford Mustang years ago." He got a devilish look in his eye.

"Ah." Her father's face lit with understanding. "The one that always got stuck in the rain."

They said something inscrutable and laughed. Dani guessed they were reliving some incident from the past not meant for a daughter's ears.

But it was her own past that still haunted her. Everything she'd ever hoped for was coming together at lightning speed. She and Kevin were starting a romantic relationship. She hadn't asked for promises. Under the circumstances—her complete honesty or lack thereof—it was best not to look too far into the future.

"You going to take it for a spin around the training center, then?" Her father opened the driver's door and jingled the keys.

"You sure it will be all right?"

"It's a private driveway, lass." Fritz motioned to her.

Dani came around and took the keys from her da. He was beaming at her with those twinkling blue eyes. She would have never believed she'd come to love him and her sisters as quick as she had. And it wasn't the possessions she'd gained because of them. They were kind, giving people. The sort of people she'd always wanted for a family since the loss of her dear ma. Tears pinched the backs of her eyes, and she hugged her father tight. "I love you, da," she whispered in his ear. "And not because of me beautiful car. You're the kindest, most loving man I know."

He hugged her tight. "Ah, me girl. I love you, too."

Standing behind her da, Fritz cleared his throat, peering at her with a pair of raised eyebrows.

Aw. Dani kissed her father on the cheek and then turned to hug Fritz. "You're a kind old man, too."

"What the hell?" Turk grumped out of the barn and came up to the group. "Can't a man plan his training schedule without all this racket?" He bunched his brows at them, sporting a scowl.

Dani wanted to laugh. He worked hard to maintain his superior air of grouchiness. Only it didn't work with her. The simple truth was Turk Bendix wanted to feel part of a bigger whole. He wanted to share in the laughter, joke with his friends, and harass in a teasing way. In the short time she'd been here, she'd learned he had one of the biggest hearts of all. Holding tight to her key, she wrapped her arms around his short pudginess and squeezed him hard. "That's for taking a chance on me."

He sputtered and tried to push her away. Dani would have no part of it. He was going to stand there like a man and take her affection.

"Now you've taken it to a whole new level of weird." Jake's sardonic voice sliced through her. Where had he come from? She made a face and spun around, her lips now razor thin.

"The Tin Man and the Scarecrow." He laughed, the sound toxic. "Turk, you're the Cowardly Lion?"

"Jake!" Bonnie swatted him.

He raised his hand, and Bonnie flinched before Jake pulled it down, realizing he had an audience. Dani knew he was belligerent. Now she wondered if he had gotten physical with Bonnie, too. Dani hadn't noticed any telling marks on her, though.

"It's okay, Bonnie," Dani said. She might be Irish but she knew the movie to which he was referring and lifted her chin with defiance. "If there's anything wicked on this training center"—Dani eyed Jake—"it would be the Wicked Wizard of Whistledown." Dani drilled him with unsmiling eyes, refusing to look away.

Turk snorted beside her.

'Twas funny. But she wouldn't laugh. She hated Jake—hated that he treated Bonnie with little to no respect. It didn't help his case that he reminded her of Tommy, either, with his jet black hair that hung provokingly past his eyes. He was hiding something Dani couldn't put a finger on, exactly, but she'd be keeping an eye on him.

Dani let it go for now. Keeping a line of separation between them would be her best option. "Bonnie, let's take it for a spin." Dani grabbed the open driver's door and motioned for her to get in the other side.

Bonnie hesitated, glanced at Jake, and grabbed the handle, flinging the door open. Their bums landed with a thud, and they shut the doors almost simultaneously, then secured their seat belts. Dani reached over and squeezed Bonnie's knee. Their eyes connected, and Dani searched her friend's for telltale signs of drugs. They were bloodshot, but her pupils were not constricted. That didn't mean there weren't drugs in her system. Bonnie's eyes darted toward Jake who was scowling at her.

Lord she hoped Bonnie didn't have a mind to ask him to hop in the back. She'd hit the gas and leave him coughing in her dust cloud to avoid that happening. Bonnie nervously tapped the door handle with her fingers, and Dani started the car before either one of them had a change of heart. Not that she was concerned a whit about Jake. But she did care for Bonnie, and that would be the only reason she'd give in or curb her tongue.

"Dani." Turk's old hand landed on the frame of her door. "While you're taking that drive, I need you to pick up the mail."

"Sure." She looked at Bonnie. "Where would that be?"

"At the end of the road as you come in."

"Okay, then." Putting the car in drive—she loved the sporty gear shift between the seats—Dani checked to be sure she wasn't going to run over a foot. Seeing it was clear, she backed up and then tapped the gas, the car bucking like an untamed stallion. She rolled her lips in, her eyes widening and landing on her father. She shrugged sheepishly. "Pedal's a bit touchy."

Crossing his arms over his chest, he shook his head and laughed—the sound deep and infectious.

Dani laughed and waved at him, this time pulling out with ease.

She took the quick right onto the training center's private road, feeling freer and happier than she'd felt in months. The wind whipped her hair, the warm July sun warmed her skin, and Dani hit the radio knob, a popular tune filling her ears.

Glancing at Bonnie, she grabbed her hand. "Isn't she grand?" she shouted over the music.

Bonnie moved her head to the beat, smiling at her. "She's great!"

Dani shook Bonnie's hand in hers. "No, you're great!"

The end of the road came up quick. Dani made a sharp U-turn to keep from zooming out onto the two-lane highway. She screamed, as did Bonnie, and stomped on the brake, her body flying forward until the seat belt locked hard across her chest. The car skidded to a stop an instant later, missing the line of mailboxes by degrees.

Dani's heart thudded in her chest. "God, I'm so sorry, Bonnie," she said, breathing hard. Then her shoulders snaked up. "You don't think they saw me lose control, do you?"

"You're good." Bonnie turned down the radio with shaky fingers. "We're too far away."

Dani nodded, feeling like a spoiled child taking her da's car for a joyride without his permission. "That was incredibly stupid."

Bonnie rubbed Dani's shoulder. "You were excited." She smiled. "I was excited for you."

That was why she loved Bonnie. She truly was a wonderful friend, which was why this whole dark drug cloud upset Dani. "And I worry about you."

"Why?" Bonnie frowned at her.

Mentioning she knew about her accident and the pills would only upset Bonnie. Dani would stick to what she'd witnessed today. "I don't like the way Jake treats you."

She laughed, the sound uneasy. "He can be a jerk sometimes, I admit."

"He's never hit you, I hope."

Bonnie shrugged. "He gets angry. I make him angry."

Dani's fingers gripped the steering wheel hard. "Oh, now you're talking nonsense, Bonnie. You've been nothing but kind to him." Dani thought about that for a moment and couldn't help but laugh. "Except you did yell at him that night he was being a minger in the backseat of your car when I was driving it."

Bonnie laughed along with her. "You mean when you sent his head into the back window?"

Dani wouldn't lie. She'd enjoyed, in a sadistic sort of way, him bouncing around like an erratic pinball. A self-satisfied smile tugged at her lips. "He deserved it."

"Can we talk about something else?" Bonnie remained quiet for a moment. "But thank you . . . for worrying."

Reluctant, Dani nodded. She'd continue to worry, and, *no,* she wasn't fine. "You talk to Chipper at all today?"

"In passing." Bonnie's brows furrowed. "Was she supposed to talk to me about something?"

Dani fidgeted in her seat. "Not that I'm aware." It was a lie, and Dani hated herself for it. Still she'd let Chipper talk to her. She'd known her longer. It would be best coming from someone who knew Bonnie's history firsthand. But Jake . . . Jake could be dealt with. Dani turned sharp in her seat. "If Jake ever hits you, I want you to tell me. I'll have Kevin talk to him."

A silly grin tugged at Bonnie's lips.

"What?" Dani jerked her head back in challenge. Bonnie, obviously, didn't know Kevin at all. That night she'd shown up at Grace played back in her mind in living color. "He'll arrest him same as me."

Bonnie's lips sputtered. "Sheriff Tightass arrested you?" Her eyes widened.

Shite. The words had fallen off her lips before she could stop them. Dani gave a nervous chuckle. She'd have to come out with the truth. "I was caught trespassing on me family's farm." She waved a dismissive hand. "He took the cuffs off once he realized Daniel Fallon was me father."

"Did he put the cuffs back on you last night?" She narrowed in on Dani with a pair of speculative green eyes.

Dani's face twisted with confusion. "Last night?"

Bonnie laughed out loud. "Relax. I was just kidding about the kinky sex." She leaned in conspiratorially. "Is he a good kisser?"

Ah. She must have seen Kevin drop her off. Dani's stomach tumbled sweetly, remembering his good night kiss. It had made her just as shivery as the one under the colorful fireworks at the farm. She nodded, feeling vulnerable and awkward and wondering if she should have admitted to anything. Dani reached over, grabbing Bonnie's hand, squeezing it hard. "Please don't tell anyone."

"Your secret's safe." Bonnie gave her a quick hug. "I'm so happy for you."

"Me, too," Dani said, her eye catching the time on the clock in the console. They'd been jabbering on for at least ten minutes. "I better get the mail." She hopped out, checked the numbers and names on the row of mailboxes several steps away, and retrieved the mail. She recognized Cloverdale's box but not the box with the name Delhaven. Eventually, if she kept her job with Turk, she'd get to know the other racing stables at the training center. Once back in her car, she handed the banded pile to Bonnie. "Can you hold this for me?"

"Yep." Bonnie placed it on her lap.

Dani took the gravel road back toward the barn, glancing over at Bonnie. "If something was bothering you, you'd tell me?"

"Yeah. Of course." Bonnie gave her a peculiar look. "Something bothering *you*?"

Dani shook her head. She'd said enough. If Bonnie wanted to open up to her, ask for her help, she'd made it clear she could come to her. There wasn't much more she could do except confront her. For now she'd let Chipper handle it. "You and Jake going to Penn National with Chipper and Turk on Thursday?"

"Yep. How about you?"

"Turk said I could sit in the grandstands since I don't have me credentials to be on the backside." Dani pulled into the parking area and frowned at Jake still talking with Turk and her da.

"How'd it go, sweetheart?" Her da opened up her door for her and helped her out.

"She's a dream." Dani gave him a kiss on his cheek. "Thank you again."

"I'm glad it makes you happy, then." He checked his watch. "Bren and Kate are on their way to talk about getting you all squared away so you can get that license. I'm going to head on home." He hugged her one last time and winked. "I'm a wee bit tired." He crossed the parking lot at a slow pace and got into his truck.

"Let's see what we got in the way of bills." Turk came up alongside her, his hands out in a gimme kind of way.

"See you tomorrow," Bonnie called to them and started toward the bunkhouse with Jake.

"Bye."

"Flynn? I need you . . ." He waved several envelopes in her face.

Totally lost with misgivings over Bonnie and Jake, she'd tuned everyone out, including Turk. "I'm sorry." She gave him a conciliatory smile. "What was it you wanted, then?"

"The mail. It's Bailey's. Confounded mailman is always mixing it up."

Dani took several envelopes from him. "Would you let my sisters know I'll be right back?"

"No problem." He turned to go inside the barn and then swung around. "Make sure he doesn't have any of our mail while you're at it."

"Okay. I'll check with him." Dani headed toward Cloverdale's barn conflicted. She was the happiest she'd been in a long time. She had a good paying job, a boss she liked, a nice place to live, even though it was a bit cramped, and the man of her dreams. Oh, and a car. That—reliving her near collision—she couldn't drive. Her shoulders sagged. And to learn she needed her citizenship. She wouldn't let that technicality bother her. It would be an easy fix soon enough.

"Dani?" Fritz said, his voice a little concerned. "You all right?"

She waved and walked over to where he stood next to his pickup. "Some of your mail got mixed up with ours."

"Oh." His expression softened. "It happens from time to time."

"Turk wanted me to ask if any of Starlite's ended up in your box." She handed him the envelopes.

"I'll have to ask Zelda in the morning. She's in charge of it."

Right. She'd seen his blue-haired secretary moving in slow motion to her car on occasion.

Fritz flipped through the envelopes, a few falling to the ground. He made a move to pick them up.

"I'll get them." Dani bent down and gathered them up, brushing the grit of the gravel drive off them when her eyes landed on the words PAST DUE stamped in red. Her gaze lingered on the envelopes. One was from a feed company, the other a saddlery.

Fritz cleared his throat.

Dani's head shot up. Something between embarrassment and maybe a touch of annoyance flitted in his usually smiling eyes. "I'm sorry. I wasn't prying." She handed them over, her hands shaking, unsure if he was angry or more uncomfortable.

He chuckled. "Ah, lass, it happens quite a bit." He leaned in like he was about to share a secret. "I need a younger assistant."

Dani laughed, too, but mostly at her own foolishness, and the feeling that something was amiss vanished. She'd gotten plenty of past due notices herself.

Only she didn't have a Zelda to blame.

Chapter Thirty-Two

When Dani returned, Turk directed her to her room by way of a wave. "They're waiting upstairs." He locked the door to his office, effectively keeping news from Rosslare an absolute mystery, and headed out the barn for home. She guessed with all that had happened, this would be a common practice from here on out.

Climbing the stairs, it hit Dani like a magic power she'd had all along but didn't realize she possessed until now. The iPhone Bren had lent her was a computer. It might not be able to read a thumb drive, but she could search the Internet. She'd ask Bren to show her how. Rounding the stairs, she traveled down the short landing. Raised voices—and not at all amicable ones—came from her room, and she opened the door. Bren and Kate turned, their expressions grim.

"What is it?" Panic rose in Dani's chest.

"Dani, we need to talk." Kate motioned her to take a seat next to Bren on the bed.

She sat down, her legs trembling.

Bren gave her a stern look. "How did you come into the States?" Her severe tone demanded Dani be forthright.

Dani swallowed hard, trying to decide what she could tell them. If they went to Kevin, she had to be sure she was telling them something he already knew. "I-I hopped a freighter." Dani's head swiveled from Bren to Kate. "Illegally."

"*Shit,*" Bren hissed. "A freighter? Why would you do such a thing? You could have been killed!" A look of disbelief—or was it anger?—tinged her usually warm eyes. "We're so screwed."

Dani hung her head unable to explain herself further.

"You're not helping, Miss High and Mighty," Kate snapped at Bren. "You snuck into Mexico through a damn drug cartel's tunnel yourself."

"You're no better." Bren narrowed in on Kate. "You faked your death, changed your identity, and left me." Bren's voice hitched, and she began to cry.

Kate's mouth fell open in disbelief. "Oh, my God. That was your idea."

"To escape your husband and save your life!" Bren cried harder.

Oh, dear. They both had two husbands? Dani's head was reeling. Her forehead creased with bewilderment even as she felt closer to these women than ever before. She had no idea how similar she was to her sisters. It would seem the word "trouble" was genetic. One day she was going to sit them both down and demand to hear the sordid details of *their* illicit pasts. But for now she'd work on restoring peace and driving the conversation back to her citizenship.

Dani pulled Bren to her and patted her back. Dressed in cute matching shorts outfit and maternity top with horses, she made for an adorable expectant mother. It truly upset Dani to see the stronger of her two sisters break down. She'd attribute it to hormones and the stress of an impending birth. "Let's not fight." She handed Bren a Kleenex from the box on her headboard shelf and eyed Kate.

Kate pushed her lips out into a pout. "I'm sorry." She knelt down in front of her and Bren, placing her hands on Bren's knees. "Forgive me?" she said, her contrite brown eyes searching Bren's.

Bren nodded and blew her nose.

"What is it you came to talk to me about?" Now that everyone had made nice, Dani needed to move the conversation forward. She knew based on Bren's outburst it was no longer a matter of signing on the dotted line and having the United States bestow her with citizenship.

"I made a few calls this morning. Just to make sure I wasn't missing anything." Kate stood up, leaning her bum against the chest of drawers. "Dad needed to legitimate you before your eighteenth birthday."

"What? I don't understand." A lump formed in Dani's throat. "But I'm his daughter."

"It's a jackass law," Bren said, dabbing her eyes.

Kate gave Bren a look of reproof. "But it's still the law."

Dani released Bren and concentrated on the lawyer in the family. "What do we do, then?"

Throwing up her hands, Kate paced back and forth in the cramped room. "It's a problem because you entered the U.S. without inspection, meaning with no passpor—"

"But I have one!" Dani jumped up. "It's in the lock box." She went for the wardrobe.

"Dani," Kate said softly. "You need a passport with a valid visa, honey. That's been stamped by U.S. immigration as you legally entered the country."

Dani rolled her lips in, tears hitting the back of her eyes. "I can't go back!"

"It would only be until you get your green card," Kate said, trying to be reassuring.

Dani shook her head, wrapping her arms around her waist. "I'll take my chances here. No one knows my immigration status." Blake's threat loomed dark and forbidding, and she threw her head back in distress. "*God.* Except Blake Lansing."

"You told him?" Bren's voice sounded accusing.

"No! He figured it out."

"Is that what you were arguing about?" Bren leveled a hard gaze at her.

Dani shrugged. "Not exactly."

"What exactly?" Kate folded her arms. "We need to know."

Dani took a huge breath through her nose. "He's electrocuting his horses."

Bren's eyes filled with alarm. "You know this for a fact?"

"Not firsthand. But judging by his reaction after I accused him, I think it's true."

Dani couldn't say, but the revelation seemed to hit Bren especially hard. Dani took her hand and squeezed. "He'll not do it again. It's me hope, anyway." She tried to smile. "I'm gambling that me illegalalienship—" She tried to laugh. "It's not a word, I know. But the point is Blake and I both have something on each other. I'd say we're at a stalemate."

"Dani," Kate said on a heavy sigh. "It's too big of a risk. If it's not Blake, it could be someone else. As it is now, you can return and apply for your green card and be back in six months. *Legally.*"

She wouldn't even survive twenty-four hours on Irish soil—much less six months.

Kate took a step toward Dani, scooching onto the bed. Her serious brown eyes locked onto Dani's anxious blue ones. "If you don't go back now and someone does turn you in, we really are screwed here." She cocked her head. "What day did you arrive in the States?"

Dani had to think back. "I think it was almost two weeks ago." She counted the days backward. "June twenty-first."

Kate nodded. "If you're discovered after you've been in the States for more than six months illegally and you're deported, they—U.S. immigration—won't allow you back for ten years. If you're lucky."

Dani couldn't breathe. Ten years. Her da could be dead by the time she was allowed back in. It seemed so unfair. She had every right to stay. She loved her new life—loved her sisters. The bond she now shared with them would shatter with the distance. Then there was Kevin. So much for finding her true love.

But if she were dead . . .

Wringing her hands, Dani stood up and faced her sisters. They were beautiful women with full lives and loving hearts. It wouldn't be fair to bring them into her nightmare without leveling with them first. "There's something you both need to know." This was where it was going to get a bit tricky. She needed to give them bits and pieces—enough to understand the danger without making them targets, too. "I'm a witness to a murder in Ireland."

Kate's and Bren's eyes widened with horror.

"I've shocked you." Dani was numb to it all. She'd been living the hard, cold reality of it for weeks. "It was an accident that I ended up anywhere near Grace. I shouldn't have come." She shook her head in utter disbelief of what she was going to say next. "And I shouldn't stay. I'd be putting your lives at risk."

Bren laughed while Kate tried to hide a smile.

Dani's mouth fell agape. "What's so bloody funny?" Dani looked from one to the other with irritation. "I'm completely broken up about it. And you're . . . you're . . . *laughing*."

Bren wiped away tears. Only they were from laughter. "It's not that it's funny . . . exactly."

Kate shook her head, smirking. "I think it's more of history repeating itself, again."

"Again?" Dani was truly perplexed. "I don't understand."

"For now all you need to understand is this." Bren looked pointedly at Dani. "Whatever happens, we're in this together."

"And you're staying put. But no more secrets." Kate wagged a finger at her and sat down on the floor, leaning her back against the chest of drawers. "How many we talking . . . murderers, I mean?"

"Two." She looked from one to the other, unsure. "But I'm only concerned with one of them."

"Would he follow you here?" Kate said.

Dani bit down on her lip. Yes, yes, he would to get to the thumb drive. She was sure. "He wouldn't know where to look." It was an honest answer—just not the one that should be rolling off her lips.

Kate nodded. "Then your job is to keep a low profile."

That would be easy enough. America was vast. Even if he had figured she'd crossed the Atlantic with the freighter, he wouldn't know where to look for her. She wasn't noteworthy to begin with. Even if she, in the end, was arrested and deported, the news agencies were more interested with the influx of illegal immigrants through Mexico. Or so she'd seen on television back in Ireland.

"What about keeping an eye on this guy in Ireland?" Bren's voice shook with concern.

Kate frowned and looked about the room, her eyes narrowing on the edge of the borrowed iPhone, hanging over the chest above her. She snagged it. "This has Internet access." Kate fooled with the phone. "What would you look up for news from home?"

"*Wexford People.*"

"Do you know how to use this to do an Internet search?"

"If you show me."

"It's simple." Bren took the phone from Kate. "See this icon that looks like a compass?"

Dani nodded.

"Just hit it. A search bar comes up at the top, and you type in *Wexford People.*"

"Let her try it," Kate said.

Bren handed her the phone, and Dani followed the simple steps until she was on the newspaper's home page.

"Search it now." Kate motioned with her hands.

Dani scrolled through, nothing catching her eye. "I don't see anything."

"What exactly are we looking for?" Bren gave Dani that older, wiser sister look.

Dani's eyes grew wary.

"I think she's afraid to involve us," Kate said.

"He-he killed me best friend." She looked to them beseechingly. "He'll not hesitate to kill again."

"Okay." Kate stood up. "I get it. I went through something similar. That's why I changed my identity." She gave Bren a knowing smile. "To protect my family."

Dani had a weird thought. "Are you not really my sister, then?"

Kate laughed. "No, I'm your sister. And I am Kate Fallon Parker."

"Just not Kate Reynolds, thank God," Bren said, her voice a little irritated.

Kate cleared her throat. "I think we can leave my tortuous past for another time." She gave Dani a conciliatory smile. "Maybe a name and a description of this guy would help us. Just in case he should ever show up looking for you."

Dani thought about that. If she gave them a name, especially Kate, she'd use that probing lawyer brain of hers to find out more information about Tommy. But there was one thing that would give him away, should he ever show up. "He's Irish same as me. You'll know the moment he opens his mouth."

"Okay." Kate nodded her understanding. "What about a description?"

"Dark hair, long over a pair of piercing, evil gray eyes . . . average size and weight but muscular."

Kate nodded to Bren. "You making a mental note?"

"Yeah. I'm guessing we're not sharing this with anyone else," she said a little uneasily. "I hate keeping secrets from Rafe."

Kate shrugged. "What are the chances he'll show up?"

That was what Dani kept asking herself.

"I don't think we should worry the rest of the family about something that isn't, in all likelihood, going to happen," Kate said.

"So what's the plan?" Bren leaned in conspiratorially, resting her elbows on her knees.

"I head back to Colorado tomorrow. Lay low while I'm gone." She directed that to Dani, then to the both of them. "I'll be back in a few weeks for the birth, and we'll see where we are then." She rolled her lips in, considering, and then took a heavy breath, turning toward Dani. "I wouldn't even ask this of you if I was one hundred percent sure this thing won't go south on us. But if Irish law enforcement is looking for your friend's killer, it might be possible to arrange some type of immunity for your having entered the U.S. illegally—if you were in fear for your life and could offer an eyewitness account."

If only she had a body to prove it. Dani nodded but said nothing more. Everything they'd discussed as a unit, she'd have to rehash in her own mind. She still wasn't completely convinced the decisions they were making today would be in the best interest of her family tomorrow.

Kate hugged Dani to her. "It's going to be okay, honey."

Dani hugged her back, the warmth of her sister's embrace giving her comfort until a glaring stab of conscience radiated cold down her back. Shivering, Dani pulled away. "What about this citizenship issue and telling Kevin?"

"No!" Bren's eyes filled with alarm, and she pulled herself up, holding her belly. "Especially not Kevin."

CHAPTER THIRTY-THREE

K EVIN WOULD GO WITH HIS GUT AND SAY THE LOOK BETWEEN SISTERS
was conspiratorial. Maybe it was him standing in the doorway of
Dani's bedroom, dressed in summer loafers, nice shorts and shirt—the
shirttails pulled out to conceal his gun—and smelling of aftershave, that
didn't seem in keeping with the sheriff of Washington County who, a few
weeks ago, had her prone in the dirt, handcuffed, and wishing like hell
their paths had never collided.

"What?" He gave Bren the evil eye. Of all people, she knew damn well
what he was up to.

"Ah. Nothing. You look . . ."

"Very sharp." Dani smiled up at him, wearing a hot, curve-loving
halter dress and strappy-sandals that, now that he thought about it, were
turning him on. "Would you like to come in?"

The room barely fit the three of them already. Hell if he was going to
invite any more scrutiny from Bren or get pinned with questions he didn't
have the answers to. He'd stay on the outside looking in. He did a double
take at the room. Although small, it was cozy, comfortable, and looked
nothing like the pine box he'd seen the last time he was here. "You do
this?" he said to Dani.

"With me sisters." She beamed at him.

Damn. "You must have spent—"

"It was our treat." Bren pulled herself up from an actual bed with a
frame and headboard. She motioned to Kate, the two moving toward the
door.

Door. Shit, he'd missed that, too.

Some investigator he was, which reminded him. "You figure out this citizenship thing yet?"

Kate hugged Dani. "I'll see you late August, sweetie." Then she slipped by him, squeezing his arm. "All taken care of, Kev."

That seemed too pat an answer. Bren made a move to slide by him, too. Only the little beach ball couldn't fit as easily as the trim general contractor who was already at the top of the stairs, trying to avoid him.

Kevin grabbed Bren by the arm. "Whoa, little mama. Not so fast." He eyed Bren and caught Kate nervously wetting her lips—something she did a lot when they were kids *and* when they were in trouble *and* lying to avoid detection. "Do I need to remind the two of you," he started as he zeroed in on Dani—she knew not to lie to him, especially after how they'd left things last night, "that I'm taking a huge risk with my career." He didn't have to go into specifics.

"There's nothing more to do but wait." Bren gave him her most sincere expression.

Why did he feel like she was playing him? Although . . . it did make sense. He'd run into bureaucratic red tape on a few government grants for the sheriff's office. Why would immigration be any different, especially now with the influx of Central American kids hopping the borders in countless droves?

"I want to know when the paperwork goes through." He leveled a hard gaze on all of them. He'd dealt with a few illegal aliens, done what he was supposed to do—arrested them on failure to possess documents or entry without inspection, both of which Dani had admittedly trampled when she hopped the damned freighter and snuck into the U.S. He now knew the point of entry to be the Port of Philadelphia and the name of the freighter. Oh, yeah, he'd taken what little he had learned last night and spent a little while this morning at work digging for more answers. He was unraveling the details of her exit from Ireland, slowly but surely.

Only he was at a definite loss when it came to Dani's extenuating circumstances—namely, Daniel. Of course that was a bunch of bullshit, too. Laws were like chameleons—they were always changing. It had never stopped him before. Research was part of being a cop, except for once this cop didn't want to know the truth—or a future without Dani in it. But this immigration detention thing still bothered him. "So with this caveat of being born to a U.S. citizen, Dani is free to remain in the States until this acquisition goes through?"

Bren glanced down at Kate, her expression questioning.

"Pretty much," Kate called back from the top of the stairs.

Kevin let go of Bren's arm, feeling like a bully. "Be careful on the steps."

She winked at him. "Why don't you take Dani for a spin in her new convertible?" She leaned in. "Big Pond is a romantic spot," she whispered and then made her way down the stairs with Kate, the two giggling.

Kevin shook his head and closed his eyes for an infernal moment, trying to collect his thoughts. The car pissed him off. She didn't need it, didn't have a driver's license, and, he feared—based on his last encounter with her on the road—couldn't drive it without a few lessons.

He entered the room and shut the door behind him. Dani stepped back and lowered her lashes.

"Hey, I'm okay with the car," he said, even though, technically, it was a lie.

She lifted her face to him, long black lashes fluttering open. "I had no intentions of really buying a car. It all got a bit out of hand last night at dinner."

He caressed her warm cheek. "I guess it's a father's prerogative to lavish his children with gifts."

"It's not a gift." Her eyes blazed back at him. "I already told him, and I'll tell you: I'll be paying him back. I'm not a moocher, if that's what you're thinking."

Kevin pulled her into his arms and kissed her pouty mouth. "Relax." He looked down his nose but in an appreciative way and smiled. "You're kinda cute when you're angry."

"I'm not angry, Kevin." She pulled away. "I just want to get on with me life."

Meaning she wanted all the things an American citizen was entitled to. He understood and wanted those things for her, too, and it started with a simple drive. "Come on, Irish." He took her hand in his. "Show me your snazzy convertible, and we'll take it for a ride on the open road."

"You mean it?" Her expression brightened. "I thought for sure you'd be—"

"Mad." He motioned her out the door. "I'm trying not to be that cop who's always looking for the negative."

She grabbed her key ring from the chest. It jiggled in her hands. He guessed having keys that unlocked doors was a good thing. He only hoped one wouldn't slam on his fingers for trusting her.

Kevin waited for her to lock her door. Taking her hand in his again, they took the steps down to the barn and made their way out to the parking lot. From what he could see, now that the sun had sunk below the horizon, on the outside at least, it looked to be in good condition. "What year?"

"Two thousand and two."

Twelve years old. But it was German. "How many miles?"

"One hundred thirty-two thousand. I know you think it's too high," she went on anxiously, "but it's—"

"It's okay. Why don't you get in and pop the hood? I'll check your oil."

If he was going to take it for a drive, he wanted to make damn sure all her fluids were topped off and her paperwork was in order.

Dani scooted into the car and reached down. "Got it."

The hood gave a hard thump, and Kevin reached under, searching until he found the lever and opened the hood. "Where'd Daniel buy it?"

"A used car lot in Hagerstown called Reliable Autos."

Kevin chuckled. He knew the place. It wasn't far from where he lived, and he knew Bob Ford, the owner. Good guy with a sense of humor, considering he sold mostly foreign jobs. The engine was cool to the touch, and he checked the radiator. It was topped off. He glanced at the window washer fluid, its blue coloring indicating it was full. Last he checked the dipstick. "You could use a quart of oil," he called out. Pulling out a handkerchief, he shut the hood and wiped his hands.

She nodded. "Is it okay to drive, then?"

"Yeah. It's fine for now." He motioned toward the glove compartment. "How about you show me your registration and proof of insurance?"

Her brows snapped together, her eyes getting that worried look.

He laughed, coming around to the driver's side door. "I'm not going to give you a ticket. I just want to make sure you have the proper paperwork."

Her expression lightened, and she retrieved the documents, handing them to him. Registration was in her name, the insurance in Daniel's with Dani as an authorized driver. He handed them back to her. "You're good."

She carefully returned the papers to the glove box, and Kevin opened the door, pulling her out. His hands went around her slender waist, and he pulled her toward him. "Remind me, and I'll add a quart of oil the next time I'm here."

"Thank you." Her eyes were filled with appreciation. "She's a beauty.

Don't you think?" she said, her voice bubbling with delight.

Kevin couldn't help but share in her excitement. The car was nice. But it had nothing on its owner. He took her hand and led her to the passenger side of the car, opening the door for her. She sat down, but not before giving him a nice shot of her legs.

"Kevin?" she said, her voice unsure.

"Hmm?" His eyes lingered on her smooth dove-white skin, and he remembered how the lights of his patrol car had left nothing to the imagination.

"What are you doing, mister?" Catching on, she gave him a lift of her shapely sable brow.

Kevin only grinned, shut the door, walked around, and got in beside her. He leaned over and gave her a quick kiss. "I kinda like when you're mad at me for a change."

She swatted him. "You can't go around ogling me in public. I don't want your father to think we're . . ."

"What?" A smile tugged at the corner of his mouth.

"It's funny to you, I see—me virtue." She looked away somewhat offended.

"It's called dating." He cupped her chin and brought her face even with his. "And he'd approve because, well, I think he likes you better than me."

She smiled at that, her shoulders relaxing.

He kissed her, turned on the ignition, and checked the clock on the dash. "It's eight fifteen. You want to grab a bite at the diner?" It might not be a five-star restaurant. Hell, this was Clear Spring, not Bethesda, but it was about as public as you could get. He wanted to show her off—wanted her to know how happy he was to have her in his life. "Crab soup's the best."

She made a face. "You're not going to make me pick me own meat?"

Kevin laughed out loud and checked the gas. It was close to full—plenty to get them to town and the ten miles to the lake and back to the training center. "No. But if you want, I'll take you to a nice restaurant over the bay bridge this fall when it's still warm and teach you how to eat them."

Something flitted in the depths of her gorgeous blue eyes, and Kevin had the overwhelming need to protect her and make sure she never wanted for anything.

"Do you have your phone on you?" He stroked the back of her neck.

"In me purse." She grabbed for her handbag and pulled it out.

"Do you mind?"

She shook her head and gave it to him.

Kevin entered his home phone, cell, and, for good measure, the sheriff's department main number and then flicked through her contacts to make sure it was there. "I think it's a good idea for you to have my numbers stored in your . . ."

A familiar name flew by the screen, and Kevin backed up, doing a double take. What the . . .

"Something wrong?"

His brows knotted in aggravation. "Not unless you have a habit of dating two men at once." He jammed the phone at her.

She laughed, her eyes widening. "I had nothing to do with that. He put it in himself, under the Bs, no less." She leaned into him, her gorgeous eyes filled with mirth. "He's got a bit of an ego, I think."

Kevin's shoulders leveled off, and he snorted. "That's a nice way of saying it." He wouldn't have been as charitable. He handed it back to her. "It's one of the reasons I'm attracted to you."

Her brows wrinkled. "Excuse me?"

"Your kindness." He gave her a quick kiss and put the car in drive, musing.

He never knew he had a jealous streak, until now.

Chapter Thirty-Four

"Y OU MAKE ME NERVOUS." DANI SAT BEHIND THE WHEEL OF HER convertible with Kevin next to her in the passenger seat in the parking lot at Big Pool Lake. It should be romantic with the moon overhead, its reflection rippling over the cool, placid water, after just coming from dinner at the Clear Spring Diner—a place where local food, local charm, and local people came together. That had been the problem. He'd introduced her to everyone. If only she didn't have a target on her back. She felt sure Kate's orders to "lay low" didn't include getting to know all of Kevin's constituents.

Maybe immigration wise, Kevin believed they'd crossed that divide from illegal to legal, pending a stamp of approval. But after her meeting with her sisters, it was clear to Dani that leaving a memorable impression with those she met could be a "dead" giveaway if Tommy was casing the establishments, looking for a young dark-haired Irishwoman.

She needed to lose the accent. Americans were enamored by her dialect. But first she needed to relax. She'd already checked tonight for word of Tommy on her iPhone. He wasn't lurking about. If anything, he was doing what he'd always done—only with two different women, at the same port, with the same type of clientele—under the guise of running a legitimate shipping company.

"Dani, sweetheart." Kevin's arm slipped behind her back, his fingertips massaging the base of her neck. "You're doing fine. Let off the brake and drive around the parking island in front."

Easy for you to say. She was nervous. From what he'd said at dinner, Kevin'd been driving on her da's farm since he was eleven, had been taught defensive driving by the sheriff's department, and knew the motor vehicle laws like they had been tattooed on the inside of his head.

She should be grateful, excited even—but not after today. The coveted driver's license would remain elusive, her racy jewel of a car a taunt. Dani let off the brake and touched the gas. The car began to move. She took the turn slowly around the parking island, looped about, and pulled into a parking space facing the lake. "How was that?" She turned toward him, her heart ticking like the second hand of a clock.

"Perfect." He unclicked her seat belt and scooped her out of her seat.

Dani squealed, landing with a thud onto his lap.

"Shh. Someone's going to think I'm taking you against your will," he said, his voice low and seductive and filled with laughter.

She knew better. But perhaps an unsuspecting visitor would think otherwise. "With your position, I think it's best I remain in me own seat." Dani made a move to climb back to the other side gracefully, which was a bit impossible with the shifter in the middle and the halter dress with its pretty scalloped edge riding dangerously higher.

"Hold up." Kevin's arm came around her, and he opened his door, getting out with her still enveloped in his one arm. "I know a private place we can go."

She wet her lips. "To . . ."

He took the keys from her, removed his gun, shoving it in the glove compartment. Locking it, he pocketed the key and shut the door. Kevin pulled her close, his fingers smoothing down the wrinkle between her brows. "We're not going to do anything you're not comfortable with."

She nodded. "Do you come here a lot?"

"Not in a long time." He took her hand. "Let's go for a walk."

"Where do you take your other dates?"

He gave her a sideways glance. "Not to my local diner. Or a park full of my childhood memories."

"Oh." Dani lowered her lashes. The waitress's words—she believed her name was Mary Beth—filled her ears.

You finally brought us home a girl we can meet.

Dani regretted her question immediately. "I didn't mean to imply—"

Kevin grabbed her around the waist and lifted her from her feet. Dani squealed and landed with a thud on top of some metal utility box at the beginning of the park's grassy, manicured lawn. She slapped her hand to her mouth, her eyes wide. "I'm so sorry. I'll not squeal again," she said, her words muffled.

He pulled her hand down and kept it in his. "Irish, we need to get a couple things straight." He looked pointedly at her. "When I ask you to do something it's because there's a good reason—not because I'm some prick who gets off on ordering a woman around."

He was talking about last night at the party. She realized now how stupid she'd been, but at the time, she was upset and trying to avoid him. "It was lucky you came after me. Otherwise I don't think I would have found me way out of the woods."

"You knew I would." He dipped his head. "Just like you know I'll never lie to you."

Meaning he knew she was keeping secrets of her own. Dani fidgeted under his intense gaze. "I'm . . ."

"Afraid. I get it." He shook his head. "I know I've said this before, but eventually you're going to have to trust someone." He lifted her chin with his finger. "That someone is me."

She nodded. "It's not so easy. I don't want to remember. I want to forget."

His hands went around her bum, and he took a step closer so he stood between her thighs. "Then be honest with me from here on out about this," he said, the rasp of his voice urgent before he leaned in.

His eyes remained open like he might miss some telltale sign in the depths of her eyes as he moved closer. If he did or didn't eventually shut them, she couldn't say, because hers were closed the moment he pressed his firm, perfectly sculpted lips to her mouth. Dani tingled and drew her arms around his neck. He was older, experienced, yet trembling in her arms. Kevin Bendix could teach her the finer points of lovemaking, she was sure. His kisses were deep and ardent, making her stomach flutter with the newness of a budding, starry-eyed relationship. But tonight, under a nearly full moon with only the gentle breeze as witness, Dani learned that he was just as vulnerable as she.

The revelation brought tears to her eyes. She didn't want to hurt him. Dani pulled away, whisking a tear from her cheek. "You're going to make me fall in love with you." She gave a nervous laugh and caressed the rough angles of his face. "It's not fair, you know. Being so bloody handsome and kissing a woman like you really mean it."

Dani pushed against him. He stepped back, his hands that had been intimately massaging her bum, moving to his sides. His eyes, questioning, held hers, and she turned away and hopped down. She didn't want him to see the tearful emotion welling up in her. Dani took the asphalt path directly in front of her, wiping the corners of her eyes.

"Dani?" In two strides he was taking her hand. "You okay?"

"Yes." She sniffed and then shook his hand playfully. "Show me where you played as a boy." She smiled at him. "I've missed so much not growing up with you."

They strolled down the path, twisting through stands of fragrant pines, the sweet scent of honeysuckle all around them. Glancing up, she smiled at him. "What was it like growing up with me sisters?"

Kevin raised his eyebrows and looked down his nose at her with mock distress. "Frightening."

Dani laughed. "I know you're telling a tale. I see the bond you have with them, especially Bren."

Kevin led her toward a playground with slides, jungle gym, metal roundabout. "I could always count on her to come up with some half-baked scheme"—he motioned Dani to take a seat on the swing—"that would get me school detention or grounded."

She kicked off her shoes and sat down, grabbing the chains. "You're lucky that you had someone to conspire with."

Kevin stood directly behind her. "How high do you want to go?" He kissed her bare shoulder.

His lips were warm, his words open to interpretation. It wasn't how high, necessarily, but how far—she wanted all that America could offer. She smiled, kicking off her wedges. " 'Til I reach the sky."

His hands came down on her hips, his fingers distinctly male against the feminine curve of her waist and semi-sheer, delicate stitching of her dress. He pulled her back, giving her a big push.

Dani flew up, her toes reaching for the stars. Her stomach tumbled on the way down, and she laughed. "Higher."

Kevin propelled her into the air. "I bet you had the boys standing in line to push you." He chuckled.

There were no playgrounds at the track—mostly hard work. As for boys, she was too busy surviving after the death of her ma to take notice. Dani pumped her legs, her stomach dipping before the freefall back to earth. When she did, she was surprised to find she was on her own. She looked back. Kevin was gone. Her heart thrummed in her chest. "Where did you . . ."

"Over here."

Dani's head spun around.

Kevin stood in front of her with his arms out. "Jump."

"I'm moving too fast. I'll knock you on your bum."

"Trust me."

Dani swallowed. All she had to do was let go.

Kevin's arms remained out.

Dani shook her head, the momentum pulling her back. "Let me slow down."

"No. Now." Kevin moved closer.

The little booger. Dani swung toward him. "You're insane." Closing her eyes she let go, her body launching from the seat. With her hands out, she said a prayer, opened her eyes before hitting his chest hard. Her arms went around his neck.

Kevin hugged her to him, tottering on the uneven black rubber chips. He fell flat on his bum before taking her with him the rest of the way, his head missing the metal roundabout by degrees when he landed on his back, moaning.

Dani sat up in alarm. Her knees wrapped around him. "You hurt?" Her hands hovered around his handsome face. "I told you this would happen." Her voice hitched.

His eyes remained shut, and he gritted his teeth, laughing. "You're kind of heavy."

Her mouth fell open with disbelief. "Here I am beside meself, worried you've broken your—"

"Ass bone." He laughed.

"You're not the least bit funny." Dani made a move to get up.

His arms went around her. "Wait. I am hurt."

"Where?" She said it like she didn't believe him.

"Here." He gave her a crooked smile and pointed toward his perfectly formed lips.

"Ah, so it's a kiss you're wanting?" She shook her head. "Then stand on your own two feet, so I know you're not paralyzed." She started to push up off of him.

"Hold up." He kept his arm around her and reached for one of the bars from the metal roundabout. Grunting, he pulled himself up to a sitting position with her in his lap and leaned against the metal bar. The teasing in him was gone when a pair of serious, if not sober, brown eyes held hers. "This guy from Ireland who might come after you . . . were you . . ."

"Involved?"

"Yeah."

She shook her head. "No. He was a mistake." Her voice little more than a whisper, she caressed his cheek and kissed him softly. He kissed her back with the desperation of a man trying to erase a bad memory. The frisson of heat she'd come to expect from his touch scorched her very soul. Dani's hand glided up his chest, stopping at the rapid beat of his heart. It was then she pulled away, breathing heavy, her own heart in her throat. "One I've regretted."

"I guess I should thank this guy?" Kevin lifted his brows.

She lowered her head and smoothed down his shirt, refusing to look at him. "You're worried about me past."

He cupped her chin, his eyes searching hers. "Irish, I worry about a lot of things." He kissed her softly at first, then more deeply, like her lips could ease every burden he'd suffered or would.

Dani's arms went around his neck, and she kissed him back. He'd only told her bits and pieces of his childhood—mostly the times he spent at Grace. Her da had treated him like a son, her sisters like the brother they never had. Dani slowly pulled away, her eyes fluttering open. "He hurt you."

"Who?" Kevin pulled his head back, his expression unreadable.

"Your father."

He blew out an agitated breath. "He tell you that?"

Dani shook her head. "Not in so many words."

The mood shifted, his arms tensed around her, and his hands that had been sending a fiery thrill through her clenched slightly on her thigh. "My father, if nothing else, likes to play the martyr." He moved his hand that had been tinkering with the scalloped hem of her dress and scrubbed his face hard, his head falling back with agitation. "He was always looking for that big break—that winner that was going to change him from the mediocre horse trainer he's always been."

Dani sat up straighter on his lap. "I think you're being a bit harsh."

He shrugged. "You don't know him like I do. He's an alcoholic."

Ah. It all made sense—the friction between father and law-upholding son. She'd had an inkling herself when she'd met the ruddy-complexioned trainer. Only she didn't believe he still drank. The smell of alcohol would have given him away.

Even so, he was a good man. She knew that now. He'd taken a chance on her, showed a compassionate side she didn't know existed until she learned the truth about Solley. As she recalled, something close to fondness—perhaps for a kinder, gentler Turk Bendix—flitted in those brown eyes of Kevin's the day Turk had called her out on the peppermints only to find he'd bought a bag himself.

She remained quiet, giving him space to think.

"I've forgiven my old man for a lot of things—the alcohol being one of them. Addiction's a bitch. But he's managed to stay sober for almost ten years." Kevin took a heavy breath and pushed back a wayward strand of her hair. "He took my mother's death hard. Blamed himself."

"Did you blame him?"

He seemed to be lost in thought, or was it in old memories? "He's always been trying to prove his self-worth. He didn't have to with me. He was my dad," he said, his voice thick with emotion.

"He still is," Dani reminded him.

He kissed her hard. "Chocolate donuts."

"Excuse me?" She eyed him speculatively. "Did anyone ever tell you that you are an odd one?"

He gave her a boyish grin. "That's what I remember. Every Sunday he'd swing by the bakery and spend what little money he had in his pocket on chocolate donuts for me and my mom." He shook his head and laughed. "Of course he ate one, too. He loves his sweets."

She suspected as much, but that wasn't the point. Her eyes locked onto his with purpose. "He's always loved you, Kevin," she whispered. "I see it even if you don't."

He cupped her face. "Always looking for that rainbow, beautiful." He chuckled. "And my father's always looking for that pot o' gold." He kissed her.

Dani smiled against his lips. She and Turk were a pair. She saw nothing wrong with Turk's ambition. She only hoped, for all their sakes, they walked away with a win at Penn National.

Kevin fluttered kisses down her neck, each touch of his lips a hot spark, turning her to flame, and she fought to keep her mind about her. "I'll let you know Friday if we get to keep some of that gold."

His hands rode up the back of her thighs. "You're soft," he said huskily, the scalloped edge of her dress rising along with the heat simmering between them.

A mass of quivering nerve endings, she concentrated on finishing her last coherent thought. "When I get back."

His head shot up. "You going somewhere?" Sheriff Bendix said, his voice clipped. He stood, taking her up with him.

Dani's eyes widened. She struggled with the clash of her hot body against his cold words, and her footing. "Chipper's racing at Penn National. Your father said I could come and watch from the stands." Her forehead creased with consternation. As usual, she was relegated to being an onlooker. Dani pulled away so she could stand on her own two feet. "I don't have a pass for the backside." Her voice rose a notch.

He seemed to be processing all that she'd told him.

Maybe leaving the state of Maryland wouldn't be at all smart, considering her status. "If it's a problem, I won't go."

"No, it's fine. I'm glad you told me." A smile tugged at the frown on his lips. "It's about time I showed you and the old man my support."

Dani's mouth dropped in wonderment. "Are you saying you want to go, then?"

He laughed. "With you, alone, and in my car."

"But what about your father?"

"I'll work it out with him tomorrow." He jerked on her hand. "Come on."

"Wait!" She remained rooted to the ground, her bare feet digging into the cool rubber mulch. "You're moving so fast. I need my shoes."

"You don't need them." He scooped up her shoes and led her down a grassy hill to a different section of the lake. They passed a boat launch and pier and then traveled the edge of the bank. He stopped at a secluded cove, a canopy of trees rustling overhead with moonlight, its beams of light ethereal, the way it glittered down on the outcropping of rocks, ideal for lounging on hot summer days.

Her breath caught. "It's lovely."

"And perfect for swimming." He dropped her shoes on the rock and kicked off his own.

Dani's heart beat faster. "You're not thinking of taking a dip, are you?"

"You can swim, can't you?"

"Yes . . . but . . ."

He gave her a boyish grin. "Last one in is a rotten egg." He stripped out of his shirt, his sinewy upper body tantalizing in the moon's glow, and then started to unzip his shorts.

"Wait!" Dani giggled and came up on him, her eyes searching his. "What have you done with my serious-minded cop?"

Laughing, he kissed her, stripped out of his clothes, and jumped in. Dani caught sight of his firm white bum as it hit the water with a splash. He came up and flung his head back, water flying from his drenched hair. "I think you should enjoy this guy tonight."

Dani bit down on her lip, twirling her finger. "You'll have to turn around, then."

He did as she asked.

"And I'm not getting naked if that's what you were hoping for," she called after him and pulled her dress up over her thighs past a pink pair of black lace panties and matching strapless bra. She moaned. They'd more than likely be ruined. Like she could afford a new—

"Dani?"

She lifted her head and laid the dress down with care on the rock. "I'm . . ."

Kevin's eyes roamed her body, from her bare feet, past her thighs, to the lacy triangle covering her sex, and then lingered on the slopes of her breasts, pushing against the thin fabric of her bra. Their stares collided. "God, you're beautiful," he said, his voice rough with desire.

That should have relaxed her a little—the attraction thing—because she was totally into him. "You weren't supposed to peek."

He swam over toward her and the rock she stood on. "Come here," he said, his voice a bit severe.

She walked over.

"Sit down." He patted the rock.

She took a seat, the stone cool against her bum, and let her legs sink into the crisp water. Her body trembled.

"Hey." He looked at her. "It's just you and me. No one's going to bother us." He pulled her in the water and into his arms. "You're the first."

Dani laughed. "You honestly don't expect me to believe that." She gave him a lift of her brow.

He chuckled as he treaded water with her. "I know you're just a kid. But I thought you understood how I feel about you." He gave her a quick hard kiss on the lips. "I wasn't talking about sex. I want to share everything with you. This is where I hung out with Bren, Kate, and Tom." He kicked off through the water, taking her with him, and they swam to the other side. Pulling her toward him, he brought her to a ledge a few feet under the water's edge and sat down, positioning her between his thighs. "They say you never miss what you don't have." He caressed her face, his soulful eyes holding her mesmerized. "But I missed a lot not growing up with you."

The sincerity in his voice brought tears to Dani's eyes. She scooched up and kissed him tenderly on those tough-guy lips of his. "You're going to make me cry." Whisking away a tear, Dani laughed. "Anyway you probably would have considered me a nuisance."

He grinned. "Maybe. I definitely thought you were that first night."

Dani gave him a pout. She'd been extremely difficult. Nuisance didn't even come close to the hellion she'd been. "I'm sorry for that. I don't like to be held down."

Something tender and sincere registered in those eyes of his. "Someday I hope you'll feel differently about that with me."

"When you make love to me." Dani searched his eyes under the moonlight. They were warm and loving, and she couldn't imagine sharing something so intimate with anyone else.

Kevin nodded, water dripping from the tip of his nose. "Is it too fast?"

She shook her head no. Only there was something to be said for taking it slow and savoring every moment she shared with him.

"It's not a race." He pressed back her hair, which hung in heavy, wet waves about her shoulders. "I'm a patient man, Dani. When it's right, we'll both know."

Sitting in the strength of his arms, the sharp angles of his face cutting an impressive profile, she'd be lying if she said she wasn't at all curious what he looked like down there. If he was half as wonderful as he looked from his narrow hips on up to his expansive muscled chest, then he truly was gorgeous.

He dropped a kiss on her shoulder, scooped her up in his arms, and stood on the ledge.

Dani's eyes widened. "What are you doing?"

"Having fun with you." He gave her a quick kiss and jumped in with her in his arms amidst her shrieks.

They came up laughing and reaching for each other. Dani relaxed and explored the swimming hole with him. He showed her the general vicinity of the underwater rock formations he'd hid beneath as a child until his lungs burned—all in an effort to frighten her sisters. Told her of riding bareback with Bren when they were eight and the relevance of a horse named Smiley. The significance of Bren's horse pendant sunk in along with something else.

Kevin was beginning to trust her . . . even love her.

CHAPTER THIRTY-FIVE

"I THINK IT'S A WEE BIT TOO BIG." DANI TRIED NOT TO LAUGH, STANDING in the parking lot of Hersheypark.

"It'll fit," Kevin assured her, shoving the oversized red—to match his little Mazda Miata—stuffed Scooby Doo between the seats.

More like a puff of wind was going to find Scooby flying out onto the highway on their seven-mile drive to Penn National to watch the evening races at six.

It didn't seem to deter him. She should have known he'd have bungee cords at the ready. Dani grimaced as he stretched one end of the cord from the loop next to the headrest, across to the other side. She didn't want to see him lose an eye because of it.

It was important that Scooby made it back home. Not because she was especially fond of the oversized beast that would take up half her little room. It was because Kevin had won it for her.

Dressed casually in shorts and a bright yellow T-shirt, he turned with a triumphant smile. "See, I told you."

Dani had never taken the time to consider Kevin's inner child until a few nights ago, when they'd gone swimming. She should have known it existed if he remained friends with her sisters who were fun-loving adults.

Dani walked toward him, dressed in her khaki shorts, white tank top, and the trainers Kevin had bought her. She put her arms around him and went up on tiptoes and kissed him. "Thank you for today and"—she eyed the red Great Dane he must have spent a day's pay on winning and smiled—"Scooby."

"You're welcome." He kissed the top of her head and led her to the passenger door. "It's not over yet, sweetheart." Opening it, he motioned for her to take a seat. "And don't smash Scooby," he said with a teasing grin as he walked around and got in.

He started the car, slipped on a pair of sunglasses that she could see only from the rearview mirror because Scooby was sitting between, blocking her view. They drove the ten minutes down Highway 473 and parked in the vast parking lot of the Hollywood Casino at Penn National Race Course, with Kevin taking the time to pull up the top and lock Scooby securely inside.

He came around the car and took her hand in his. "Do you want to see Chipper before the races start?"

"I don't think that's possible. I don't have an ID to get onto the backside."

He winked at her. "I gotcha covered."

"You're not seriously thinking about sneaking me in?" Her hand tightened on his. "I don't think that's wise, Kevin."

"This coming from the woman who hopped a freighter?" He gave her a mock look of surprise.

She leaned into him. "Okay. But you're the one who's going to be explaining to security when we get caught." That last word concerned her. She had no identification in the event that happened. What if they did what Kevin hadn't the heart to do? Arrest her.

With her hand tucked securely in Kevin's, she let her worries go. This time it would be different. She was with him. She smiled at that. Funny how the serious-minded cop, after picking her up this morning in his sporty coupe, had reverted back to that carefree, playful date from a few nights ago.

They walked toward the stable gate. Behind the fence were rows of green barns with white roofs. Dani took a big breath, preparing herself to stand casually next to him at the gate while he, she guessed, talked his way in or flashed his police badge.

Kevin tugged her hand hard. "Not that way." He hooked his chin toward a clump of trees about fifty yards past the gate. "This way."

Dani picked up the pace and followed him into a small wooded area that ran up along the fence. He pulled her toward him and kissed her. Dani's arms went around his neck. His hands slipped under her tank until he touched bare skin. She'd never tire of the way he made her feel when she was in his arms.

He broke the kiss and pressed his lips against her ear. "You're soft," he whispered, and then pulled away, pressing a wisp of her hair behind her ear. "You trust me?" His warm eyes searched her face.

She nodded, her eyes darting from him to the fence. "But I'm a little concerned." She leaned into him conspiratorially. "Why the woods, then?"

"Because." He drew her further down the fence. "I used to come here as a boy with my dad. I did a lot of exploring." He grimaced. "Mostly from boredom. And there was one thing that always remained consistent."

Dani lifted a speculative brow. "What's that?"

He motioned her toward a section of the fence. "Holes."

Sure enough, a section of the fence had a hole that ran from the bottom to about a third of the height of the fence. Easy enough for her lithe body to slip through, but she wasn't so sure Kevin's broad shoulders would make it unscathed. She frowned. "You're too big."

He pulled on the fence with his hands, the muscles in his forearms flexing.

"Kevin!" she whispered harshly. "You'll cut your hand."

He let go and turned toward her. "You worried about me, Irish?"

Worried about a lot of things, yes. This little caper that he seemed to find incredibly amusing could cost her freedom, if they were detained for trespassing.

She connected with those brown eyes of his—usually serious—now more amused than anything.

Dani gave him a stern look. "I don't find you the least bit funny." She took his hand in hers. It was warm and strong and ruggedly handsome. It covered hers completely and possessively, and she couldn't bear to see him cut it on a damned jagged fence. Plus, he knew better. And now she was just plain mad. "Have you lost your head?" She beaded in on him. "Wouldn't it have been more practical for me to flash me passport?" Not that she had it with her.

"Too risky."

"This is too risky. You're an officer of the law. I'll not have you risk it all for a visit to the backside for me." She tugged on his hand. "We're buying a program and entering like any other spectator."

He laughed and pulled her toward him. "A promise is a promise." He yanked on the fence with one hand and pushed her through with the other.

Dani bit down on a squeal, her body transported effortlessly through the sharp, angry barbs without so much as a scratch, until she found herself alone and spitting mad on the other side. "You are in so much trouble, mister, if you try a stunt like that again." She placed her hands on her hips and narrowed in on him.

"I like your bossy side," he said with a grin and angled his body through. His shirt caught one of the sharp points. With a grunt, he made it the rest of the way, tearing a small hole in the shoulder of his T-shirt. He gave it a look out of the corner of his eye and laughed. "You have me breaking all the rules."

"*Aww,*" she said with disbelief and a little irritation. "I told you not to do it."

He only laughed harder, the sound melodious and carefree, and it warmed her heart to see him relax. Although slipping through a fence in an area where they were not allowed was still incredibly stupid in her book.

"Come on." He took her hand in his, and all her misgivings floated away. He led her to the back of one of the barns and brought his head even with hers. "Just act casual. We don't have one of those badges they wear around their necks," he whispered.

Dani automatically glanced down like one would miraculously appear—stupid. As much as she wanted to see Chipper and share in the excitement that only comes from being on the backside, her nerves were having a terrible time.

They rounded the corner with Kevin going into a believable act of *I belong here.* They strolled down the dirt road that housed barns with different racing teams. Jockeys milled about in front of the jockeys' quarters, wearing their festive racing colors. She couldn't wait to put on Starlite's silks in October for this Maryland Millions Stakes. Dani shivered. Looking too far into the future was a frightening prospect. Something had to change in a positive way for her to legally be allowed to remain in the U.S.

It put a huge strain on her. She longed for nothing more than to be that honest girl Kevin wanted.

He shook her hand in his. "Did Dad tell you the barn number?"

"Uh"—lost in thought, Dani had to think about that for a minute— "nineteen."

He hooked his chin to the right. "I think it's two more down."

They passed the two barns, the stalls clamoring with activity. Dani hesitated when she recognized Lansing dressed in a suit, talking with his trainer.

Kevin recognized her apprehension and followed her line of sight. "He's not giving you any trouble, is he?"

Dani shook her head. "No. I haven't seen him since the fireworks." That she didn't get to see, thanks to him.

They came up on the next barn that should be nineteen. Turk stood outside, waving. "Hey, you made it." He smiled and patted Kevin on the arm and then leaned into Dani. "He find that hole in the fence?"

Dani's eyes widened. She pulled her head back, dubious, and gave them both the evil eye. "I can't believe you two." Now it was clear this had been a conspiracy all along. They should have called the backside the dark side for all the goings-on it took to get her within steps of Starlite's barn. Not that she was mad. Just astounded.

"Go on in." Turk motioned for her to enter. "Chipper's in there with Bonnie and Jake."

Dani frowned. She'd more than likely have to curb her tongue if she ran into him. She ducked into the barn and found Midnight in his stall, picking at his hay. Georgie, the chestnut, was in the stall next to him. She gave them both a pat. "You seen Chipper, the two of you?"

"She's around back with Bonnie."

Dani cringed the moment Jake's bossy voice filled her ears. She turned. "Thanks." She made a move to head in that direction when he took a step closer.

"You seen Turk?"

"Outside with Kevin."

He nodded. "You and the sheriff dating now?"

Like she'd ever confide in Jake. "No. Turk asked him to bring me." Dani walked away. The less she engaged him, the safer it would be. She wouldn't put it past Jake to turn her in if he knew of her circumstances.

"You're here!" Chipper came toward her with her riding crop in hand.

They gave each other a big hug.

Dani stood back. "Look at you. You look grand in your silks." She loved Starlite's colors. They were different hues of blue—turquoise, a sky blue, and a rich, dark navy. "You're going to tear up the track tonight."

"I'll be exhausted by the end of the night, but it's what I've trained for."

"And you'll be brilliant." Bonnie came from somewhere to the right, carrying a bucket of water. "How was Hersheypark?"

Dani cringed and gave Bonnie a look.

Bonnie's eyes widened, totally offended. "What? I didn't tell. Turk told everyone on the ride up in the truck."

Shite. Jake had already known the answer to his question before it left his conniving lips. Dani took a deep breath through her nose. She needed to stop worrying. She was here now, and they all now knew that Kevin and she were . . . *dating.*

Dani smiled. "He won me an immense stuffed Scooby Doo."

Bonnie laughed out loud. "He didn't drive his patrol car, I hope?"

"No." Dani laughed, too. "That would have surely turned some heads. He drove his red sports car."

Chipper snickered. "I can't imagine it fitting. Those things are huge. I tried like crazy last year to win Hannah one." She pushed out her lips. "I ended up with a tiny silver stuffed kiss instead."

Aw. Dani grabbed Chipper's hand and squeezed it. "You're a good ma to Hannah."

"I try. Now if I can put some bacon on the table."

"Chipper, time for the scales," Turk called to her from the shed row, standing next to Kevin, looking like a proud papa bear with his cubs.

"On my way." She waved a hand to him and turned toward Bonnie who had sat down the bucket of water and gone to get Chipper's saddle.

Kevin motioned to Dani. "You ready to make that wager?"

She hadn't discussed placing a bet, not that it mattered one way or the other, but she felt sure this was his way of letting her know it was time to step into the land of law-abiding citizens.

Bonnie handed Chipper her saddle just as Dani went to give her one last hug. They all laughed when Dani found herself hugging leather.

"Hug me when I win," Chipper said with a grin.

"I will. That's a promise." Dani turned, and her heart beat a little faster. Kevin was gone. She headed outside and relaxed when she spotted him talking to—of all people—one of the stewards and an older woman she didn't recognize, dressed in a nice dark pantsuit. Dani hung back. That serious expression she had come to recognize lined his face. Her anxiety bumped up a notch.

Milling about, nervous and with good reason, Dani caught sight of Chipper emerging from the scale room, carrying her saddle. She'd get that hug. Dani started in her direction when Blake came up on Chipper and took the saddle from her. Dani's mind struggled to put the two together. They had been cordial to one another the few times she'd seen them together—except for Chipper and an occasional glare—but nothing to suggest they were more than business acquaintances.

Chipper grabbed for her saddle, Blake pulled it away. Their voices rose, and it was clear this wasn't a friendly conversation. Fingers laced her elbow, and Dani jumped, swinging around.

"Whoa." Kevin's lips thinned. "What's going on?"

"It's . . ." Dani glanced back toward the scales. Jockeys were entering and leaving, but there was no sign of Chipper or Blake. Dani swallowed the frisson of alarm riding up her throat and turned toward Kevin. "Nothing. I-I think I'm ready to place that wager."

"Yeah, me, too." He seemed rattled as well.

He led Dani past the barns and back toward the opening in the fence. They slipped through, making their way to the other side of the track and the grandstand area, where they paid admission and bought a program. It wasn't until they reached the teller area that she pulled on his arm. "What's the matter? You seem troubled." She frowned. "Are you upset with me?"

"No."

"Why were you talking to the steward and that older woman?"

"Not by choice. That woman owns one of the stables at Whistledown."

That was odd. She'd never seen her before. But then again, there were about seven stables, and she'd only really been introduced to two. "Which one?"

"Jane Delhaven's."

Delhaven. Where had she heard the name? Oh, on one of the mailboxes that she'd almost smashed to smithereens with her car.

"She knows you, then?"

"As the sheriff of Washington County. She recognized me and introduced me to the steward."

"Why?"

"They were talking about one of her mares. They had to put it down. They just got the necropsy back."

"The poor thing. Was she sick, then?"

"Dani." He gave her that look that said *too many questions.* "She died of arsenic poisoning."

Dani's hand flew to her mouth.

"I know, right." His jaw tensed. "It all seems to fall in line with my father's wild notion that someone is tampering with the Thoroughbreds at Whistledown."

Dani couldn't stop from shaking. It was true, then—all of it. She beaded in on him. "What are we going to do about it?"

"Not we, Sherlock." He motioned her to move up in the line. "Me, and I'd appreciate you keeping this between us until I can talk to Dad tomorrow."

She nodded. "It wouldn't do any good to upset him tonight."

"You know him well."

She gave a half smile, though she wasn't at all happy. "I like your da. You know where I stand on that."

He pulled her next to him, his hand going around her waist. "Are you having a good time, Irish?" He kissed the back of her head.

"With you." She angled her head and tried to smile.

He nodded his understanding, stroking her hair. "Let's place that bet."

Chapter Thirty-Six

"**S**HE'S GOT A GOOD CHANCE OF WINNING." DANI'S VOICE BUBBLED with excitement, her pretty profile tense when Chipper took the lead on the straightaway as the horses barreled toward the finish.

Kevin squinted at the track. This was the fifth race of the night and the second of the three races Dani had bet—all wagers on Chipper to win, of course. She'd already come in first in the second and *damn* if she wasn't making her move now. There was no catching her or Dani, who jumped off the bench next to him in the picnic area of the grandstand. She ran up to the rail for her own photo finish, the smile lining her face when she angled back turning his heart to mush. Kevin walked toward her, pulling her into his embrace. "Two for three." He kissed the top of her head, his stomach growling.

Dani pulled away and grinned. "Is that your way of telling me you're hungry, then?"

He grimaced. "Subway at Hersheypark is not what I'd call filling."

"You're a more steak and potatoes kind of guy?"

He nodded. "Want to grab dinner in the restaurant before the last race?" He pointed to the grandstand's picture windows above.

Dani's brows furrowed. "Will they let us in wearing shorts?"

"Sure." He put his arm around her and led her to the entrance of the clubhouse. "Let me treat you to a nice steak dinner."

They stepped into an elevator, and she leaned against him. "You're spoiling me, you know."

He laughed. "I'm buying you dinner, Flynn, because *I'm* hungry."

His real hope was that some casual dinner conversation would take her mind off Delhaven's mare and the implications its arsenic poisoning brought when it came to his father's theories.

Her arm slipped around him and she squeezed. "You keep telling yourself that. But I know differently."

She was beginning to figure him out. He guessed their little talk at the lake had started to sink in. He only wished she'd begin to share her past with him. They exited the elevator and entered the Mountainview Restaurant. He asked for a two-top with a TV, directly in front of the large windows that looked out onto the track. The maître d' led them to their table and gave each a menu.

Dani fooled with the silverware and the gold linen table napkin. "I've never eaten in such fine surroundings."

Kevin opened his menu. "Personally, I prefer a home-cooked meal."

"Aye, you have a wonderful kitchen. It'd be a dream to cook in." She scanned the menu and frowned. "I haven't a clue what to order."

"How about I order for you?"

"Grand." She shut her menu, her attention diverted to the TV which showed the horses leaving the paddock for the track. "They're getting ready to start the seventh race."

Kevin was still contemplating her previous comment. He rolled his lips in, considering. "You cook?"

A smile touched her lips. "Were you afraid I didn't?"

"You didn't answer the question."

She took a labored breath and grimaced. "Not a bit."

His face must have dropped because her eyes widened. "Does that mean your feelings for me have changed?"

"No. But I won't lie." He grinned. "I was hoping." He closed his menu and tried to ignore the hunger pang ripping through his gut. "I can make a sandwich—cook a steak on the grill. We'll get by."

"Aw." Dani reached over and squeezed his hand tight, looking contrite.

"What?"

"It was a joke. Me ma loved to putter about the kitchen, I know a few dishes to make your mouth water, Kevin Bendix. Rosemary and garlic roasted lamb for one. It's delicious with colcannon." She cocked her head. "Do you like lam—"

"Remind me to paddle your behind when we get home." He narrowed in on her, trying not to laugh when the lanky waiter came to their table.

"Good evening, my name's Corey, and I'll be your server tonight." He sat down two coasters. "What can I get you to drink?"

Kevin eyed Dani. "I think we're ready to order."

She nodded and sat back in her chair.

Kevin ordered a T-bone for himself, a petite filet mignon for Dani, and mashed potatoes and green beans—a classic dinner that would fill them up for the ride home. "What would you like to drink, sweetheart?"

"Sweet tea? Is that . . ."

"Iced tea with sugar, ma'am," the waiter said.

Dani nodded. "That'd be fine."

Kevin handed the waiter the menus. "Make that two."

"Yes, sir." He took the menus from Kevin. "I'll put that in and be back with your drinks."

"Thanks." Kevin sat back in his chair after the waiter left and checked his watch. Dani sat across from him, almost in a trance, staring out the window to the track. "Time's getting away. You okay watching Chipper's last race from here?"

She turned toward him and smiled sweetly. "There'll be more races," she said and then became thoughtful. "What did you mean earlier, 'We'll get by'?"

It had been on his mind. Even though her room had a fresh coat of paint and a real bed, it was far from being a home. But that wasn't his main concern. "It's not safe."

She leaned into the table. "I don't think it's the humans they're after from what you told me earlier. Besides, I have a door now and . . ." She pulled something out of the pocket of her shorts. "A key. I'll be plenty safe."

"You didn't seem to think so after finding your pretty little ass on the ground the other day."

"The horseshoe, you mean. I thought that through, too. It's the horse that usually suffers because of it, not the rider." She shrugged. "I was unlucky." She took a deep breath. "I'll not be bullied into leaving by you or the creep who's behind this. I'm a lot stronger than you think." She sat back. "Besides, I'm your eyes and ears. I can keep a lookout."

He'd been afraid of that. She'd do what she damned well pleased. Kevin dropped back into his chair, irritated. "Anyone ever tell you you're an unbridled woman?"

"A horse connotation." She laughed, lifting her chin to him. "I don't think it's me you have to worry about."

Yeah, he owed his father an apology. Kevin had assumed, like everything else connected with his old man, this thing at the training center was just another of Turk's failed attempts to be front and center in Kevin's life.

Kevin had been wrong, and it was going to sting like hell when he pulled his dad aside and admitted he'd been right all along. Worse than that, Dani had pegged him. It would be hard to contain Turk Bendix once he knew the truth. He would want justice. Kevin did, too. But he was a realist—justice could be slow or not at all.

"Dani, I'm counting on you to defuse the situation with him, not escalate it."

She opened her mouth then shut it when the waiter set down their ice teas and a basket of fresh-baked bread.

Kevin handed her a piece and then grabbed his own soft crusty goodness. Popping it in his mouth, he devoured it, washing it down with his tea. "Dani, I don't want to fight tonight." He held her hand in his. "I'll have a full day tomorrow with this investigation and meeting with animal control, along with all my other duties."

"I know. I'm sorry." She shook his hand in hers, her attention drawn to the TV again. "They're getting ready to start the eighth race—there's Chipper in the post parade."

Kevin leaned in to take a look at the screen. "How many minutes 'til post time?"

"Seven."

Kevin made a move to get up. "Come on." He hooked his chin toward the stairs. "If we hurry we can make it." He led her up the steps and out the door to a waiting elevator.

"I don't want you to miss dinner," she said, her eyes full of concern for him on the way down.

"We'll eat when we get back—it's always so much better to be in the front row." The elevator doors opened, and they exited from the building and onto the patio of the outdoor grandstand area, heading for the rail.

"Look, it's Chipper." A smile lit Dani's face, and she waved to her friend on Midnight Edition and tugged Kevin toward the track.

Kevin shook his head and grinned. Who was he kidding? This was her life. This was what she enjoyed. He wasn't happy about her living arrangements, but they'd work something out. He had access to surveillance cameras. For starters, he could put one in his father's barn. He'd been contemplating the idea since hearing about Delhaven's mare. He'd have access to the live feed, even on his home computer. If something didn't feel right, he could fly up Interstate 70 and be there in five.

"Hey." Chipper smiled at them. "Wish me luck."

Dani reached over the rail and gave Chipper a high five when she passed by on her way to the gate. "We'll celebrate tomorrow when you beat the pants off Lansing's horse."

Chipper laughed out loud. "It's a deal," she called back and disappeared behind the gate to load up.

Huh? Kevin hadn't realized his father and Lansing had entries in the same race. More like he'd been too consumed with the death of the mare to pay attention to the program. He let it go for now and put his arm around Dani. "What vantage point do you want?"

Dani looked around and nodded to one of the tables and grimaced. "On top would be nice. I'd be able to see more."

"Lady." He put his hands on his hips and looked down his nose at her in mock distress.

She gave him a sweet smile and batted those baby blues at him. "The race lasts but only a minute."

She was a pretty little pint-sized package, and he was finding it hard to deny her anything. He hooked his arm around her neck playfully and kissed her. "You're not happy unless you're causing me trouble."

She laughed at him. "Don't be a stick in the mud." She grabbed his hand, and they walked over to the first empty table. He helped her up onto the bench.

She beamed down at him. "I'll wait until they're off before I find that vantage point we were talking about."

"Sweetheart, it's fine." He guided her up onto the tabletop and laughed when she towered above him. "Let me know how the air is up there."

She peered down. "How about I let you know when we win?" A triumphant smile played on her lips.

Before he could respond, the bell went off and the gates flew open. The announcer went into his normal rhetoric, calling the race. There was a decent-sized crowd, lots of cheers and jeers when they hit the first turn.

Dani craned her neck. "She's in front!"

"Where's Lansing's horse?" Kevin hated the son of a bitch. He'd love nothing more than for his father's racing team to stick it to him. Even sweeter with Chipper in the saddle.

"Third," she called down in a panic. "I think."

She thinks. For once he felt like he had a stake in this. He chuckled to himself. That would be Dani's doing. Kevin lifted his chin and squinted toward the track, his excitement growing. Hell, he was over six feet, and he was having a hard time seeing the backstretch. Maybe Dani had the right idea. Kevin put his foot on the bench and tested his weight.

Dani, catching him out of the corner of her eye, grabbed his hand to help steady him. "She's ahead and coming around the far tur—"

The air around him exploded, the reverberation of the blast disconcerting. Kevin's grip on Dani tightened. "What the hell!" Kevin hopped up on the picnic table next to her, adrenaline coursing through his body.

Dani ripped her hand away. "God in heaven!"

He turned toward the track. Something was sprawled on the ground, horses trampling it, dirt flying. He squinted hard but couldn't get a clear shot. He grabbed Dani by the shoulders. "What's happening?"

Her terror-filled eyes met his. She blinked at him. "It's . . ." She shook her head unable to speak.

"It's okay." He pulled her toward him, the table wobbling from the crowds swarming past. He guided her down with him, first to the bench and then to the ground.

Dani thrashed against him. "Let go of me." The words tore from her throat.

He sat her down amidst shouts and blaring sirens—he guessed from the ambulance the track had on standby—trying to make sense of everything, but she jerked free and bolted through the crowd.

"Dani!" He went after her, searching for her familiar sable ponytail and slender shoulders, but she'd been swallowed by the sea of spectators who had run amuck within sixty seconds of the blast. Kevin couldn't say with certainty what had happened but this was the world of terrorist attacks—a bomb seemed likely. He'd missed the moment of impact though.

From the snatches of conversations all around him, speculation ran the gamut—bomb, firework, backfire. He pushed his way closer to the rail. Considering the Fourth of July was only a few days ago his money was on someone who couldn't get enough of the star-spangled holiday. *Idiot.* Horses were skittish as shit.

Kevin came up on the rail. The track was the last place he wanted her. His eyes darted from one end of the track to the other, the far turn—the last articulate words that had left Dani's lips before the explosion—his focus. He gritted his teeth. Other than a disjointed herd of horses and riders that had no real direction coming toward the outside rail, he couldn't see a damn thing. His pulse quickened like the beat of a tom-tom. Where the hell was she?

"Folks, we have a rider down," the concerned announcer's voice emanated from the speakers.

Shit.

"Dani!" Elbowing his way through, he searched the rail for any sign of her, moving toward the paddock. Riders were starting to come in, their expressions blank—most likely shock. Hell, he guessed so. They'd more than likely had a part in trampling the rider who went down. Straining his neck, Kevin caught sight of Bonnie on foot, leading Midnight Edition off the track, minus its rider. Heart jackhammering in his chest, he forced his way through, slipped under the rail, and grabbed Bonnie by the arm. "Is it Chipper?"

Bonnie swung around, tears rolling down her face. She tried to speak, but sobs racked her chest. "I-I don't know."

Christ. He'd answered his own question. Midnight Edition was the only riderless horse. "You seen Dani?"

She nodded. "P-passed her when I caught Midnight coming toward the finish line."

He cursed under his breath. Of course she was on the track. She'd had the best vantage point of anyone down where they were—and she'd had her eyes glued on Chipper. She'd seen it all. Kevin, ran down the homestretch in the opposite direction, toward the small crowd gathered at the far turn, his heart lodged in his throat. *God.* Dani must be distraught.

People were running, shouting orders. An ambulance flew by him, its emergency lights creating a red haze against a darkening sky. Kevin searched the faces of those hovering in a tight circle. Some stood, others were bent at the waist, and some were on their knees. But it was the woman sitting on the ground he concentrated on. The tiny dark-haired form rocking Chipper's lifeless, battered body in her arms.

"Our Father, which art in heaven, hallowed be thy—" A sob rolled up Dani's chest, her grip tightening when an EMT moved in to take Chipper's vital signs.

There wasn't anything the young paramedic could do. Kevin had witnessed death, knew the stages. Chipper's usually tanned skin had become gray in color, her lips pale, almost paper white. And the callous cop he believed he was sniffed hard and blinked back tears.

Get it together.

He wiped his eyes, took a deep breath, and pushed his way in. Dropping to his knees next to Dani, he put his arms around her trembling body. Kevin nodded to the paramedics to take over and scooped Dani up. She moaned and fell against his chest.

"It's going to be okay, baby." Kevin kissed her cool forehead and cleared the crowd. All sorts of warning bells went off in his head. This wasn't his state or jurisdiction, but he wanted answers. First, he was getting her the hell out of there. He strode toward the backside and let one damn security guard try to stop him. He'd seen Bonnie, didn't know where the hell this Jake was or his father. Kevin's jaw clenched. His old man was probably a wreck. Now he had two he had to worry about. He'd figure it out and get them all the hell back to Maryland.

Kevin glanced down at Dani with her sable hair pulled up in a ponytail, wearing clothes he'd bought her from Walmart. She was more beautiful than any woman he'd ever known, and he couldn't take his eyes off her. "Talk to me, Irish."

She remained stoic, still in shock. He couldn't begin to know what was going on in that brain of hers. *Shit.* His brain wasn't working on all cylinders. So it was only now that he realized this scene had played out once before in his mind, when Dani had told him about her mother's death.

Okay. Minor setback. Dani was strong, vivacious. She'd bounce back. He shook his head, completely consumed with worry. To think he'd cursed her very existence that night at Grace. Now he didn't think he could live without her. That little nugget of truth snuck up on him, and damned if he knew what to do with it.

CHAPTER THIRTY-SEVEN

AIR RUSHED IN, RAINDROPS PELTING DANI'S SKIN LIKE ICY SPIKES. SHE struggled to open her eyes against the zigzag of glaring light when a warm hand came down on her back.

"Where am I?" Her voice was hoarse, her throat incredibly dry.

"My house." Kevin lifted her into his arms from his car.

Dani reluctantly let go of the plush red stuffed animal pillowing her body when the air around them exploded, the ground rumbling. She clung to him. "Is that thunder?" Her voice trembled.

"Yeah, just started." He ran with her in his arms.

Fat raindrops splashed her skin. "What time is it?"

"Almost three thirty."

Dani's body jolted awake. "I have to go to work soon."

"Relax. You're off for a few days." Kevin climbed the steps, opened the door, and kicked it closed behind him. He sat her down in the foyer.

"Why?" Dani rubbed her eyes. They were crusty and swollen.

"Dani," he said softly, pulling her into his arms. His tired, bloodshot eyes searched hers.

"What's the matter?" Dani caressed his cheek, trying to place what she'd done with the last twenty-four hours of her life when it all came screaming back. A cry bubbled up her chest, and her stomach roiled. She grabbed the doorknob to Kevin's powder room and flung it open. Dropping to the floor, she gripped the cold porcelain. She gagged, her body heaving. Nothing came out.

Chipper's pretty face and bright smile flashed in her head. Only to go dark then reappear death-white and stiff.

"She's dead!" A sob tore from her throat, tears rolled down her face, and that afternoon in Penn National's barn played in her head with overwhelming regret. "I didn't get to give her one last hug." Dani's head hung like a broken flower from its stem. She wanted to wilt away and die.

Kevin knelt down, his arms slipping around her. "Dani, honey," he whispered against her ear. "I'm so sorry."

Every awful moment twirled in her head. She'd have remained in that catatonic state if it weren't for Hannah and Suzanne Grant. Their grief had filled the cramped space of the hospital room. Dani grabbed for Kevin's hand. "Thank you for having them move her to a room."

"I didn't want her mother and daughter to see her like that."

Hannah. A familiar ache came over Dani. She nodded her understanding, unable to speak. She'd been grateful to Kevin for making that call to Suzanne Grant and arranging to have one of his deputies drive them up to Hershey Medical Center.

It had just been Dani and Kevin at the hospital keeping vigil over Chipper's body after the nurses had cleaned her up and tucked her under a blanket. Turk had stayed behind at the track with Bonnie and Jake, answering a police investigator's questions. His blank stare still shook Dani.

She angled her head back toward Kevin. "I'm worried about your da."

"I've already checked on him. They made it back around one."

"I should have helped him with the horses."

Kevin kissed her shoulder, his rough cheek coming to rest there. "Trust me. He knows you took on the hardest job of anyone tonight."

Dani's face crumpled, and she wiped the corners of her eyes. "When will they release her body?"

Kevin pressed her hair behind her ear. "Later today after the autopsy."

Dani shook her head. "I don't understand why they need to cut her open." It had been obvious how she died.

Only it was more of the why that bothered her.

Something or someone still didn't make sense—Lansing. He'd argued with her before the start of the races and then showed up at the hospital, demanding to see Chipper's body.

It was only then that her grief-fogged brain remembered the argument at the scales. She'd told Kevin straightaway about her misgivings. Or was it suspicions?

Did Blake need to see for himself that she was dead?

Dani stared at the blank rose-colored wall of the powder room. "What did you make of Lansing tonight?"

"As a cop . . . suspicious . . . until he fell apart," he said, his voice rumbling against the blade of her shoulder.

Dani didn't think Lansing could have faked his overwhelming grief to throw off the cops if he'd had a hand in what happened at the track. They'd know soon enough. Kevin had alerted the lead investigator. They'd detained Lansing at the hospital. "You'll let me know what they say about Blake?"

He pulled away and turned her toward him, his lips thinning. "There are things you will become privy to by the very nature of our relationship. I expect you to hold the answers to Lansing's behavior, and any other cases, in confidence."

Dani nodded. For all her cloak and dagger theories, there could be a simple explanation. "You think it was just kids playing with fireworks near the track that spooked the horses?"

He shrugged. "It's a theory."

"But you don't believe it." She flashed a pair of determined eyes at him.

"Trust me. The state police up there are thorough." He kissed her temple and helped her up. "Let's hope it was just a senseless act with no malicious intent."

Meaning he hoped the explosion, backfire—whatever it was—wasn't connected to the odd things happening at Whistledown because if it was, they were now dealing with a murderer.

Wind whistled against the creaking old Victorian, the rain heavier now. Lightning flashed. Dani clenched her teeth, waiting for the boom, moving closer to Kevin. His arms encircled her, thunder exploding all around them. It rattled the windows and shook the floor. Dani whimpered and shoved her face into Kevin's chest, her fingers digging into his hips.

Of all nights.

Kevin peered down at her, his eyes sympathetic. "You all right?"

Dani nodded. "Fine." She pulled away from him, embarrassed, and tugged down her white tank, stained with Chipper's blood. "Will I be staying with you tonight?"

Kevin nodded and then tried to cover up a yawn. "Come on. I'm beat." He led her out of the powder room and toward the stairs. "Let's get a shower and get some sleep."

Dani hesitated, her eyes growing wide. Did he mean together?

He laughed. "I'm too tired tonight to ravish you in the shower. You can use the one in the hall, and there's a guest bedroom across from mine."

Her shoulders leveled off, the heat receding from her cheeks. "I didn't mean to imply . . ." Lightning flashed again, and Dani reached for the banister.

"Yes, you did." He chuckled and motioned her up the steps amidst a crescendo of thunder. It was angry and rolling, and she clenched her teeth, wondering if it would ever stop.

Dani went ahead, her heartbeat racing. *Damn storm.*

Kevin gave her a peck on the cheek when they reached the top, turning on the hall light. "Nothing wrong with a woman protecting her virtue." He sidestepped her, popped on the light to the hall bath, and gave her a tired smile. "If I remember correctly, I've been accused of running lights and siren trying to do the same thing."

Dani gave him a lift of her brow. "Yes, and you embarrassed me because of it."

He snorted and opened the cabinet below the sink, pulling out shampoo, conditioner, and a box of soap. He placed it on the counter. "Fresh towels and washcloths are hanging up."

"Thanks."

He moved out of the bathroom. "Bedroom's up and on the left."

Dani smiled at him and then slammed her eyes shut when a streaming white-hot bolt lit the upstairs hall. "Shite!" She gripped the door jamb, trying to ride out the rumble beneath her feet.

Kevin gave her a pained expression. "You going to be all right in the spare bedroom?"

"Ah . . ." She'd be up, but she'd be dry, unlike the last storm she'd endured, which was at sea.

"You can sleep with me if you want."

Dani rolled her lips in. Not that the thought hadn't crossed her mind. He seemed to have a calming effect on her. But lying next to him would create a whole new set of complications. "It's kind, but no." She gave him a quick smile. "I'll see you tomorrow morning, then?"

"Good night," he said, something flitting in the depths of his eyes before he turned and headed down the hall.

Was he hoping she'd say yes? He'd said he was tired. She was, too. But after tonight, she'd made a promise. No regrets.

Torn, she threw her head back and entered the bathroom, shutting the door. She tossed her dirty clothes onto the floor and stepped into the shower. Letting the warm water cascade down her body, she ruminated over the day's events, trying to piece together all that had happened and wondering—as she had so many times with her ma's death—if she could have changed the outcome. Maybe if she had ridden up with them or confronted Blake. If he was planning to hurt her, he might have reconsidered.

Again, the bloody question was why?

Dani frowned, turned off the shower, and got out, her bare feet sinking into a cushy bathmat. *It doesn't make sense.* She dried herself off and wrapped the towel around her body. Rummaging for a toothbrush under the sink, she came up with a new one in its cellophane wrapper. If he'd offered his soap, she guessed the toothbrush was up for grabs as well. Opening up the side medicine cabinet, she found a small tube of toothpaste and comb.

She brushed her teeth and combed out her hair, gritting her teeth when she hit a knot, thunder rocking the small bathroom. If she had some way of muffling the noise, she'd be better for it. *Cotton balls.*

Dani bent down again and searched the cabinet. She found a sample pack of lotion—probably something he'd received in the mail—a can of men's deodorant, mouthwash, and a small travel dryer. At least she could use it for her hair.

Dani brought it out and quickly dried her hair. She applied the travel pack of fragrant lotion, luxuriating in the silky feel. Body lotion—even a bargain brand—was a luxury.

Dani tidied up, pulled her hair into a loose bun, and eyed herself in the mirror. He hadn't said anything about sleepwear. She could beg the use of one of his T-shirts, but it had been a good thirty minutes since he'd gone into his room. She'd more than likely wake him. Dani glanced at her clothes, deciding they were best suited for the garbage. She'd never slept in the nude, but she guessed she could do it for one night.

She checked that her towel was securely tied, then opened the door and stepped out into the hall. The rain continued to assault the roof like a barrage of bullets, the lightning and thunder becoming more like an affliction the way her body contorted every time it flashed and rumbled.

Dani scurried across the hall when the hall lights flickered. *Shite!* She eyed Kevin's bedroom door. It was cracked, a sliver of light running the length of the doorframe. She bit down on her lip. She was stronger than this. It was a freakin' storm—not the end of the world . . . *Tell me beating heart.*

Taking a deep breath, she took a step in. A blast of light illuminated the still black room, thunder shaking the house without mercy, lights pulsing until everything went pitch black. Dani swallowed a scream, made an about-face with her hands out in front, pushing open Kevin's door.

The lights popped on.

"Dani!" Kevin froze walking out of the bathroom. "Shit!" He fumbled for his towel, wrapping it around his hips.

Dani sucked in air and closed her eyes. "I didn't see anything!" That was a lie. She'd seen enough to know she liked looking at him. She opened her eyes and grimaced. "I'm sorry. It was dark, the lightning—the lights . . . They went out."

He walked toward her, grinning. "How about I get a few candles from downstairs? I'll put one in your room in case it goes out again."

He strode past her bare-chested, his blond crew cut glistening from the shower, and entered the hall. He thought she'd done it on purpose. *The nerve.* If she wanted to see, she would have asked. He could be quite an exhibitionist when he wanted—he'd more than likely have accommodated the request. Dani paced his bedroom. The walls were a warm butternut with mocha-colored drapes—the contrast very sharp and masculine with the deep-toned wooden chest and coordinating nightstands.

Dani bit on her lip when another surge of lightning struck, and she hunkered down on the edge of his bed to ride out the thunder. This sucked. She'd been afraid of thunderstorms for as long as she could remember. If God thought he was helping her to overcome her fear by not giving her a minute's peace tonight, he was sadly mistaken.

"Hey, you okay?" Kevin entered the room carrying a large candle in a glass jar in one hand and a lighter in the other.

"Yeah." She stood and tightened her towel. "I'll go to me room now." She passed by him.

He set down the candle on the chest next to the door, tossing the lighter beside it, and caught her in his arms. He tilted her chin up, his eyes holding hers. "You're really scared."

She nodded. "It's a silly fear."

Kevin touched her cheek, their gazes colliding. "Dani," he said, his voice low and urgent, and then he kissed her. His lips moved against hers like a timeless waltz, practiced and fluid.

Dani's nether region tumbled sweetly.

His hand cradled her neck, the other, positioned on her lower back, inching their bodies closer until she was pressed up against his smooth, muscled chest. Her fingertips slid to his shoulders.

His hands fell away from the dip in her spine. He jerked his towel off, letting it fall to the ground at her feet.

She trembled. Hers would be next.

His lips left hers, traveling down her neck to her shoulder blade where he dropped a single kiss. Tilting his head toward her, the flame of the nearby candle reflected in his impassioned brown eyes. "You taste good."

Dani swallowed and reached for her towel.

Kevin took her hand. "Let me."

She nodded, letting her hands fall to her sides and looked away.

"Hey." He angled her chin toward him. "I'm here, sweetheart."

"I know," she whispered. "I'm a bit nervous you won't find me attractive."

He chuckled. "I already do." He kissed each swell of her breasts pressing against the white terrycloth towel and then tugged on the last stronghold, leaving her naked and tremulous. His eyes swept over her with a hunger she'd not seen before. He touched her breast, rolling a nipple between his fingers.

"Oh, God." Dani's breath caught, and the rose-colored nub stiffened.

He kissed her long and deep, his hands fiddling with the band in her hair until sable waves fell past her shoulders, dusting her back. He broke the kiss, creating space between them, his focus her . . . all of her. "My sweet, sexy Dani."

Dani's shoulders curved in. He was older, wiser, and experienced. "I don't think I can compete with the other women you've had."

"It's not a competition." His eyes turned serious. "There's no one else I want, Dani."

She nodded. "I feel the same about you."

He lifted her into his arms. "Stay with me." With little effort, he shucked down the bedding and climbed in, placing her beside him on the cool sheets. He laid next to her on his side, his bronzed hand tantalizing the way it rested on the pale curve of her hip. "I want to take it slow with you."

"Aye. Slow is good." Dani caressed the sharp angles of his handsome face rough with whiskers. "All I want is to make you happy."

"You do." He tasted her again, his hand riding up her waist, her rib cage, cupping her breast. His lips moved down her neck, and he kissed each tender peak.

She rolled into him, arching her back. Her hands explored the contours of his broad shoulders, pecs, and distinct muscles of his stomach.

He kissed her forehead, straddled her, pressing her into the mattress. "Nice and slow," he whispered against her ear and spread her thighs with his knee. He settled between her legs, the tip of his penis against her.

She was wet and warm, like nothing she'd ever experienced before. Every nerve ending she possessed seemed to pool and throb in that very spot where he would enter her.

He took her hand in his, kissed her palm, and brought her arm above her head. His fingers remained threaded with hers.

Her heart beat faster.

He moved onto his elbows, hovering above her, hands still locked with one another. His eyes smoldered, locking onto hers.

Dani's lashes fluttered shut, afraid he'd see something in the depths of hers he didn't like—deception, maybe.

"Open your eyes." The rasp of his voice made her tingle.

Her eyes flickered open. "What do you see?" She wanted to know, his gaze intent and a little unnerving.

He kissed her mouth. "You."

Her eyes remained open, as did his. They kissed, and his grip tightened on her hand incrementally, like he was afraid to let go. The only way she'd ever leave him would be against her will.

She loved him with all her heart.

Dani stroked his arm, his skin smooth and taut over flexed muscles. Although sexy, it was his inner strength she was attracted to most. She felt safe and protected with him.

His kisses intensified. They were longer, deeper. Dani arched her back and moaned into his mouth. His lips fell away, and he stroked her hair, his eyes still intent on her face. "This isn't about sex. You know that, right?" His words were low, controlled, and spoken with complete sincerity.

Dani's eyes began to tear up. She nodded, her lips parting. "I love you."

His thumb brushed over her bottom lip. "Me, too." He thrust into her.

Dani let out a soft cry and clung to him.

Kevin kissed her hard, then slowly until she began kissing him back. The last thing he wanted to do was hurt her. Breathing heavy, he broke the kiss. "You okay?" His voice was hoarse.

Her eyes remained open. They blazed back at him. "Don't stop."

That he could do. Kevin bent his head and again touched his lips to hers. It was like lighting a match, and he burned to taste her. He kissed her, caressed her, and started moving slowly in and out as her hips rose up to meet him, then his thrusts became more urgent.

Her breathing became erratic. Her hand squeezed his tighter. Then her eyes closed, her lips parting.

She was sexy, flushed, and his. "Open your eyes, beautiful."

He had a thing for her baby blues. They were what drew him to her that night when she lay beneath him, struggling to free herself on Grace's gravel drive. Not even three weeks later, he found himself in the same position, only she was in his bed with him inside her.

He rocked above her, his own climax rising.

"Kevin." Her voice hitched, and her eyes opened. "It's welling up in me, I fear," she said, breathless.

"Relax and don't fight it, baby. I've got you." He cupped her breast and drew the rosy pert nipple into his mouth.

Dani's back arched. She was warm and wet and convulsed around him. Her fingers dug into his shoulder blades before her lithe, tight body sunk luxuriously into the cushy mattress. Her once fiery eyes now sated and heavy.

She whimpered, the feminine sound turning him on. Kevin kissed her hard. "I love you, Dani." He thrust into her again and again. Cresting, he had just enough sense to pull out, his semen squirting onto her translucent skin and the well-trimmed swirl of ebony curls between her thighs.

He reached down and grabbed a discarded towel, cleaning her and then himself. Tossing it back on the floor, he dropped down next to her and pulled her into his arms. He pressed away a damp wave of her hair and kissed the column of her neck. "I want you to move in with me."

She rolled into him and glanced up. "To protect me."

"A deputy could do that, Dani." He dropped a kiss on her lips. "It's a selfish request. One I hope you'll consider."

"Like playing house, then?" She wrapped her arms around him, laying her check against his beating heart.

He settled against her, surprised at the calming effect she had on him.

"No." He laughed and kissed the top of her head, then adjusted himself so he could see her clearly. "Like I love you and want to come home to you every night."

She kissed him. "I'd like that, too. I would. But what of the horses?"

He caressed her cheek. "I thought about that. The department has surveillance cameras. Thinking of installing one in the barn to keep an eye on your horses."

"Twenty-four seven, then?"

"You got it." He tweaked her nose. "Technologically more foolproof than *your* eyes and ears." He hadn't forgotten her fierce stance on the subject that night at Penn National.

She nodded but remained quiet.

"What?"

"I'm a package deal, you know." Her lips quirked.

Kevin thought about that for a minute. "Ah, you're talking about that damn cat."

"Jimmy," she corrected.

"Right." He snuggled her to him. "Whatever makes you happy." He yawned and pulled up the covers, his eyes growing heavy.

This would be the first night in a long time he'd sleep like a stone, knowing she was with him.

It had been that day in his kitchen. He knew then she was the only woman for him.

Chapter Thirty-Eight

Bonnie flitted by Dani at the Huntsmen's Club, wearing a revealing dress and laughing with a glass of—it looked to be—bourbon in her hand.

What the bloody hell is wrong with her?

They'd just come from sticking Chipper in the cold, hard ground, amidst the cries and wails of her family. Dani had searched the faces at the gravesite, hoping to find Bonnie amongst the mourners. She might as well have wished into the wind for all the good it had done. Dani clenched her jaw.

Nice of her to show up for the food and drink.

Dani caught up with Bonnie and grabbed her by the arm, jerking her around. The gold-colored liquid sloshed out onto her fingers.

"Hey! That cost me money!"

"Shut up," Dani whispered hard under her breath and dragged Bonnie's unsteady body through a pair of swinging doors. The room was a small bar, reminding her of the pub with its dark paneled walls and wooden tables. "That's a lie." Dani took the glass from her and slammed it down on a nearby table. "The racing stables chipped in for the luncheon as well as the open bar." She narrowed in on her. "But you wouldn't know, I imagine. You haven't been around."

Bonnie sucked her fingers, Dani guessed trying to siphon what little liquor was left on her hands. She truly was pathetic. Dani took a breath through her nose, trying to find her compassion. She loved Bonnie like a sister—understood the closeness she'd shared with Chipper. They'd been friends long before Dani had come on the scene.

She took Bonnie's trembling hands in hers. "I know you're hurting."

Bonnie's chin shot up. "Don't tell me how I should . . ." Her hollow green eyes tunneled into Dani's, the seconds ticking by. "Feel, damn it."

Dani grabbed her defiant chin. "What are you on, then? You can barely finish a thought."

"Nothing." Bonnie's head dropped to her chest like she'd fallen straight to sleep.

Shite. Dani pulled out a chair and pushed her down in it. "You need help before you—"

"I've got her, lass." Fritz came from behind in his dark suit and trademark suspenders.

"There, there." He pulled Bonnie up like a ragdoll. "She needs a little fresh air is all."

"It's more than that." Dani grabbed his arm, nailing him with an incisive gaze. "You know it as well as I."

His usually warm eyes flashed with contempt. "It's none of your business, lass." He jerked his arm away and dragged Bonnie to the back door.

Maybe Fritz felt a responsibility for what had happened to Bonnie. He was being a fool, though. Like the fresh air was going to cure her.

She'd likely die of an overdose. Dani closed her eyes. "May God protect her," she prayed, her eyes flying open.

Fritz propped open the door with his elderly frame, struggling through it with Bonnie's dead weight. Every ion she possessed wanted to help him—but not like this. *Let them go.* She would talk to Bonnie again— *Lord willing*—without her enabler. Dani clenched her hands.

Nice of him to talk about things he hadn't a clue about.

"She is me business!" Dani flung at him, tears pinching the backs of her eyes.

Fritz left, leaving the door to slam behind him.

Dani shoved the chair under the table. *Eejit.* Spitting mad, she hit the double doors hard with her hands. They flew open like a pair of saloon doors from one of those old American westerns with her looking nothing like a rough and tumble cowboy in her black high heels and pretty little black dress.

"Jesus." Kevin pulled his head back, the corner missing his head by degrees.

"Oh, luv." All that bravado dwindled, and Dani rushed to him.

He pulled her back through the double doors, his arm going around her. "What's wrong?"

Everything, she wanted to say, except for what she shared with him. They'd been together for the past three nights. If it weren't for the fairy tale playing out under his roof, she'd be beside herself with grief.

Dani gave him a quick kiss and pulled away, waving a dismissive hand. "It's nothing. Bonnie's not handling things well. Fritz took her back to the training center."

"Yeah." He scrubbed the back of his neck. "I was thinking about heading that way myself."

"Oh?" Dani's brows rose.

He took her hand in his and shook it. "Just want to check on my old man."

Since leaving the gravesite, she hadn't seen Turk. She assumed she'd run into him at the luncheon.

"I'm worried about him, too. He didn't seem at all his grumpy self at dinner the other night."

Kevin pulled loose his tie, popping the top button of his dress shirt, and hooked his chin toward the door Fritz and Bonnie had left through. "Let's get out of here."

She'd already spent time with Suzanne and little Hannah. They'd be too busy with other friends and family to notice she'd left with Kevin. She'd see them again and soon. They'd promised to come by the track next week for lunch.

Dani nodded toward the door. "I'm ready."

He placed his hand on the curve of her lower back and led her out into the scorching sun's rays.

He helped her into his patrol car and then came around the other side and got in. He smiled at her and started the car. "How you holding up?"

Dani shrugged. "I miss her."

He nodded and drove out of the parking lot and onto the highway. "I'm here for you." He turned toward her, a serious expression lining his face. "You know that, right?"

"I do, yes." She gave him a weak smile.

He turned his attention to the road and reached over, patting her thigh. "You look very pretty."

Dani looked down at her dress, shaking her head. "I bought it for you."

He laughed. "Me?"

"To woo you."

"I got news for you." He chuckled. "You had me that day at my house, weeding my garden in your bare feet and the clothes I bought you from Walmart."

Dani frowned. "It seems like a lifetime ago."

They rode in silence the rest of the way. She wouldn't be at all surprised if their thoughts didn't mirror one another. She worried about a lot of things, but there was only one person on her mind now.

Dani had seen Turk briefly at the gravesite and before that on the night after Chipper's death. She'd cooked that lamb she'd teased Kevin about, on one condition—he invited his father. Turk had eaten his meal, his expression a mix of loss, worry, and was it guilt?

Somewhere deep within, Turk seemed to be trying to find fault with himself. The few times he did utter words at dinner it was to question the trip up, the care of the horses, the scales and the weight of the saddle, and the deadly race.

He'd done nothing wrong.

Try telling that to a man who has become—as amazing as it is—a sort of surrogate father to the women that worked under him.

It was the subject that came up next at dinner—Delhaven's mare—that had Dani holding her breath. Turk had listened, only to shake his head. The suffering between father and son had been painful to witness.

As for Lansing and the content of his interview with police, Kevin did get a four-letter word out of Turk, beginning with an "F" and followed by the word "him," after learning from the police the argument between Chipper and Blake had centered round Blake trying to get Chipper to jump stables. Dani assured Turk that from her vantage point Chipper's answer—although she hadn't heard it with her own ears—had been no.

For all the anger the three of them shared toward Blake, he seemed an unlikely suspect. Although Dani would remain skeptical until she unearthed the reason for his odd behavior at the hospital. She wouldn't leave it to the thorough and final state police report Kevin had received this morning, ruling Chipper's death as an unfortunate firework mishap.

Kevin put the car in park next to her Cabrio, which had been left to languish, nodding toward his father's pickup to the right of it. "He's here." The relief was palpable in his voice.

Dani grabbed for the door, opening it.

Kevin reached behind him. "Go on and check on him." He pulled up a quart of oil from the floor. "You have the keys to your car?"

"Aw." Dani dug out her key ring from her purse and handed them to him, a pout on her lips. "I love you, you know." She gave him a quick kiss on the mouth and then placed her leg outside the car.

"Show me tonight," he said on a laugh and squeezed her bum as she got out.

Dani shut the door, her body tingling at the thought. She picked her way through the gravel in her high heels, headed toward the barn doors. She glanced back. Kevin was out, minus his tie and navy blue suit jacket, rolling his sleeves up past sinewy forearms. Dani wet her lips. She didn't think she could wait until tonight. It didn't matter if the man was wearing a towel or a fine tailored suit—looking at him sent a fiery thrill through her.

Dani tamped down the rushing warmth of attraction for him and entered the barn, stopping cold at the open doorway of Turk's office. He sat at his desk, still in his suit, staring at an unopened bottle of whiskey and a shot glass. Dan's stomach dropped like a stone into a bottomless well.

She knew a thing or two about alcoholics. They were either going to take a drink. Or they were testing their resolve.

She hoped it was the latter and walked right in, snagging the bottle off his desk. "Ah, is it a drink you're wanting?"

His eyes widened, but he didn't utter a word.

She checked the bottle. "Irish." She couldn't help but smile. "I see you have good taste, then." She uncapped the bottle, the tamper-resistant black label tearing in her hands.

She waited, hoping. But when he didn't protest, she placed the tip of the bottle to the glass and filled it to the brim.

Turk jumped up. "What the hell are you doing, Flynn?" His blue eyes looked as if they'd pop straight out of his head.

She wouldn't lay off just yet. She pulled her own head back, giving him a look of rebuke. "Sharing a drink with me old trainer." Dani picked the glass up, the woodsy amber-colored liquid teasing her nose. "To Chipper, may she rest in peace." She tossed it back and swallowed. Like warm lava oozing down a mountainside, it scorched her throat. Dani leveled a hard gaze at him.

Tears filled his eyes. "How does something like that happen?" He shook his head. "She was on top. She would have won the eighth, been a real contender in the Travers." He started gathering up racing books from every corner of the tight office, throwing them in a large trash can by his desk.

When he went for the old silver tray he'd won at Belmont in '95, Dani jumped in his way. "What the devil are you doing?" Her eyes flashed.

His blazed back, his lips thinning. "I'm a wash up—a has-been." He laughed, the sound pained. "A never been, if you ask that damn son of mine." He plopped down in his chair and closed his eyes.

"That's not true." Dani came to him and crouched down.

His eyes popped open. "He tell you about that?" He tossed his head toward the desk and the bottle of whiskey.

"Even if he did, what does it matter? I know you wouldn't have taken a drink." She put her hand on his knee.

"Kid, I wish I had your faith." His hand came down on hers. "He's a fool if he ever lets you go."

Dani smiled at that. "Let's worry about getting Starlite back in the saddle."

"I got a horse that ain't worth a shit after Penn National—skittish as hell and another mouth to feed 'cuz I'm not giving up on him." He took a belabored breath, falling back in his chair. "It doesn't matter. I'm done."

"Mr. Porter let you go?" Dani's voice caught. There was no other trainer she wanted to work for. Of course, it was silly to even assume she still had a job.

Turk's head fell to his chest. "There is no Mr. Porter."

Dani's mouth fell open, and she dropped back on her heels. "You're pulling me leg."

"Wish I were."

"But who owns Starlite?"

"You're looking at him."

It all made sense—the reason she'd never seen or heard from Mr. Porter was that he didn't exist. Turk called the shots all along.

She gave him a stern look. "Please tell me Kevin knows this."

"Hell no!" Turk grumped.

Damn it. Dani should have closed her ears to that. Kevin had warned her about leveling with him. "You're going to fill him in, I suppose."

He gave her a disagreeable look, shaking his head. "He's one of the reasons I invented Porter."

"I don't understand."

"When I lost my ass I could pretend it was Porter's money." He sat there for a while deep in his thoughts. "That kid of mine, well, hell, I never gave him a reason to respect me."

"That's not true. He loves you."

"Does he? Will he if I lose it all? " Turk shook his head. "I'm going to lose it now." He clucked his tongue. "Probably his childhood home, too."

"Kevin's?"

"He thinks it's paid in full from his mother's insurance pol—"

"How's it going in here?" Kevin set down a suitcase he'd brought for her things and swung in, his attention diverted by the oil on his hand and a rag he used to wipe them.

Shite! Dani grabbed the shot glass and whiskey, the bottle going behind her back, the glass in the can, thumping on the way down. "Horse talk."

He nodded with one of those glad-to-hear-we're-moving-on nods. "That's good."

Turk gave her a wink, turning in his seat toward Kevin. "I think a cable came loose on that camera you installed in the eave yesterday."

"I'll check it out." He walked in with the rag, looking for the trash can, stopping short when Turk stuck out his hand.

"I'll take that."

"Okaaay." He looked from Dani to his father as he stretched the word out. "Something going on I should know about?"

"Not unless you want in on this gig I have with Porter."

"A trainer?" He snorted. "I'll check the camera." Then he looked at Dani. "Thinking about heading back to the office, making a few calls and finishing some paperwork. You have things to do here until about six?"

"I'm still paying her, aren't I?" Turk harrumphed. "While you two have been playing house, we've been losing time, right, Flynn?"

Dani's brows furrowed. "Ah . . ."

Turk raised his eyebrows at her. "I guess you forgot to tell him you and Solley are training for the Travers in six weeks."

Dani's mind scattered. *Training . . . Travers?*

"R-right. I'm taking Chipper's place." She gave Kevin a quick smile.

"Huh, huh." Kevin looked at them strangely and picked up the suitcase. "I'll drop this off at your door and check the camera while I'm upstairs." He strode away and took the steps.

They waited until he hit the second floor.

Dani zeroed in on Turk. "Where the bloody hell did that come from? First you tell me you're Mr. Por—"

"Shh." Turk cringed. "He'll hear you." He motioned up with his eyes.

"Brilliant," she whispered, then shook her head. "I suppose I'm to keep your confidences until they foreclose on your home, then?"

He wagged a finger at her. "The purse is over a mil." His eyes glittered. "Enough to cover my mortgage, give you about 60K in your pocket, and get this stable back in business."

Chapter Thirty-Nine

WHAT THE DEVIL HAD SHE BEEN THINKING? DANI FLUNG OPEN THE door to Chipper's locker and cursed. She should have said no. *No, I can't.* She was illegal with no chance of getting her citizenship anytime soon and running from a killer who wanted her dead—after she gave him a thumb drive she'd hidden in her sister's home.

She needed to get that back. Dani gritted her teeth. She had a car—a lot of good it did without a license. She banged the metal door a few times against the locker next to it and grimaced when two photos fell off the inside of Chipper's locker and wafted to the floor. Dani scooped them up, a whimper escaping her lips at the one with Chipper sitting in the front seat of her car with Hannah behind the wheel in her lap. The other was of the three of them the night of the ball.

Dani leaned against the cold metal lockers, wiping at her face. She didn't feel at all right going through her things. She pushed off, eyeing the contents inside—jockey helmet, saddle pads, an extra pair of silks. Dani ran her hand along the smooth fabric.

I'm not wearing it.

The last time she'd seen those silks before today they were covered in muck and Chipper's blood. The colors made her physically ill—she would ask Turk to consider changing them. She'd pay for it from her own money if she had to.

First, she was putting the locker back the way she'd found it. With the photos in her hand, she searched the locker for tape. On the top shelf, a small dispenser sat close to the edge. Dani rose on tiptoes and grabbed for it. The tape fell to the floor, along with several scraps of paper fluttering like delicate butterflies in a spring meadow.

Dani sat the tape dispenser down on the bench next to her. Picking up the paper, a tune began to play, her bum rumbling. She grabbed the phone out of her back jean pocket, the name startling her. She took the call. "Kate?"

"Don't you ever check your voice mail?" Her sister's voice was clipped.

"I-I don't know how." Dani rolled her lips in. The mobile she'd brought from Ireland wasn't complicated like the iPhone Bren had given her.

"It's okay." Kate's voice softened. "It's important you keep in touch with us."

Dani continued to gather the loose papers, placing them on the bench like pieces to a puzzle. It had been a week since she'd talked to either one of her sisters. "A lot's been going on."

"Dad told Bren. I'm sorry."

Dani nodded, unable to speak. She cleared her throat and grabbed the tape dispenser. "Are you back, then?"

"No, not until August 30."

"What was it you called about?"

"This person who was killed in Ireland—was she a woman?"

Dani's hands stilled in the middle of ripping a piece of tape off. "Yes."

"Was her name Kara Gilroy?"

Dani pressed a long sticky strip against several pieces of paper, her hands trembling. "How did you know?"

"They found her body—one gunshot to the back of the head," Kate said at the same time the paper on the bench started to take form.

"Oh my God."

Her past and her present clashed like a mighty cymbal. It was deafening. Her head ached, her mind thundered, trying to decide which was more important.

"Dani? You all right?"

"I have to go." Dani disconnected the call and seized the tattered, taped document in her hand. How was it that Chipper had a check for five thousand dollars written out to her from Blake Lansing?

Dani's hands flew to her mouth. "No. I can't believe it," she said on a whisper. Dani shook her head hard. With her phone in her hand, she snatched up the check and tore out of the bunkhouse. It couldn't be more than half past four, the sun perched high in the summer sky. People were still milling about, some on the track, others—she scanned the buildings and parking lots, narrowing in on the silver sporty convertible Mercedes—were still here.

Dani marched toward his barn. Thinking better of it, she paused and texted Kevin two short lines. *Blake's been bribing Chipper. I'm headed to his barn.* She shoved her phone back in her jean pocket and entered the barn. Deep in conversation, two grooms' heads shot up.

"Blake Lansing. Where can I find him?"

The one with curly blond hair pointed toward the back of the barn and a handsome six-paneled wooden door. *Ah. The king and his royal chambers.* Well, he'd better take court with a commoner or he'd find his door in splinters. Dani stomped toward it, her boots biting into the dirt floor of the barn, and jerked the heavy wooden door open.

Surrounded in dark, warm-toned paneling, Blake sat on the edge of a gorgeous mahogany desk wearing a pair of riding breeches, one booted foot dangling. He zeroed in on her, his forearm tensing below the sleeve of a white T-shirt.

Dani took a step in.

His brows rose as he continued speaking into his cell phone. "I'm going to have to let you go, Mark. I have someone in my office." He disconnected. "I thought we had an agreement."

Dani strode over and jammed the check in his face. "Did she get tired of doing your dirty work for you?" Her brow rose over an irritated blue eye. "And maybe she told you to go to hell that day at the scales?"

His face reddened. "What the hell are you talking about?" He snatched the paper from her, his eyes scanning it for a brief moment before his lips thinned. "Shut the door."

Dani tensed, icy tingles riding down her spine. *Relax.* There wasn't much he could do to her with his employees outside in the shed row. She walked to the door, keeping him accounted for. She shut it and took measured steps toward him. "I suppose you can explain."

His eyes blazed back at her. "I don't owe you or anyone an explanation." He walked around his desk and sat down in the high-backed chair. Resting his head against the leather grain, he pinched the bridge of his nose. His eyes closed. "But you're only going to get Bendix involved in my shit." They opened, his gaze uncertain. "Aren't you?"

She already had. If he had something to say before Kevin arrived, he'd better start talking. "A large check written to a woman you know professionally seems a bit suspicious and something he'd want to know about, considering his investigation and that of the state police in

Pennsylvania. Don't you think?"

"If it were a bribe." He ripped open a drawer to his desk, grappled with files until he flung one on the top of his desk.

Dani eyed it.

"Go ahead. Open it."

Leery, Dani took a tentative step forward and flipped the folder open like it was a venomous snake getting ready to strike. *Only documents.* She lifted the folder from the desk, thumbing through check stubs, all made out to Charlene Taylor Grant for the same amount. She lifted her eyes to him, then back to the stubs, checking the dates. The ones on top were written this year, all dated the first of the month. "I don't understand."

He stood up abruptly. "Nor should you." He shoved his hands inside his pockets and motioned with his chin. "There are three more years of checks, each written the first of the month for the same amount." He gave her his back. "I've been a selfish man with little patience. It was easier for me to pay than to give of myself or my time."

"Pay? Pay her for what?"

"There's more than checks in the folder."

Dani sat it down and flipped through until she found a single sheet of paper that was heavier than the rest. Her fingers gripped the parchment, her breath catching when she read the document. "You're Hannah's father." It came out in hushed disbelief. But it made sense, now, his interest in her that day before the ball.

He angled his body away from the window. The late day sun, filtering through the wooden blinds, landed on his tanned face. Lines bracketed his mouth, others fanned out from his tired eyes. "I gave up my parental rights the day she was born and agreed to pay child support with one stipulation—that Chipper keep my playboy image intact."

Dani didn't believe Suzanne knew. She chewed her bottom lip.

"What?" He looked at her pointedly.

"You seem to take issue with this image you've worked so hard to perfect." She shrugged. "Do you still feel that way?"

His forehead creased. "Excuse me?"

"Selfish and impatient?"

"Would it matter? Parental rights are not something you get back."

Maybe not. Hannah would be better off with her grandmother whom she adored. Reminded of her own father, a smile touched Dani's lips. "Someday she may be receptive to learning who her real father is."

He lifted his chin to her and gave her a half smile. "You talk from experience." He sat back down on the edge of the desk. "It takes a tragedy to see your life for what it is. I've done some unscrupulous things, which you already know."

"You threatened to have me deported, Blake."

"I was angry." He laughed. "No one's ever put me in my place." He seemed to be lost in thought. "Barring Chipper, of course."

Dani's romance with Blake started to take shape in her mind. He'd met her on the track and asked her to go to the ball with Chipper and Bonnie looking on. Chipper's reaction when she had returned with Solley made sense now. Then he'd miraculously showed up after Chipper walked over, helping her to save face with Kevin.

Whose attention had he really hoped to gain?

Dani's bottom lip dropped. "You weren't the least bit interested in me." She narrowed in on him.

He chuckled. "You're beautiful, but, no. I've only had one woman on my mind since leaving the well-heeled Oak Ridge Equine Center of Ocala to come to this backcountry farm you call a training center." He seemed to be calculating things in his head. "Almost a year ago."

Blake's behavior that night at the hospital played in her head like a frenetic instrumental full of pain and loss. "You still loved her."

He shrugged. "Doesn't matter now."

Dani nodded. "If it's any consolation, I think she was still in love with you, too."

"Funny way of showing it." He raked his fingers through his dark hair and eyed the taped-together check. "She refused to cash July's check. Said she didn't need *my* money."

"Jealousy, I fear." Dani shook her head. *Men.* They were so clueless when it came to women. If he'd only sat Chipper down and told her what was in his heart, things may not have turned out the way they had. Maybe she would have given him another chance, become part of his business instead of Turk's, and wouldn't have been on that bloody track that night. "The part about jumping stables wasn't true, I take it?"

He shook his head. "This wasn't something I wanted spread around town."

She understood. Hannah needed to heal. It would be difficult if her mother's death was a topic of conversation for the local gossipers.

"Your secret's safe with me." Dani handed him the file. "You'll be heading back to this Ocala, I imagine."

He shook his head. "Whistledown has more appeal for me now."

"Hannah."

"She's my child." He took a heavy breath. "Not that I have any claim to Hannah. But I want the best for her. Chipper has her in a Montessori school in Clear Spring. Tuition isn't cheap." His brows furrowed, and he remained lost in thought.

"Blake?"

His head shot up. "Yes?"

"Would you like me to talk to Suzanne Grant?"

"You'd do that?" He looked at her with skepticism.

Dani shouldn't want to help him at all. He'd used her, threatened her, and now—now he only pulled at her heart.

"It'd be me pleasure. I'm sure she'd welcome your help in affording Hannah's special school." Dani walked toward the door and turned. "They're meeting me for lunch here next week. Maybe you could join us. If Suzanne is agreeable to you meeting her."

He looked affright. "I-I don't . . ."

"Only if Suzanne agrees, and"—she winked—"as me good friend."

His shoulders relaxed, and he pushed off from the desk and walked toward her. "You really are a gem." He opened the door. "You have my number?"

She laughed. "Yes, and you've caused me a lot of explaining because of it." Dani turned to leave, past the curious eyes of the two grooms, and headed out of the barn. She couldn't seem to stop smiling. Blake Lansing a father—Hannah's father. *Who would have believed?* She passed Fritz's barn, the warm glow of charity dimming. She'd seek him out tomorrow and make things right. As for Bonnie, she doubted she'd remember their encounter.

Dani entered Starlite's barn and climbed the steps. She pulled her keys from her front pocket, unlocked her door, and grabbed the suitcase off the landing. She was starting a new chapter of her life with Kevin. Even small, the room with its warm daffodil walls held bittersweet memories for her. Dani sat her mobile down on the chest. "Oh, shite!" Her hand came to her lips. "Kate."

Dani dialed up her number and waited. The phone clicked. "I'm sorry," she said before Kate could say a word.

"You okay?" Concern filled her voice.

"There was something I needed to take care of—a bit of an emergency." Now that the whole episode with Blake was resolved—and much better than she could have ever imagined—her past commanded her complete attention. "Kate?" Her voice shook slightly.

"Yes, sweetie."

"Where did they find Kara?"

"She washed up along a strand of beach not too far from the docks in Rosslare Harbour."

Dani blinked back tears. To think she'd actually held out hope. It was stupid. Garda would be looking more closely. They'd wonder what became of Dani. They'd start at the docks. Putting pressure on Tommy was never a good thing.

She sniffed and wiped her nose with her hand. "How did you escape your first husband?"

She took a heavy sigh. "An FBI agent took him out."

"Killed him, then?"

"Before he could kill me."

Kate's words resonated with Dani, and she trembled. "I think it's only a matter of time before Tommy finds me."

"That's his name."

Dani sat down on her bed. "Tommy Duggan. Kara stole a thumb drive from his office. She gave it to me before she was killed." Dani's voice hitched. "Kate, I had it that night at the picnic and tried to read it on Bren's computer. Kevin walked in, and I hid it in the Irish clock."

"Grandma Maeve's?"

"Yes. I guess. I need to get it back. I'd never forgive meself if something were to happen because of it."

"It doesn't matter, honey. If he finds you, he'll use us like bargaining chips regardless if you move it. I'll tell Bren. If she agrees, we'll leave it there for now."

A light rap hit her door. "Someone's here."

"You know who it is?" There was tension in her voice.

"It's not Tommy." She wet her lips. At least she didn't think. That last night in Ireland came back to her, the door swinging open in the warehouse. She relaxed. "He's not the type to knock on doors."

"Been there." She laughed. "Seriously. I know you've been distracted, and with good reason. But be vigilant, check word from home on the iPhone, and check your messages."

"I will."

A light rap hit the door again. Dani covered up the phone. "Coming."

"Love you," Kate said in her ear.

"Love you, too." Dani disconnected and answered the door.

"Forgive me?" Bonnie stood in the doorway, her expression contrite.

Dani nodded. "Come in."

Bonnie stepped in, Dani shut the door behind her.

"You're forgiven." Dani hugged her tight.

Bonnie's arm went around her, her body trembling. "I'm so messed up right now."

"I miss her, too." Tears filled Dani's eyes. "She told me about the accident and the pills. Let me help you."

Bonnie nodded against her. "I thought I could handle everything. I'm going to get help," she snuffled.

Dani rested her chin on her shoulder. "Don't be sad, Bonnie. She'd want you to be chipper."

Bonnie snorted in her ear. "Please tell me you didn't just say that."

Dani pulled away, giving her a disagreeable look. "What is so bloody amusing?"

Bonnie wiped tears of laughter from her face. "Think about what just came out of your mouth, Flynn."

Dani tried to recall her words. When she did, she snickered. "It wasn't at all what I meant, well, I did, but not—"

"I know what you meant." Bonnie gave a pout. "I'm going to miss having you around."

Dani unzipped her suitcase. "That's silly. I'll be working me regular schedule." She opened her top drawer, pulled out a mix of underwear, shorts, and tops and hesitated. She might still need the use of the room to change in and out of clothes. She left a few items in her drawer and shut it. The jar of peppermints shook above. Dani frowned. She'd miss giving the horses their bedtime treats. She spun around with the clothes still in her hand. "But I won't be here in the evenings." She dumped her clothes in and grabbed the glass jar. "Will you give them their nighttime treat?"

"Sure." She took the jar from Dani. "I'm really happy for you—for everything."

"You ran into Turk, then?"

"I saw him earlier. He told me you and Solley are going to take Chipper's place at Travers."

She grimaced. "Six weeks. It's not very much time, I think."

Bonnie waved a dismissive hand. "You'll tear up the track." She sat down the jar and opened up Dani's wardrobe. "What are you taking from here?"

Her pretty dresses, a pair of black slacks, and a white fluttery top hung in a neat row. "They're not clothes for working in the barn."

Bonnie handed them out one at a time, bending down to grab a shopping bag folded at the bottom of the wardrobe. "I'll put your shoes in this."

Dani placed a finger to her lips. What else was she missing or forgetting?

"Oh, the peppermints." Dani shut her suitcase and took the bag of shoes from Bonnie, nodding toward the jar. "Only one before bedtime. Turk's rule."

Bonnie laughed, picking it up from the bed. "And we know how he is abou—" Bonnie moved closer to the small window. "Dani . . . ah . . . is that Kevin running lights and sirens?"

Puzzled, Dani moved to the window. A patrol car, its red and blue lights flashing, swerved around the bend of Whistledown's gravel drive.

Her heart pounded, and it was then she remembered the text she'd sent.

CHAPTER FORTY

BAREFOOT, DANI WALKED OUT OF THE STEAMY MASTER BATHROOM and into the slumberous, earthy tones of Kevin's bedroom. He sat propped up in bed with a pad and pen, jotting something down. That fastidious cat he talked about, now a reality, sitting at the end of the bed cleaning himself.

Kevin glanced up, his eyes taking her in from the flirty short hem of her sheer coral pink nightie to the swell of her breasts pushing against the lacy demi cups.

"Sexy." He sat down the pad and pen when she moved to the edge of the bed.

Dani motioned with her eyes toward his notes. "You taking Lansing off your list of suspects?"

"They're talking points for tomorrow night's council meeting. But, yes I have, and you"—he grinned—"I should have put over my knee and spanked for scaring the shit out of me tonight." Turning off the light, he nudged Jimmy off and pulled her into his bed.

Dani giggled on the way down, remembering his indignation earlier when she'd flagged him down after he flew out of his car. "It's one of my flaws, I think." Her body hit the plush pillow-top mattress, and she rolled into him.

"Stirring up trouble?" Bare chested, Kevin smiled down at her under the moon's glow from the window. His hand rode up her thigh. The sheer material of her nightie crumpled in his hand, and he kissed her tenderly on her lips. "Stop taking matters into your own hands. It's taken me a lifetime to find you. I don't want to lose you now."

Dani's insides tumbled sweetly at the roughness in his voice. She'd waited a long time for him as well. She couldn't bear the thought of losing him to her lies, if they ever caught up with her.

"You're a wee bit quiet." She nudged him in his ribs.

"I was just thinking." He kissed her forehead. "Lansing's got a kid, huh," he said wistfully.

"Hannah," she corrected him.

He pressed a dark wave of hair away from her face. "What do you think ours will look like?"

Lying in the strength of his arms with only the beat of his heart, she couldn't speak for fear she'd cry.

"What?" His eyes searched her face.

Dani was relieved they were in shadow. "Don't tease me, Kevin."

"I'm not." His heart beat faster under her palm where she caressed the smooth muscle of his chest, and he pulled her still closer. "I'm in love with you."

"So you say." Dani laughed, trying to make light of it, all the while wondering how many women he'd spoken those very five words to. "I bet you've used that line for a tumble in the sheets before."

"But I mean it now." His voice was low and controlled and earth-shatteringly sincere.

After what she'd learned from Kate today, she should tell him of Kara before he read it himself. "I suppose you plan to marry me tomorrow, then?" She rolled over giving him her back and snuggling her bum into him.

He slid the thin strap of her nightie down her shoulder and dropped a kiss on her warm skin. "Not tomorrow, no. But the question is, would you even have me, Dani Flynn, from Ireland?"

His poor attempt at an Irish brogue made her smile. "If you're asking, the answer is with all me heart." She peered over her shoulder. "But it's not only me heart you're wanting."

"The deal was"—he turned her in his arms so she was facing him—"that you're honest with me from here on out."

Dani nodded, and she closed her eyes to the thoughts rolling around in her head.

You need to start trusting me.

Her lashes fluttered open, and she was met with Kevin's curious gaze. She caressed his rough cheek. "Kevin."

It was like jumping off that swing. She needed to get on with it. This was a solid step in the right direction. Dani swallowed. "I don't know the particulars, but Kara Gilroy turned up dead."

His body stiffened, the angles of his face becoming sharper and more defined beneath her hand. "Look," he said pointedly at her. "I'm not interested in solving some international espionage ring you've got going here." He raked his hands through his short-cropped hair. "Just tell me this. This guy you're running from. You think he killed her?"

Dani bit her lip and nodded.

"*Shit.*" Kevin sat up and turned on the light. "What's his name?" His eyes tunneled into her. "I know what I said. But this is some serious shit, Dani."

Dani swallowed hard and moved away from him. "It was different for her. She remained in Ireland. He's not going to find me here."

"And this race in New York . . ."

"You think I can't win?"

"Hell no, sweetheart. That's what concerns me."

"Then you have more faith than I. Losing the Travers isn't going to lift me into the international limelight." She gave a hard laugh. "I'm only racing for your da. It's fierce competition. I haven't a chance of winning. But I'll not live me life in a hole, hoping the bastard steps right over me."

Dani got up, trembling, and moved toward the small desk and computer. Starlite's shed row, captured in real time, gleamed back at her in the dark.

"What of this damned DVR?" She hadn't a clue what it stood for. But for all its technology, it hadn't captured a single suspicious moment since he'd installed it last Friday. "I'd think you'd be worried more about the goings-on in your own county than the ones an ocean away."

Kevin came up behind her. "I care about you," he said roughly against her ear. He scooped her up in his arms and carried her to bed. Laying her down, he shucked off his bottoms and climbed in next to her, unabashedly naked. "About making you happy." He kissed her forehead. "Keeping you safe." He dropped another on her nose. "Loving you the rest of my life." He found her lips and kissed her.

"Me, too," she said against his mouth.

His hand burned a trail of heat up her leg, traveling under the whimsical hem of her nightie. With deft fingers, he slipped her panties down her thighs, past her knees and then her ankles, the lacy undergarment finding its way to the foot of the bed.

She was tremulous and wet between her thighs. He touched her there against the swirl of ebony curls. Dani moaned and arched her back. "I could never go back to Ireland." Her breath caught when his fingers slid inside her.

"I'd follow you." He kissed her hard on the lips, his tongue licking its way inside her mouth. He teased, stroked, slowly pulling away. "Wait," he said, breathing hard, his mouth hovering over hers like he wanted to taste her again. "I'm not ready to start that family just yet." He turned off the light and reached for the top drawer to his nightstand. She waited all shivery, her own breaths coming in short pants before he thrust himself inside her.

"God," she murmured.

His mouth came down on hers, his hips rocking hers like the gentle roll of the sea. The tide of pleasure rose, cresting higher. She couldn't breathe, couldn't think. He loved her in spite of her past, in spite of what she'd told him about Kara. Kevin hiked up her nightie, crushing it between them. Her breasts heaved over the delicate neckline, the strap sliding down her arm.

His hands were tangled in her hair, the gentle tug erotic. She moaned into his mouth. He released her lips, breathing heavy. "I want to see you come, Irish."

"Oh, Kevin, I'm almost there, luv." She wrapped her legs around him, her body rippling like a flame starved for oxygen—starved for him. He thrust into her again and again. "Kevin," she whispered, digging her fingers into his shoulder blades. She came in a fragmented explosion of pleasure and warmth with him kissing her mouth, her neck, the slopes of her breasts.

Breathing hard, his impassioned eyes, lit by the moon's light, clung to her. "Irish," he said as he sought his own release. "Trust me to keep you safe." He came with the same raw emotion he'd begged of her—honesty.

Under the glimmer of moonlight and a breeze filled with sweet honeysuckle wafting in from the window, his plea tore at her heart. Tears filled her eyes. She would find the courage to tell him everything, in time.

He rolled off of her, took care to clean himself up, and enfolded her in his arms. "I love you," he said on a yawn and snuggled his chin into the curve of her neck.

But not tonight.

Chapter Forty-One

"L IZARD ON A LOG!" TURK'S GRUFF VOICE SHOT THROUGH HER
earpiece. Dani clenched her eyes shut, her eardrum ringing. *What
the bloody hell?* She was riding high and tight. If she moved any higher,
she'd tumble over Solley's head. It wasn't her form that was the problem
anyway. Solley was nothing like the horse she'd breezed over a week ago.
His starts were slow, and his breathing, although heavy as expected after
three-quarters of a mile, seemed erratic.

Dani held tight to the reins with one hand and dug frantic fingers into
her back pocket. She relaxed when she brushed up against the warm
metal of her ma's coin. Dani grimaced. It was silly to think it had any
mystical powers, but having it along was like having her ma right there
with her.

Leaning over the saddle, she patted Solley's neck. "Are you not feeling
well, boy?" Dani slowed their pace and came in, lifting off her goggles.

"What the hell was that?" Turk narrowed a pair of turbulent blue eyes
at them like they'd just cold him out. "I coulda walked faster than that."
He lowered his head to jot something down—their time she supposed.

Dani made a face at him. He wasn't the only one with something to
lose—and it wasn't the bloody race. "Maybe we're training him too hard."

His head shot up, and he waved a dismissive hand at her. "Bah. You're
soft, Flynn. Last week you couldn't slow him down." He scowled and
flipped her the bird.

"What the . . . ?" Dani's mouth fell open. *How incredibly juvenile and
vulgar and so unlike . . .*

The clomp of hooves came up behind her, and she recognized the tip of Blake's riding boots.

Dani shook her head, somewhat relieved, realizing now who the insult had been directed to.

"Give him a bath and cool him out." Turk gave them his back and trudged up the hill toward the barn.

"I take it you didn't tell him about what we talked about yesterday," Blake said, his voice edged with amusement. He reined in next to her by the outside rail.

Dani swung on him. "You're not the least bit funny. He still thinks you tried to steal Chipper away from him."

He shrugged. "I would have if she had been willing."

Dani's hands tightened on the reins. "You haven't changed a bit." Solley pawed the ground and snorted. Even the horse agreed. Sensing Solley's nervousness, she pulled him past Blake and his mount. "I need to go."

"Wait." He came up alongside them. "I meant that was the old me." He dipped his head, trying to get her attention.

Dani stopped, her own curiosity growing. "What is it you want?"

"I'll help you train him."

Dani laughed. "Like Solley's going to listen to the likes of you?"

He chuckled. "But you will."

Dani gave him an incredulous look. "And you'll do this why?"

"I don't have a horse running, for one." He grinned, his expression changing to one of repentance. "And I owe you."

"Turk's not going to let you train a horse you abused," she hissed. Her gaze swung toward the hill in search of him. Turk ducked inside the barn. Dani turned sharp in the saddle. "Or a jockey he thinks you may try and steal away from him." She frowned. "Plus, he's a man."

He nodded his understanding. "I don't have to be present."

Dani mulled that one over in her head. Solley had won stakes races in the past under Blake's stable. She gave him a sideways glance. "So it's pointers you'll be giving me?"

He nodded. "I'll be on the track while you're training." He moved closer. "I'll watch you work out, and, afterward, when it's convenient, give you some suggestions."

Dani threw her head back and moaned. Everything she was about was marred by secrecy. "All right." She leveled a hard gaze at him. "But let him catch on, and I'm telling him the hard truth about you and Chipper." She gnawed the inside of her mouth, feeling like a bully. "You must think me ungrateful."

He shook his head. "I'm finding you to be a good friend." His expression softened. "I don't have many."

Emotion rode up her chest. *Bollocks.* The last thing she needed was to feel sympathy for Blake Lansing. Dani wagged a finger his way. "This change in you better be permanent."

He winked. "It's a new leaf, to be sure, Dani Flynn." He laughed and reined his horse to the left. "See you tomorrow on the track." He kicked his horse in the sides and galloped away.

Dani hopped down, giving Solley a big kiss. "It's because he wants something from me." She mulled that over. Putting off that call to Suzanne was no longer an option. Dani grabbed the reins and led him through the gate and up the hill toward the barn. "But let's first get you smelling as fresh as a sweet meadow and your legs wrapped with some soothing poultice." She tweaked Solley's forelock and leaned into him. He was a sound horse. That she knew. Although a frightening prospect if Turk found out, they'd turn this thing around with Blake's help. She had no doubt.

"Isn't Kevin picking you up?" Turk walked out of his office with his key in hand.

"After his council meeting."

He blew out an agitated breath. "Biggest waste of taxpayer money." He motioned her to follow him. "Those things go on for hours. It's almost seven. I'll give you a lift."

Dani grabbed her mobile from her back jean pocket and motioned upstairs. "I'm good. I need to charge me phone and give Suzanne a call and see how's she's doing."

"I gave her Chipper's last paycheck at the funeral." Turk's expression dimmed. "She seemed to be disappointed by the amount."

"She said something?"

"Nope. But I can read people." He clucked his tongue. "She needs anything, let me know."

"I'll ask her. I will." She had to be hurting for money without the five thousand dollars she probably believed came from Starlite.

Turk's mouth twisted like he was debating, and then he shuffled on his feet. He handed her the key. "Use the phone in my office." He leaned in like he was about to share a secret. "And check that damned DV-whatever-it-is, and let me know what the hell's going on around here at night."

Dani took it, the key radiating cold through her hand. "What about tomorrow, then? I won't be in 'til quarter of six. How will you get into your office?"

"I'll be late myself." His eyes gleamed. "Thinking about stopping off at the bakery. What kind of donuts you like, kid?"

Dani smiled at that. "Chocolate."

He clucked his tongue. "One of my favorites. I'll see that I pick us up a few." He looked as if he were recalling something. "Bonnie strikes me as a powdered donut kind of girl."

She wanted to say, *Only if it were crushed oxycodone.* But that wouldn't be at all charitable, and she didn't believe Turk had any inkling about her troubles. "It's a good choice, I think."

He nodded. "The rest of them will eat anything sweet."

Dani didn't doubt it. Although she'd prefer a jelly-filled for Jake. The thought of him wearing it made her mouth quirk.

"I'll see ya." With nimble feet, he took out through the barn to his pickup.

Dani entered his office and shut the door, locking it behind her. Kevin had given her and Turk strict instructions about keeping the office locked. He didn't want it getting around that there was a surveillance system in place. He'd gone through great pains to surreptitiously install the camera in the eave of the barn. Maybe no one could see it, but the DVR on Turk's desk, although hidden under a stack of papers next to the computer screen, could be detected if someone had a mind to snoop.

She sat down in Turk's chair, placing her phone and the key on the desk. Spinning from side to side, she contemplated how to begin the conversation with Chipper's mom, her eyes on the office phone. It was more of the telling that had her hesitating. It would be a shock. She'd have to ease her way into the conver—

Her mobile rumbled against the wood. She checked the name, smiled, and scooped it up. "I miss you."

"Yeah, same here." He sounded distracted.

"How's it going? Your meeting, I mean."

"Hasn't started yet. I wanted to check on you first. I won't be available for a few hours. You okay if I don't get there until ten?"

"Sure. I'm in your father's office. He gave me the key."

He snorted. "You've got him wrapped around your finger."

"I'd like to think it's more a matter of faith." Dani's brows furrowed. "But the truth of it is I fear I'll only fail him."

"Hey, that's not going to happen."

She smiled at that. "You're biased."

"Damn right. You're my girl," he said, while voices rose in the background.

"You're busy."

"I can talk for a few more minutes. Anything else bothering you?"

Dani rolled her lips in. "You have time to check out the video from last night?"

"No. Things have been crazy here all day." He paused. "You sitting in front of the computer?"

"Yes."

"I'll walk you through it."

"Grand."

Kevin got her into the program and then helped her to select last night's recording. "Just click on it to view."

"I'll do it after we hang up."

"They're walking in now. I'll call you when I'm leaving."

"I'll charge me mobile meantime, then."

"All right. See you soon, sweetheart."

"Bye." Dani disconnected and hit play. She found the fast forward and clicked it. A body zipped across the screen. Her heart jumped, and she stopped it, running the tape back. *Eejit.* It was only Bonnie doling out peppermints. Dani let it play for a good twenty minutes after Bonnie left for the night. Nothing remarkable. She hit the fast forward and jolted up in her seat when a dark form passed by the screen again. She rewound it and let it play, her shoulders relaxed when she recognized Bonnie.

Odd, the time.

It had to be . . . Dani checked the clock on the recording—half past three.

A bit early. The horses didn't stir until five.

Dani let it play. Bonnie walked up to Solley's stall. She seemed to be coaxing him up from a deep sleep. His head popped over the stall, and she fed him something from her hand—and not just one.

Peppermints? Dani clenched her hands. She'd told her only one. She should have known not to trust someone with little self-control. Solley especially liked the sweet minty candy. If Bonnie were feeling at all sorry for him, she wasn't doing him any favors. Dani stopped the tape and stood. *Damn her.* He was in training and seemed miserable this morning.

Dani made sure the DVR was well hidden and locked up. She made her way across the gravel road and ducked inside the bunkhouse, passing Arturo in the small recreation room that held a table with chairs, small kitchenette, couches, and a TV.

"Have you seen Bonnie?"

Dressed in a nice pair of jeans and polo, he smiled at her. "Hey, Dani. She and Jake left togetter. I tink an hour ago."

She nodded. "Where might you be going, then?"

"Meeting them . . . how you say, funny bar called Cow?"

"The Purple Cow?"

"Tat's it. Pur-ple Cow." He cocked his dark head. "Joo wanna come?"

"Thank you, but no. You'll let her know I was looking for her, then?"

"Sure. See joo later." He headed out the door.

It seemed everyone who lived in the bunkhouse had left for the night. Dani peeked inside the bunkroom to her left. Judging by the scantily clad, heavy-breasted Carmen Electra poster pinned between the two rows of bunks, she guessed this to be the men's side. Dani turned and passed by the table and skirted the couch, entering the bunkroom on the other side. She flipped on the light. It was smaller than the men's with only two sets of bunks and four separate shelves with garment racks positioned below.

She should go. Only that left another night of Bonnie indulging Solley with his sweet tooth. Dani couldn't say for sure, but plying him with sugar could have contributed to his lackluster performance on the track this morning. Maybe taking the peppermints back would be the best solution until she talked with Bonnie tomorrow. They hadn't been in the barn that she could see. That left the bunkhouse.

Dani eyed the shelves. No peppermints. She checked the clothes hanging from the racks, trying to determine which section was Bonnie's, when she caught the familiar pattern of the dress Bonnie wore to the luncheon. Dani started for it and dropped down on her knees in front of a metal footlocker.

She ran an unsteady hand through her hair. Never one to snoop herself, Dani hesitated. Her eyes swept the room, and she relaxed when she spied the jar at the end of the bunk to her right. She ducked under and pulled it out, her head smacking the edge of the metal frame.

Something rattled, and it wasn't her aching brain. She rubbed her head and glanced up, searching the poorly lit area underneath. Her eyes widened on a corner of the frame. Sandwiched between reinforced metal and the mattress sat an amber-colored pill bottle.

Dani yanked it out, her blood simmering. Bonnie'd promised to stop taking them. Slipping out from underneath, she sat her bum down and leaned against the bunk. She turned the bottle around and checked the label. It had been filled three weeks ago. She popped the cap. Only two pills remained. Dani threw her head back. This was stupid. For all she knew, Bonnie had forgotten about her stash. She lifted her head and noticed a ceiling tile askew directly above her. Now that was odd. Dani got up, dropped the bottle on the mattress, and climbed the ladder to the top bunk. Reaching out over the bed, she pushed the tile open and peered up inside. A bright yellow box sat on its side, the bold words printed in red shaking her senses.

"What are you doing?" Bonnie's voice rose in alarm.

Dani swung her head toward the door. Bonnie stood next to Jake, her complexion growing pale, fingers gripping the leather strap of her handbag.

Jake walked toward her. "I'll help you down." His words were strained.

Dani trembled. "I can get down on me own." She turned her bum around and took the ladder. "I was looking for the peppermints." She turned to face them.

"They're on the floor." Jake hitched his chin toward the clear, glass jar next to the bunk where the unmistakable red and white candy sat for the world to see.

Dani glanced down and chuckled. "So they are. I must have missed them."

Jake took a step toward her when Bonnie grabbed his arm. "She's lying. She's been on my case about the pills." She eyed Dani nervously, her expression changing to one of warning.

Bonnie had to know what she'd seen in the ceiling. It was above her bunk—maybe not her specific bunk because it was apparent to Dani she slept on the bottom.

Dani's stomach churned. "Aye, you promised me you were done with them."

Jake looked from one to the other and jerked his arm away. "Pills, huh?" He jumped up and moved the ceiling tile back inside the metal track. "I think we need to take a walk." He motioned them outside the bunkroom.

Dani went first with Bonnie not far behind. Jake remained. The bunks dragged and scuffed along the wooden floor. What else had she hidden inside the ceiling that Jake seemed bent on retrieving? Dani reached behind to her back pocket for her mobile, panic seizing her. She'd left it in Turk's office.

"I can explain," Bonnie whispered with desperation.

"Rat poison." Dani swung on her. "What the bloody hell are you involved in?"

CHAPTER FORTY-TWO

JAKE CAME UP BEHIND THEM OUTSIDE THE BUNKHOUSE. HE GRABBED Dani's arm, shoving something rigid and unyielding into her back. "We're going for a walk." He pressed his bristly cheek against the side of her face. "You and me," he whispered hard against her ear.

"I-I don't understand." Fear held her in its vise, and she couldn't move. Dani's eyes grew wider, and she looked to Bonnie. "Tell me what this is all about."

Bonnie only stared back at her, fidgeting with a gold bracelet and then the hem of her shorts, perspiration popping out along her hairline like tiny water droplets. She'd be no help to Dani with Jake. What an incredibly inconvenient time for Bonnie to finally listen to Dani about her addiction—going cold turkey was going to get her killed tonight.

Jake shoved the gun against her spine. "Move it, Flynn." His hand slid to her neck, and he muscled her forward down the gravel road.

Dani took an uneasy step. "I'm going." She tried to throw his heavy, sweaty hand off her. The weight of it made her nauseous. She glanced back. "Like I've never seen rat poison at a training center." Well, not hidden in the ceiling of a bunkhouse, for sure. But most stables used some type of rodent control.

Bonnie caught up to them. "Let her go, Jake," she said out of breath. "She doesn't know anything."

"Shut up," he growled at her. "You're the dumbass who left it out."

"I-I didn't. It was in the—"

"God you're stupid. Shut up already and call him."

Bonnie kept walking next to them, shaking her head, her expression one of a scared puppy dog trying to do everything right for her master.

Dani's stomach turned like spoiled milk at the sight of her. It rolled up her chest, and she couldn't get the awful taste of weakness out of her mouth. Bonnie grabbed her phone from her purse and walked away, putting it to her ear. They navigated the deserted road that split the training center down the middle like an open book. Only the truth of what these two were about remained hidden in whatever sordid pages they'd written along the way. Bonnie stopped when a voice came on the line, and Jake kept moving her further toward the next barn. Bonnie's incoherent words floated on the breeze, which had cooled considerably since the sun had set. She hung up, and then scurried back like the obedient dog she had become. "He's still here."

"Must have parked around back." Jake chuckled and angled his head sideways to get a better view of Dani. "Grand, isn't it." He sneered in her face, his features turning hideously familiar.

Fear, like tiny pins, pricked her senses, and she slowed her steps. She needed time. Time to escape him—both of them. Before she could formulate a plan, Jake made a sharp left with her, driving the barrel of his gun into her back until they came to the first barn. Before she could piece it together—the barn and its owner—the door rumbled open.

Dani blinked. "Fritz?" Her voice trembled with uncertainty.

He shook his head, his expression grim. "Bring her in."

They entered the barn, and Dani noticed something peculiar. "Where are your horses?" She wondered about the handsome gelding she'd ridden. "What of Delicate Maneuver?"

"Claimed or sold them. He was the last."

Dani's brows furrowed. "But I just rode him. You just raced at Delaware Park. You said so yourself on Fourth of July."

Fritz shook his head and frowned. Was he conscience-stricken? Dani wasn't so sure.

She looked to Bonnie with bewilderment. She'd worked for him, lost her job when he'd downsized, and obviously conspired with him. But on what, Dani wasn't quite sure. "You knew this."

Bonnie bent over and hugged her middle, looking as if she'd vomit on the spot.

Dani narrowed in on Fritz. "You never had any intention of keeping your stable. You got rid of your grooms, your horses." She'd never gotten a look inside until now. The closest she'd come was that day when she delivered his mail. "How did you manage it? The grooms, I mean? You can get rid of a horse here and there—they're not going to talk. But a groom?"

"Ah, lass, I did what I had to do—gave them some severance, found them a better paying job. But on the West Coast, far enough away so they couldn't bend anyone's ear here."

Now that she thought about it, she hadn't seen Zelda and her immense car for a while, either. *Err.* He was a piece of work. Lying piece of work. He'd told Turk a little over a week ago his feed had been tampered with. Dani fisted her hands; she wanted to belt him in the mouth. There had been no horses to speak of. He'd lied to Turk. But it was what Turk wanted to hear—needed to hear. Knowing he wasn't the only one would keep Turk from eventually casting a suspicious glance toward Fritz.

Fritz pulled the door shut, the pink and blue hues of twilight snuffed out like a candle. They stood in the eerie glow of fluorescent emergency lights high in the eave of the barn. Their hum grated on her fraying nerves.

Fritz pulled out a chair. "Let her sit down for God's sake."

Jake shoved Dani in the chair, the gun trained at her.

Fritz jumped back the moment he realized Jake was armed. "Jesus, you have a gun?" Fritz placed his hands on his hips. "Put it away. You're scaring her."

Jake raked his free hand through his dark hair, his eyes glinting down at Dani before he swung his head toward Fritz. "You gotta be fuckin' kidding. *She* knows." He nailed Bonnie with wild eyes, the barrel now aimed at her pretty blond head. "I should shoot you in that stupid little skull of yours."

Bonnie gasped. "But you love me?"

"Money, Bonnie," he bit back. "I love money."

A cry bubbled up Bonnie's chest. Jake repositioned the gun on Dani. "Where do you want to do this thing?" He shot a predatory look toward Fritz.

Dani shuddered. He was going to kill her, and the two who seemed squeamish at the prospect didn't have any leverage or control to stop it. She needed to clue them in and fast. She wouldn't be his only victim tonight. "He's going to kill us all." She looked from Bonnie to Fritz. "You'd be a fool to think otherwise."

"He's not killing anyone, lass." Fritz paced like he was in charge. Dani knew better. Whatever control he'd had slipped away with every step he wore into the ground.

He could think all he wanted—strategize even. But it wouldn't change the outcome. Jake had the gun. Jake would call the shots.

Fritz stopped, grabbed another folding chair against the wall, and sat down in front of Dani. "It's not what you're thinking." He leaned closer. Light streamed in from the slats of the barn walls and landed on his face—more haggard and old than she'd remembered. She couldn't tell what side he was on. It was his eyes. The warmth she'd come to expect from the old trainer was replaced with indecision. If he were weighing his own mortality against that of hers and Bonnie's, she couldn't say. His eyes hardened just then like cold, hard crystals. "I needed the money. It's that simple." He shrugged. "Lost it in stocks years ago. It was just a bet here and there to get me on my feet." Fritz looked behind him at Jake, who scowled at them. Fritz waved him off, his contrite eyes now holding Dani's. "Can't we just look past this? It can be our little secret now."

Jake gave a hard laugh. "You on drugs, man?" The same long dark hair that reminded her of Tommy hung past his uncaring eyes. "She knows." He smacked his head several times, looking more crazed than she thought possible. "Get it through your thick skulls. She'll run to lover boy the minute we let her go." He looked directly at Dani. "You think that fall *you* took was an accident?"

Bonnie whimpered in the corner. "You weren't supposed to ride her."

"Shut up!" Fritz stood up like he was going to slap her.

Bonnie cowered in the corner, the fall of her blond hair shielding her face.

Dani swallowed. "You loosened the mare's shoes." It wasn't a question.

"No. Your friend Bonnie here did that." Jake gave a vicious laugh.

"You made me." Bonnie pointed a shaking finger at Fritz. "Told me you wouldn't get my pills if I didn't."

Fritz frowned at her, his eyes now on Dani. "You weren't supposed to get hurt."

"You must think me a fool." Dani gritted her teeth. "You wagered on me—wagered I'd fall."

Fritz scrubbed his face hard and narrowed in on Bonnie. "I didn't know until after the fact." He turned toward Dani and shrugged. "If you'd held on—"

"You bollocks." Dani jumped up, spitting mad. "And *you*." She swung on Bonnie.

Bonnie took a step back. "I didn't know you'd ride her."

Fritz pushed Dani down hard in the chair. "You're alive. Be grateful." He glanced over his shoulder and then back to her, his eyes panicked. "It was only a couple of horses—nothing serious that wouldn't mend."

He was a fool. A horse had died, and if the box she'd found in Bonnie's ceiling had anything to do with it, they were all guilty of murder.

Ignoring Bonnie's quiet sobs to the left, Dani looked from Fritz to Jake.

Jake's dark eyes tunneled in on her. "Go ahead. Dig your own grave."

"What are you rambling about?" Fritz swung his head back at Jake.

"He . . . she"—Dani's distrustful eyes landed on her friend—"killed Delhaven's mare."

"Killed?" It fell off Fritz's lips with quiet disbelief. "I hadn't heard she'd lost a mare." His murky eyes turned confused.

His reaction seemed genuine, giving Dani every indication that this was the first time he'd heard of it. Perhaps it was. She and Kevin had just learned of it last Thursday. The only news swirling about Whistledown was Chipper's untimely death. They'd only buried her yesterday. If Jake and Bonnie had acted alone, Fritz's behavior made sense.

Dani nodded toward Jake. "Ask him." But her question was directed toward Fritz.

Jake shrugged. "Just a little side action."

Fritz's hands gripped the top of the chair, but he said nothing, which clued Dani in. He was afraid of Jake, and it wasn't just the gun.

Dani lifted her chin to Jake. "Did you win, then?" she said, her voice razor sharp.

He gave her a cheeky smile. "Most."

"You make me sick to my stomach." She gnashed her teeth. "How'd you go about it?"

"Stupid mick!" He took a step toward Dani, the gun becoming an extension of him. "You found it in the ceiling."

Fritz angled his head back toward Jake. "Damn it to hell. What's she talking about?"

"Rat poison," Bonnie said, like she'd awakened from a trance. "He made me put it in the Delhaven mare's feed."

"Shit." Fritz stood, his body quivering. "That's jail time. You idiots."

"Not going to jail. Not for some fucking horse." Jake leveled the gun on Fritz.

"Put that damn thing down." His eyes flashed at Jake. "Horses are one thing. But people, I didn't sign on for that." His voice grew harsh, and he swung his arm back, trying to grab for the gun.

Jake stepped back. "Too late for that."

Fritz tottered and fell back a step, dazed.

"Penn National, old man."

Fritz's head tilted like he was trying to recall something. "I didn't bet Penn National."

"You don't call all the shots." Jake smirked at him.

Dani sat up in the chair, sweat running down her back. "What are you getting at?"

He swung on Dani, the gun targeting her center mass. "You're dead." He spoke matter-of-factly and jerked the gun away and then pointed it at Fritz. "You open your mouth, let her walk, we'll all go down for murder one."

"But we haven't killed anyone." Bonnie wrapped her arms around her waist like she was trying to ward off the cold—only it was stifling in the barn. "Let her go. She won't tell, Jake."

"Shut up! You think that was some fucking kid?"

Kid. Penn National. Dani tried to connect his phrases. What did it mean? Then that day came at her like a speeding comet, its tail awash with fuzzy memories of her day with Kevin.

"Christ," Fritz hissed. "You idiot! *You* killed her."

"Yeah. What a fuckin' waste of my time." Jake groused.

Bonnie fell to her knees. "Ch-chipper," she sobbed. Her body caved, her blond hair falling past her shoulders, hiding her face.

Dani kept an eye on Jake and the gun when it swiveled toward Bonnie's head. There were too many of them. He'd need to reduce the threat. He'd start with the one coming unglued on the floor. Dani wanted to cry, too—wanted to tear his eyes out and shove the bloody gun in his mouth and pull the trigger. He'd gambled with Chipper's life. She died for a couple grand that never even paid out.

From the chair, Dani reached with her booted foot and kicked Bonnie hard. "Get up," she growled.

Her head popped up, hair sticking to her tearstained face. "That hurt." Eyes shooting daggers at Dani, she rubbed her backside.

Dani jutted her chin toward Jake, her expression deadly serious.

Bonnie's head turned, and she scrambled to her feet, moving next to Dani in the chair.

Fritz pushed off the wall. "Let me have the gun."

Maybe Fritz was the mastermind, but it was clear this diabolical turn wasn't part of his plan. Now was not the time to be a hero. They needed cool heads.

"He'll not give it up that easily." Dani remained in the chair. "Will you, Jake?"

Jake took his eyes off Fritz.

"Give me the damned gun." Fritz dove for it.

Bonnie screamed, and Jake swung, firing one shot. Fritz's body jerked back against the barn wall, his eyes wide, hands grabbing for his belly where the blood began to saturate his shirt. He slithered to the ground, falling forward. The acrid scent of gunpowder filled the air.

Dani's stomach roiled. "Fritz!" She came out of the chair and dropped to her knees, rolling him over onto his back. Blood oozed from a hole in his stomach. It was jagged and black where the bullet had entered. Dani shook her head. *So stupid.* He'd been kind to her—tried to diffuse the situation. He hadn't a chance of winning.

Bonnie threw herself at Jake, her arms a windmill. "You killed him!" She smacked him in the head, the shoulders, until he got his arm around her neck, jerking her back hard against him. "Stupid, bitch," he hissed and shoved the gun under Bonnie's quivering chin. His eyes flared at Dani. "Get up, or she's next."

Dani stood with her hands up. "Where is it you think you'll be safe after this?"

"You don't give a fuck about me!"

No. But she did care about Bonnie. She was so much like Kara. Misguided, troubled. She didn't want to lose her the same way. "Let me help you, then. To get away."

He gnawed on his bottom lip. "Get her car keys." He motioned with his eyes toward Bonnie's leather bag. "They're inside."

Dani kept her hands up. "I'll get them." She didn't know the time. She'd left her mobile in Turk's office. Kevin would be here soon. She had to stall. Finding Bonnie's bag on the ground, she shifted through the inside. Her hands stilled on the metal keys. "I can't seem to find them."

Erratic eyes bounced from Dani to Bonnie. "You've got to the count of five."

She waited while he counted, and then at three, pulled the flower key chain out. "Got it."

"You drive."

Dani's mouth fell open. "You can't be serious."

He eyed Bonnie, a blubbering mess who, if it weren't for his muscular arm holding her up by her neck, would have crumpled to the ground.

This was insane. She couldn't drive. Not with him. Not like this. "I'll only wreck it, for sure."

He pointed the gun at Dani, his eyes desperate and holding hers. "Drive or die."

"Where?" Her throat went dry.

"Big Pool."

The lake?

CHAPTER FORTY-THREE

Pretty and soft... Dani was the opposite of him. Kevin chuckled. Even when he'd nicked himself with his razor this morning after she'd used it to shave her legs, he hadn't complained. He liked sharing his house with her, his bathroom, but especially his bed.

Kevin pulled into Whistledown's gravel drive. Dani made him think. He wanted that lasting future with her. The family he'd always envisioned had begun to take shape in his mind. She was the woman he wanted to bear his children.

Hell, I'm ready to propose.

He scrubbed the back of his neck. Forking over about six grand for the perfect diamond wouldn't put a dent in his nest egg. It wasn't that. There wasn't a jewelry store that had what he wanted. The only person who could give him that was his father.

Platinum band, flawless one carat heart-shaped diamond, it sat in an Irish Claddagh setting—a timeless symbol of love, friendship, and commitment. His lips thinned. "Didn't exactly turn out for its previous owner," he grumbled under his breath, taking the turn sharp on 68. Didn't matter. It was how he felt about Dani. Even with all the shit surrounding her immigration status, he knew the woman to be inherently sweet and innocent. She'd somehow gotten herself entangled in something. He doubted she set out looking for trouble. He shook his head. It just naturally seemed to find her. He chuckled. She was every bit a Fallon girl.

He wouldn't let that deter him. He was going to marry her, make her legal, and the hell with going through the bureaucratic red tape that Kate and Bren were busying themselves with. First he needed that ring. But it was his mother's. He'd have to approach his father. Last he saw of the engagement ring and matching wedding band—he wanted that too—was in his mother's jewelry chest in his childhood home, where it sat cushioned in its original Tiffany's satin box like a sacred body in its crypt. Which told him it was off-limits.

Kevin pulled into Starlite's parking lot, his headlights bouncing off the barn before he turned off the ignition to his patrol car. He opened the door and, with the aid of the interior light, checked his watch—9:42. He'd told her a little after ten. But he'd slipped out early after he had his turn at the podium, giving the council the rundown on his budget and his proposed plan to reduce the rise in burglaries. His jaw clenched. The bastards were screwing with his crime statistics. They'd been on the rise—not a good thing during an election year.

He'd begin beefing up patrols tomorrow during the hours of ten and two when most were at work and school—prime-time for an uninterrupted break-in. But tonight he had other things on his mind, like collecting the raven-haired beauty who had stolen his heart, making breakfast together—one of his favorite meals for a late dinner—and then taking her to bed. Kevin got out and straightened his crotch, which had become increasingly snug. Just the thought of her wriggling beneath him, calling his name in that sweet Irish lilt made him rock hard.

Shutting his patrol car, he strode to his father's barn, sliding back the door. He entered, first checking the door to the office—locked—then heading toward the steps. "Dani, sweetheart," he called up the stairs. "You ready to go?" He waited, checked the aisle, even took a walk down it. She'd mentioned a horse named Solley—the one she would ride in the Travers. Her gorgeous blue eyes glimmered with warmth when she talked about the black horse. He wouldn't call himself a horse person, but if they were important to her, they were now important to him.

He found Solley's stall and peeked in then backed up when the black stallion—colt, whatever you wanted to call it—came toward the opening of the door. Kevin's eyes widened. *Big ass horse.* Then it hit him—the horse and his father's reaction when Dani had stuck out her hand to pet him that first day. *Shit.* He didn't like it. His phone peeled at his hip, and he took the call, thinking it was Dani. He frowned at Bren's name.

"Yeah?"

"You seen Dani?"

"I'm at the barn picking her up. Something you want me to relay to her?"

"Nothing important. Thought I'd stop by and take her to lunch. Haven't seen her for a while." She seemed anxious.

"Something wrong?"

"No. Just been calling her cell the last hour. She hasn't picked up."

"The doting older sister." Kevin smiled. He'd soon be related to this one—if Dani would have him. "When are you going to relax, little mama?" He chuckled into the phone. "Not everyone's your responsibility."

Bren huffed in his ear. "Just tell her I'll be by the barn around noon tomorrow." Her voice was tinged with aggravated amusement. Something he'd come to expect.

"I'll see—" He jumped back when something soft and wet licked his ear. He angled his head sideways and caught the black muzzle of Dani's horse. *"Shit."* He wiped at his ear.

"Kev, you all right?"

"Hell no." He eyed the horse. The stallion whinnied and shook his head like he was laughing. "Damn horse tried to kiss me."

Bren laughed into the phone. "Where are you?"

"I told you. In the barn waiting for *your* sister." Which reminded him—she hadn't come down. "Hey, gotta go."

Before Bren could reply, he hung up, placed the phone back on his hip, and strode over to the steps. He climbed them two at a time. Traveling down the hall, he came to her door. He tried the knob—it didn't budge. He should have expected that. He'd told her to keep it locked.

Kevin rapped on the door. "Dani, it's me."

Nothing—no movement. He knocked harder. "Open the door." His adrenaline rose with every soundless second that ticked by. She wasn't in there. Thinking better of it, he put his shoulder into it. The wood split and he peeked inside. Empty. He grimaced. Now he owed his father a new door.

He moved down the steps, checked the barn one last time, and then came to the door of his father's office. She'd been in there around seven thirty before the meeting had started. He knocked and didn't get an answer. His chest tightened.

"Dani, open the door," he yelled, banging on it. Kevin grabbed his wallet and pulled out a credit card. If he wrecked two doors, his father would have his head. Sliding the card between the door frame and bolt of the lock, he worked it while holding the knob until it clicked. He opened the door and flicked on the light. The office seemed like it always did, untidy but organized with piles of *Racing Forms* for a scatterbrain like his father.

Kevin stepped in and checked the desk. Every nerve ending in his body went on high alert when he noticed Dani's cell phone sitting on the edge of the desk. He picked it up, checked recent calls, and found his buried under about twenty of Bren's.

What the hell?

The volume of calls didn't jibe with a damn lunch date. Bren had been worried. Bren knew something he didn't. He fell back on his heels.

Or did she?

Kevin clicked into his father's computer and checked the video from seven thirty on. With the angle of the camera, he'd only caught a partial of her head when she left the office around eight eleven. It was hard to tell if anyone else was on the other side of the frame. He wouldn't jump to conclusions. *Right. Tell my jackhammering heart.*

Check the bunkhouse.

She was friends with his father's groom. She could be visiting until he picked her up. He was early—and he'd forgotten to call before he left.

Kevin shoved her phone in his back pants pocket and headed out the door. He hustled across the gravel road and entered the bunkhouse. A couple of grooms sat in the lounge area watching an Orioles' doubleheader—one he had hoped to catch on the radio during the drive home from picking Dani up. "You seen Bonnie or Dani?"

They swung around. "Tey left togeter," said one of his father's Hispanic grooms whose name escaped him.

"Together?" Kevin took a step closer. "Her and Bonnie?"

He shook his head. "No. Jake, too."

"How long ago?"

He shrugged and looked at the other man. "When we come from ta Purple Cow?"

The second groom looked at the clock on the wall and then spoke to his friend in Spanish. Kevin only making out the word nine.

The first groom rocked his head back and forth, debating. "Nine tirty. Give or take."

"You know where they went?" His blood pressure rose. Dani didn't like Jake. Kevin couldn't see her getting in the car with him.

Both of them shrugged, with one eye on the TV afraid they'd miss a play.

"What car?"

The groom he'd spoken to first turned. "Bonnie's."

Kevin nodded, made a mental note of the yellow Volkswagen, and grabbed his phone. He dialed up his father.

"Yep."

"Meet me at Starlite's barn."

"When we talking?" Turk said around a mouthful of food.

"Now."

His father swallowed and cleared his throat. "What is it?"

"Dani's gone. Left with Bonnie and this guy Jake."

"Probably wised up and got tired of waiting around for you."

"I had a meeting."

"Yeah, yeah." A door shut and something clattered to the floor on the other end of the receiver.

"What the hell was that?"

"My balls," he huffed. "*Jesus*, you're up my ass. I'm on my way."

Kevin disconnected and went back to the barn. He checked every stall, the tack room, bathroom. Went out the back door and checked the Dumpster. Sick to his gut, he was even contemplating finding her lifeless body. He checked his watch. *Twenty minutes.* Where the hell was Turk? Kevin came back in and paced the shed row, agonizing over whether to put out a BOLA for the yellow bug. He was reaching. There had to be a good explanation why she'd leave—without her phone and without telling him. Kevin shook his head. His father had hit on something earlier. The woman couldn't move without checking in with him first— he dropped her off, he picked her up, he made her wait. Well, his father didn't know the whole of it.

"This better be good." Turk's grumpy voice filled the still barn.

Kevin swung around. "She's not here." He handed her phone to him. "Found this on your desk."

"Dani's?"

"Yeah. One of your grooms said she left with Bonnie and Jake."

He rolled his eyes. "More like Bonnie and Clyde when she's with him."

Kevin threw his hands up. "That's just great, old man. Why's he on your payroll?"

Turk waved him off. "You want to tell me how to run my business? Or do you want to find her?" He gave Kevin his back and walked out in knee-length shorts, white T-shirt, and a pair of hard soled slippers. What little hair he had left stuck up like after a bad night's sleep.

Kevin went after his father, catching him moving toward Bailey's barn. "I thought he knocked off at six."

"Thought so, too. Looped around when I came in to see if I could spot Bonnie's bug."

"You find it?"

"Nope. But I did see Fritz's truck parked around back." He glanced up at Kevin. "Thought it was odd. Usually parks in front."

They snuck up to the barn. His father stopped and glanced up, his eyes agleam. "So, we go in guns ablazing?"

Kevin gritted his teeth. "Just open the door."

His dad pulled it open, the heavy barn door rumbling like a clap of thunder. Kevin immediately thought of Dani. His body tensed. He was losing precious time.

"Son of a bitch!" His old man charged in, dropping to his knees. "Jesus, it's Fritz." His father hooked his chin over his shoulder and swallowed hard. "He's been shot," he said like he couldn't believe it himself.

Kevin grabbed his phone and called the emergency center. "Sheriff Bendix here. Send an ambulance and a few deputies to Whistledown. We got a man shot." He hung up and went down on his knees next to his father. He checked for a pulse. It was faint. "He's alive." Kevin studied the wound. One gunshot at close range, judging by the powder burns. "He's lost a lot of blood." A dark pool saturated the ground underneath his torso—probably the exit wound.

"Is Fritz gonna die?" His father's voice shook, his eyes filling with alarm.

"You got anything for pressure?"

"The tack room."

"Get it."

His dad scrambled to his feet, heading down the aisle.

Kevin fell back on his heels, his cop senses tingling. Something was up. Where the hell *were* his horses? *Shit.* He glanced down. Eyes closed, shallow breathing, Fritz was Kevin's only chance. "Bailey," he growled. "Where's Dani?" Kevin shined a penlight into his face. "Come on, old man," he growled.

Nothing.

Damn it. Kevin grabbed his phone and called the emergency center.

"Sheriff Bendix. Put out a BOLA for a 1960s yellow Volkswagen Beatle. Maryland tags, registered to a Bonnie Dunn, three occupants, one Irish female dark hair, one number two blond female, and a number two male dark hair. Last seen on—"

"What do I do?" His father came up behind him holding a cloth.

Kevin pointed to the wound, covering up his phone. "Put pressure on it."

His dad nodded and got down on his haunches.

Kevin reconnected with the operator. "Last seen on 68 in Clear Spring." He hung up just when the swirl of emergency lights lit up the gravel drive of the training center. "Keep up the pressure. I'll be back."

Kevin met his deputies outside. "Just put out a BOLA for a—"

"Heard it on the radio," Harmon said as a couple of EMTs rushed over from a waiting ambulance.

"Inside." Kevin waved them toward the barn, then pulled both Harmon and Ramirez aside. "Need to set up a perimeter with the state police. If I had to guess, the shooter's Jake Griffin—number two male, dark hair, muscular build, about five ten."

"Any idea where he's going?" Harmon said.

Not far was the optimal answer. Realistically, as far as he could get. Griffin would keep the women with him to bargain with or execute. Panic—white-hot—flashed across his chest and he felt as though he was having the big one. *God, I could lose her.* He wanted to cave, drop to his knees.

"You okay, sir?" Ramirez tilted his head, his expression one of concern.

"Fine," Kevin snapped. "What are you standing around for? Get that perimeter. Take it as far as we've got manpower. Alert the surrounding counties."

He walked away, trudging up the slight incline of the gravel drive to his car. Tears burned the backs of his eyes, and he wiped his nose hard. *Damn woman.* Why didn't she call him if she was in trouble? He gritted his teeth. *Because—jackass—you made it clear you couldn't be disturbed.* Kevin swung open the door to his patrol car and slammed the hood with his fist. "Fuck."

Gravel crunched to his left, and he jerked his head around.

His father rounded the corner of Starlite's barn. "Damn it, boy. I've been looking for you," he said, out of breath. "Bailey started talking. Big Pool."

P. J. O'DWYER

"Big Pool what?" Kevin demanded.

"How the hell do I know?" Turk threw open the back door to his pickup, scrambling for something in the rear.

There was the town . . . Kevin's gut twisted. *He means the lake.* Ripping the phone off his hip, his frantic fingers punched in numbers until the operator answered. "Send as many units to Big Pool Lake."

The pump action of a shotgun came from the right.

Kevin stiffened, grabbed his gun, and swung toward it. "Damn it," he seethed.

His father stood at the patrol car's passenger door armed with a shotgun, scowling under the emergency light of the barn. "*Damn,* you're jumpy."

"Balls my ass," Kevin grunted.

He shrugged. "Man's gotta protect himself." He beaded in on him. "You need to deputize me or something?"

"Get in," Kevin ordered, holstering his gun before he dropped into the driver's seat.

His father's brows rose, and he jumped in.

Kevin started the car and tore out of there. If this were any other case, he'd be detached, able to think and act decisively. It wasn't. He was crumbling inside—hollow at the prospect of living his life without her.

His father grabbed his shoulder. Kevin gave him a sideways look.

"He won't let us lose another one." His father's usually gruff voice quavered.

Kevin nodded. He knew what he meant. It had been the closest they'd come to discussing the loss of his mother. The old man had loved Lindy Bendix. Kevin knew that now. Just as sure as he knew Turk Bendix loved Dani like a daughter.

"I'm going to ask her to marry me."

" 'Bout damn time." His father settled back in the seat, both hands on the shotgun, his expression one of consternation. "What d'ya make of it?"

Kevin wished he knew. But he had a sinking feeling his father's childhood friend wasn't an innocent victim in all this. Looked to be some serious shit he'd been involved in—enough for someone to want him dead. He gripped the steering wheel hard and took the exit for Ft. Frederick State Park and Big Pool.

"What do you make of his barn?"

His father gave him a questioning look.

"No horses."

"Damn fool had me believing he had them. Told me they were off their feed same as mine." He shook his head. "I must have had my head up my ass. I should have noticed things weren't right."

Yeah, well, his father had been preoccupied with other things— namely, his own horses.

Kevin kept his foot on the accelerator. He wouldn't be surprised if, in the end, it all had something to do with Delhaven's mare—even Chipper's death.

The last thought had him burying the needle. This guy Jake had nothing to lose.

CHAPTER FORTY-FOUR

BONNIE DROPPED TO HER KNEES ON THE PIER, SHOVING HER HEAD over the side. She gagged then vomited. Dani wrinkled her nose. She could have done the same, but she wouldn't give Jake the satisfaction. Her only concern was survival. He'd brought them here for one purpose.

The lake made sense. Deep and dark, it would be her final resting place. Jake had made sure of that. He'd made them tie their boots extra tight—well, her boots. Bonnie wore sandals that matched her jean shorts and top. Dani would go down first, once her boots filled with water.

Jake pointed his gun toward Dani. "Get one of the boats."

The canoes had been dragged onto the grassy bank for safekeeping and strung together with some sort of steel rope and large padlock. "It's impossible. They're locked." Dani wrung her hands.

He jerked the gun down toward the ground and squeezed the trigger. The air around her detonated as the cord snapped, and she flinched, ears ringing. *Eejit.* That was two. She didn't know how many bullets his magazine held. Kevin had said his held twenty-one. If they were similar, he had nineteen left. Dani's shoulders sagged. He only needed two well-aimed shots to kill them. It'd be hard to miss sitting across from him, only a few feet away in a boat.

Jake's eyes darted from Dani to Bonnie and back to Dani. She would be his Achilles heel—aware and full of hate. She'd been plotting against him, looking for an opportunity to overpower him. As much as she wanted to run, she wouldn't leave Bonnie.

She hadn't asked to fall off Fritz's damned horse all those months ago. Her only mistake was trusting him. With everything Dani now knew, she wouldn't be at all surprised to learn Fritz had somehow caused Bonnie's fateful fall, got her hooked on painkillers, and pawned her off on Turk so she could do his dirty work. The Bonnie she'd come to know, during the lucent moments, didn't have it in her to hurt anyone. What she needed was a friend.

More so after this played out. She'd be arrested. Dani only hoped they'd be lenient. From what she'd gleaned back at Fritz's barn, Bonnie and Fritz had no knowledge of what Jake had caused at Penn National. Still. Chipper's death would haunt Bonnie. It haunted Dani.

Jake shoved her hard. "Put it in the water."

Dani slipped on the wet grass and fell backward onto her bum. She gritted her teeth. *Arsehole*. Getting up, she flipped a dark green canoe over and dragged it through the weeds, pushing it into the water. The metal hull scraped against the tall, stiff stalks of cattails.

Bonnie whimpered to her right. Dani peeked over her shoulder to find Jake waving his gun at Bonnie. "Get her in."

Bonnie sat curled in a ball at the beginning of the pier. Dani went over and touched her shoulder. She jerked, swinging her head toward Dani. Her eyes, full of tears, glistened under the nearly full moon.

Dani leaned down. "Can you swim?" she whispered.

Bonnie's swollen, frightened eyes clung to hers. She shook her head an emphatic no.

Smashing.

"Come on, we'll take our chances in the boat," Dani whispered and helped her up. The ground squished beneath her boots the closer they got to the bank. Dani held Bonnie by the arm as she got in. She skittered in her sandals, the canoe wobbling under her weight.

"It's going to sink." Bonnie squealed and dropped to the floor of the canoe, cowering between the benches on either end of it.

Sinking was the least of their worries. "Move up on the bench." Dani motioned with her hands.

Jake came up behind her. "Paddles?"

They'd be in the boathouse. Just like in Ireland, those things tended to walk away unless they were locked up. "I don't know."

His eyes bounced off the canoe, the pier, and landed on a small shack several yards to the right. "Come on." He grabbed Dani by the arm, dragging her up the hill. He glanced back several times to check on Bonnie. Her sobs filtered up the grassy incline. *Damn it.* This was her opportunity. *Run, Bonnie.* Jake shoved Dani away from the door, aimed, and fired. The bullet ricocheted off something metal—the lock.

Dani jumped, splinters flying.

"Go!" Jake aimed the gun at her.

Dani pried the door open. Life jackets hung on hooks, and the bloody paddles he needed to get them out to the deepest part of the lake sat in a large garbage can. She grabbed two and hesitated. He'd likely get the shot off before she could deck him.

"Move it." He pushed her out in front. His hand landed on her shoulder hard, and he shoved her down the hill. When they made it back to the canoe, Bonnie remained frozen on the bench. Dani gritted her teeth. *Stupid girl.* She could have easily slipped away, giving Dani only herself to worry about.

"Put them in."

Dani dropped the paddles in the middle.

Jake climbed over the edge of the canoe, keeping the gun trained on Dani. "Push us out and get in."

Dani gripped the canoe on either side of the pointed end and pushed, walking it forward. Cold water seeped over the edge of her boots, filling them. The canoe swayed and Dani debated rocking the boat. If Jake were standing, she might be able to make him fall, but like Bonnie, his arse was glued to the seat. He didn't seem to like the water. Strike one for him. She was a sea nymph—had been since she was a babe living on the coast.

"Get in!" Jake nailed her with predatory eyes.

If she gave a big enough push, he'd float a fair distance. She might escape him. But he'd kill Bonnie. Dani bit down on her lip.

She'll die like Kara.

Dani hopped in. The canoe shook, and she fell to her knees.

"Dumb, bitch! I should shoot you now." Jake's grizzly voice filled her ears.

On her knees like she was, he'd have no problems executing her. But he'd forgotten one thing. "You plan to paddle out all on your own, then?" She snorted and shook her head. "Lots of luck with that."

"Shut up and grab the oar." He kicked one at Bonnie. "You, too."

Bonnie whined, her hands scrabbling for it. She hung it over the side, dipping it in the water. It caught the current. "I don't know how," she cried and stirred the paddle like a spoon in a teacup, the current pulling it from her grasp.

"God, you're dumb." His eyes swung on Dani. "Get us out to the middle."

Dani paddled, doing her best, working only the one side of the canoe. Bonnie hiccupped next to her while Jake sneered. Covertly, she took in her surroundings. She and Kevin had passed the boat launch that night. The cove couldn't be too far away. She'd keep paddling, get closer, and then make her move. Now that her eyes had adjusted, it was fairly bright with the moon overhead. But the water remained dark and choppy with the wind coming in from the west. Dani shivered. The water was the last place she'd want to be. As luck would have it—their only refuge if they wanted to survive. She needed to engage him in conversation. Give him a reason to talk to her.

"I don't believe he was actually dead," Dani said like she was thinking aloud.

"Who?" Jake snapped.

"Fritz." She shrugged. "He was pretending, I think."

Jake's Adam's apple bobbed above the collar of his white T-shirt. He hadn't considered the possibility. Not that she knew one way or the other. Jake had jerked her up and out the door before she could be sure. She'd keep him guessing.

"You think he heard you? About the lake, I mean?" She eyed him speculatively.

He gnawed his bottom lip. "Keep paddling and shut up." He leveled the gun at Bonnie. "Open your goddamned mouth again, and I'll shoot her."

Bonnie pulled at her hair with both hands and whimpered. Her eyes darted all around her. Her breathing became erratic. "Solley's going to die!" Bonnie wailed.

Dani jerked back on the oar. "What did you say?" Her eyes tunneled into Bonnie's.

They were wild with fright—crazed even.

"The-the peppermints." She scooted away from Dani. "He-he made me—"

A gunshot exploded. Bonnie screamed, her shoulder slamming into Dani. She moaned, blood seeping through her fingers, and pitched sideways toward the water. Dani gripped the paddle and swung it, cracking Jake in the head. Like a well-placed uppercut, his head rocked backward and he moaned. But the gun remained firmly in his hands. *Shite.* Dani pushed Bonnie into the water and jumped in behind her. Her mind raced as she held her breath and reached frantically into the dark abyss for Bonnie's body when soft, weightless hair brushed her fingers. She clenched it, wanting to rip it from her scalp. Patience and understanding, she was all out of. Bonnie'd poisoned her horse—of that Dani was sure. Something whizzed past her underwater—a bullet. Several. She counted seven more. Dani's lungs burned for air and she kicked, but the added burden of lifting Bonnie to the surface created a huge drag.

She was sinking.

Chapter Forty-Five

PULLING INTO THE SERVICE ROAD TO THE PARK, KEVIN CUT OFF THE lights and sirens and snaked up and into the parking lot. He jammed on the brakes and turned off his headlights. Giving Jake Griffin a calling card could force his hand.

Kevin keyed his mic. "Come in slow—all emergency equipment off."

Gripping his shotgun, his father's eyes tunneled into him, and he unlatched his seatbelt. "We just going to sit here?" He reached for the door handle.

Kevin grabbed his arm. "Slowly."

A sedan pulled in beside him, fireball swirling in the dash, brakes squealing.

Shit. Kevin shot daggers at the unmarked state police cruiser.

"Guess your strategy's been blown to hell," his father said dryly and opened the door, getting out.

Kevin gritted his teeth and cleared his patrol car. The air around them exploded from gunshot. He ducked, pulled his service weapon, and motioned to his father, running toward Archer's cruiser.

"What we got?" Archer said, crouched down, head on a swivel and weapon extended.

"Shooter—number two male, five ten, dark hair." His father's earlier comment came back to him. *Shit.* "Possible number two female, five four, blond. Don't know if she's armed."

"What about the third?"

"Victim—number two female, five two, dark hair."

Archer nodded. "Shot came from the lake. Far right."

From their vantage point, Kevin couldn't see squat. The area of the lake where the shot had been fired lay down a slight incline behind the tree line. They'd have to use it for cover.

Another round pierced the humid night air, his heart jackknifing in his chest. "I'll go right."

Archer nodded and began moving left.

Kevin eyed his father holding the shotgun next to him. A car peeled wheels into the parking lot. Kevin glanced over his shoulder. *Delgado.* His deputy got out with shotgun in hand. Two more units rolled in, one sheriff the other state. Kevin waved Delgado over. "Johnson follow the ambulance to the hospital?"

"Yes, sir. Last I heard, they were wheeling him into OR."

Bailey was alive. Good. Hopefully he'd survive, and they'd be able to question him later. "Who's working the crime scene at the barn?"

"State boys."

He didn't like that. But under the circumstances it was best. He was too connected to this thing. Kevin peered back at his father. This was the end of the line for the old man. Nodding to Delgado, he grabbed the gun out of his father's hands.

His dad's brows shot up, lips thinning. "What the hell?"

Kevin handed it off to Delgado. "Secure it in your trunk and keep him here." He turned toward his father with emotion he didn't think he possessed welling up in his chest. "I'm not taking a chance on losing you, too."

Turk nodded, his expression softening. "Be careful."

Kevin rapped him on the shoulder and motioned for his deputy—who'd retrieved a bullhorn from his vehicle—and the trooper to follow him toward the lake. They came to the playground where he'd recently brought Dani. One day he'd hoped to come as a family. His throat went dry.

I might never get that chance.

They jogged past it, ducking into the tree line. Archer—who looked to be coming back from the lake—met up with him.

"In one of the canoes."

"How many?" Kevin said.

He shook his head. "One. The male." Archer pulled him aside. "Your girl know how to swim?"

She'd kept up with him that night in the cove. "Yeah."

Archer motioned them down the hill. "He's been shooting into the water."

Kevin's grip tightened on his gun, his insides doubling over like a sucker punch to the gut. "Anyone in the water?"

"Not that I could see."

Sweat pooled between his shoulder blades. *God where is she?* Griffin had stopped shooting. That was the other thing that concerned him. Kevin shook it off, the dread. She had to still be with him. He'd have felt her passing away. She had that kind of hold on him. He'd know. Kevin motioned to the men. "Fan out along the bank and watch your crossfire."

Kevin's radio went off, and he keyed it at his chest. "Go ahead."

"DNR's here with a boat, sir."

"Have them head toward the boat dock. Let them know it's their call." He got along with the Department of Natural Resources Police's Area Seven commander, Captain Bill Giles. Kevin would trust him and his men to handle Griffin on the water if it came to it.

Kevin glanced over at his deputy, hand out. "Bullhorn."

"Yes, sir." He handed it off.

"I'll try and talk him back to shore."

They each took a position on this side of the lake. If he had to estimate, Griffin was about twenty-five yards away, on his knees, his head pivoting back and forth. Dani was resourceful. She'd survived her ordeal at sea. She'd outsmart Griffin.

He'd cling to that hope.

Kevin clenched his teeth. It was about time the son of a bitch realized *he* was now in the line of sight. Kevin tore through low lying brush until he came to an opening not far from where the bank turned right toward the cove. Bringing the bullhorn up to his mouth, he said a silent prayer and keyed the mic. "Griffin, throw down the gun."

His belligerent head swung toward the bank, the canoe rocking. "Fuck you!"

Kevin shook his head. "You're surrounded. Put the gun down and raise your hands."

Something—a fish, maybe—jumped, creating a ripple effect to Kevin's right. Griffin jerked his gun in the general area and squeezed off a round. The blast reverberated across the lake. *Damn it.* Could Griffin see something he couldn't? Was she still in the water?

Kevin's gut clenched not knowing if she were alive or dead. If he could, he'd unload his gun on the piece of shit. But Griffin wasn't shooting at a target he could see. He wasn't shooting at one of them, either.

Ker plunk.

Kevin jerked his head to the left. Same ripple. Griffin responded but with a double tap and two rounds into the water. *Jumpy bastard.* This lake was loaded with fish. But if the natural habitat of the lake helped to empty his gun, he'd be easier to take down.

Kevin again keyed the bullhorn. "You're surrounded. Drop your weapon and put your hands up."

"No fucking way!" Griffin's gun swiveled to the right, and he pointed it at Kevin.

Kevin dropped the bullhorn and went for his gun. "Drop it," he yelled with Griffin lined up in his sights.

Click.

Son of a bitch. Kevin squeezed off a round, hitting Griffin in the shoulder. Griffin's shot veered to the right of Kevin, striking a nearby tree. This was going to turn into a shootout. Griffin would be killed in the end. But flying bullets could also hit an unintended target. If Dani had somehow made it back to the bank, she'd be in the tree line same as him. Kevin's heart raced, and he keyed his mic. "Hold your fire."

Smack.

It came from the right. Griffin dropped down in the canoe and shot off four rounds.

"Hold your fire!" Kevin's panicked voice echoed through the trees. *Jeez.* He scrubbed his neck hard. His skin was hot and sweaty, and his stomach roiled.

Get it together, man.

Kevin took a deep breath. He'd fished on this lake—seen beaver. They were resourceful and smart. After the first shot, they'd have hightailed it to their dens. It wasn't a beaver . . . a frog . . . or a fish.

Ker plunk.

Water rippled to the right, and Griffin—with a brain the size of a pea—unloaded his weapon. He threw it down in a fit of rage, signaling he'd run out of bullets and chances.

An electric motor zinged to life to the right and around the bend of the bank. A johnboat with three DNR police cut through the water, guns drawn.

Snap.

Adrenaline coursing through his veins, Kevin spun around and leveled his gun toward the thick vegetation and outcropping of rocks of the cove.

"Don't shoot," said a shrill voice.

Before Kevin could connect the lilt, Dani climbed over a flat plateau of rocks—barefoot, breathless, and soaked to the skin. Dani staggered toward him.

A moan rolled up his chest, and he holstered his gun. He charged toward her, riveted on her blood-streaked white tank, his fear so cold he trembled with it. "God, you're hit." His voice quavered, and he held her by the shoulders. His eyes tore past her chest, and he tilted her toward him to get a look at her back. No exit wound. *What the—?* "You need to sit down."

She raised a feeble hand. "But I . . ."

Kevin keyed his mic, trying to lower her to the ground. "Need an ambulance. One victim. Gunshot wound to the chest."

"Pulling in now," radioed one of his deputies. "What's your location?"

Dani fought against him. "No." Her anxious blue eyes darted from him to the deep vegetation behind them.

Kevin keyed the mic. "The cove."

Cold, wet fingers held tight to his hand. "It's Bonnie."

His arms went around her. "What is it?"

Her eyes clung to his. "*She's* shot." Dani jerked his hand hard.

Rustling came from the right, Archer clearing the trees. "She okay?"

"Fine," Dani shot back. "It's Bonnie."

"The blonde?" Archer said.

Dani nodded. "She's behind the rocks."

A deputy trudged through the tree line with two EMTs. One carried a backboard.

Archer waved Kevin on. "We got this. Take care of her."

He nodded his thanks and scooped Dani up in his arms.

"Wait!" Dani's eyes grew wild.

"*Damn it.* My heart's racing, you're covered in blood. Let me think!"

Her face crumpled, and she began to cry.

Shit. "I'm sorry. Don't cry, sweetheart." He slogged through the woods, avoiding tree stumps and vines. Last thing he wanted to do was fall on his ass. He held her to him. She was sobbing, muddy, and trembling. But she was alive.

"Put me down!" She thrashed in his arms. "You don't understand. It's Solley."

Add hysterical.

"Not a good idea and Solley's fine." The damned horse had tried to kiss him earlier. His grip tightened on her, and he angled his head past her legs. "How are your feet?"

"Me boots," she moaned. "I kicked them off. It was that or drown. I'll replace them."

"I don't care about the—"

She elbowed him in the ribs. "Let me down!"

"No!" He slipped through the last stand of trees, his blood simmering. "What the hell's wrong with you?"

She bit down on her lip, tears streaming down her face. "Me horse. They p-poisoned him."

"Who?"

"Bonnie. They made her. Threatened to take away her pills." She hiccupped, trying to catch her breath. "Same way they poisoned Delhaven's mare."

"Pills?" He narrowed in on her. "What kind?"

"Oxycodone."

Great. An addict. They—he could only guess she meant Bailey and Griffin—were behind the pills, the mare's death . . . Kevin got a sick feeling low in his gut. "They have something to do with Chipper's death?"

She again bit down on her lip and nodded, snuffling.

Kevin strode to a nearby bench and sat her down. "Don't move." He pointed a finger at her.

Her shoulders caved in, and she curled into a ball.

Kevin keyed his mic. He couldn't bring Chipper back, but he could try and save the stallion. "Let me talk to my dad."

"Yes, sir."

"Hello." Something bumped the mic. "This thing on?"

Kevin clenched his hands. *Stop keying the mic.* Finally met with silence, Kevin keyed his. "Dad. Shut up and listen. They—your buddy Fritz, Griffin, and Dunn—poisoned your stallion."

"What the shit! I don't care about the damned horse. What about Dani?"

Kevin smiled at that. "She's fine." He gazed at her. Multi-faceted eyes, the color of exquisite sapphires, held his. They were worried. "Check on her horse."

"Need a car for that."

Right. "Let me talk to one of my men."

The mic bumped again. "Yes, sir." Delgado came on the line.

"Take him back to Starlite's barn. We'll be right behind you."

"Need my shotgun, too." His father grumped in the background.

"Clear the chamber before you give it back to him."

"I know how to handle my own—"

Kevin released the mic and crouched down in front of Dani. Their eyes connected. "I thought I'd lost you."

Her arms went around him, her body shaking. "His name is Tommy Duggan. I worked for him on the docks of Rosslare Harbour." She gulped in air. "He shot Kara. I'd held out hope she was alive."

Wet tears ran down his uniform shirt, and he held her.

"I-I didn't know for sure she was dead until her body washed up."

Kevin picked her up and sat down with her in his lap on the bench. He'd hoped she'd come to trust him—trust him enough to tell him the truth. Now he'd nail that Irish son of a bitch, too. Then they could be together free and clear.

Chapter Forty-Six

I T WAS PURE LUCK.
Dani would have never believed six days after Solley had last ingested the tainted peppermints laced with arsenic, she'd lead him out onto the track for the second day in a row to train. The vet said the concentrated form of arsenic—a dry powder—Bonnie had used most likely didn't adhere well to the hard candy. But for good measure, he suctioned out the contents of Solley's stomach with a gastro tube, followed by a charcoal slurry to suck up what trace amounts were left.

It'd been an exhausting couple of days for everyone, including her horse. But a true miracle for sure.

Dani's forehead creased with consternation. She was still ambivalent about Bonnie. Had Dani not witnessed it with her own eyes on the tape, Bonnie would have continued to ply Solley with his favorite sweet until he dropped over dead. She couldn't forgive her. Bonnie'd had options. She could have come to her—told her the raw truth of it before the tragedy with Chipper. Dani believed Jake had acted alone that night, but it could have been avoided.

Dani shook it off. For now the trio remained in the hospital recovering from their gunshots, under police guard. She'd let the courts decide their fates.

The clouds overhead crowded the sky. They'd said a chance of rain. She didn't doubt it. The air was damp. Her hair was a testament to that. Even in a ponytail it curled.

Dani held tight to her riding helmet and dug her boots into the dirt leading down to the track. She was in a mood—darker than the skies.

After the lake, when she'd broken down and told Kevin about Tommy and the dock, he'd been so tender and sweet. But then he seemed indifferent toward her the next day. He'd made love to her that night, but it had been rough—like he expected her to prefer it that way.

She didn't.

They were a couple—lived in the same house. But he hadn't touched her since. When she asked why, he brushed it off. Told her it was the investigation. She didn't believe it. She'd overheard him one night on the porch with his father—while she tidied up after dinner—telling Turk the state police were handling it.

So he didn't like that she'd worked for Tommy. So much for telling him the truth. Only she still hadn't told him everything. With his attitude Hades could freeze over before she'd confide in him about the thumb drive. It remained in the clock for safekeeping for now. She and her sisters were keeping tabs on Tommy. Well, they were monitoring the news from her village. Garda still hadn't connected Kara's death to Tommy or O'Shea.

"Dani." Suzanne Grant waved at her from outside the rail. At least there was a bright spot to all of it. She'd had that talk with Suzanne. It'd been a shock. But Chipper's mother was open to Blake visiting with his daughter as a friend of Hannah's mother and one Dani Flynn.

The four of them—Blake, Dani, Hannah, and her grandmother—had gone for ice cream earlier in the week. Blake had been nothing but charming. Only this time it was genuine. Fatherhood agreed with him—too bad only a select few knew. It would stay that way for now, maybe until Hannah was eighteen.

"How's it going?" Dani smiled at Hannah, sitting atop of Bart with Blake. "Look at you, Miss Hannah. A real horsewoman like your dear ma."

The words—so hauntingly familiar—had Dani fighting back tears. She missed her ma and Hannah's, too, for that matter.

"Uncle Blake's teaching me to ride."

"Uncle Blake, is it?" Keeping Solley accounted for, she tied him off on the rail, and shot Blake a curious look.

He shrugged and gave her a sheepish grin. "It's less formal than Mr. Lansing." He hopped down, helping Hannah out of the saddle.

Dani couldn't help but notice how he hugged her tight and took a sniff—a sniff of her hair. *Of all the things.* He caught her eyeing him, turned a shade of red, and handed her over to her grandmother just as

Turk moseyed down from the barn.

Grand.

"Hey, smiley." Turk tweaked Hannah's nose, put his clipboard under his arm, and pulled something out of his pocket. He made two fists. "Pick one."

Blake sidled up next to Dani. "What?" he said under his breath.

Hannah looked up at her grandma, eyes big and brown. "Which one?" She placed her little finger against her lips, debating.

"You were sniffing her hair," Dani whispered back like he'd lost his head.

Turk nudged his right fist toward her. "Pick."

"She smells good and clean like . . ."

"A fresh meadow."

"Sort of—yeah."

"You're hopeless." Hopelessly in love with his baby girl, she wanted to say. Dani snickered. "She'll have you wrapped around her little finger in no time."

"Wouldn't have it any other way." He folded his arms and grinned.

"Flynn." Turk waved her over with Solley. "Less than two weeks. Let's go."

She lifted her chin to him. "Let me say me goodbyes."

He waved her off and slipped through the rail and onto the track.

"I'll be watching from the rail," Blake said. "Use the whip to remind him to switch leads on the inside when going into the turn."

"Aye." She raised the whip. Dani would only be tapping him on the shoulder, a gentle reminder to switch up. She neared the gate.

Turk opened it, shutting it behind her, and then pulled her aside. "Taking pointers from Lansing?"

She didn't miss the edge to his voice and glanced back at the threesome.

"Bye, Uncle Blake." Hannah lifted her arms to him.

He scooped her up and gave her a kiss on the forehead and sat her down.

"Come on, sweetheart. Grandma's got a few errands to run."

"Suzanne." Blake pulled something out of his pocket, handing it to her.

She peered at it, her head snapping up. "Ten? *Blake,* it's too much."

"Nonsense. You've got school tuition. College won't be too far behind."

Turk leaned into Dani. "What the hell's he talking about? You'd think he was the kid's—"

Dani jerked him down the track by his arm.

Turk stumbled, pulling his arm away. "I'm not a piece of meat."

She wasn't lying for Blake or anyone else anymore. Dani nailed Turk with unsmiling eyes. "He *is* her father. He didn't try to steal Chipper away from you. They argued about his child support that day outside the scales at Penn National."

Turk got that pompous look that came when he thought he was right. "Figures he didn't want to own up to his responsibilities."

Dani growled at him. "He fought with her because *she* wouldn't cash his bloody check for five thousand."

"Jeez." His face reddened, and he rubbed the back of his neck. "You telling me Suzanne meant 10K back there?"

She nodded. "He's being responsible. Wouldn't you say?"

Turk shrugged. "Still an asshole."

Dani clenched her teeth. "One you'll be working with, starting tomorrow." After everything that happened, she hoped those that were left could learn to play nice with one another.

He laughed. "He my new groom?"

"No." Dani jammed her helmet on her head and stormed over to Solley and slipped through the rail. She untied him, opened the gate, and led him in, shutting the gate behind them. "He's training right alongside you, starting tomorrow."

Turk's cheeks puffed out. "Oh bull . . . *shit.*"

Dani got up in his face. "I've kept your secret about the mortgage. I'll not keep it another minute unless you accept Blake's help."

"What's in it for him?"

"Not a bloody thing. He's turned over a new leaf."

"A rotten one," he huffed.

"I mean it, Turk. I'll not train or race unless you agree to let him help us."

"Yeah, I've seen his methods."

"That was the old Blake."

He gave her a look of disbelief. "You really think fatherhood's made him a new man?"

"You're not to mention it to a living soul." Dani pulled him close. "Hannah doesn't know."

"Not doing it." He gave her his back. "Not working with him."

Dani hopped up into the saddle, her bum landing with a thud. "Then lose your house, you old goat." Dani dug her fingers up along the left, inside of her helmet and jerked the wire out, her face twisting with anger. "I'm done with you screaming in me ear, too." She tossed it to the ground and kicked Solley in his sides, galloping away.

Let him fire me.

Chapter Forty-Seven

"You're not going, then?" Dani zipped her suitcase closed and sat it down by the bedroom door.

Kevin shrugged and got into bed with Jimmy right behind him. "Got too much to do around here."

"I see." Dani checked the alarm clock on his nightstand—11:32 p.m. Nice of him to give her a little advance warning. "I don't suppose you've told your father."

"Called him while you were in the shower." He fluffed his pillow, took off his black diver's watch, and sat it down on the nightstand, turning off the light on his side of the bed, leaving her standing in a dusting of moonlight from the window. "He's picking you up at three thirty."

Dani clenched her fingers. With the way he was acting, she wouldn't be at all surprised to find all his fancy words of love and support for her career had been only a ruse to get her into his bed. Now that he had, he didn't care a whit about her.

"I'll move my things into the spare bedroom."

His light popped on, and he scowled at her. "Why?"

Dani stormed over to the bed. "Because you've been nothing but mean to me since I told you the truth. The truth you said you could handle."

He raked his hands through his close-cropped hair. "Can we not do this tonight?"

Dani clenched her teeth and smiled. "How about we not do it, ever?" She gave him her back and marched into the bathroom. He flicked off the bedroom light, plunging her in darkness.

The bastard.

She left the bathroom door open, flipped on the light, and smiled when she caught him squinting in the mirror, the light a beacon on his angry face.

Her humor faded. She didn't want to fight with him. She loved him and hoped he'd have jumped out of bed to apologize, telling her he still loved her with all his heart.

Bah.

It was hopeless. His chilly behavior had crept in on her like a phantom in the night. Dani gathered her toothbrush, soap, shampoo, and conditioner.

That's it.

Other than the existence of the thumb drive, she'd told him everything he needed to know.

Whatever. He'd never had a problem telling her his mind. If he wanted her out of his life, he would have said so. Wouldn't he? The last thing she wanted from Kevin was pity. Dani juggled her toiletries in one arm and shut off the light. She padded across the bedroom, a slight breeze from the open window ruffling her nightie. Spying Jimmy at the bottom of the bed, she clucked her tongue. He stretched and rolled over, ignoring her.

Grand. Even the cat was on his side. Snagging her suitcase off the floor, she headed down the hall, feeling ignored and unloved.

She wouldn't give him *or* her turncoat feline the satisfaction of a good night.

At 3:27 a.m. Turk pulled up and blew his horn.

Dani cringed and grabbed her suitcase and overnight bag, shutting the front door. She locked it with her key. Glancing up to the second floor, she checked the window to Kevin's bedroom. If he was watching her leave, she couldn't say. It remained dark.

"Good morning, sunshine," Turk called from the open window.

"Shh." She gave him the evil eye. "He's still asleep." She grabbed the door handle to the back door.

"Ah . . . You might want to throw your gear in the bed."

She nodded, a bit perplexed. There should be plenty of room with only the three of them. "Arturo getting Solley ready?" she called back.

"Yep. Picking him up now with the trailer." Turk's voice floated through the back slider.

Dani threw her bags in the truck's bed. "What about Blake?"

"Got some open house at school with Hannah and Suzanne at noon."

Latching onto the passenger side door, she yanked. It didn't budge. "You need to—"

"How 'bout you sit in the back. I got my box of papers up front." Turk popped the lock. "Blake's meeting us at the hotel later tonight for dinner."

Grand.

Her love life was shattering like a piece of fine crystal, and Turk had decided she—even though she was the one putting her arse on the line, saving his house and his business—wasn't good enough to sit up front with him.

Err.

She ripped open the back door. The tension drained from her shoulders, her body filling with warmth. "Da!"

"Sweetheart, I'm surprised meself." He hooked his chin toward Turk. "But a little birdie told me you were in need of a bigger cheering section."

She'd have loved to have her sisters, too. But Bren was due soon, and Kate didn't fly in from Colorado until next week.

Dani gave Turk a feigned look of annoyance for making her feel unwanted. "You're not the least bit funny."

"Hop in, Flynn," he said and laughed.

She did and plopped down next to her father, shutting the door. His arm went around her. *Funny.* She'd forgotten it had been her family she was in search of after finding herself in America—not the man of her dreams. Dani snuggled into her da. He was pudgy and warm and she loved him with all her heart. She couldn't imagine sharing the next few days with anyone but him and Turk.

Oh! *And* Blake—the man with the bankroll who was going to save them all.

CHAPER FORTY-EIGHT

ELECTRONIC FINGERPRINTS. DANI GLANCED BACK TOWARD TURK, HER heart in her throat.

He sat in a chair in the commission office at Saratoga Racetrack, yawning from their early morning, seven hour drive from Maryland to New York. The clock above his head read 10:02 a.m. His brows rose over his glasses. "Standard."

Maybe for him. She'd been nervous about the entire process. If she wanted to race, she needed a license. She'd brought her passport, knowing if the steward, clerk—whoever—flipped through it, they'd find her expired visa. They hadn't. After they'd gotten a good look at her *valid* passport, she fumbled and dropped it. By accident, mind. But her nerves played in her favor. Before she could pick it off the floor, they moved her on to where she stood now—the fingerprint line.

"Next." A clerk named Rick waved her over. He was older, somewhat attractive and, it would seem, impatient, tapping his foot.

Dani tensed. She could say the hell with it right now. Grab the application she'd filled out with her social security number and head straight out the door. But the old man sitting in the waiting area who believed in her, believed she could make everything right in his life, would be devastated. She couldn't do it, and with everything wrong in her life when it came to Kevin, she was feeling a bit reckless. Dani shuffled toward him.

Rick the clerk opened the swinging door and smiled at her. "First time?"

Her shoulders leveled off. "Y-yes."

He nodded. "Slap and roll."

Dani swallowed hard. It sounded painful. "Excuse me?"

"Fingerprints." He chuckled and took her hand.

She flinched.

"Relax." He straightened her fingers on her left hand. "Spread them."

Kevin used that term on her that night at Grace when he arrested her, and Dani straddled her legs, waiting for the pat down.

"Flynn," Turk grumped from the waiting area.

It was the first gruff word he used with her since their departure. Dani turned. Turk shook his head, his bum halfway off the seat, giving her a disagreeable face. Well, she wasn't a mind reader, and she hadn't a clue what he was trying to say. She turned her back on him.

"Your fingers—not your legs," Rick said, trying not to laugh.

"Oh." Her cheeks warmed, and she pulled her legs together. "How do you mean?" She tried to flex her hand in his tight grip.

He pressed her four fingers flat against the glass with the bright light for a few seconds and then pulled her hand back. "Right hand." She gave it to him freely, knowing that everything she'd done to avoid detection in the U.S. was slipping away.

She glanced back at Turk. He'd been giddy the whole ride up, he and her father talking nonstop. Tired with little to no sleep, Dani dozed the seven hours. When they arrived, they shipped Solley into the Clark Barn, settling him into his stall. Before she could take a breath or consider what she was about, Turk gathered her up, making a beeline for the commission office where he remained antsy yet still smiling.

"Loosen your finger." The clerk shook her pointer. "Just let me roll it from side to side."

Dani took a deep breath and tried to relax. Within five minutes, the clerk was on her last digit—her thumb.

"Where do they go from here?" Dani asked, trying to be casual.

"State of New York and the FBI."

Dani jerked her thumb away like she was in fear of losing it. Maybe not the finger. But definitely her anonymity and quiet way of life in Clear Spring were in jeopardy.

"You okay?" Rick narrowed in on her.

"Ah, the light. It was burning me finger."

He gave her a strange look and touched the glass. "It's warm."

Dani shrugged. "We done, then?"

"No," he snapped. "I need to retake your thumb." He grabbed it—

none too gently—and rolled it against the glass.

She pulled it away from him when he was through, placing her hands behind her back. "What do they do with it—the FBI, I mean—when they get them?"

He laughed. "Check to see if you're on the Ten Most Wanted list."

"You can't be serious!" Her heart seemed to skip a beat.

"He's kidding." Turk stood, leaning over the swinging door. The smile he'd worn since leaving Clear Spring disappeared. "Hey, listen. I'm traveling with this horse. She's"—he pointed toward Dani—"staying on the grounds, if I can find space for her, and you're gumming up the works with your jokes. How 'bout getting us the hell out of here so we can race?"

Dani hid a smile. She'd wondered when the real Turk Bendix would show himself. She was a little concerned with the time, too. As nice as it would be to sleep in a bed in a hotel, she didn't want to leave Solley. She'd prefer a cot in the tack room near his stall if they'd let her. But she thought Turk meant the bunkhouse or something similar. She'd clue him in on her preference later.

Rick's lips thinned. "Need to take her photo for her license." He grabbed a camera off a desk and motioned Dani out and followed behind. "Stand against that wall with the gray background."

Dani complied and smoothed down her hair. She tried to smile.

"No smiling," Rick snapped, scowling from behind the lens.

Dani's eyes narrowed. She was losing her patience. Spread your fingers, roll your fingers, no smiling—*what the bloody hell?*

"You gotta be kidding me." Turk got to his feet.

"Face recognition camera. Smiling changes contours of the face." He pulled the camera down. "This one goes to the FBI. The second is for your badge." Rick glanced at Dani from behind the camera. "You can smile for that one."

Grand. Dani wanted to slither to the floor. She'd filled out their paperwork, answered their questions to the best of her knowledge, and tried to quell her erratic heart when she checked off the word "no" to the question: Do you or any immediate family members have any criminal charges against you?

As far as she knew, the answer was still no. That would soon change though, thanks to this new and emerging trend in security. *Saints preserve me.* Dani stood still, didn't smile, and he snapped her photo. The next shot was for her badge. She managed a grimace before the flash blinded her for the second time.

"Let me check the fingerprints—make sure they're clear. And get your license and badge." Rick motioned them to the waiting room chairs. "I'll be with you in a minute."

More than ready to flee, although the waiting room wasn't what Dani had in mind, she sat down.

Turk took the seat next to her. "What's up, Flynn?"

"Nothing." Her hands remained restless in her lap. "I want it to be over is all." She angled her head down. "Get you your money and go," she whispered.

"Back to Kevin?"

Dani rolled her lips in, considering. "I think it'd be best if I move back into the barn."

Turk took a heavy breath. "Can't say I blame you." He rested his head against the wall. "Damnedest thing. You'd think the way he acted that night at the lake he couldn't live without you."

Dani reached for his hand. That night at the lake hadn't only affected her. "I'm sorry about Fritz."

He shrugged. "Me, too. But what he did . . . did to Chipper . . . you." He shook his head. "Even using Bonnie with all her troubles—it's unforgivable."

She nodded. "Da feels the same way. About Fritz, I mean. You have to go with your heart. Feelings change." Like Kevin's for her. Dani's grip tightened on Turk's hand. "You still feel the same about me?" She laughed, a little embarrassed. "Not the can't-live-without part."

"I know what you meant." He patted her hand, his eyes becoming moist. "I'll put it to you this way. I was ready to dust off Lindy's heart-shaped diamond engagement ring." He nudged her. "In a platinum Claddagh setting—and the matching wedding band—and give it to that son of mine."

"Engagement ring?"

He shrugged. "Thought that's where the two of you were headed."

Not anymore.

He nudged her shoulder with his. "You're the only one I'd want to have it. So he's shit out of luck."

Dani pursed her lips. "That's sweet of ya to say."

"Might just be cashing it in when this plays out, any old way." He leaned in. "There's no hiding behind Starlite or the invisible Mr. Porter on this one. Gotta race under the owner's name."

"Your name."

"You got it. Joseph William Bendix, owner." He pointed to himself with his thumb, fell back in his seat, his head coming to rest against the wall.

Dani grabbed his hand and squeezed. "You're a grown man able to make decisions for yourself. If Kevin can't handle . . . to hell with him."

"My sentiments exactly."

Nice the two of them could talk it up now. The truth of it was, they both feared what lay ahead of them after the race.

"Perfect prints, little lady." The clerk called from the counter, holding up a lanyard with her badge attached to it.

Brilliant. With lightning speed her photo and fingerprints would be sent into cyberspace. She wouldn't be at all surprised if she were standing on Irish soil by the end of the week.

"Let's go, *little lady,*" Turk said, poking fun at the clerk and grabbing her hand. "You're only licensed as an exercise rider until you're named on a horse."

Dani jerked her arm away, her mouth falling open. "But I have a horse."

"Come on, Flynn. Didn't they draw post positions when you worked at Tramore?"

Yes, they did. But it was the way he'd said it. She nodded.

"Okay, then." He grimaced. "Granted, it's a circus. They draw post positions on Wednesday, they'll announce you, and then you'll get your apprentice jockey license before the race."

Her heart sped up. "I have to come back for that?" That was the last thing she wanted to do—be under more scrutiny.

He cocked his head, giving her an *I'm thinking* look. "Ya know. I think it's automatic here." He waved it off. "Don't mean shit without a gate card anyways." He tugged her along. "Come on, kid. Let's show 'em what you got."

Oh, Lord, the starting gate. If she couldn't prove she could get out of it, they'd never let her back on their precious track for the actual race.

"Flynn, let's go."

"Coming." She pulled her hand away. "I can walk on me own two feet."

He put his hands on his hips and sized her up. "Just show 'em you can ride." He sauntered over to the barn like a man half his age with Dani in his shadow.

She had so much to lose . . . so much to prove. This should be an exciting time, an experience to treasure the rest of her life. Instead, her stomach was coiled in knots. Having her da meant the world, but her sisters were her safety net. Not that they agreed with what she was doing. But they'd understood once she explained it. She wouldn't forsake Turk now, not after everything he'd done for her.

They entered the barn. Solley was up with his head over the stall door. She gave him a quick kiss, saddled him, and led him out. Turk met her outside, and they traveled over to the track.

"Have you heard from Blake?" Dani asked.

"Nope." He gave her a sideways glance. "Forgive and forget, right?"

She gave him a quizzical look. "I don't understand."

"Let's just say, I'll look the other way for now when it comes to his past. He shows up tonight—does his part like he has for the past two weeks—I'll give him the benefit of the doubt."

She nodded. "Fair enough."

Only on the inside, she had her misgivings, especially with their little agreement Turk knew nothing about. If he reneged, she'd be in a world of shite.

Chapter Forty-Nine

"**G**ATE THREE."

"Aye." Dani nodded to the outrider.

She'd galloped for him on several horses after leaving the commission office. Now it was almost noon and time for them to shove her and Solley into the bloody gate. She'd practiced it with Solley numerous times that last week with Blake. She only hoped she could do it when it really counted—now and at the start of the race.

He led them in. The metal bars were cold and restricting, like a jail cell. Solley blew out an agitated breath through his nose.

"It's okay, boy." Dani patted his neck. "You were born for this, sweetheart."

The starter shut the back gate, the slam of metal against metal giving her heart a jolt. Her hands were sweating, the reins damp between her fingers. She'd knotted them like she always did to keep her grip from slipping. The bell went off. The gates swung open. Dani clicked her tongue at Solley, and they were off, speeding down the track toward the first turn. A thrill shot up her spine, and she laughed.

She should rein him in. But they were gliding. With the wind at her back, she settled down in the saddle. She'd been right. He was born to do this. She smiled at that. They were *both* born to do this. She knew that now. Knew it with every beat of her heart.

Dani took the far turn, coming toward the homestretch. Turk walked out onto the track, waving his arms over his head like it was the end of the world—her world.

Shite.

Dani slowed her mount and came in. Adrenaline coursed through her veins, and she shook from exhilaration and fright. By the time she neared the rail, he had joined a group of men. One was her father. He must have made his way over from the hotel after his nap. He worried her—his age. If only she'd listened to her ma all those years ago and sought him out.

She reined Solley in, leaning over. "See, nothing to it, luv."

"Dani!" Turk called over.

Tell me beating heart.

Emotion welled up in her, and Dani whisked away a tear. The last time she had been here, it was with her ma. She'd won, too. It was more than just Turk's finances now. Dani wanted to win. But not only for herself for her ma.

She dismounted and handed the reins to Arturo who had stepped onto the track. "Could you see that he gets a warm bath?"

He nodded with excitement. "Joo did great!" He gave her a wide smile and led Solley off to the barn.

"Thanks," she managed, trying to catch her breath. Dani lifted up her dusty goggles. The one in the summer fedora made her a wee bit nervous. She sighed. Turk had mentioned something about pleading their case to the judges on their way over. She just assumed registering for the race was enough.

Dani cleared the track and started their way. Her legs shook like she'd run the mile and a quarter on foot. She wasn't fool enough to think they were letting her race on her own merit. Everyone in the business had heard about the tragedy at Penn National. It was sympathy that got them here, along with Solley's racing stats before he'd soured and Turk's experience as a trainer that had convinced the judges to let her take Chipper's place. Turk had been to the Belmont. She made a point of not bringing it up because of what happened to his wife while he'd been away.

Turk pulled her aside. "Ever hear the saying, *This race isn't won on a Monday?*"

Dani grimaced. She knew better. But they were in a groove, and she'd been . . . showing off was more like it. "It was stupid, and I'm sorry for it."

"Don't let it happen again," he said out of the side of his mouth and then smiled at the man in the fedora. "Dani, I want you to meet Mr. Bud Tillsdale." He raised his brows at her. "He's one of the judges."

She got his covert signal and tried to smile. "Pleasure, Mr. Tillsdale."

She shook his hand.

"The pleasure was watching you on the track." He laughed. "Turk tells me your mother raced here."

"Aye. It was years ago. She raced the summer here in '05. Won the Woodward, if you can believe it."

He looked as if he were trying to place something. "Must have been at the Belmont before they moved it here in '06."

"You might be right. It's been a while. I was a young groom at the time, working that summer here. Didn't get off the backside much."

He pulled on his chin. "She was Irish like you?" He seemed to be considering something when he slapped the side of his leg. "Her name was Rory Flynn."

"You knew her, then?"

"You bet." His hand landed on her shoulder. "Your family, kid." He shook his head and grinned at Turk, his hand falling away. "It was back in the day. Great horsewoman, great lady. I might've run into her once or twice at the Parting Glass. As I recall," he said with a devilish smile directed at Dani, "she liked her beer."

Dani grimaced. "You mean Guinness."

"That, too." He rapped Turk on the back. "She's in."

"I-I'm in?" She could hardly believe it.

"Of course you're in." Her father came up alongside of her and put his arm around her. "You're a Fallon, me girl."

"No," Mr. Tillsdale said. "She's a damned good jockey." He tipped his fedora at her. "Enjoy your time here, Miss Flynn, and good luck on Saturday." He said his goodbyes and hopped in a waiting golf cart.

Dani wanted to pinch herself. It was really going to happen, and like the fizz in a bottle of champagne, she felt herself rising to the top.

Lord, bless me and save me from meself.

She was going to pop the cork right off this thing and make a frothy mess of her life.

The reality terrified her.

She really would have her head on a swivel from here on out. It wasn't just deportation she feared—they had a name, her fingerprints, social security number, and face recognition photo now. If she won—which they'd banked on, literally—the name Dani Flynn would be in circulation until the hubbub died down.

Tommy's chilling words slapped her hard. "It's a pity I have to kill you, love."

Dani stood on the perimeter of the paddock under a fragrant pine tree, away from the crowds and the media, which she'd successfully avoided for the past two days, while an NBC Sports commentator continued to announce the post positions for Saturday's race. Under the warm afternoon sun, they'd filled all of them except for posts two, seven, and eleven.

"Number seven, David's Goliath, three to one favorite, owned by Del Ray Farm, trained by Vince LaDecco, ridden by Joe Dalia," he said.

A pretty young woman in a summer dress and heels stuck the cute magnetic replica of Del Ray Farm's silks on a white magnetic board under the seven spot.

Please not the outside. It'd be the devil to get to the rail.

"Number eleven," the commentator said, taking the entry form from the gentleman to the right of him. The form slipped through his fingers, falling onto the paddock's lush green grass.

Dani stood frozen, her fingers digging into the bark of the tree.

Someone from the track scooped the entry up and handed it back to the commentator.

"Sorry about that, folks. And way on the outside, post position eleven goes to Solitary Confinement, owned by Starlite Racing, trained by Turk Bendix, ridden by Dani Flynn."

Dani's head fell to her chest. *Of all the luck.* She might as well turn around and head back to Maryland. The odds were . . . Her head shot up. *Grand.* She'd missed the odds because she'd been consumed with losing a race that hadn't even started. She shook her head. If she had to guess, it was probably a hundred to one. She was a no-name jockey on a washed up horse. Considering her status, it wasn't a bad thing necessarily. Keeping a low profile while in New York was paramount.

Dani checked the board. All eleven post positions had been drawn. Turk answered a few questions from the commentator and then headed in her direction.

A male reporter stopped him, shoving a microphone under his nose. "Turk, can you give us some information about Dani Flynn?"

Panic rose in Dani's chest. She hadn't a clue what would come out of Turk's mouth.

"Nothing to tell. She's a damn good jockey."

Dani's shoulders relaxed.

"Where'd she come from? There're no stats on her."

"She's Irish—worked as a groom at Tramore." He laughed. "The grooms here are only good for one thing. But this lass gallops him, rubs him, walks him."

"Huge purse, Turk. It seems a huge ri—"

"This isn't a charity case here." He twisted his neck, rubbing the back of it. "I've been around a long time. This horse and her are good for each other."

"But is *he* ready. Last we've seen or heard of Solitary Confinement was—"

"I'm not here to run third. He's shown us—shown her—flashes of his past brilliance."

"Why the Travers?"

Turk shrugged. "Hey, we know the horse likes the track, don't we? He won up here last year."

"That's your story."

"There is no story." He waved them off. "We're here to win."

"Where can we find Dani Flynn? It's a great human interest story."

"She's around," he called back, moving in her direction.

"That's her!" A reporter jabbed his finger at Dani from no more than twenty paces away.

Shite.

Dani slid a pair of dark sunglasses down her nose. Turk hooked his chin toward the barn, his message clear. Dani turned and ran straight into a microphone and a reporter from ESPN.

"Dani Flynn, right?"

"Ah . . . aye." Her eyes flew to Turk. Not that he could see her panicked expression.

"Turk says you're a seasoned jock."

"I-I wouldn't say seasoned. Solley and I are—"

"You call him Solley?"

"It's a nickname. He's not at all like the dark name he was given."

"There'd been a rumor he soured."

Turk's hand landed on her shoulder. "He's sweet on her. Loves her like no one else."

Camera flashes went off, and Turk steered Dani left, his arm coming around her. "Give a nice wave and a smile, and let's get the hell out of here," he whispered under his breath.

She'd love nothing better.

"We'll see you on Saturday, then." She lifted her hand and smiled. Every fiber in her being wanted to run—not walk—to the nearest exit and forget the whole bloody thing. They traipsed across the thick grass and onto a sidewalk, reporters traveling with them with large cameras. They shoved microphones under their noses and continued to fire questions at them.

"Who did you work for in Ireland?" a female reporter said from NBC Sports.

"Turk, foresee any problems with the post position?"

"He'll run for her. Don't matter outside, inside, or in-between," he shot back.

"Were you a jock or is it only now that you're in the States?" That came from ESPN.

"Who is your agent, Dani?"

Dani threw up her hand to ward them off. *Bollocks. I should have stayed back at the barn.*

She'd become the news today—all five foot two, one-hundred and ten Irish pounds of her. The sunglasses wouldn't fool anyone who knew her.

They certainly wouldn't fool Tommy.

Chapter Fifty

"Twenty to one." Blake shoved the racing book under Dani's nose.

"Not very good odds." She continued to brush Solley outside his stall in the Clark Barn, hoping to relax him before the race, a little more than an hour away.

"They are if you're betting on a long shot."

"Glad to see you have such confidence in me."

Blake laughed out loud. "You kidding me? I know this horse. I know what he can do." His hand came down on her neck. "I know what you can do, Dani," he said, his voice softening, fingers moving hypnotically against her skin.

If it weren't for the fact it was Blake, she'd have relaxed and let him work the kinks out of her tense muscles.

She shook his hand off and gave him a stern look. "You're not thinking of starting up where we left off, I hope."

He chuckled. "We were fighting as I recall."

Good that he remembered. They would remain friends and, she was afraid, co-conspirators until she crossed the finish line. "What are you betting, then?"

"Ten to win on number eleven."

So much for being family. Not that she expected them to fix the draw. It was just her luck. "I don't want you wasting ten thousand of your hard-earned money. I only need a hundred thousand to pay off Turk's mortgage and give him a cushion until the stable is back on its feet." She shook her head. "Five'll do."

He cocked his brow at her. "The other hundred grand is for me."

Dani's mouth fell open. "You really think I have a chance of winning?"

"You bet."

She couldn't help but laugh. "Then you better place that *bet* before the start of the race."

"Dani!" Turk called from the doorway of the barn, glancing at his watch. "It's a little after one. Time to see the doc, get changed, and weigh out at the scales."

"Aye. On me way." She slapped Blake on the back like a drinking mate of her ma's. "I'll see you in the winner's circle with me money." Dani winked at him.

If only I had the same confidence in meself.

She gave Solley a big hug. "I'll see you in the paddock soon, boy."

He'd been under tight security since Wednesday. Now she would be under the same type of security—or was it scrutiny—until five when they came to get her for the race, starting at five forty five. Dani headed out the barn toward the jockeys' quarters. She didn't much care for being prodded and poked by the race course's doc. They'd check her vitals, but they were more interested in the results of her Breathalyzer. Not that she'd had a drop of alcohol. But they were wise to double-check them all. She certainly didn't want to be out there tearing up the track with the other jockeys if one was under the influence.

Dani entered the jockey's quarters, her heart thrumming in her chest. Turk motioned her through a door. He remained on the other side. She stood in line with other jocks for the Breathalyzer test. They stared her down like they'd never seen a woman jockey before. Dani kept her head up and didn't break eye contact with a single one.

"Hope the hell she knows what she's doing," one jock whispered, two up from her.

"Not looking to get killed out there by some no-name girl who thinks she's a jock," the one next to him chimed in.

Dani clenched her hands. She'd had just about enough. "The name's Flynn—not she or some no-name girl." Dani narrowed in on them. She had every right to be here, same as them. "I've waited all me life for this. Worked hard in Ireland as a groom since I was sixteen. Me ma won the Woodward. It's in me blood."

"Joe Dalia." The jock next to her put out his hand. "Number seven. Good luck."

"Ah . . . Dani. Dani Flynn." She shook his hand, considered *her* post position and grimaced. "Aye, I'll need it. Eleven."

"Flynn, you're up." Rick the clerk from Monday hitched his chin at her.

"Good luck to ya, Joe." Dani passed the others in line, glad to be moving on, her shoulders sagging when she noticed Rick from the commission office. "So you're a jack-of-all-trades, then?"

"Master of none," he said on a laugh and raised a tube up with a mouthpiece attached to the end. "Can you give me one nice big breath?"

Dani nodded and blew into the Breathalyzer, a little surprised by his lightheartedness.

"Good girl." He took it from her, his eyes widening. "I mean Dani."

"I'll let it slide," she whispered.

He nodded. "Next stop first aid to see the doc." He leaned into her. "Good luck and don't let them get to you."

"Thanks." Dani went out the way she came and met Turk. "First aid."

"I know where it is." He patted her shoulder, and they walked a ways, passing a few buildings. "How you feeling, kid?" He gave her a sideways glance.

"Nervous."

"Good. That's normal." He stopped in front of a building marked First Aid. "Last stop before we get you back to the jocks' quarters and get you dressed." He led her in and dropped in one of the chairs. "Have a sea—"

"Miss Flynn," said a man in jeans and a white polo, holding open another door. "Dr. Chase Carroll, can you follow me?"

"Aye." She headed that way and slipped past him into the room.

"Can you take a seat please?" He smiled, motioning her to the examining table.

She used the aid of a step and took a seat.

"So you're the one the reporters have been after. Can you take a few deep breaths?" He pulled on her shirt and placed the cold stethoscope on her back.

She'd tried to keep a low profile after that day in the paddock. She had nothing more to say to them. Nor did she want another photograph floating around or another sound bite of her being broadcast to who knew where.

"You'd think they'd never seen a female jockey before." Dani took several deep breaths.

"They're curious about you."

Well, they could stay curious. "I just want to do what I've been trained to do."

He laughed. "Get on with it. I get it." He took her wrist with his thumb and two fingers and checked her pulse. "Low."

"Is that bad?" Alarm rose in her chest.

"No. You're fit." He patted her knee. "Have a few more tests and then you're good to go."

He took her blood pressure, checked her throat and then her ears. "You're in good health."

Thankfully, he wasn't inside her head. Otherwise she might not pass the nerves-of-steel test—if they had one.

"So am I free to go?"

"Yes, ma'am." He opened the door. "Good luck, Miss Flynn."

"Thank you." Dani cleared the door, meeting Turk on the other side.

"Everything go all right?"

"I'm fit as a fiddle."

"Good. I'll show you to the women's jock quarters." He took her outside.

They passed the same buildings, traveling the same sidewalk, passing the commission office until they came to the jockeys' quarters.

Turk opened the door. "Women's quarters to the left."

Dani nodded, hesitating. "I'll see you after the race, then?"

"You bet." He turned to leave and then swung back. "Dani?"

"Yes?"

"Ah, hell." He hugged her to him. "I love ya, kid." He pulled away and wiped at his eyes. "I'll see ya."

Before she could find her words, he was out the door, walking a brisk pace away. Dani smiled. He must. She did, too—love him with all she had in her.

Dani entered the women's jockey quarters and made her way to her assigned stall. She opened the door. Her silks—nothing at all like Starlite's old colors—that the valet arranged for her were vibrant and full of new promise. It had been a hurdle to get the Jockey Club to agree to the change, last minute, before the race. But after Turk explained the circumstances—just like he had when it came to switching Dani and Solley in the Travers—they'd understood and agreed.

Dani ran her hands along the smooth fabric. Yellow like the bright sun. She only hoped Chipper would shine down upon her. Dani was running this for her, too. Her chest tightened, and she wiped away a tear.

She slipped out of her clothes and grabbed her ma's coin out of her jean pocket.

She kissed it, tears filling her eyes. "Wish me luck, ma. I miss you terribly." Checking her silks and not knowing where to put it, she tucked it inside her sports bra, shivering at the coldness of the metal. Dani then donned her shirt and pants. They were snug, but like a second skin, they fit perfectly. She slipped on her riding boots, grabbed her helmet and whip. She barely had to remind Solley to switch up. But she'd tap him just the same. She didn't want to jinx herself.

She took a deep breath, said a prayer she'd make the weight again today, and sauntered over to the scales where she met Arturo with her saddle and Turk and her father.

"Where's Blake?" Dani leveled a hard gaze at Turk.

"Placing his bet."

She relaxed and lifted her chin toward her father. "How about you, Da?"

"Done." He dusted off his hands, his cloudy blue eyes twinkling under the mid-day sun. "Fifty dollars on eleven to win, sweetheart."

"And you?" She gave Turk a questioning look.

"You and I got the purse money to split."

Dani swallowed hard. If he only knew they might take his money back once they found out she wasn't legally in the States. She frowned. Even if Turk placed a bet, they'd probably take that away from him, too. Didn't matter. If she won, Blake's winnings would solve that problem. She wouldn't concern herself with disqualification for immigration status. It didn't affect those placing a wager. They wouldn't connect Blake to Starlite Racing, either. He wasn't on the payroll.

He was simply a good friend—though she could hardly believe it—and a gambler who liked a long shot.

She'd wait to see if she won before she told Turk the truth. If she didn't place, well, then she'd keep quiet. If they did get second or third, she'd have to tell him before he spent the purse. And if she won, she certainly would tell him. He might not be able to spend the seven hundred and fifty K, but he'd have half of Blake's winnings. The cash would pay his debt on the house. He'd breathe easier knowing he wouldn't have to tell Kevin about his poor money management skills.

As for her relationship with Kevin, she'd be moving out as soon as she returned, relinquishing him from his bloody chivalrous responsibilities.

She'd made herself a promise long ago. *Too bad it is in the reverse now.* She'd make no promises to a man unless *his* heart followed, and, sadly, Kevin's hadn't.

With her helmet firm atop her head and her whip in her hand, Dani followed the pomp and circumstance of the other ten jockeys as they led them out from the jockeys' quarters and into the crowds. She kept to the narrow sidewalk, trees swaying in the warm summer breeze. She could almost believe it was just a day in the park with red and white tents, blankets strewn about with people picnicking—some dressed for leisure and others decked out in pretty dresses and fancy plumed hats, the men wearing suits like Turk, Blake, and her da.

The magnificent wooden structure of the grandstand loomed above, its spirals topped with glimmering crosses reaching skyward toward the hands of God. She only hoped He didn't send a thunderbolt zinging her way for all the lies she'd told to get her to this point.

"Need a leg up?" A groom stood next to Solley. He was tethered to the outrider in the paddock.

"Aye. I'd appreciate it." Dani held tight and hoisted herself up with his help. She settled into the saddle and let the outrider take her through the paddock and onto the track.

Trumpets filled her ears. Panic—pure panic—seized her just then. The crowds had swelled since a few hours ago, their cheers growing with each passing second 'til post time. The announcer's voice echoed out over the track. Dani was oblivious to his words. This couldn't be over fast enough. 'Twas a pity something she'd dreamed about as a young girl— and that had come true—she wanted to wish away.

The outrider led her toward the gate. Solley pranced on his tiptoes. She leaned over and patted him, trying to allay his fears, her hand trembling. "I'm depending on you to keep me from passing out," she whispered.

The outrider nodded toward her helmet.

"Oh." She placed her whip under her knee, her fingers scrabbling for her goggles. She brought them down and blinked, opening her eyes.

Leading her in, the outrider released his hold on Solley, the assistant starter taking over. Solley nickered, then snorted. He seemed ready for this to be over, too. Gates slammed one after the other, hers deafening when it banged closed behind her.

Her heart raced. In a few seconds—

The bell rang, the gates shot open.

"And they're . . . *off.*" The announcer's voice echoed all around her.

Solley tripped, gaining his footing. *Good Lord.* They'd broke late. It'd be the devil to catch up. She pulled her legs up. *Lizard on a log, lizard on a log.*

". . . his pace is strong." The announcer's voice bumped up a notch.

Whose pace? Whose pace? Dani's heart tripped in her chest. She'd missed the name. They passed one, then another. Sleek, his hide glistening with sweat, Solley poured it on.

"David's Goliath is the front runner with Dam Straight in second."

Dani took the turn, forgot the whip, and held on. He'd switched on his own. She tried to count the furlongs in her head, but they were nothing more than a blur. They were gaining. She needed to get them to the inside. She pulled on the reins, nudging him toward the left.

"Solitary Confinement is making his move to fifth. He's coming to the inside rail."

Dani let him go. He pushed out the number four spot, edging up to third. Dirt flung back, slapping her in the face, goggles, her beautiful silks. She didn't care. She was going to win—*they* were going to win. And she didn't want it to end. The wind whipped at her face, her hands.

They rounded the far corner, turning back toward the grandstands. A small crowd of nameless faces hung over the rail, cheering. She trembled with exhilaration. They were coming to the homestretch, inching their way into third. "We can take 'em. You best believe it, boy. We can take him."

She couldn't breathe.

"Twenty to one Solitary Confinement makes his move in the final turn," the announcer yelled with shock. "He's a longshot, folks, keeping pace with Belmont winner David's Goliath."

Don't fall back, don't fall back. Dani clenched her teeth.

"David's Goliath ahead by a neck entering the homestretch." The announcer's voice strained. "Solitary Confinement is surging. Here he comes, Solitary Confinement but David's Goliath still leading by a nose!"

She had to hold it. They were neck and neck now. Solley's nostrils flared. He grunted, giving his all. He'd prove to everyone today this was his race to win.

"It's . . . it's . . ."

The finish line loomed, they were dead even with the other horse.

"It's . . ."

Dani urged Solley forward not knowing what he had left. He surged but so did David's Goliath next to her.

"It's . . . it's . . ."

They crossed the finish line, Dani's heart in her throat.

"Too close to call," the announcer's voice trailed off in dramatic fashion.

Dani's head fell. *Of all the things.*

She was betwixt and between. Dani yanked up her goggles and slowed Solley down. She hugged him around the neck. "I love you, boy. It doesn't matter what they say. You were magnificent."

She needed to catch her breath. Sweat poured down her back, the silks sticking to her damp skin. A woman mounted a horse outside the rail directly across from her. Dani blinked at her trendy short blond hair. It glimmered like a halo.

Chipper?

She donned a helmet, took something into her hand, and road out onto the track.

"Dani," she called, rode up alongside her, and shoved an NBC Sports microphone at her. "Great race. You two upset the apple cart today," she said, her voice bubbly with excitement.

"He's a keeper, this one." She patted Solley. "It was all him. I was only along for the ride."

"Solitary Confinement had his challenges. A graded stakes winner until he fell off the racing circuit."

Through no fault of his own, she wanted to say. But the slight would only harm her new relationship with Blake. "He's back. Doesn't matter if we win today or not. He's back and he's more than proved himself," Dani said, trying to catch her breath.

"What an upset! We certainly have to pay tribute to Turk Bendix. Won the Belmont nearly twenty years back and sadly lost his wife of twenty-seven years the same day."

Dani clenched the reins. *Reporters.* They were always dredging up the past. Turk didn't need to be reminded. Now it would forever be captured on film.

"He's a wise trainer," Dani said. "He's taught me all I know."

"How do you feel about the photo finish?"

"We'll wait and see with everyone else."

Turk, her da, and Blake all stood on the rail near the winner's circle, waving her in.

Dani nodded. "If you'll excuse us."

The reporter backed off, and Dani hightailed it back to the rail. "So close." She frowned down at them.

"It's not over yet," Turk said, twisting his *Racing Form*. "Just stay on and walk him around the track until they announce the winner."

Blake patted her thigh from the rail. "Hard fought race, beautiful."

Her eyes widened, trying to let him know hard fought didn't mean a win.

"You all right, sweetheart?" Her father cocked his head, looking at her strange.

She guessed she looked like a goldfish out of water. "Just fine, Da. Nervous is all."

"Get out there." Turk motioned with his head like he had horns he was going to poke her with if she didn't move.

"I'm going." She turned herself around and paced more than circled along with David's Goliath and his jockey.

"We have the photo finish." The announcer's voice reverberated over the track. Lights flashed on the Jumbotron. The official finish line photo flashed up on the board for all to see. Dani blinked, her mouth fell open, and she held tight to the reins. "And it's Solitary Confinement by a nose." The photo disappeared from view, and the number eleven flashed up on the screen, blinking.

The crowds cheered, a swath moving toward the rail. Turk waved her over like mad toward the winner's circle, smiling so wide it looked unnatural. Dani laughed and trotted over.

Arturo headed her way from the rail. "We win, we win!" He grabbed hold of the reins and directed them to the winner's circle.

She was happy for Arturo, too. She'd make sure he got his cut out of Blake's money as well.

Someone threw a floral blanket of red carnations over Solley, the fragrance tickling her nose. Her team surrounded her and her fine steed—Turk, Da, Arturo, and Blake.

The announcer chuckled. "Whoever said the best things come in small packages must have been talking about Starlite Racing. We're used to seeing a swarm in the winner's circle."

The track photographer held up his camera. "Smile, folks."

Flashbulbs went off all around them. Spectators hung over the winner's circle hooting and hollering. It was insane, and Dani loved every minute.

"Very eventful race. I'm still stunned." The announcer laughed. "Pinch me."

Pinch him, someone pinch me.

After the reporters and photographers backed out of the winner's circle, the jockey who placed third on Dam Straight rode up next to her. "Congratulations."

She recognized him from earlier. He'd been the one mouthing off about her—the second one, she believed. She lifted her chin to him. "Thanks. Good race, yourself."

He nodded and smiled. "Welcome to the club, Dani." He reached out his hand. "Duce McCoy. We'll see ya in the jocks' room for a little initiation."

An Irishman. Dani shook his hand. "Aye. I'll see ya soon, then."

He trotted off toward the paddock with her crazy team still celebrating below. Turk jumped like a leprechaun, and her father danced a jig next to him, the two hugging. Dani hopped off, her legs wet noodles when she touched the ground.

Shite. Dani reached for Solley.

Blake grabbed her instead. "I got ya, beautiful."

Music played, the crowds were partying it up in the grandstand, spilling out around the winner's circle.

Dani pinched herself.

"What are you doing?" Blake eyed her.

"Making sure it's not a dream."

Blake chuckled. "You're crazy, Flynn."

"I know." Dani laughed like she'd not laughed before. "I don't believe it. We won! We won!"

Blake twirled her about. She tottered as she came full circle, Blake catching her in his arms, giving her a big kiss on the lips. It . . . it was unexpected and completely innocent. That she knew. But she had a sneaking suspicion Kevin—if he was watching—would think otherwise.

To hell with him.

She could have been in his arms sharing this moment with him, if he weren't being such a miserable bollocks.

CHAPTER FIFTY-ONE

Turk drove up along the sidewalk in front of Kevin's house. They'd spent another night in New York partying it up in the posh Pavilion Grand Hotel. She'd met celebrities, the governor of New York, the mayor of New York City and drank until she was numb to it all.

Today, she had a splitting headache. The dark clouds overhead only added to her foul mood and a homecoming that would find her packing her bags.

"Give me a call when you're ready, and I'll pick you up."

Dani's head fell against the seat back. "Just as soon as I'm packed." She squeezed his hand tight. "You're like a second da to me, Turk. I'm sorry about the purse."

"Damn it, girl." He narrowed in on her. "I put you in a bad position. Not the other way around. You should have told me, *and* let me give you your cut."

"I'll not take a penny of it. It's yours." She closed her eyes. It all came flying back to her—the crowds, her jittery nerves, the race, her exhilaration. Her lips quirked. "I wouldn't have changed it for the world." Well, except for the purse—seven hundred and fifty K wasting away in a bank account that couldn't be spent for fear it would have to be paid back. He'd be worse off for sure. Her lashes fluttered open, and she gave him a stern look of her own. "Pay off that house of yours tomorrow. So I'll not worry about it being taken away."

He patted his pocket with Blake's check. "The bank's still open. It will be paid in full before the close of business today."

She nodded, pulled her head up off the seat back like she was carting around a boulder, and opened the door. "I'll just grab my things." Dani yanked her two bags out of the back. They'd already dropped her da off first at his house. When they passed Bren's on the way out, she'd thought to ask Turk to drop her off there. But she'd still have to gather her things, and the timing of it today would be perfect—Kevin was at work. Plus, Kate would be arriving next week for the birth of the baby. She'd see them both soon enough.

Dani waved goodbye to Turk. She smiled for a brief moment at her Cabrio that sat parked out front since she'd moved in with Kevin. She'd get her life back, manage that driver's license, and get on with living. Somehow. She took the brick pathway to the house and glanced back. She'd been doing that a lot since the bloody press conference—looking over her shoulder. Turk pulled out, and Dani tensed at the compact silver car parked across the street. She'd seen it earlier when Turk pulled in. Only she hadn't gotten a good look until now at the rental car sticker running along the back quarter panel.

It was silly to think she'd find Tommy standing there in the flesh. She doubted seriously he'd announce his arrival. Dani's shoulders leveled off, and she continued down the brick path. The house with its whitewashed siding and striking black shutters would be a distant memory. The flourishing garden around back she'd nurtured from its weedy existence would languish. Kevin wouldn't keep it up, she imagined. He'd be busy looking for that perfect mate—preferably American, blond, and tall.

Dani gritted her teeth. She wouldn't be at all surprised to find he'd go back to Kristen the bank manager. Dani slid her key into the lock. It couldn't be more than about half past three. She'd gather her belongings—which weren't many—and give Turk a call before five. She patted her phone in the back pocket of her shorts, making sure she hadn't lost it along the way, then fished in the front pocket until she could make out the familiar hard disk that was her ma's coin. She relaxed knowing she had both, and then her mind fast-forwarded to the next step— packing. Kevin normally arrived home between six and half past. She'd be gone by then.

She turned the key and opened the door. Dani jerked back. "Shite! What are you two doing in here?" She stepped in, glanced around. "Kate you should be… Is Kevin with you?"

"No," her sisters said in unison with Bren shaking a key in her hand. "I have his spare."

Kate grabbed her bags. "You haven't checked your damn phone for two days."

Dani held her aching head between her hands. "I've been busy."

"*God,* Dani." Bren grabbed her hand and dragged her into Kevin's living room and sat her down in the paisley winged-back chair. "Celtic Trans-Atlantic Shipping. Ring any bells?"

Dani gripped the arms of the chair hard, her knuckles turning white. "Tommy's."

"They're investigating him." Kate set down her suitcases.

Dani looked from one to the other with her beloved kitty—she'd missed since leaving almost a week ago—jumping in her lap. She hugged his soft body to her, his rumblings calming. "What's come of it, the investigation?"

"They're looking for him for questioning." Bren put her hands on her hips.

Kate narrowed in on her. "They have a man by the name of O'Shea in custody."

"You're afraid he's here." A lump formed in Dani's throat.

"He *is* here." Bren handed her an iPhone.

Dani read the headline in the *Wexler People*. DUGGAN SPROUTS WINGS, FLIES TO NEW YORK IN THE WAKE OF PROSTITUTION RING SCANDAL ROCKING PARLIAMENT.

The names on the thumb drive took shape in her mind. But it was the women from the boats that swirled about in her head. Her stomach roiled, and she jumped to her feet, Jimmy scurrying off, disappearing around the corner. Dani followed that way, slid on the runner in the hall, grabbed the door frame of the powder room, and flung herself onto the floor. She gripped the cold porcelain and heaved.

"Dani!" Shoes scuffed against the hardwood floor.

A door opened, then slammed. "What the hell is going on in here?" Kevin's voice boomed in her head. Or was it above her? She couldn't even begin to turn her head to be sure.

"Out!"

There was a ruckus behind her. Her sisters' protests mixing with Kevin's angry shouts. Dani pushed herself up from the floor and rinsed her mouth. Grabbing the towel, she dried her face. The sour aftertaste of vomit lingered in her mouth.

Kevin jerked her out of the bathroom, his face bloodred. "You sleep with Lansing?"

Dani yanked her arm away. "It was a congratulatory kiss."

"Yeah, I bet."

"Don't believe me." She swung on him, getting in his face, which—because of his height—had her craning her head up in an uncomfortable position. "You shoo me sisters away. Give me the silent treatment for weeks with not even a reason."

"I think you have a pretty good idea why."

Dani shrunk back. He had her there. Only she'd just now learned of it. "I don't have to listen to this. If you don't want me, *Kevin,* then show me the door."

He gripped her arm, pulling her hard against him. "You lied to me." His eyes swept over her, filled with simmering rage.

Stone cold and terrified, Dani trembled in her white tank and khaki shorts. "What the devil are you blathering on about? I told you about Tommy. Tommy had lied to me. I didn't know about the human trafficking." Anger coursed through her veins, making *her* blood boil. Dani ripped her arm from him. "*Bah.* You're lying to yourself. You can't feckin' handle the truth."

"I know the truth, whore." He choked back tears and reached behind his back. The edge of his handcuffs caught the light from the chandelier high above in the hall.

"What are you—" Dani backed up, maneuvering toward the door, her eyes wide with alarm.

He clawed at her, trying to snag her arm.

"You're going to arrest me?" Terror edged her voice. Dani's eyes bounced off his hands, the cuffs, the table in the hall. His keys glittered. She grabbed for them and pulled the cherry table in front of him. It clattered to the floor. She jerked open the door, glancing back. Kevin stepped over the table, his back foot catching between the legs. He fell, cursing.

Dani slammed the door behind her and ran toward the street, the keys jangling in her hand. She glanced down but a second and recognized her key to the Volkswagen on his ring. *He was so afraid I might drive off without permission.* Well, she was doing it now, and to hell with his bloody laws. She hit the automatic door lock. It chirped when she slid around the rear of the car. She flung open the door just as Kevin flew down the stairs of the porch.

Dani jammed the key into the ignition, her hands unsteady. It started, and she slammed her door shut, hitting the door locks a second before Kevin grabbed for the passenger door.

He jerked on it. "Open the son of a bitch," he seethed, the veins pulsing in his forehead and neck.

She clenched her teeth to stop them from chattering and put the car in drive. In the rearview mirror, he ran back up the walkway to his house. Dani checked the keys dangling from the ring and relaxed a bit when she noticed the funny-shaped one to his little Miata. She already knew she'd snagged the keys to his patrol car. But he could have spares in the house. She wouldn't concern herself with it now. She needed to concentrate on getting out of his neighborhood. She'd done it several times in the passenger seat over the past several weeks since moving in. She only needed to get out and onto 70 and then 68. Grace was a few miles from the exit. Dani hoped her sisters had returned home after Kevin had kicked them out.

Concentrating on the signs, her hands slick on the wheel, she took the exit for the interstate. She tried to relax her shoulders. They were bunched, her fingers cramping from their death grip on the wheel. Tears slipped down her cheeks. They were warm and salty when they reached her mouth. Dani wiped hard at her face. He'd called her a whore just like Tommy had.

Only it stung coming off Kevin's lips.

Kevin paced the front porch with a pair of irritated eyes trained on the tree-lined street. She couldn't drive worth shit. Wrapping her pretty little neck around a tree in her sporty Volkswagen was a certain outcome. He shouldn't care what happened to her. If he was lucky, he'd walk away from this thing with a bad case of chlamydia worst case full blown AIDS.

A fucking prostitute.

How the hell had he missed the telltale signs? Because there weren't any. She was charming, sweet, and had seduced him like any other john. Kevin slammed his fist into the front door. She never loved him—she used him, made a complete mockery of him and his position to the point she'd left him immobile. Literally.

Sirens wailed in the distance. It wouldn't be long before his deputy turned onto his street with the extra set of keys. Let Harmon smirk once and the bastard would find himself on permanent midnights.

Harmon pulled behind Kevin's patrol car and hopped out. All the passenger doors swung open. *What the hell?* Did he bring the entire shift to gloat?

No . . . suits. *Shit.* He'd told the feds to let him handle Dani. They'd only scare her. Kevin snorted, his jaw tensing. He'd done a pretty good job of scaring her all on his own. He'd been pissed—about a lot of things. But the one thing that kept replaying in his head over and over was the news coverage clip and the precise moment Lansing had kissed her. The image was ingrained in his mind. Instead of being that professional lawman he prided himself on, he'd acted like a jealous fool. He assumed she'd slept with him. Why the hell not after what he'd learned about her in the last few days from Garda and the FBI? He couldn't stop the slight that had fired off his lips.

So he was hurting. He'd have to learn to get over it. She was going back to Ireland, and, based on the list of charges against her, it would be years before she would be released. Didn't matter. He could forgive a lot of things. But not this.

"Ah, sir. I tried to keep them in your office," Harmon whispered, sending a covert glance behind him. "They want to talk to you." He handed Kevin the keys.

He'd have met them in his office with their prisoner as planned. But like everything else in his life—his job, his reputation, his relationships—it was going to shit. The three strode down the brick path toward his house.

"Sheriff Bendix." A broad-shouldered, stocky agent with dark hair held out his hand. "Agent Jeff Dawson, we've been speaking by phone."

Kevin nodded, shaking his hand. "Thought we had an agreement."

"We gave you that chance," the other suit said, his expression one of complete aggravation.

"Carter." Agent Dawson glared at him. "Things have changed, remember?" He hooked his chin toward the red-headed gentleman. "Garda Inspector Tim Cleary."

"Nice to meet you, Sheriff Bendix." He nodded. "I see you have a fine place here. Sorry to intrude."

"No problem."

"Do you have a place where we can talk?" Cleary held a file under his arm.

Kevin's hands clenched. He needed to get on the road. But he'd gone through a great deal of trouble to portray his and Dani's relationship as a purely platonic one after contacting the FBI—who then contacted Garda—about this Tommy Duggan two weeks ago. He knew her family, helped her find employment—that was it. Racing out of here, acting like his world was coming to an end—and in a sense it had—would tip them off.

Duggan was out there, no thanks to his call to the FBI and Dani's blatant disregard for her safety after her see-and-be-seen worldwide televised interviews.

Kevin opened his front door. "Living room to the right as you come in." He held it until the last one—his deputy—cleared the threshold and then shut it behind him.

Harmon hung back in the corner, standing. The other three took a seat. Two on the couch and Cleary in the winged-back chair next to Dani's suitcase—*and* the luggage tag he'd filled out with her name and his address. Kevin shook his head. "Let's not waste time. She's out there. Your only living accomplice." The last word he said through gritted teeth.

Cleary looked to Dawson and sat down his file. He flipped through it. "O'Shea—Duggan's mate—rolled over a few hours ago. We're looking for a thumb drive. Miss Flynn may have it."

Kevin shrugged. "As far as I know she never mentioned it. I can't speak for her family." Although something told him Bren and Kate already knew of its existence.

Cleary made some notes, glancing up. "That would be her father, Daniel Fallon, and her two half-sisters."

He nodded. "But if I had to guess, she's headed for the training center."

Cleary turned over the paper. "Would that be this Starlite barn?"

"Her room's on the second floor. If she's got this thumb drive, she may have hid it there."

Dawson clucked his tongue. "If it was there, I'm afraid Duggan's already found it."

Kevin's gut clenched like a tight fist. "You saying he's been there?"

"Unless Miss Flynn has a habit of trashing her room and sleeping standing up—the mattress was up against the wall," Carter said with disdain.

Kevin's adrenaline spiked. How long had that been? Grace was only two miles down the road. He'd hit the farm next. "Let's go." Kevin charged out of the living room and swung open the front door. Behind him, the men scrambled to their feet, the heavy soles of their shoes clattering on the wooden foyer.

Kevin dashed toward his patrol car and hopped in. Cleary grabbed hold of the passenger door and swung it open. "I think it's best I ride with you. If you don't mind, Sheriff Bendix."

"Get in." Kevin jammed the key into the ignition.

Cleary jumped in, barely managing to shut the door before Kevin peeled off.

"I sense she means more to you than just that of a relation to a family friend."

Kevin gave a hard laugh. "Try again. She's endangering that family friend."

"I see. Then it wouldn't interest you to know that along with giving us important information about this thumb drive, O'Shea clarified one important aspect of this case that has baffled us."

"What's that?"

"Dani Flynn's just as she seems. She's innocent."

Chapter Fifty-Two

"**B**REN! KATE!" DANI RAN UP THE STEPS AND JERKED OPEN THE screen door. "Bren!" She ducked inside the living room, formal dining room. Nothing. Moving down the foyer, she checked the kitchen to the right, her eyes landing on the butcher block and the one lone knife. She tore into the kitchen and grabbed it. She frowned at the small blade. *Of all the luck*—a paring knife.

It would have to do. Tommy wasn't stupid. The race Kevin had warned would only gain her unwanted notoriety had done just that. It wouldn't take long for Tommy to link the Fallons to her.

She'd have to find him first. Only she wouldn't go it alone, and she wouldn't be involving Kevin. With everything that had happened, she still loved him and wouldn't put him in danger. Tears filled her eyes.

He doesn't love me.

She sniffed and set down the knife and grabbed the cell phone from the back pocket of her shorts. Her hands scrabbled across the screen, trying to access the Internet and a phone number for the state police. It only remained cold and dark in her hand. *Bloody hell*. She'd forgotten to charge it.

Dani shoved it back in her pocket and picked up the knife. She crossed over into the family room and Great-Grandmother Maeve's clock. She turned the key with the tassel. It clicked, and she opened it. The thumb drive fell out onto the end table. She scooped it up right as the screen door creaked open and then slammed.

"Dani?" Kate's sandals slapped the hardwood floor in the foyer, growing more distinct.

Dani wiped away her tears, shoved the small knife in the front of the boot between the laces and the tongue. It was secure, somewhat concealed, and hopefully wouldn't find its way in to her foot. Dani straightened. She wouldn't get into the thumb drive. This was no longer about the three of them and some grand plan. The risk was too great. Dani tucked the thumb drive inside her bra and entered the hall.

Kate seemed to float toward her, arms open like an avenging angel. "You okay?"

Emotion welled up in Dani's chest. She shook her head. "He thinks I'm a prostitute."

Kate's arms came around her. "Dani," she whispered in her ear. "Tommy's got Bren and Charlie in the barn."

Her head snapped back. Panic surged to every corner of her body. "Where is he?"

"With them . . . with a gun." Kate's voice shook.

Dani looked past her, the door, to the barn. "He let you go?"

"He saw the car pull in, watched you enter the house."

"Sent you to find me, then."

"I'm not offering you up like a sacrificial lamb." Kate's eyes darted from the living room to the dining room and back to Dani. "We need a plan here."

"He's too slick. We can't outsmart him." Dani moved toward the door. "I'm done running, Kate. If it's the thumb drive he wants, I'll give it to him straightaway." She swung back at Kate. "But not here, not with me family."

"What are you saying?" Kate took measured steps toward her.

"I'll lure him away from you—the farm. He'll follow like the shark that he is."

"You take the thumb drive?" Kate glanced down at Dani's hands.

Dani clenched her fingers tight. "Earlier when Turk dropped off Da. You weren't here." It was a bald-faced lie. But a necessary one, if she wanted to keep them safe.

"Where is it?" Her voice bumped up a notch.

"What does it matter?" Dani reached for the door.

Kate grabbed for her, swinging her around. "I know this kind of guy. He'll kill you with or without the thumb drive." Kate's intense brown eyes darted to the door and back to Dani.

"We're wasting time." Dani pulled her arm away, bolted out the door and down the front steps. When she was dead center of the barn doors, she put her hands up. "Duggan! Come out, luv, and we'll talk about a little ocean voyage and a certain thumb drive." She flung his fateful words back at him—the ones he'd used on her all those many weeks ago on the dock—and waited, her legs trembling.

The barn door screeched open, and Dani's breath caught. He held Charlie in his arms with Bren next to him, the gun at his side. The threat was so real she could taste the bitterness in her mouth. Bren knew it, too. She couldn't disarm him—pregnant or not. The risk to Charlie was too great.

"Talk." His chin shot up, his way of letting her know he was in control.

"Not here, mate. The old ball and chain is on me arse. I wouldn't be at all surprised to find he'd brought the Garda with him."

"Fuckup."

Dani winced. *Same belligerent bastard.* "You away in the head? He's a cop, Tommy. Come to bring the whole bloody Garda down on us." She treaded backward. The corn with its long billowy stalks, danced and rustled in the wind to her right. She'd have a fighting chance in there.

What a fool she'd been. Even if Kevin thought to follow her here, he couldn't.

"Up the yard with ya, then." Dani waved him off. "Not looking to be sent back. I'm illegal . . . no thanks to you." She turned and started running toward the cornfield, dark clouds rotating overhead. She kept her ear to the ground. Nothing—except for the roll of thunder in the distance. *Grand.* The storm had caught up with her. She gave a hard laugh.

I knew he would.

Dani refused to look back. *Follow me, arsehole.* Her heart pounded in her chest. It was a split-second decision. She'd die a million times if he killed her family. What he needed was some incentive.

"I've got your bloody thumb drive on me, mucker." The friendly slur that rolled off her lips made her stomach roil. He wasn't her friend or her mate. Dani ducked inside the drying stalks still tall enough to hide in. It would make for a fine maze.

"I'll kick your head in, Flynn." His voice pierced the humid air around her.

A baby whined. "I've got you, sweetheart." The relief in Bren's voice was palpable. Charlie was safe.

Running footsteps crunched against the gravel drive behind her. "Give it up. All I want is the thumb drive."

Eejit. He'd kill her first.

Dani pushed her body deeper. Rough dry leaves scratched her bare legs, arms, her face. She didn't care. She needed to put space between them. The ground was uneven, the rows of corn tight, making it difficult to pick up speed. Tommy would be fighting against it, too.

A bright bolt of lightning slashed across a menacing dark sky. Thunder quaked, the ground shaking beneath her feet.

But he has the gun.

Dani stopped and bent down. Shaky fingers pulled at the laces of her boot, trying to free the knife. She tugged hard, the knife flying up. She'd kill him before she gave up the thumb drive.

Rustling came from in front. He should be behind her. Terror wound itself deep inside her, and Dani stood frozen.

Kevin jerked his patrol car onto 70. "Innocent?" He glared at Cleary.

He shrugged. "It's a hard truth . . . to find you've been wrong."

"But you said . . . you told Dawson she was on Duggan's payroll."

"Come to find out not for very long—a week or two."

"Doing what?"

"This guy's a slick one. Seems he had Ms. Flynn and Ms. Gilroy believing they were some sort of meet and greeters. Unbeknownst to them, their job was to keep the women from panicking when they boarded the buses—even had the two dress conservative like lawyers. If you can believe it." He scrubbed his face hard and turned. "Do you understand what I'm telling ya, mate? Flynn and Gilroy had no inkling about the darker side of Duggan's operation."

Kevin's shoulders caved.

He'd been so angry, livid with the woman for weeks, knowing—believing, thanks to the Garda's shoddy intelligence—Dani had been Duggan's girl and every other john's, willing to pay for her services. Kevin groaned. She'd looked at him like he had stabbed her straight through the heart.

"I called her a whore." The words fell from his lips in quiet disbelief, and he punched the steering wheel.

Cleary winced. "Apologize, then. Tell her . . . tell her it was the guard's misunderstanding. She'll have a mind to take you back."

Kevin gave him a sideways glance and jerked the car to the right and the exit for 68. "What makes you think—"

"Come off it. I saw her luggage, mate. Looked to me she was returning home." He shrugged. "You're living with her."

"She'd been up in New York . . . won the Travers."

"Aye. Tell me something I don't know." He dipped his head, trying to catch Kevin's attention. "She ran a damn fine race. Beat out the favorite, I hear."

Kevin shook his head. He didn't have a chance of salvaging their relationship. He'd been an idiot. She'd told him everything in the end. Well, except this thumb drive. *Damn it.* All she wanted was his love and support, and he couldn't even give her that. Kevin pulled down Grace's driveway, his emergency lights bouncing off the walls of tall oaks with Harmon on his bumper.

"What do you know about this Duggan?"

"He's a prick. Dirty as they come—a real scumbag if you know what I mean."

Kevin's muscles tensed, his gut churning. "Do I even want to know how she got ahold of this thumb drive?"

Cleary shrugged. "From what Duggan's mate O'Shea said, it was Kara Gilroy who'd stolen it. She must have given to Dani for safekeeping."

"What's on it?"

"Transactions, mostly. List of buyers. It's disturbing. A gangster of the worst kind and some of his best paying clients are members of parliament."

"Christ." Kevin slammed on the brakes in the middle of the parking area, Harmon pulling to the right of him. "That's some serious shit."

He nodded. "A bunch of dodgy oonngoro milling about in decent society that will get what's coming to them." He frowned. "If we can get ahold of this thumb drive before Duggan."

Kevin didn't give a damn about the thumb drive and jerked the door open. "Her sister's farm." He motioned for Cleary to follow him.

Several more doors swung open. Kevin motioned his deputy and the two agents over. Dani's car wasn't here. He strode toward the front porch, noticing half the snowball bush on the corner of the house was missing. He veered off in that direction, his heart thrumming in his chest when he recognized the blue Cabrio. "She's here."

Kevin unholstered his gun. He'd thrown the girls out of his house. Bren's truck—he hadn't noticed until now—remained in its usual parking space in front of the barn, Kate's rental parked next to it. They were here, too. Kevin motioned them up the steps when a clatter came from the house. The screen door swung open. Bren leveled a shotgun at them.

Kevin jumped to the left, Cleary, armed, to the right.

"Hold your fire!" Kevin's eyes darted from Bren to Cleary to the three armed law enforcement officers behind him with their weapons drawn.

"They're in the cornfield." Kate came behind Bren, carrying a revolver.

Shit. Kevin ripped the gun out of her hand. "Give me that."

Kate's mouth fell open. "What the—"

"Which direction?" He handed the gun to Harmon who moved up the steps.

"To the right of the tulip poplar." Bren's shaky finger remained on the trigger of the shotgun. "He's going to kill her."

"Little mama, give me the gun." Kevin came toward her, his arm going around her back. He holstered his gun and grabbed the barrel. "Ease off the trigger, Bren."

She nodded and then swallowed, taking her finger off like she was in a trance. "She's got the thumb drive, led him into the cornfield to save Charlie and me." She swung on him, eyes wide with fear. "Don't let her die, Kevin." Tears flowed down her cheeks. "She's one of us now."

"I know." His voice hitched, his mind fast-forwarding to a life without her. Panic rushed him. *Stop it. Do your job.* Kevin eased the rifle from her grasp and handed it to Cleary. He then waved Kate over who had moved to the railing, searching the field. "Take her in the house and stay there." He eyed Harmon. "Secure the house. If he doubles back, use the radio."

"Yes, sir."

Kevin radioed for backup and then took the steps and stopped, glancing back. "Kate, what's he wearing?"

"Black T-shirt and jeans." He'd already seen a photo—belligerent looking piece of shit with shifty eyes and long hair. He'd learned all he needed to know about Tommy Duggan in the past two weeks. He wasn't screwing around with this prick. Kevin glanced back and nailed Harmon. "Take him out."

"Yes, sir." Harmon opened the door to the house and led the women in.

Cleary came up alongside him. "Alive is preferable."

"His choice." He was on American soil—his laws. They'd get their precious thumb drive, and they'd get a body to go along with it. But it was going to be Duggan's—not Dani's.

The air exploded around them. Kevin's heart jackhammered in his chest, and he ducked, pulling his gun from its holster.

"Storm rolling in!" Dawson lifted his chin to the skies.

The ground quaked beneath his feet. Kevin waved them over. "Cornfield's about four acres. A utility road for farm equipment runs down the middle of it. Cleary and I will take this side. You two take the other." This was asinine. What he needed was a helicopter—visibility, on foot, sucked in a cornfield. They'd end up in each other's cross fire. "Duggan's in a black T-shirt and jeans. Dani's in khaki shorts and a white tank. Don't shoot unless you see the target."

The wind began to whip, stirring up dust and debris. The corn swayed, its stalks bending from heavy gusts. *Hell.* The air crackled around them. It was supercharged. A wall of gunmetal gray clouds filled the sky. No aviator would fly in this. "Cleary, you think your man Duggan will give up, given the chance?"

"Way off the mark, mate. He's deadly."

The air detonated around them. It was distinct. "Gunfire!" Kevin ducked, his heart in his throat. There was no time for reasoning. "Duggan! Sheriff Bendix of the Washington County Sheriff's Department. I've got FBI and Garda with me, too. You're surrounded! Give yourself up!" Kevin angled himself between two rows of corn, moving sideways, his head on a swivel—ear to the ground.

CHAPTER FIFTY-THREE

Dani dove for the dirt and crawled into the corn row and then into the next. Lightning sizzled across the sky, thunder rocking the earth beneath her. The small paring knife shook in her hand.

Too close.

But she wasn't alone. She should be grateful. She guessed prison would be preferable over death. Now she wasn't so sure.

"Caught your interview, luv, thanks to O'Shea!"

Tommy wanted to engage her in conversation. She wouldn't be the bastard's homing device. Dani clenched her mouth shut and brought herself up to a squat. With rows on both sides, the shot coming from somewhere in front, she pushed up to her feet and crossed over several more rows.

"Did you know he owns part of a racehorse?"

She knew it—knew it in her quaking heart that day of her fatal error in New York, when the damned reporters cornered her. Dani shook it off and kept moving. When she'd come in June, the corn had only been knee high, planted in two sections. A dirt road ran between them. She'd be in the open. But if she got there first, she could run faster. Tommy was a jack in the box, popping up on her when she least expected. She'd die straightaway of a heart attack if she remained in this network of unending, identical rows of withering green.

"You're real photogenic, luv." His voice seemed to come from all directions, and Dani trembled with indecision.

God is truly punishing me for me sins.

The faces she'd tried to forget morphed into a kaleidoscope of frightened eyes. They'd all been anxious. She'd calmed the women and young girls the best she could—took time with some, over those few weeks, explaining the many opportunities awaiting them in Ireland once they got to where they were going. It had all been an elaborate scheme—one she'd been a part of unknowingly.

It doesn't make me any less guilty.

Dani couldn't bring herself to think about what had happened to them. She knew. Bile rose in her throat. She gagged, covering her mouth. Tears filled her eyes, and she blinked them away—only to have them roll down her cheeks. Dani ran, straddling rows of corn, the leaves nicking her flesh, making her damp skin burn. In a green blur, she kept running. She tripped, her body sailing through the air. She landed hard, hitting her chin, the knife flying out of her hand.

Shite.

Dani's chest ached, her chin throbbed, and her skin stung like a million tiny paper cuts. Dani clambered onto her haunches, her hands scrabbling across the dry earth in search for the knife. Without it she was dead. Men's shouts and more sirens swirled about her head. The fool. He was beyond reason. In the end, Tommy would return to Ireland—in a pine box along with her.

Corn rustled from the left. Dani could make out the tip of Tommy's black boots several meters away, standing in a corn row. They shuffled, and then he moved with determined strides in her direction, chewing up ground at an alarming rate. A shiver ran down her spine.

Shaking—scraped and bleeding from knee to elbow—Dani rose to her feet. Something glinted, and she ducked down, searching the ground around the stalks, her fingers brushing against the sharp blade of the knife when something gold glimmered.

Shite!

Dani grabbed for her pocket, patting it. Nothing. She dug inside it, her heart in her throat. The coin.

A shot rang out. Dani ducked, her ears ringing.

"Fuck." Tommy stilled, took a few steps in her direction, the tip of his boot millimeters from the coin.

Gulping, Dani snagged the knife. She couldn't bear to leave the coin, but it wouldn't save her life. She ran with the blade, busting out from the cornfield, stumbling into the dirt road when a dark force flew out of the cornfield behind her.

Terror raced to every recess of her body. She turned and backed up, the knife clenched in her hand and down to her side—immobile.

Tommy soared toward her like a wicked spirit, eyes pulsing. He jerked her by her hair. Dani cried, her boots scraping along the red clay road until he had her within a breath of his snarling, pockmarked face.

"You fucking hoor." He raised his gun, shoving it against her temple.

It dug into her skin, merciless and unyielding. Dani's life sped past her like the windows of a fast moving train. She could barely make out the images—but for one. Everything slipped away. She was back in that cozy Victorian kitchen, eating, conversing, and laughing with a man she could easily fall in love with.

She *was* in love. She'd *seen* the tears in Kevin's eyes when he'd tried to handcuff her earlier. Somewhere deep within him, he still loved her—had to love her.

Dani stared into the steel gray eyes of death. Tommy Duggan had caused her a great deal of trouble. She wouldn't die a martyr.

Dani jerked up the knife.

Kevin rounded the cornfield and froze dead center of the dirt road that divided the two sections. Duggan had Dani cinched up by her hair, the gun positioned at her temple. The beat of his heart echoed in his ears, sweat pooled between his shoulder blades, and Kevin swallowed the bitter taste of certainty.

Duggan was going to die, and he wasn't going alone.

Dani knew it, too.

She'd die thinking he despised her.

Damn it. He loved her with everything in him and would mourn the life he'd never share with her. Kevin gritted his teeth. He'd hate himself a little more each day, knowing had he believed her, trusted her, confronted her with the intelligence he'd been gathering since she'd leveled with him, she wouldn't be facing a non-survivable gunshot to the head.

Kevin raised his Glock. His hands trembled. "Let her go!"

"Say goodbye, ya fuckin' peeler!" Duggan jerked Dani onto her toes and repositioned the gun against the center of her forehead.

Dani jerked. The gun went off, and Kevin's world exploded. Dani's body slumped, and the bullet that couldn't miss felt as though it had entered his own flesh, shattered his own bones, and punctured his own heart.

No!" Kevin charged Duggan. Raindrops began to fall like the teardrops of angels. They were coming to take her home.

Duggan had Dani by the arms like he was holding her up, the gun still in his hand. Kevin aimed his Glock. Duggan turned, his eyes rolling back in his head. "Hoor," gurgled up his throat, and he slithered down the front of Dani.

Dani turned, tears streaming down her cheeks, blood soaking through her white tank, a bloody knife shaking in her hand. "I'm not a whore. I'm not a whore," she cried, her eyes clinging to his. "You were the only one." Her voice was little more than a whisper.

It had been his first thought that night when he'd made love to her. What an asshole he'd been.

Agents and deputies spilled out of the cornfields in both directions and into the road. They rolled Duggan over, handcuffing him.

Sidestepping the melee, Kevin reholstered his gun and reached Dani, taking the knife from her trembling fingers. He handed it off to Dawson who came up beside him. Kevin pulled Dani's tremulous body into his arms, the feel of her solid against his chest, and his legs buckled with relief.

"I know, baby. I'm sorry. Please forgive me." Tears burned the backs of his eyes. She was shaken but alive.

"I didn't know. I didn't know." She wept into his uniform shirt.

"Shh. Shh." He rested his lips against her ear. "I know. I know." He kissed the side of her head.

She glanced down at Duggan. Her breath caught. "Is he dead?"

They'd rolled him back over, his position unnatural with his hands still cuffed behind his back. His black T-shirt was saturated in his own blood, his glassy stare indicative of death.

"Yes, sweetheart. He can't hurt you anymore."

A moan roiled up her chest. "I-I killed him."

Kevin pulled her away from the gruesome scene, holding her by her upper arms. "You had no choice."

She nodded, sniffed, and nodded some more. "He was going to kill me family."

He caressed her cheek. "It's over."

Cleary strode toward them. Kevin tensed. *Well, maybe not.* He knew the protocol here—knew she'd be extradited back.

Kevin put a protective arm around her waist, pulling her next to him. "Give us a minute?"

Dani clung to him. "I don't want to go, Kevin," she whispered.

Dawson nodded, eyed Cleary and then Kevin. "We'll meet you at your deputy's patrol car."

"Don't forget the evidence, mate," Cleary murmured.

Right. It was their focus—more so than Dani. "I'm on it."

Sirens wailed in the distance. More suits than Kevin could count descended into the cornfields, he guessed to locate the bullet that had missed Dani's head by degrees and any other evidence they deemed essential to their high profile case that had gone international.

A wave of panic came over him. He didn't have much time with her.

"We need to talk." He drew Dani into the cornfield, through several rows, and finally into the dirt that brought them to the edge of the field where they'd have some privacy and a view of Grace's driveway and the circus forming with reporters, their television vans, and—he did a double take, his jaw tensing—several county council members.

Great. I'm screwed.

He shook it off and concentrated on the woman he'd let down in a major way. He cradled her pretty, tearstained face in his hands. His throat tightened, and his breathing became shallow. "Can you forgive me?"

Dani's teeth chattered. "So cold."

Kevin's arms went around her, and he pulled her into his embrace.

Pressed against him, Dani glanced down at their bodies—her bloody tank. "Y-your uniform shirt." She tried to pull away.

"I care about *you*. Not my damn shirt." He peered down, lines fanned out from his tired eyes. They bracketed his strong mouth.

Dani nodded and snuggled into his broad chest, taking advantage of his warmth. "You must think me an eejit."

"No. I'm the eejit for believing you could be anyone other than who you really are."

Dani frowned and released him, her shoulders slumping. "I'm just as guilty. I knew Tommy brought them in illegally. He paid me cash. Told me they—the women and young girls—had paid a pretty penny for a new life in Ireland and the UK." She shook her head, tears filling her eyes. "I should have known there was more to it. They were right to be frightened." A moan rolled up her chest. "What do you think has become of them?"

He shook his head. "Let it go, Dani."

She nodded her head. But she didn't think she could let it go that easily. She had a fair idea. But for now her mind refused to cross that dark abyss. She held tight to Kevin's upper arms. "I know what it's like to find meself in a strange country. Not knowing a soul." She blinked, tears slipping down her cheeks. "But I found me family, a job—thanks to you—and fell in love."

"Don't cry." Kevin wiped the tears from her face with the pads of his thumbs and then hugged her to him. The side of his face came to rest on the top of her head. "I've been conflicted since I met you. Conflicted with the information the FBI and Garda were feeding me. I should have come to you. "

"I don't blame you, Kevin." Dani pulled out of his embrace, reaching inside her bra. "I haven't been completely honest with you." She fished out the thumb drive. For something so small, it'd caused her a lot of trouble. "Kara took it and she gave it to me that night on the docks before they killed her. I hid on the freighter. Fell asleep in the lifeboat waiting until it was safe. I woke up at sea." Her lip quirked, and she wiped away a pesky tear. "It was the best decision I ever made." She handed it to him. "Will you see to it the Garda get this?"

Kevin took it from her shaky fingers, shoving it in his front pants pocket. His hands cupped her face. "We don't have much time, sweetheart." Frantic eyes darted about her face. "You understand you have to go back . . . for the trial?"

"You can't come?" It was out before she could take it back. She shook her head. "That was a mindless question. Your life is here."

"My life will be in Ireland." He placed his finger under her chin. "Under some sort of witness protection program."

"Witness Security Programme. I know what it is. They change your name, your profession." Dani couldn't breathe. "I don't want a new identity."

"Just do what they say. I need to know you're safe until this thing plays out."

"That could be months." Dani jerked away from him. "What about me family?"

"Dani." Kevin reached for her, pain evident in his voice, his eyes.

Dani backed up. "I'll take me chances here. They have the bloody thumb drive. Duggan's dead. What more do they want from me?"

"This thing's huge. It goes as high as the Irish Parliament." He grabbed her by one of her wrists. "You need to testify, put them behind bars. If you don't, you'll always be looking over your shoulder."

"How will I talk to you?"

"I haven't figured that out yet." He scrubbed his face. "I'll talk to Inspector Cleary."

"The guard?" Dani laughed derisively, jerked from his grip, and waved him off. "Bah. I don't trust them."

"Trust me." Kevin pulled her toward him, and his eyes swept over her. "I love you," he said, his voice rough before his lips crushed down on her mouth. His kiss was urgent, maybe a little fearful—for her . . . him . . . both of them. For a hulk of a man who fought injustices, protected the weak from predators like Tommy, he trembled in her arms.

He knew it as well as she. Knew that once she left American soil, he'd have no say. The Garda could tuck her away and shove the bloody key under their bureaucratic red tape.

Dani gave into his kiss and the future. She'd go months without his touch, the sound of his voice.

The rain intensified. Water droplets smacked her face, arms, even reaching the backs of her legs. Reality pinched her hard. There'd be no telling when she'd see him again—if ever.

"We have to go." He mouthed against her lips.

Dani's eyes sprang open. His were on the crowd behind them. Kevin broke the kiss, and Dani turned. Her heart beat faster.

Reporters.

"Let's not give them anything to use against us." He took her hand in his, gave her a quick kiss, and led her out.

"But how will I know how to—"

Cleary came toward her, grabbed her wrist, putting it behind her back.

"Wait!" She couldn't breathe.

Cleary's eyes were on Kevin as he ratcheted the last cuff tight around her wrist. "They're asking to talk with ya, mate." He hooked his chin toward the bright lights of several television crews, the reporters skulking about like vultures getting ready to partake in a fresh kill.

"Yeah, I see 'em." He rubbed the back of his neck, glanced their way, the tendon in his jaw flexing. "I want to see her before you go." Kevin's eyes locked onto Dani's. They were wary. "I want a way of contacting her."

Cleary visibly blanched. "That's not how it works."

"Figure it out," he shot back.

"Can I see me family?" Dani's throat burned. She looked from the guard to Kevin, trembling.

Kevin looked pointedly at Cleary. "She needs a change of clothes." He eyed the crowd coming their way. "I'll get her sisters. They can give her something to wear." Kevin motioned toward one of his patrol cars. "Put her in—"

"That won't be necessary. We have a ride to the air—"

"Just give me a minute." Kevin strode away like a man bracing himself for an all-out war. He glanced back once and then disappeared into a sea of reporters."

"This is mad." Cleary angled her toward an awaiting sedan and tucked her inside, shutting the door.

Left alone, Dani could only stare out and wait. Her teeth were back to chattering, and her clothes were wet and smeared with Duggan's blood. It made her skin crawl.

I need to see me sisters—me da. Tell them I love them—will see them soon.

The driver and passenger doors flew open. Cleary and another—she guessed one of those FBI agents—got in, slamming the doors.

Cleary leaned over the seat. "I'll do everything in me power to see that he gets word of ya. But there's no promises. I'll only be taking you as far as Dublin." He shrugged. "After that it's up to the Witness Security Programme you'll be going into."

"What if I don't want to?" she bit back, her stomach in knots.

He frowned at her. "If you want to end up like Veronica Guerin, suit yourself, Miss Flynn." He turned his back on her. "Get us to Dulles Airport."

Dani shook, tears washing down her face. She'd been all of about ten when this crime reporter he spoke of had been viciously murdered at a traffic light by a drug cartel in broad daylight, no less, near the outskirts of Dublin. She was the reason they'd created the program Dani would just as soon opt out of.

They pulled around a television truck, and Dani caught a glimpse of Kevin fielding what looked to be a barrage of questions.

I've left him a fine mess to clean up.

Dani fell back against the seat more deflated than she'd ever been in her life. She'd had a taste of family, the love of a good man. It was hopeless to think she'd ever get it all back again.

Ah. Dani's head fell to her chest. *And me ma's coin lost to me forever. Bollocks.*

She'd leave as she arrived—penniless, the clothes on her back, and shackled.

They wouldn't let her reach out to Kevin or her family until they'd gotten what they needed from her. It could even take years. She was going up against some highfalutin parliament types.

Dani's stomach roiled. *Who's to say they won't get off in the end? The end . . .*

By then they—Kevin and her family—would have forgotten that Dani Flynn ever existed.

CHAPTER FIFTY-FOUR

A COLD NOVEMBER WIND BLEW ACROSS THE IRISH SEA AND INTO Devlin's Pub the moment Dani opened the heavy wooden door to come in for work. At half past three in the afternoon, it had begun to fill up with people milling about, chatting at the bar, and Darcy shuffling chairs to accommodate a large group of tourists. Fall in Ireland was a bargain.

"It's a fine day for a turf fire." Dani relished the heat of the flames as she stepped in, snuggling inside her new sweater. It was the least they could do—the government—after she'd put her life on hold for almost three months.

She wouldn't be seeing another shilling, though, after she'd said a kind no thank you to a new identity and their lifetime armed police protection.

Dani Flynn was who she was and would forever be, and the cop *she* wanted to protect her for a lifetime had decided she wasn't worth the trouble. Dani frowned. It was like Kevin Bendix never existed in the flesh. She guessed after he'd taken inventory of his life and the drama she'd caused the two months she'd known him, protecting himself was more in his best interest.

His own sort of casualty insurance.

"Shut the door, luv." Pat motioned, pulling a pint for John Murphy, the owner of the local hardware store. "Get yourself settled," he called from the bar, holding up a note. "A Patricia Gilliam called ya this morn'." He glanced at it. "Something about your green card."

"Aye, she called the pub, then?"

He nodded. "I'll leave it under the bar for ya."

"Grand." Dani passed by the bar on her way to the back room. She'd been expecting the call. It had been months since her initial contact with the embassy in Dublin. She smiled. Cleary, it turned out, wasn't as tough as he'd made himself out to be and had taken her to get her papers in order *before* he'd handed her over.

Dani hung her sweater and pulled down the sleeves to her white blouse, turning up the cuffs. She gave a swift yank, smoothing the shirttails over her jeans and made a face at the fitted blouse. She didn't believe showing a little cleavage—Darcy's bright idea—was going to sell more pints.

Dani closed her eyes. That night at the ball spiraled toward her. Her lips quirked. She'd protested about her cleavage then, too. Only the dress was beautifully made. It had shimmered when she walked. Dani's eyes popped open. She'd have to settle for the meager wage of a barmaid and trying to finagle her old groom job back from Carrigan. From what she'd heard, winning the Travers wasn't enough to garner a jockey position with his stable.

Me luck.

It didn't matter. There was only one trainer and stable she'd want to work for, and it wasn't in all of Ireland. Dani tied an apron around her waist. She would check the message out front and shove it in her back pocket for safekeeping. Tomorrow she'd call this Ms. Gilliam and see where she stood with the coveted green card.

What she needed was a mobile. They'd confiscated Bren's, and her mobile—the one she'd brought with her to the States—remained there with all her belongings she'd bought thanks to Turk and his kindness. She missed him. Not that she didn't miss her family. She did. But the friendship, trust, and respect she'd built with Turk had been unexpected. He had become a second—more cantankerous—da to her in those eight weeks. She missed him and her beloved Solley and mourned what could have been a great run on the track had she been able to stay.

From what Bren told her two weeks ago—it was the first she'd spoken to anyone since her release—Turk had hired a new exercise rider and groom to replace Bonnie and Jake. They'd recovered and remained in jail awaiting their trial, along with Fritz.

Bonnie was the only one she cared about. She hoped, in the end, Bonnie would get her life back the way it was before her fateful fall. But it did beg the question—about Turk. Why hadn't he found himself a jockey?

It wasn't a question she had put to Bren that day on the phone. Turk's racing stable would be the least of Bren's concerns. Not that she had concerns. If anything, Bren was the cheeriest Dani had heard since she'd met her. Had she been allowed to stay for just one more day, Dani would have witnessed the birth of her niece. They'd named her Deidre, after Bren and Kate's ma.

Dani's shoulders sagged a little. All she had left of her ma—her lucky coin—she'd lost.

Dani sniffed and wiped at her eyes. She wouldn't cry. She might not have her ma or anything sentimental, but she did have her da and her sisters. She loved them. She'd see them soon. Dani's lips thinned. But not Kevin. He'd made it clear, without saying a word, he'd moved on. Last she heard he was gearing up for the election. That was over two weeks ago. She'd been curious about the outcome—concerned even. But she didn't have the nerve to go searching the Internet on Pat's computer. Not that he wouldn't let her use it. It was the knowing that bothered her. If he lost, she would have had everything to do with it.

Bah. He was a popular candidate. He was probably partying it up the past two weeks with that bank manager. Dani knew her sister. Bren and Kevin were tight. If he wanted to call, Bren would have already given him the pub's number, told him to call, and let him know she had declined an alias and a life of protection.

She was still Dani Flynn.

Dani gritted her teeth. *Probably why he hasn't called.* Dani hit the swinging door with her open hand and entered the pub.

She slipped behind the bar and smiled across it. "Good afternoon to ya, John. How's the hardware business, then?"

"Grand, Dani. It's good to see ya back."

"Can I get ya another Guinness?"

"I've had me fill, darlin'. I'll just be needing me tab."

Pat winked at her from across the way while he tested the microphone for tonight. "I printed it out already. It's under the bar on the shelf."

Dani nodded. "Who's coming to play tonight?"

Sean Hennessey slapped the bar and laughed. "Why, it's Pat himself."

A group came in, and Darcy got them seated. It looked like they'd be serving a crowd tonight. Word must have gotten around about his performance. She'd always loved the few times he'd sing a tune. He'd done it that last night with Darcy on the fiddle before she'd gone to the docks. Dani lifted her chin toward her boss. "And it's a fine voice you have there, Pat. Will Darcy be accompanying you, then?"

"Don't go lettin' his head swell," John whispered and then grinned. "Now Darcy—she's a different story."

Darcy winked at Dani and looped her arm around John. "And you're a fine man for telling it straight." She gave him a big kiss on his bald head.

Dani chuckled. There was something to be said for working at Devlin's—they were a fine bunch with a good sense of humor. "Let me get that tab for ya."

Dani bent down in search of it right as the pub door creaked open. She found the message from Miss Gilliam and stuffed it in her apron and then spied the thin receipt one shelf down underneath an empty shot glass.

"One, two, three, testing." Pat's voice filled the bar.

"Give me a shot of your best Irish whiskey." A voice from above filtered past her ears.

Dani jerked. It was American. At least she believed it was amidst Pat's echoing voice. She'd had the same reaction a few nights ago when another Yank had ordered a sandwich with his family at one of the tables. It was stupid and something she was going to have to reconcile with herself.

Grabbing a bottle of Black Bush from underneath—a top shelf brand the locals rarely drank—she filled the shot glass, stored the precious gold liquor back in its rightful place inside the dust ring, and pushed up from her crouched position. She handed John his tab. "Whenever you're ready."

She swung around to the next gentleman. Her hand trembled, the whiskey spilling onto the bar.

Lines bracketed his eyes and tough-guy mouth. The same tired lines she remembered that day in the cornfield.

Dani slammed the shot glass down. "And here I thought you fell off the face of the earth," she said through gritted teeth, her eyes spearing him.

"Make it a round." Kevin held up his shot glass and spun around in his stool, looking at her out of the corner of his eye. "I'm getting engaged today."

Patrons clapped, a few hootin' as they held up what drinks they had in their hands.

"Engaged?" Dani laughed out loud. "It must be a leap year, then. No woman with half a mind would say yes to the likes of you." Her stomach fluttered, and she cursed her womanly hormones. He was just as bloody handsome as she remembered with his deep brown eyes, chiseled face— more whiskery than before—and blond hair he wore a bit longer now. Dani narrowed in on him. "Unless she was doing the asking." She turned toward John. "You ready to pay your tab, then?"

John looked to Kevin and then Dani, his gray brows rising. "It's early yet. I'll take another pint. If you don't mind, darlin'."

Irish. They were a nosey lot, too.

"Put his on my tab, darlin'." Kevin winked at her from across the bar.

Dani clenched her hands and pulled John a pint, sitting it down in front of him.

"John Murphy, I run the local hardware store." John stuck out his hand. "It's very kind of ya."

"Kevin Bendix from the States and soon to be hitched." He turned his stool toward Dani, his brown eyes wary.

Don't make me feel anything at all for ya.

Dani turned her back on him and fooled with the shot glasses. She lined them up, debating if he'd been serious about buying a round for everyone in the pub.

"To Dani Flynn," Kevin said behind her back.

What the devil?

Dani's shoulders tensed. She worked here. She didn't need him spreading rumors about some impending nuptials.

The bollocks.

Pat came from behind the bar. "What are ya doing? Fill the shot glasses," he snapped and grabbed the bottle of Black Bush from underneath the bar.

"You can't be serious? *He's* not serious." Dani looked out of the corner of her eye at Kevin. "He's only grandstanding."

"For you, and I'm taking full advantage of it." Pat began to fill the glasses to the rim.

I'm not doing this.

Dani yanked on the tie to the back of her apron and threw it on the bar. "You can serve them yourself," she bit back and flew around the bar. She dodged Kevin's outstretched arm and tables and whimpered when she caught sight of Turk coming in from the parking lot.

"Kid." He reached out to her.

She hugged him. "I missed you."

He hugged her back. "What's wrong?"

The tears she'd tried to keep from falling flowed down her cheeks. This was only the second time he'd ever hugged her back. The first being before the race that changed everything. "I have to go," she whispered. She pulled away from Turk and gave one last look at the bar.

Kevin had his bum half off the stool, his expression one of indecision.

"What are ya waiting for?" Pat motioned with two shot glasses in his hand. "Go after her, lad."

Kevin's bar stool scuffed across the floor, and Dani threw open the wooden door to the pub. He'd said he'd find a way to contact her before the trial. He hadn't. Maybe they'd given him the runaround. But she'd been sprung over two weeks now. What was his excuse for not contacting her? Did he think he could come to Ireland and embarrass her in front of her employer and friends?

If he wanted to ask her hand in marriage, there were other ways to go about it. Dani crossed the small parking area. The door to the pub flew open. Kevin stepped out. Dani turned away, the wind whipping at her hair. She didn't want to talk to him. Not like this. Dani ran toward the bluff. It was foolish unless she could sprout wings. The sea crashed against the rocks below, churning into a turbulent mix like her stomach. Dani twisted her hands, the air damp and cold on her face.

Strong fingers encircled her upper forearm, jerking her backward. "Are you nuts?"

She rolled into Kevin, her hands landing on his soft flannel shirt.

His chest muscles tightened. "You have a death wish?" His eyes, pained and hurting, held hers, then veered downward to the fitful sea and back up until they reconnected with hers.

She ignored the urge to cradle his handsome face in her palms and clenched her teeth instead. "I certainly wouldn't jump to me death for the likes of you."

His eyes swept over her face. "You look the same." He took a step back, his hands falling away. "You're beautiful."

Dani snatched her hands off his chest. "Sweet talk isn't going to . . ." The door of the pub creaked open. It was distinct, and she peeked around Kevin's broad shoulders. *Shite*. Dani nailed him with unsmiling eyes. "Now look what you've done. They're all spilling out of the pub."

"They're expecting to witness a proposal, remember?"

The wind caught her hair, making it to fly about her head. "There's not going to be an engagement," she said, clipped.

"Cut me some slack. You left me with an angry mob of reporters and council members *and* a pile of shit I needed to clean up." He dug into his pocket and held something out in the palm of his hand. "FBI found it in the cornfield."

"Me ma's coin," she said with hushed disbelief and scooped it up like a missing doubloon from a treasure chest. She'd never been more relieved. "I should thank you, but . . ."

"You're mad at me."

Dani shoved the coin into the front pocket of her jeans for safekeeping and then placed her hands on her hips. "You think I was enjoying meself the last three months locked away from the outside world? The least you could have done was called after the trial."

"You don't have a phone."

"You could have called the pub."

His lips thinned. "I wanted to."

"Then why didn't you? Bren told me you were busy with the election. I waited, hoping . . ." God she was pathetic. Dani looked away.

"I lost the election."

Dani whipped her head back. "You're not the sheriff any longer?" She swallowed at the dejection in his face.

"You were hoping I was."

Not for the reasons he seemed to think. He loved his job. It was who he was. Dani let her head fall to her chest. "It was because of me."

Kevin slipped his finger under her chin, raising her face to him. He pulled her toward him. "I lost the election. It doesn't matter how or why. What matters is that I don't want to lose you, too." He pressed a wisp of her hair behind her ear. "Would you have wanted me—a man who couldn't provide for you?"

Dani caressed his bristly cheek. "I'm not about money, Kevin. I would have loved you if you were a poor man."

"Would have?"

Tears filled her eyes. "I've never stopped." Her voice hitched.

"Then marry me." He held her hands in his and dropped to one knee.

Dani's eyes widened. "What are ya doing?"

"What he should have done before you left." Turk grumped and trudged up the hill and handed Kevin something from the pocket of his corduroy blazer. He winked at Dani, looked down his nose at his son. "Don't screw it up." He walked the ten paces or so back and joined the crowd from the bar, rapping Pat on the shoulder. "She's a damn fine jockey." He gave Dani a thumbs-up. "A million in winnings to *spend.*"

His voice rose a notch on the last word, and he winked at her. "Sorry I'm going to have to steal her away."

Dani's brows furrowed. "What the devil is he talking about?" *Lord has he spent the purse?* Dani yanked on Kevin to get up. "You didn't let him spend the purse, did ya?"

Kevin shook his head. "I know he's stealing my thunder," he groused and got up, looping his arm around her waist. "Go ahead, old man. I can see it's killing you."

Turk nodded and pulled out his glasses, slipping them on his head. He then reached into his breast pocket and pulled out a slip of paper. "Due to the heroic efforts of Dani Flynn in the capture of Thomas Duggan—an Irish fugitive suspected of running a human trafficking ring—I hereby pardon Dani Flynn for competing in the Travers Stakes without proper documentation and allow U.S. citizen Joseph William Bendix, the owner of the Thoroughbred Solitary Confinement, to retain the one million, two hundred and fifty thousand dollar purse effective immediately. Sincerely, Senator Patrick Malloy of New York."

The group from Devlin's cheered, slapping each other on the back. Pat gave Turk a big hug and kissed him square on the lips.

Dani's legs began to crumble beneath her. "I don't believe it."

"Believe it." Kevin held tight to her and kissed her on the cheek. "You're a millionaire, sweetheart."

She wouldn't be spending a dime of it. It was Turk's money. "You owe me nothing."

"A million and a quarter," Turk shouted. "And you'll take the million, or I'll give it back."

Technically, they'd received sixty percent. But it was close to a million. She was having a hard time of it. She'd struggled for so long.

She looked to Kevin with a mix of confusion, distress, and disbelief. "He can't be serious?" Dani whispered, and then something else began to sink in. She grabbed for Kevin's hand. "He told you, then. I mean about him being the owner of Starlite? And you're okay with it?"

"He did, I am, and he is serious about the money." He squeezed her hand. "Now say yes so I can get what I came for."

"And what is that?"

"A wife," he said, his voice thick with emotion, and then a smile tugged at the corner of his mouth. "And a mother to that damn cat you foisted on me."

Oh, she'd thought of Jimmy often and wondered how he was getting along. "Ah, you still have him, then?"

He gave her a look of disbelief. "Of course."

"Grand. Excuse me a moment." She put up a finger and then angled her head past Kevin's broad shoulders. "It's a fine offer, Turk," she called to him. "One I'll not turn down."

The cheers started again with Pat waving them toward the pub. "It's a celebration. All drinks are on the house." They fell over each other with laughter and headed in. Pat was the last of them. He glanced over his shoulder. "You've got some privacy." He waved at them with his fingers. "Go on, lad. Ask her to marry ya so we can celebrate that engagement you were talking about, too."

He entered, the door shutting behind him.

Kevin clucked his tongue. "I guess you think I want you for your millions now."

"More like seven hundred and fifty thousand American dollars," she corrected and straightened his collar. She loved the column of his neck. It was strong and handsome like the rest of him. "The thought had crossed me mind, yes."

"I'm not touching a penny of it."

"How will we survive with you not having a job, then?"

He laughed. "You saying you'll marry me?"

"I think I have to. Now that you're destitute."

His arms went around her. "That's what took me so long. You're looking at the new director of security at the Rocky Gap Casino."

"Casino?" Dani's lips sputtered. "A law enforcement officer running a gambling establishment? You can't be serious?"

"Previous law enforcement officer, and you bet—close to home, less headaches, more money, *and* . . ." He pulled her against him. "More time to spend with you and start that family." He kissed her tenderly on her lips, his arms falling away, his hands slipping inside hers. He bent down on one knee, again.

Dani's hands flew to her mouth, tears filling her eyes. She trembled. Not because of the chill in the air, but because everything she'd ever wished for was coming true.

Kevin let go of her one hand and reached in his pocket. The setting sun glinted off something shimmery in his hand. "I've thought of you every day, Dani. Second-guessed everything I did, thinking what I could have done differently to avoid being separated from you."

"Kevin." She stroked his head. "You did nothing wrong, luv. I'd go through everything again to be with you."

"Not everything." He gave her a knowing look.

She snorted. "Well, no."

He kissed her hand, his beautiful brown eyes still nervous and locked on hers. "Will you be my wife, the mother of my children, and the love of my life, Dani Flynn?" He held up a gorgeous Claddagh engagement ring with a perfect heart-shaped diamond.

Dani rolled her lips, trying not to cry. She nodded. "I love you," she said on a whisper.

He slipped the ring on her left ring finger, letting out a sigh. "It's a perfect fit."

Oh, if only her dear ma were here to see it. It was times like this she missed her most. She would forever be in her heart and so would Ireland.

She held up her hand. "It's beautiful, Kevin." She knew how important that ring was to him. It was his mother's. "I'll treasure it."

He rose from bended knee. "I'll treasure you," he said, his voice a bit hoarse. "I love you." He kissed her breathless, his arms slipping around her waist.

Under an autumn sunset with the Irish Sea as witness, its waves battering the jagged cliffs and rocks below, she'd come full circle.

She would leave her homeland, this time of her own free will. But richer than she'd ever been. It wasn't the money, although—her lips quirked against Kevin's—she'd have a grand time spending it. The untold wealth—her family, Kevin, working for his da, and a future filled with promise and children of her own—was what mattered most.

She'd be back for a visit—many visits. But home wasn't necessarily a place. Home was where she'd thrive, where she'd no longer be alone, and where a man named Kevin Bendix would cherish her forever.

Affection, passion, and devotion, she tingled with it. Dani kissed him back, tears wetting her lashes, sliding down her cheeks. She was in love and filled with happiness.

You have me heart, luv—for as long as I live.

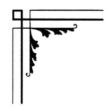

Keep reading for an excerpt from P. J. O'Dwyer's next novel

LINGER

The first book in the
SATIN AND STEEL
Women of Law Enforcement Series

Available from Black Siren Books Summer 2015

LINGER

CHAPTER ONE

DRIVING RAIN ASSAULTED BRIT GENTRY'S PATHFINDER ON Interstate 68, her fingers tightening on the steering wheel when she took the curve too fast through Cumberland Gap.

Slow down.

Brit eased off the accelerator. Smashing into the side of Cumberland Mountain, although tempting, wouldn't bring Sergeant Beau Crenshaw—a highly decorated vet from the Afghan war—back from the dead.

Nope. But she wouldn't have to live with the guilt of killing him, either.

Brit glanced down at the semi-automatic inside the pocket of the driver's side door. She hadn't wanted to bring it, hadn't wanted to look at or handle another firearm, but black bears were a common occurrence in the mountains. If she ventured out once she made it to her cabin in Deep Creek, she wanted the added protection. The sentimental piece of metal had been her father's and the first gun she'd ever shot. She'd almost tossed it into the Chesapeake two weeks ago, the watery grave the perfect resting place for everything and everyone who had ever caused her pain.

The skies grew darker, fog rolling in as she approached the town of Cumberland. The wind picked up, buffeting her SUV, making it a challenge to keep from swerving into the next lane. The interstate, now more circuitous, cut a path high above the old brick city once known as the gateway to the west. Brit would usually crane her neck to catch a glimpse of the ornate spires of the courthouse and the churches that seemed to stretch toward the heavens. But not today. Her hands remained clenched on the steering wheel, the gorgeous fall colors of October a blur through the rivulets and cascading water the wipers couldn't seem to catch up with.

Trucks whizzed by on her left, a wall of water swamping her vehicle. She fishtailed, her heart in her throat until she regained traction. *Damn it.* She wasn't prone to anxiety attacks. She couldn't fall apart—not with her job. Only she had been slowly succumbing to an all-out breakdown since that night in July on the Chesapeake in what was to be the maiden voyage of a Sun Odyssey 33i sailboat she'd had her eye on for years.

And Sergeant Beau Crenshaw and a little thing called a financial disclosure investigation had been the cherry on top of the melting tower of ice cream that was her life.

Brit swallowed, the pressure from the elevation lessening in her ears. She needed to stay alert the next few miles. Fringed with dense trees on both sides, westbound 68 and its constant grade, either on the incline or decline, could be treacherous with the rain. First she'd get past the two idiot truckers up in front who were playing cat and mouse with each other. They might just find themselves utilizing the runaway roads made of sand strategically positioned on the downgrade, if they could even find them in the fog.

Wipers going full speed, Brit pulled around the semi to the left, its height making it difficult to see the road up ahead. She pressed down on the gas pedal, gritting her teeth, and sped past him. A dark compact car behind her seemed to have the same idea and came up on her bumper, then eased off. Damn good thing. One tap of the brake and he'd find himself fishtailing like she'd done earlier or in a three sixty.

Brit put her sights on the next truck up ahead that remained in the right lane, at least for now. It was a double tandem—two trailers hauled by one lonely cab. Now *that* made her nervous. It was like a train on a collision course and the worst piece of highway legislation they'd passed to date.

A white pickup flew by her in the right lane, then zigged over in front of her. Brit tapped the brake, holding her breath. *Shit.* Not good. The idiot better not try that around the—

Too late.

The truck darted in front of the tandem, and Brit tensed. Air brakes screeching, brake lights activated, the trailers tottered on their wheels and swung across the highway like a giant metal gate.

Brit sucked in air and jerked her Pathfinder to the left, aiming for the shoulder. She squeezed through, tree branches like spears attacking her driver's side window. They clunked and scraped her SUV, the uneven ground bumping her up and down. Something clipped the right rear of her quarter panel. She stiffened at the crunch of metal on metal. The SUV spun, and a hot flash of panic radiated up her chest. Like a merry-go-round, everything whirled—trees, roadway, the semi—except for a black projectile coming toward her at lightning speed.

I'm going to die.

Brit shut her eyes tight, waiting for the impact that would shatter her bones and tear her flesh. *God. Let it be quick.*

Her SUV stopped, rocked a few times until she sat motionless in the right lane. A thunderous clap came from somewhere—maybe behind her—the ground shaking. Brit's eyes popped open. The awful groan and whine of metal bending and twisting echoed around her. The black projectile she now knew to be the compact lay flipped on its roof on the left shoulder, smoke billowing from its hood.

Vehicles collided, broken glass shattering. Brit's body jolted at each horrific impact until there was only the eerie sound of manic wipers going a hundred miles an hour. She flicked them off. Her head fell back against the headrest, her eyes closing while she worked through the sharp pains radiating up her back.

She was sore but alive.

Her eyes fluttered open, and she scrabbled for her cellphone sitting in the console. Shaking fingers stabbed at the keypad—pound seventy-seven. She knew the call would go to the closest state police barrack and didn't hesitate.

"Multi-car pileup, tandem on its side on 68." Her breaths came in waves, and she squinted against the fog. She tried to find a mile marker, anything, when a wisp of fog thinned and lifted above a green highway sign. "Grantsville exit," she almost shouted into the receiver.

"You say Grantsville?"

"Yes!" Brit swung her head around toward the wreckage on the shoulder. She couldn't determine the make of the compact. "One fatality." At least she thought. Brit got out. The highway in front was a proverbial ghost town, the fog enveloping her in its misty shroud. She turned behind her and gasped. Flames shot above the semi, left to cool on its side. "Vehicles on fire." She clicked off and threw her phone onto the driver's seat and bolted toward the compact.

She'd do what she could until the emergency responders arrived. Then hightail it out of here. No way was she staying for the media circus that would ensue or the boys from the Cumberland Barrack. That was all she needed—to be recognized and linked to a deadly pileup and possibly the only survivor. They'd blame her. Find some way to pin this tragedy on her. Why not? They'd love to parade her photo on national TV. They'd been doing it for the better part of two weeks.

Brit edged around the compact and crouched down. With the windows blown out, she'd know if this one survived. The quiet unnerved her—not even a moan. With her hand on the frame, she peered inside, shoulders slumping when she found the vehicle empty until she noticed the missing windshield and the shards of broken glass glistening on the gravel shoulder. Brit skirted the wreckage. Her hands began to tremble at the blood and dark hair embedded in a spidery piece of windshield in the grass. Her breathing became erratic. She clasped her hands together and tried to control her airflow.

In, out, in, out.

That night on the hill came flooding back. The grizzly hole in Crenshaw's forehead, his wide-eyed stare, the blood.

Get it together, Brit. Find the driver.

Right. Probably up in the tree line. She shivered at the prospect and hugged her draping black sweater around her. A trendy style, it had kept her comfortable in the SUV with the heat but wasn't functional out in the elements. Neither were her lacy cami and thin straight leg jeans. And her footwear—forget it. She wouldn't get far traipsing through the woods in her high-heeled, over the knee suede boots.

She'd do her best.

Brit rounded the mangled metal and headed up the grassy, wet incline. She hovered at the tree line. "Hello!" She took a few steps into the low-lying brush, its leaves a golden brown rubbing against her legs. "Are you hurt?" Brit shook her head. Now that was stupid. She knew whoever it was would be in bad shape, if they had survived.

No answer, except for the pitter-patter of rain hitting the crown of trees above. Brit moved deeper and grimaced at the suction her designer boots made as they sunk into the mud.

Whatever. If she could help this person she would. She continued through the woods, cupping her right ear. Still nothing. The wail of sirens grew more distinct. They'd be here soon, faster than she wanted if she continued to search in vain for a victim she felt sure was no longer of this world.

Turning around, she then maneuvered back the way she came. Her vehicle was maybe fifteen yards ahead, parked at an angle in the far right lane where it had finally rested. The pickup that had caused all the problems had vamoosed. Lucky for him.

Brit crossed the highway, grabbed her phone from the seat, and hopped inside—the Pathfinder still running. Same as she, once she put it in drive and got the hell out of here. Brit clicked her seat belt, did an inventory of her truck. Suitcases in back, her small cooler, with essentials until she got to the market, on its side in the passenger footwell. She righted it and then angled her head to check her driver's side mirror before taking off. Brit lurched backward, her scream, shrill and curdling, drowning out any conscious thought except—*holy shit!*

Heart racing, eyes widening, she tried to decide if he was man or beast standing outside her truck. But it was the pistol aimed at her center mass that had her going into survival mode. Her gun sat a grasp away in the pocket of her door. Easy access if it weren't for the fact she had one try at getting it into a position that would allow her to get off a shot.

Her door flew open, her eyes darting toward her gun and back to his hairy face.

"Move over," he shouted.

Brit's hands went up. "Okay." She eyed Sasquatch—head full of curly raven hair, bearded, broad, and bleeding from his forehead down to the hole in the knee of his jeans.

"Move it." He used the gun as an extension of his arm and snatched her phone from her hand.

Brit's eyes narrowed when he shoved her only means of communication into the left front pocket of his windbreaker. *Awesome.*

He jerked the gun at her, his meaning clear.

"Going." With her hands up, she did her best to climb into the passenger seat, which was difficult with the cooler taking up space in the footwell.

He slid into the driver's seat, moaning when his butt hit the leather. Slamming the door, he kept the gun trained on her. "Where we going?"

Brit pressed back into the door. Was he kidding? He wasn't going anywhere with her. She eyed the door handle. Damn boots. She'd skate on her heels onto the highway like a skittish deer, and he'd shoot her in the back.

"Hospital?" She shrugged, hoping he'd consider his injuries, especially the jagged pieces of glass glittering from his knee. "Got a lot of tendons running through there." She pointed toward the gaping hole in his jeans covered in blood.

"No hospital." His hands shook on the wheel, his eyes filled with pain and . . . was it fear? "Where were you going?" His voice was razor sharp.

"Deep Creek." Brit took a needed breath through her nose. "My cabin."

"Secluded?"

Too secluded.

"You need a doctor." With her hands still up, she pointed toward his left temple and the bloody knot bulging at his hairline. He must be the one from the dark compact. "You could have a head injury."

He snuffled. "Don't much matter. I'm on borrowed time anyway."

Great.

The sirens increased in intensity. Sasquatch shook his gun at her and put the car in drive. He peeled wheels, fishtailed, the guardrail looming toward her before the SUV sideswiped it. Brit slapped her cheeks hard with both hands and sucked in air. "What the hell?"

He grunted. His lips, shrouded in the forest of black whiskers, quirking.

Asshole.

She didn't need this, and to think she'd tried to save his ass back there.

"Look. You can take the truck, drop me off at the exit." She pointed toward the Grantsville sign as it whizzed past. *Damn it.*

She wasn't taking him to her cabin.

"Never been to Deep Creek."

What the hell! You just commandeered my vehicle.

This wasn't a vacation, especially not for two. She needed to heal. He needed to heal, too. But—

"Know anything about first aid?"

"No!" It came out angry, exasperated, and she regretted it immediately. Rolling her lips in, she angled her body away from him, her blonde hair falling past her eyes concealing—she hoped—her true feelings. She couldn't afford to incense him, though her own blood—that was still on the inside where she wanted to keep it—was boiling mad.

A pair of green eyes tunneled into her. "This is happening, Brit

Gentry. So deal with it."

Her mouth dropped open with disbelief—real fear ebbing to every recess of her body. He *had* been following her, knew her name. Her stomach roiled. There was no hiding who she was. He'd have that gun trained on her until he decided to take the kill shot.

He hooked his chin toward her. "Buckle up." His large hand juggled the gun against the steering wheel, his other struggling with his seat belt. He yanked and came up short when the belt locked. "Son of a bitch," he hissed and then jerked it a few times like a nervous rider on a rollercoaster before it clicked in place.

She guessed he'd learned his lesson about the safety of seat belts. Brit tried not to smirk.

His shoulders relaxed, and he settled into the seat, his face—that she could see—set and determined.

"Can I put my hands down?"

"In your lap where I can see them."

Brit complied. There would be no more finagling her freedom. He wanted her for a purpose—all the more reason to start strategizing her escape. Or was it his demise?

Sasquatch had more to worry about than a malfunctioning seat belt. First chance she got, she'd put a bullet between his eyes.

So much for deluding herself about the gun—she was a professional killer. One that could squeeze off a fatal round at twenty-six hundred meters, given the command, with dead accuracy.

Only this time, this Maryland State Police counter-sniper was on her own.

PERSONAL MESSAGE FROM
P. J. O'DWYER

While it's thrilling to create that next complex character or never-saw-it-coming plot twist, I find hearing from readers the most rewarding. If you enjoyed this story or any of my other books, it would mean a great deal to me if you'd send a short email to introduce yourself and say hello. I always personally respond to my readers.

Please email me at pjodwyer@pjodwyer.com and introduce yourself, so I can personally thank you for trying my books. You will also receive notifications about future books, updates, and contests.

I hope, too, you'll consider subscribing to my blog at www.pjodwyer.com/pjwp/blog.

Thank you!

A MESSAGE FROM BLACK SIREN BOOKS

In an effort to support horse rescue organizations and their mission of rescue, rehabilitation, and education, P.J. O'Dwyer and Black Siren Books will donate a portion of all Fallon Sisters Trilogy book sales, and all future literary works purchased through www.pjodwyer.com or the publishing house of Black Siren Books, to horse rescues around the world.

ABOUT THE AUTHOR

Born in Washington, D.C., the oldest of five children, P. J. O'Dwyer was labeled the storyteller of the family and often accused of embellishing the truth. Her excuse? It made for a more interesting story. The proof was the laughter she received following her version of events.

After graduating from high school in the suburbs of Maryland, the faint urgings of her imaginative voice that said "you should write" were ignored. She opted to travel the world instead. Landing a job in the affluent business district of Bethesda, Maryland, as a travel counselor, she traveled frequently to such places as Hawaii, the Bahamas, Paris, New Orleans, the Alaskan Inland Passage, and the Caribbean Islands.

Today, P. J. lives in western Howard County, Maryland, with her husband, Mark, teenage daughter, Katie, and their cat, Scoot, and German Shepherd, FeFe, in a farmhouse they built in 1998.

P. J. is learning that it takes a village to create a writer and relieved to know she's not in this alone. She's an active member of Romance Writers of America. She also participates in a critique group, which has been an invaluable experience with many friendships made and an abundance of helpful praise, and yes, criticism. But it's all good. Improving her craft is an ongoing process. While creating that next complex character or never-saw-it-coming plot twist is thrilling, P. J. finds teaching the craft as an adjunct college professor the most rewarding. She's always eager to share her journey in the publishing world in hopes of inspiring her students to realize their own dreams of becoming a published author.

Writing is a passion that runs a close second to her family. When she's not writing, she enjoys spending time with family and friends, fits in her daily run with her husband, and tries heroically to keep up with her daughter Katie's social life. Who knew how demanding the life of a teenager could be, especially for Mom?

When asked where she gets her ideas for her stories, she laughs ruefully and says, "It helps being married to a cop." Actually, she admits, "Every day I find a wealth of possible stories and plots in the most unsuspecting place—my daily life."

P.J. O'Dwyer